Lovers
and
Scammers

TAM AHLBORN

Lovers and Scammers is a work of fiction. Names, characters, places, and incidents either are the product of the author's imagination or are used fictitiously. Any resemblance to actual persons, living or dead, events, or locales is entirely coincidental. The only exception is Susyn Blair Hunt, MsD. She does not own the fictional Crystal Corner Gem Shop and will probably never live in Florida. However, she does give fantastic spiritual, tarot card, and natal chart readings. Her ability to channel our loved ones, who are no longer with us, is always an amazing experience. You can find her on Facebook and or her website, SusynBlairHunt.com.

ISBN 979-8-3660-4414-1 (pbk)

Printed in the United States of America

Acknowledgment
♥♥♥♥♥♥♥♥♥♥♥♥♥♥♥♥♥♥

Many thanks to Susyn Blair-Hunt for her continued support and the use of her name and title throughout the book. Her readings and horoscopes are insightful. They have a perceptive and deep understanding of the problems that are all around us at any given moment in our journey through life.

Prologue
♥♥♥♥♥♥♥♥♥♥♥♥♥♥

I hate weeds, I hate weeds, I hate weeds, Keira thought. She was honored that God allowed her to pull undocumented flowers and make gardens beautiful. A few pallets of blooming beauties around a water bubble vase with a stone path and a bench; a client called it a work of art. A neighbor had overgrown bushes and too much shade in the corner between her house and garage. She complained the nook was hopeless. Keira manicured the evergreens and placed a lotus posing statue on a bed of smooth rounded rocks. The neighbor raved and insisted the makeover was bound to heighten her spiritual awareness. One man bought a full page in the Sunday paper to show how much he loved his newly landscaped parcel of land by The Landscape Architect and Lawn Care Service owner, Keira St Cloud.

Keira remembered when the robust man came huffing into her office. He wanted several of his beautiful oak trees cut down. Although there was no longer a law regulating the removal of trees on private property, these trees were healthy. It was the yard that was worn-out and dingy looking. She recalled begging the man to trust her with his two acres of land butting up against a rotten old fence.

Thinking about it brought back memories of painting the fence black, not white as expected. Keira fertilized and tilled the grounds, then finally planted dense shade grass seed. Granite boulders and small evergreens with granite boulders and small evergreens with two sections of fencing here and there added much-needed visual details. As a homey touch, she clustered wooden benches beneath a few of the beautiful oaks.

When the owner returned in fall after visiting his grandchildren, the grass had filled in. His rolling green lawn, among the oak trees and the neighboring horses grazing in the field beyond his property, was breath-taking.

As Keira's name and reputation as a landscape architect grew, so did her company. She hired more and more workers to do the digging and moving of sod. And then, one day, a landscaper was hired whose own company had gone bankrupt during one multiple hurricane season. Peter knew how to plant trees and shrubs; no training was necessary. Keira assumed the chiseled muscles, his perfectly tanned body, and sun-kissed blond hair were all due to hauling bags of mulch and laying sod. And, within weeks, he proved to be a diligent worker.

Peter was hard-pressed to impress Keira. Unfortunately, he only received cattle calls from the other workers and nothing, not even a smile from the boss. She stayed focused on her landscape company and seldom had time for light conversations. He soon realized, if he wanted to win over Keira's heart, he would have to live, dream, and breathe 'everything' terra firma and the aesthetic appeal of landscaping.

His desire materialized with a crack of lightning and an unexpected thunderstorm. Keira had been inspecting the young trees they had planted on the outer perimeter of a golf course. Her golf cart battery had died when the abrupt downpour started. She had been fearful, knowing the high statistics of lightning deaths in Florida. Thinking fast, Peter had grabbed the company truck keys and raced across acres of freshly laid sod to safe her. The rescue of one very wet boss lady secured the relationship he had wanted since he had walked into her office.

Within the year, he had proposed with the perfect emerald and diamond engagement ring. And that is how Peter swept Keira off her feet and married her.

Keira's business flourished. Her landscape blueprints were masterpieces, according to many clients. Peter hired more and more crew members as Keira took on larger and larger landscape design contracts. With extra workers on each job site, she could focus on her visions for the properties easier. It motivated her to create even more dynamic designs. However, her creativity wiped out many weekend plans.

Peter wanted Keira to cut back. He hoped to enjoy the financial freedoms Keira had worked hard to acquire thus far. He tried to persuade her to enjoy a cruise through the Alaskan waters, but she won a bid on a Zen garden. After battling to get the job, she could hardly refuse to design the grounds on the east side of Florida. He booked hotel accommodations for two weeks in the Turks and Caicos Islands. Who would have thought ruptured water mains on the grounds of an exclusive resort two days before a celebrity wedding would drown that vacation plan? He pouted when she continually bid on contracts and dashed his grandeur vacation plans.

Although it sounded like Keira was neglecting Peter, she wasn't. She flew with him to New Orleans for Mardi Gras, which turned into a four-day celebration. She bought him a Jaguar convertible for Christmas. Of course, they took mini-vacations to St Augustine, Miami, for her favorite Cuban sandwich, and Naples, just for the fun of it. He failed to mention those things.

Keira's hard work and reputation finally paid off. She bid and won the contract of her dreams. She was given carte blanche to design and totally renovate the landscape of one of the most beautiful mansions in Tampa. Keira got to work immediately and spared no expense. Her crew spent months on the project. The scenic vista of the stately home, and Keira's vision, would be featured in one of the top design magazines in the country. The last inspection with the city had passed, with flying colors. She was one step closer to signing off on the contract. Standing on the balcony, she was admiring her completed work. It was then, the manager of the estate requested her to follow him. He led her to the office of the owner of the estate.

"Please have a seat, Ms. St Cloud," the manager said, with an air of smugness Keira didn't quite understand.

"Ah Keira, thank you for joining me," the owner said as he walked into his office from a side door. "I love the vision you had for my home. You have brought magnificent beauty back to this old but majestic manor."

"Thank you, sir."

"I have your check here for you." The owner said as he dropped the check on his desk. "But first, I would like you to see something."

Keira turned in her chair as a view of the manor's sprawling lawns panned across the widescreen TV above the hand-carved credenza. The spectacular landscaping was just as Keira had promised, extravagant and beyond beautiful. She smiled and continued to watch. And then she saw it. There, among the fragrant red roses and the waterfall cascading into the glistening aquamarine pool, were Peter and Mrs. Weinsworth. His god-like bronzed body was having sex with the lady of the house. They were completely naked on the large white outdoor sofa she had picked out for the upcoming garden party.

Her mouth fell open as she clasped the sides of her face with her hands. Tears rolled down her cheeks; Keira was devastated and heartbroken. Not only was she witnessing her husband having sex with someone, but with the owners' wife.

"By the reaction on your face, you didn't have any idea your husband was pulling shenanigans with my, now, soon to be ex-wife. I took the liberty to inquire, and your, I assume, future ex-husband is not part-owner of your company. However, you are responsible for the workforce of your company. I suggest when you leave here; you stop at your attorney's office immediately. You have worked too hard to have a subterranean termite like him destroy what you have built."

Keira watched as Mr. Weinsworth ripped the quite large check in half and handed it to her.

"Good day Ms. St Cloud."

?

8

Chapter 1

♥♥♥♥♥♥♥♥♥♥♥♥♥♥

"Good morning Miss Keira. Are you spending this fine Sunday on your boat?" Old Mr. Benson asked as he cast his fishing line off the end of the dock.

"Yes, the weatherman said it is supposed to be breezy, perfect conditions for a good day sail." Keira looked up into the heavens before stepping over the side rail of her sailboat. A great day indeed, she thought.

Mr. Benson had to be in his nineties. Every Sunday morning, he stood at the same spot at the railing and cast his line from the pier. Keira couldn't remember ever seeing him reel in any fish. Of course, she never took the opportunity to look in his faded orange Home Depot bucket. And, every Sunday, he asked her the same question about spending the day on the boat. She liked the Sunday morning predictability of Mr. Benson. It was as if all was right with the world when Mr. Benson showed up to fish.

Most of the other guys who traipsed onto the dock early on the Sabbath were usually hungover. Some cursed at the seagulls that swooped down to grab the fast-food breakfast sandwiches out of their hands. The swear words were consistently quite colorful. Or, the one guy who, every Sunday without fail, tripped on the only two wood planks in the entire dock that were uneven. Each time, Keira unconsciously held breath, expecting to hear a splash. But the worst were the escapees from the honey-do list, die-hard fishermen. They had two things on their mind: not doing the trivial, long list of crap projects, wifey-poo wanted to have done and not letting the big one get away, period.

Keira quickly stowed the weeks' worth of groceries she had just purchased into the tiny refrigerator. Thank goodness there was still an unopened jug of wine and a gallon of water in the below deck storage bin. Her plans for the day were to do as little as possible. Yes, she needed to scrub the barnacles off the hull. Yes, she needed to go to the laundromat. Yet thinking about what some people possibly put in those washing machines made her stomach roll. And to watch the dryer drum go around and around, she couldn't make herself do that on such a beautiful day.

After grabbing her laptop, Keira settled back against the cushions. She glanced towards Mr. Benson as he cast his line. He had such a content look on his face. She wondered if she too would have that kind of satisfied look to her if she went fishing, probably not. It had been a while since she had a day without immediate decisions to make or crises to handle. She thought back on the past week; it had been like climbing a mountain with a backpack full of rocks. If there was a potential for setbacks, it happened last week. Not only had one of the dump trucks developed a flat tire, but it had also been carrying a ton or so of rocks. Some of the pool equipment still hadn't been delivered yet. And, one of her best workers had decided to run off to Las Vegas and elope, of all things, ugh. She tapped her fingernails across the top of her laptop and fretted about the backyard pool and landscaping contract. Her projected goal was to have it completed by next Friday. It was doable if and only if there were no more setbacks.

Keira shook her head and opened her message box. Oh, my, gosh, she thought, twenty-six new messages were waiting for her. Why had she let Marla talk her into joining one of the most popular online dating websites? It had taken her an hour to think up a catchy name and set up her profile. It was utter nonsense, she thought; she wasn't looking for a husband. She had made that mistake a while back and vowed never to repeat that again. Come to think of it. There wasn't enough time in her day for work and dating.

Instead of opening the messages from men eager to hear back from her, she scrolled through the thirty-some guys, the system's algorithm chose as most compatible with her. The first guy looked decent, but there just wasn't any spark in his eyes. The next looked old; he was almost five years younger than her, according to his profile. He had some very bad genes, poor guy, she thought. And then there was "Alexander," a picture of him standing in Times Square. There was also a photo of him at an awards banquet, and the last snapshot was him eating some breaded chicken over fettuccine. His profile said he had a master's degree in the medical, health, dental or veterinary field. He was the father of one child. He stated he stood six foot one inch, had black hair and his eyes were brown. He was interested in marriage.

This Alexander guy was from Washington DC. He said he was surrounded with love and happiness in his life and had a decent job. He loved enjoying nature and took pleasure in the beauty all around him. It inspired him to do more each day than merely existing. He made a point of saying the quality of a good relationship came with trust and sincerity. And lastly, he was searching for a woman with an understanding and caring heart, one who realized that her love was the best thing that could happen to a man.

After studying his pictures, he was cute. The problem was, he lived five states away. That was way too far for a Friday night walk on the beach sort of thing. She giggled. And so she turned to the next guy. Aah, she thought, this guy, Gene, 36 was from North Port, Florida. That was closer but still sort of difficult for a spontaneous walk at sunset. His profile said he was a self-employed entrepreneur and the father of two children. The statistics on him: six foot tall with green eyes and brown hair. He was born and raised in Stockholm, Sweden. His 'all about me' said, 'I've always wanted to come to the states when I was young, but I didn't have the opportunity until after my college years. I am a person who enjoys staying in shape, eating healthy and maintaining good health by working out. I'm a fun, positive, happy, loving life, kind of person. Having a good wholesome time with family and friends is very important to me. I enjoy being outdoors, watching movies, music, dancing, walking on the beach, traveling, hiking, cycling, and swimming. I've been a widower for three years. I am a Christian, and my faith is important to me. With God, all things are possible, my hope and dreams are to meet my best friend, soulmate, and life partner with the potential for a beautiful long-term relationship.

Alrighty, Keira signed and decided the Gene 36 guy had some strong convictions. That was good, but she wasn't ready for an intense relationship. With a slight move of her thumb to the touch pad on her laptop, she moved on. One guy said he was above average looking, um, maybe, she laughed. He said he was not looking for Ms. Perfect but Ms. Perfect for him. He solicited for only petite females to respond. Another giggle escaped Keira when she noticed he was five foot two inches. His request sounded understandable, not temperamental once he mentioned his height. Since she was five foot seven, delete was the key to press.

One profile caught her eye; the guy's name was George Z. Emmanuel. He had a home in both Dallas and Tampa. He explained he owned a painting and remodeling business for the last twenty-five years outside of Dallas. Since his brother lived in Orlando, he started visiting and ended up buying a home in Tampa. He established an extension of his business in the city, which was thriving, so he frequently came to Florida. However, as she read on, the sad part of his profile was when he noted he had three sons. One died when he was five; a car hit him. Another son died when he swerved to miss a person walking down the middle of the road. He lost control of his vehicle and crashed into a tree. Wow, Kiera thought, how do you write something in response to that? Do you send your heartfelt sympathy? Would some women try to commiserate with a story of their loss? Trying to share sorrow could sound more like one-upmanship than compassion. Yet to ignore the tear-jerking account with a 'how ya doin' yadda, yadda would be cruel. There were some tremendously sad vibes around this George Z. Emmanuel guy. She wondered if he wore the tragedies like an albatross on his shoulder, or did he treat every day as a gift and made the most of it?

It was two in the afternoon when Keira stretched and set her laptop aside. Ole Mr. Benson must have gone home for the day. Hopefully, he caught some fish.

Many of the slips remained empty, with the weekend boaters still out on the water. It was a perfect boating day. For an instant, she thought about motoring out to the Gulf of Mexico for a couple of hours of sailing before the breeze settled down for the evening. But as she debated the pros and cons of dealing with boat traffic on the Intracoastal Waterway, she saw Micah Andreas carrying towing lines and a toolbox to his jet boat. Why would the owner of the marina take heavy-duty ropes to his very pricey craft? The beast of an engine he had on that vessel was a gas-hog on a good day; towing another boat would cause extreme gas-guzzling, for sure.

Keira watched the owner of the marina for a bit of time. Micah had muscles in all the right places, plus he was tall, tanned, and had beautifully sculptured features. She had seen several of the women who frequented the marina, ogling him on the weekends. It was fun to watch as he was usually oblivious to them. Grabbing a damp mop, Keira started swabbing her mahogany deck. She didn't want the marina's owner to think she was watching or spying on him.

She loved her dock space near the edge of the marina's property line. There was shade in the afternoon, so her sailboat had usually cooled down by the time she got home from work. Since her slip wasn't on the main pier, she didn't have to endure all the weekend parties. The gatherings were loud and sometimes lasted late into the night. They grilled anything and everything remotely resembling a fish. But, the worst was the smell of the overflowing garbage can of beer bottles and rotting watermelon rinds. Keira couldn't imagine the odor at their end of the pier by Monday. She dipped her mop into the bucket once more to rinse and almost jumped out of her skin.

"Oh, my, gosh, you scared the heck out of me." Keira yelped as she put her hand over her heart. Micah stood on the dock with his hands on his hips, looking down at her. It was rumored; he was some Greek shipping tycoon's youngest son. He had the dark Grecian good looks and dark curly hair. But Keira didn't believe it. Why would he own a marina on Bradenton Beach of all places?

"If you aren't busy, would you mind helping me?"

"Keira was puzzled by Micah Andreas asking for her help. "Sure, what do you need help with?"

"Come with me; I need you to scout for me." Micah requested as he grabbed several colorful towels and a small cooler sitting on the bench. He walked swiftly back to his boat, idling at his dock space.

Keira quickly grabbed her sunglasses and locked the cabin door. She promptly walked the three piers over to Micah's dock space wondering what type of boat she would be searching for. He had already removed the lines from the cleats while he waited. It was fascinating to Keira that he watched her pull off her flip-flops before hopping into his boat. That was proper etiquette; didn't everyone do that?

She pushed the hull away from the dock and pulled in the bumpers. Micah instructed her where to store them in the bench seat box. She loved the rumbling feeling of the twin engines under her feet. It was all about the horsepower; when it came to speed boats. Micah piloted his beast of a boat, out of the marina and into the sound.

"An acquaintance of mine called in a request for a tow. Their boat lost power about a mile or so off Longboat Key. I am going out to haul them in. I am concerned because one of my mechanics worked on the boat earlier in the week. I watched it leave the marina this morning, and it was running just fine," Micah practically shouted over the roar of the engine.

Keira had listened to the guys along the docks. On several occasions, they said that Micah's mechanics were the best in the area. His men were well trained, produced fast service, and the shop costs were reasonable. She was glad he was concerned with his customers' service issues, not to mention, it was a Sunday.

She smiled as they cruised along the waterway but was puzzled. She understood the need for a second person on a tow- boat. Pulling an out-of-commissioned boat on the water was dangerous. There were so many possible obstacles. Micah knew he couldn't stop on a dime, especially if someone's boat got too close. A spotter had to watch out for another boat's wake, causing drift issues. The pulling cable could let go or snap. The disabled vessel could crash into anything in its way. But why was Micah using his personal, very expensive, and beautiful boat? Not that she was complaining, nope she had seen the marina's heavy haul boat. It sat low in the water, smelled like diesel fumes, and was a nasty heavy-duty work tug.

Laughing as Micah's boat cruised under the Longboat pass bridge, she yelled over the engine noise, "it's nice not having to wait for the drawbridge to go up." With the need for clearance for her mainmast, she usually had to idle in circles while waiting.

"I agree, and with weekend boat traffic, I bet it can be a real nightmare," Micah yelled back.

Keira almost squealed in delight when Micah pushed the throttle down and picked up speed. He maneuvered his boat south along the Longboat Key beaches but also west toward the open water. He had mentioned the stranded boat's coordinates were out about a mile or so, drifting. With the tide out, it could be closer to two or more miles farther. Time was of the essence with the tide changing, and a vessel was adrift.

The occasional salt spray, the hum of the engines, and the wind in her hair were the things Keira enjoyed about being out on the water. Sometimes she was frustrated though, she couldn't be the beautifully groomed female, who protested when her hair got windblown and tangled, or the salt spray smudged her perfectly made-up face. Keira would have loved the polished salon look of beauty, but her ragamuffin style always seemed to win out. It was an effort to keep reminding herself this wasn't a pleasure cruise; she was helping find a boat. But, hey, a day on the water was always a thrill.

Keira saw a boat bobbing in the sea starboard side about a mile out. She tapped Micah on the arm and pointed in the direction. He handed the wheel over to her while he scanned the horizon with binoculars. He slowly shook his head and made the gesture of someone drinking and smiled. She watched as he scanned the many other crafts dotting the horizon. There was a boat with a scuba flag in the water. Keira gave that vessel a wide berth. She wondered what they were diving for since the bottom depth was about forty feet and all sand. There weren't any shipwrecks in the area, well, except the sugar barge from Cuba that sank off Bradenton Beach by the Gulf Café back in the forties. But that barge had been pilfered to the point there was nothing left. It was the site where many people had received their open water certification while getting their recreational scuba diving certification through PADI. Maybe they were just scrubbing the barnacles from their hull like she usually did, once a month. She passed a boat with a couple of guys fishing or probably, more like sleeping in their seats.

She could see Micah was getting frustrated since each boat they passed was enjoying a lazy day on the water. He had tried the ship to shore radio but received static. Finally, he rummaged through a duffle bag he pulled from under one of the seats and picked up his cell phone. She saw him frown and drop his phone back into the canvas bag.

"The boat is just north of Siesta Key Beach. Hang on." Micah said as he took over the wheel and pushed the throttle down further.

Keira realized that Micah was none too happy at the moment. His jaw was firm, and the veins in his neck were very visible. Please don't have a stroke, please don't have a stroke, she thought.

The jet boat zoomed along the almost calm Gulf of Mexico. Keira loved to sail, but the speed and the sounds of the twin engines were the only way to spend a Sunday afternoon. Thank you, Micah, she thought, even if it was only a one-time thing. Monday, she would go back to being a boat slip renter. The full-time landscape architect with all the headaches of owning her own company would be back. But for now, she was enjoying herself. Within minutes though, Micah pointed out the disabled cruiser. She watched as he circled the boat, looking closely at it. The three women on board were jumping up and down. One was holding what looked like a champagne bottle.

"Can you drop the bumpers over the side, please?" Micah instructed Keira as he pulled alongside the stranded vessel.

"Oh Micah, I hope you brought some more bubbly with you; we are almost out," purred one of the nearly drunk and very sun burnt women.

Keira watched as Micah hopped aboard the stranded boat with the agility of a cat. She could hear him all businesslike, asking a couple of questions. He lifted the engine cover and then attempted to start the motor, to no avail. He tapped a couple of gauges with his finger and then turned around. She wasn't sure what he said to one of the women, who seemed like she was probably the boat's owner. But, he didn't look happy when the voluptuous chick in her very tiny bikini threw her arms around his neck and laughed. It was interesting to watch as he reached and untangled himself from her octopus-like arms.

"Here, Mikey, have a beer and cool off a bit." Keira heard the chick in a straw hat slur as she handed Micah a bottle of beer which he dropped back into the cooler at the back of the boat.

Micah turned to Keira and said, "Can you hand me the tow lines from under that seat over there, please?"

Keira dug out the heavy ropes and lifted them over the railing to Micah. She watched him head to the front of the boat. He leaned down over the front guardrail and clipped the line to the bow ring. No wonder the women drooled all over him, Micah's backside was most definitely lust-worthy. Stop it, Keira, she grinned. Whatever he had determined was wrong with the tipsy lady's boat, judging by the set of his jaw, he was not a happy man. In no time at all, he had the dead-in-the-water boat strapped and tied off to the stern cleats of his jet boat.

One of the women tried to climb over the side and asked Keira for a hand.

"No, Nita, you have been drinking. You will stay with your boat while I tow you and your friends back to Bradenton Beach." Micah said sternly.

"We are so sooorrryyy Micah, we honestly wanded you to come party wit us cuz you work toooo hard allll week," the scarlet skinned chick said as she flopped down on the now-closed engine cover.

Micah jumped back into his boat and started the engines.

Although they were about to head back to the marina, Micah's mood hadn't seemed to lighten. Had he used Keira to deter the women; if they had tried to pull any drunken female stunts? But how did he know she wouldn't side with them? Well, that thought was silly. He was the owner of her dock space, and she wasn't going to mess that up. Besides, she was just happy to be on the water. Keira could feel the initial strain on Micah's boat as the tow lines straightened and the disabled vessel followed.

"While I drive, will you please watch the ropes? And pray none of the, er, lovely ladies falls overboard. However, I might not hear you if they do." Micah looked at Keira and smiled at his own joke.

"Could you determine what was wrong with their boat?"

"Yeah, they didn't fill the gas tank."

The journey back to the marina was slow going. Many Sunday afternoon boaters were calling it a day and heading home. Keira saw Micah glancing at the distance of each boat as they zoomed by. He maneuvered his vessel with confidence and total control. Even under the drawbridge of Longboat pass with its strong currents and the wake of other boats, he kept the tow centered behind his boat. There was no drifting towards the cement pilings, while he was driving. Keira smiled, Micah Andreas was not only a marina owner; he knew his way around the watercrafts.

"You're smiling; do you care to share?" Micah asked.

"You handled the currents well through the pass. You know, the ladies don't look too happy. I think they ran out of booze." Keira pointed out as she watched the pouting trio.

"Wait till they get the towing bill!" Micah laughed.

Keira grinned at him; it was the first time she had ever heard him make a joke. But then again, she only talked to him on a professional basis. Was he the life of the party away from the marina or the quiet and reserve type she had only known him to be? Oh, good grief, stop the speculations, she thought. He was not one of the guys on the dating site.

"Keira, can you throw the bumpers over the starboard side of the boat, please? I'm going to guide their boat to the gas pump dock. I want you to jump onto the dock and steady their boat while I cleat mine".

Once she tied the disabled boat off, Keira watched as the three women scrambled from their vessel. They ran directly over to Micah and took turns hugging him. She could hear their near inebriated chatter. There were going to be some very nasty hangover headaches by those three in the morning. Keira decided between the aftereffects and sunburn, tomorrow will be brutal for sure.

Looking at Micah, she smiled and knew there was nothing left for her to do. Taking the long way around the marina past the marina's warehouse, Keira slowly walked back to her boat. She specifically walked past the scuba shop and through the parking lot, so she wouldn't have to make excuses not to eat with the grill masters of pier 2.

The sun had dipped behind the trees and buildings. The birds had headed home for the night. Weary and sun burnt boaters slowly returned their boats to their slips as Keira closed the hatch door. Usually, she sat out enjoying the evening; but with all the fresh air and sun, she headed toward her tiny bathroom for after- sun lotion.

Filling a plate full of cold shrimp salad, celery, carrots, and cheese, Keira sat down at the small galley table and opened her laptop. Now, where was she...

Wildman
34 years of age
Port Charlotte, FL
Aries
5' 11"
Blue-green eyes

Dear Mistress of Palms,

After reading your profile, I was truly impressed. I envisioned you with long dark hair flowing in the evening breeze, standing between beautiful and majestic palm trees. Very much the mistress in command of all that lay at your feet. Such beauty, I am not sure I am even worthy. But, let me tell you a little bit about myself. My name is Matt. I do not have any children, nor have I ever been married. I have lived in Port Charlotte for the last ten years however, for the time being, I am living in Turkey. I am on a two-year contract with a major company to excavate amethyst deep within the mountain caves.

I have found the most exquisite color of purple

gems and am very sure they will fetch a high price on the market.

I must close, for now, it is late, and I usually rise early in the morning to make sure the workers receive proper instructions. Besides, the internet closes down shortly for the night. I pray when I open my computer next, there will be a note from you, my mistress of palms.

I look forward to hearing from you, my dream love.   *Matt*

With a carrot midway to her mouth, Keira stopped and read the short message a second time. Wow, she thought. Was this guy for real or pulling her leg? He couldn't be; who talks like that? If he was trying to get her attention, mission accomplished.

Dear Wildman,

Thank you for your flattering letter. I am not sure if I could ever live up to the vision you embellished. However, you are correct. I do love to wander through a stand of royal or some of the lesser-known exotic palms.

Tell me more about your contract in Turkey. It sounds fascinating to live abroad for a few years; you will have to tell me about the countryside there. Excavating gems from a cave so far from home seems like such an out-of-the-box line of work. How did you get into the geotechnical engineering field? Do you have a background in gemology? I have so many questions for you, tell me more!

Mistress of Palms

Keira walked out on her deck and stretched. The docks were quiet. There was comfort in hearing the distant squawk of a pelican and the soft lapping of water against the tethered boats. She just sent an email to a guy in Turkey excavating gems from a mountain. That was truly different and not what she was expecting on a dating website.

She thought about how she spent her afternoon; it had been

interesting, for sure. Keira was happy she could help Micah Andreas bring in the boat with the empty gas tank. Why would anyone leave the docks without checking their fuel? Towing a boat up the coast from Siesta Key was brutal in cost, plus it was a Sunday! She wondered how steep the woman's bill would be. Why did her mind keep circling back to Micah Andreas? It was silly; he was off-limits to her. Shaking her head, Keira remembered she needed to review what still needed to be completed by Friday on the current job site. Getting her clipboard out, she jotted down her To-Do list for the next week.

With the plan for the week done, it was time for some fun. Keira clicked on the dating website. The first guy who popped up on her screen was a guy from Brandon. It was a bit far, but he had dreamy blue eyes. His smile looked genuine, not plastered on or forced. Oh crap, he had four kids. How old was he, thirty-three years old, and that many children? Um, no thanks! Ok, here was a nice guy. He was six foot two, that's good, thirty-six, check, no kids, oh wait, he lived in Taylor Lake Village, Texas. Where was that? After using her search engine, she found it was between Galveston and Houston.

Taking a sip of her wine, Keira realized they could take a walk on the beach together, just on different sides of the Gulf of Mexico. That would never do. Why was she looking at guys from outside her local area? It was senseless. Goodbye John from Taylor Lakes Village, you were so cute too, Keira thought.

Scanning a few more profiles, she came across Evan, 30 years of age, from Charleston, South Carolina. Oh, he was so cute. Evan had the Jon Bon Jovi long brown hair but in a controlled style look to him. Keira burst out laughing when she read an excerpt of his profile. It said:

The following expressed opinions are the opinions of Evan at this particular moment and are subject to change without notice. All rights are reserved. The readers of these opinions are free to consider them, repeat them and or use them for whatever purpose they choose. However, this does not apply to the government; its agents, assignees, employees, et al, which/who are specifically barred from

their use, etc., etc. Evan provides no warranty as to the
qualifications, accuracy, correctness, moral fiber, or other attributes
of these opinions, or their fitness for any particular purpose. Use of
these opinions in making decisions is the sole discretion and risk of
the user, who agrees and promises, by the use of these opinions, to
defend and hold Evan harmless to all for any direct, indirect,
incidental, consequential, inconsequential perceived, real or
imagined damaged caused by the opinions and their use, repetition,
or considerations, etc., et al.

Oh, my, gosh, Keira thought he had to be an attorney or at least understood how to write legal and binding documents. His profile was witty and entertaining. Evan certainly was one of those people who would have kept her on her toes. But he lived so far away; it really was a shame.

Looking at the time, Keira yawned, "Goodnight, boys, I will talk to you tomorrow!"

"Sorry I am texting you so late. I just got back into town and was anxious to say hi. I would like to talk with you. Scott"

Keira looked at the text on her cell phone. Who was this person? She didn't know anyone named Scott. It was probably some guy who texted the wrong number. Too bad, so sad, he wasn't going to hook up with the person he wanted.

"You have the wrong number," Keira's fingers tapped. She yawned again, took one last look at her cell for any new messages and then, turned it off.

Chapter 2
♥♥♥♥♥♥♥♥♥♥♥♥♥

After picking up coffee for her and her foreman, Keira leaned against the work pick-up truck and reviewed her mapped-out plan on how she would get the current job contract completed on time. She had contacted the pool supply warehouse. The estimated time of delivery of the equipment they had purchased for the pool was critical. In order to fill the swimming pool and spa and deal with any unforeseen issues by Friday, everything was dependent on the missing pool parts. She was not yet stressing over it, but the day was young.

She drove over to the Riverview Boulevard project; the site of their next landscape project to begin the following Monday. The clients were on board with the changes to their green space Keira had shown them on the blueprints. She had obtained all the permits required: the gas, cable, and electrical lines had been flagged. At the last minute, the wife wanted some additions added. So, Keira quickly made the requested modifications to the blueprints, added a clause to the project contract, and asked both husband and wife to meet her at Bradlow and Gresheim Attorney's office to have it all legalized. The husband had grumbled about having to sign the contract in front of Keira's attorney. She explained having the contract signed with the addendum of last minute changes to the documents protected their investment and held Keira and her company to their wishes. When she pointed out, it was in their best interest, how could they object? She was looking out for them. What she didn't say was she didn't say was she didn't want to be in the middle of not getting paid when the husband didn't like the last minute really ugly changes his wife wanted.

It was early afternoon when she dropped by the pool

landscaping job site. She was pleased to see the mini bull dozer had been driven onto the flatbed trailer and the pallets of sod were waiting to be laid down. She picked up a rake and started leveling out the ridges left from the dozer treads.

"The missing impeller will be delivered to the office tomorrow morning," Keira informed Kraig, her foreman. "Oh, and the Riverview contract is all set to start on Monday, so we have to get this job completed by Friday."

"Great. I have some news that will make your day."

"I wanted to talk with you last night. Did you not get my text? Or, were you punishing me for not texting before now? I was out of the country. Text me back. Scott"

"Kraig, we are on a roll today. What's your news?" Keira asked, ignoring her phone's ping while talking to Kraig.

"Marcus will be back on Monday from Vegas." Her foreman said as he inspected the cube of sod.

"What? I thought he was going to be on his honeymoon for another week."

"It seems they got married on Friday and the wedding was annulled on Sunday."

"Are you kidding me? Why?" Keira stopped raking and started at Kraig. She usually didn't listen to the crew gossip, but if this meant her manpower would increase Monday morning, she was all ears.

"From what Marcus's sister told my sister, Marcus got drunk on Saturday night. When he woke on Sunday, his new wife was having sex with some guy in the next room."

"Wait, how did he find her in the next room?" Keira asked as she picked up a dirt clod and tossed it toward the dump truck.

"You know that door that is always locked, between rooms in hotels, so you could share two rooms if you had a big family? Well, that door was open, and he saw her or rather them."

Back at the shop, Keira finished up some paperwork. She remembered the text that pinged while she was talking to Kraig

earlier. Rolling her eyes, she texted back to the unknown guy,
"Sorry, I think you texted the wrong number."

Keira felt grimy from raking the soil and hearing the dirt on Marcus. Thank goodness she had installed a shower stall in the bathroom off her office. After scrubbing the leftover dust off her skin from work, she changed into clean clothes. Reluctantly she sat back down at her computer. After completing phone calls to prospective clients, some receptive, some not so much; she took a peek at her messages from the dating site profile.

WILDMAN – Matt

Dear Mistress of Palms,
I am very excited today; my team has found a new cave full of geodes much darker purple than the ones found earlier this month. I wish you could see them, very dark and no visible flaws noted in their facets. With each chamber of the cave we explore, I become more thrilled. Some of the caverns sparkle with hints of purple gems when the generator lights are on. It motivates me to continue working; however I many have to reward the men with a long weekend off. I must remember these men are local workers and have families who miss them. I think that is why I have signed on to the dating website. It would be nice to develop a relationship. So, when I finally return to the United States, I have someone to come home to. I have told you so much about myself, yet you have said little about you. You black hair and blue eyes. I don't remember you ever telling me your name. Please tell me so I can dream of you... Matt

The guy sounded very lonely. Keira looked out the office front window. To live in a foreign country and pretty much in a cave most of the day could do that to someone, she decided. Developing a plan to occupy his mind when not working, something to look forward to when he comes home would be a smart idea.

Dear Matt,

My name is Keira. I work at a landscape company. We plant pine trees, evergreens and create beautiful green spaces for people. I love palm trees. I could tell you how many types of palm trees there are, the amount of water they need to flourish, or the nutrients the topsoil may lack here in Florida, hence the name Mistress of Palms. I will not bore you with trivial details. Most people do not care as long as their palms grow. Since you deal with geomorphology, I am sure you could relate to the nutrient/soil composition aspect.

How did you get into the field of gem excavation? Do you have a degree in gemology? It certainly is an interesting career. Tell me more about the uncovering of gems. Is there some technique in knowing what kind of gems are in the caves?

A little bit about me: I joined the dating website, like everyone else, to find that special someone. Or maybe I want to be that special someone. I am probably not like most women you know. I don't get my nails painted or spend the afternoon at the spa. I love scuba diving and the smell of sea air.   Keira

Keira didn't want to tell Matt she owned the landscape company. She didn't lie; she honestly did work at landscaping. But there were some men, like her ex-husband, who tended to see dollar signs when the word owner was mentioned. And if she told him she loved to play in the dirt, she feared he would think of mud wrestling. The thought of wallowing in that kind of glop was not her style; she was embarrassed by women who were into stuff like that. She pressed send and wondered how many seconds it took for her note to be delivered to his inbox in Turkey.

Keira stood up and walked back into the bathroom. Looking at her reflection in the mirror, nope, no wrinkles, but she did use a good moisturizer and sun-block. Her hair was healthy, with no damaged ends. She inspected her teeth; they were straight, clean, and white.

And, she shaved her legs last Saturday night. Grinning, maybe she should try a bit harder to make herself look appealing, if not even a little bit sexy. She frowned, wondering where the nearest day spa was. But after she spent a day being pampered, the next working day dropping palm trees into holes, she would return to the scruffy look within hours. With a shrug, she walked back to her desk, picked up her laptop bag, and knew a glam day would not be tomorrow's project or the next.

On the way home from work, Keira decided to stop at the Publix grocery store. She picked up a rotisserie chicken, cheese, a tomato, and some cilantro. Tonight was going to be chicken taco night! And maybe tomorrow night would be chicken quesadillas, and Wednesday night would be chicken and rice soup. After that, she would be sick of chicken for a couple of days, grinning; she couldn't wait to get home.

There was one thing Keira loved about Monday evenings living on her boat. Many of the boat dock renters excessively enjoyed the weekends. The crystal blue water shimmering in the sun was a boater's dream. Rock and roll music jamming on the radios trying to be heard above the boat engines racing up and down the coast. For those anchored on the white sandy beaches, there were never enough sun-block or adult beverages.

As the sun set, the scent of grilling meats permeated the early evening air and into the night. Sundays were the same but sometimes a little bit more family-oriented. Friends and neighbors continued to enjoy their boat along the docks. And as always, they were in a frenzy to indulge in every activity possible on the day of rest!

Monday, it was back to work and early to bed, almost like a recovery night for those post-weekend people. It was time to rest the ole liver. The marina was quiet. Almost eerie and creepy quiet; there usually wasn't a soul around. Only the hoisting of garbage cans into the garbage trucks broke the silence. This evening was no different, as Keira walked the plank to her slip in a hurry to create her favorite Mexican dish, yum.

With a plate of tacos and a glass of wine, Keira sat down cross-legged on her mahogany deck with her back resting against the side seat. The sky was a pale orange. It was a perfectly balmy evening. She could hear the siren in the distance, warning the drawbridge was about to be raised. A tall mast vessel was heading towards open water. As she took a sip of wine, her thoughts wandered. She had sailed in and all around the Straits of Florida when she was younger. Keira closed her eyes; her mind imagined the breezes along the Atlantic side of the keys. Heading north along the east coast, up into the Maritimes with the sails billowed out and her sailboat riding the waves, she held course. She would cross the Atlantic to Turkey.

As exciting as it sounded, the idea was outrageous. There were so many things to consider before even contemplating such an adventure. Keira loved her sailboat, but she never had the desire to sail across the pond to Europe. It took guts, courage, and lots of will-power to navigate the waters from the outer point of Newfoundland to Europe.

She thought about Matt. After a whole day of drilling tunnels in caves, he was probably asleep. If she remembered her trivia well, Turkey was seven hours ahead of the Eastern Time zone of Florida.

"You seem deep in thought."

"Oh, my, gosh. You scared me! That is twice in two days." Keira exclaimed, almost knocking over the glass of wine by her knee. She would have been mortified, on her hands and knees, picking up the glass and wiping up wine in front on Micah. Especially when just yesterday, the three women were drunk and slurring. "You are here kind of late this evening," Keira said, staring up at Micah standing on the plank next to her boat.

"I was waiting on FED-EX to bring some documents. Thank you for helping me yesterday."

"Not a problem. Would you like to come aboard? Maybe have a glass of wine or beer; I made tacos and have plenty. I could put together a couple for you." Keira asked.

"Thank you, that's a very tempting offer, but no. I just stopped to say thanks for your help yesterday. I appreciated it. Have a good night."

Keira had seen Micah's hesitation before he declined the tacos and beer. She watched him turn and hike her hidden path to the parking lot. Guess it wasn't such a secret if he knew it was there. Of course, he was the owner, she thought, as she listened to the sound of his sports car as he drove out of the parking lot.

While she ate dinner, she had so many questions about Micah Andreas. She knew nothing about him. The talk on the docks was exaggerated hearsay, women gossiped about the number of love affairs he had, and the men honored his badass jet boat skills. There was so much speculation. Was he married with children? STOP, she didn't want to think about him. Instead, she opened her laptop and checked her messages.

Rad & Sexy
36 years of age
Clearwater, FL
Scorpio
6' Brown eyes

> *Dearest Mistress of Palms,*
>
> *I seek an audience with you. Your profile was amazing. Share with me all that is you, for I am sure there is far more hidden behind your beautiful smile. Let me explore your inner beauty and listen to the song your voice sings.*
>
> *My name is Len. I have come to enjoy the finer things in life. It would give me great pleasure to share a bottle of superior quality wine while learning more about you. There is something very Intimate about a late evening meal by candlelight, paired with a full-bodied vino. Len*

This guy reminded Keira of a Victorian Courts of England during the 1850s. If he wanted to seek an audience with her, shouldn't he have written a letter with gold leafing and a quill pen? From the aristocratic tone of his writing, the note should have been wax sealed and hand-delivered, by his page.

Dear Len,

Thank you for responding to my profile. It is hard to express inner feelings and thoughts in a few lines on a dating website. It takes time, patience, and trust to learn what causes someone to laugh out loud or have a meaningful conversation that bares parts of our souls. Sometimes a shared bottle of wine and candlelight does soften the walls around the heart. I hope you will share more about who you are with me.   Keira

After reading over another couple of profiles, none of the guys sounded interesting. She closed her laptop, picked up her dishes, and headed for the galley to clean up her meal prep mess. The tacos were good, and tomorrow night's chicken quesadillas were going to be even better since she decided to marinate some of the meat in queso sauce.

Before Keira turned off the lights for the night, she decided to take one last look at her message board on the dating site. Rolling her eyes, she laughed out loud at the thought of becoming obsessed with reading her female chasing male messages. Yet Keira had to admit, she had a six-month contract. She was either going to find love or walk away wiser for her time spent. The thought of a romance with someone of her dreams would be nice. Someone who made her toes curl and her heart do a flip flop every time she thought of him. She wanted someone to love her, not because she owned a successful company, but because they fell in love with her. Not everyone was like her ex-husband.

Keira was amazed when a flag immediately popped up on her profile.

RAD & SEXY – Len

Mistress of Palms,

As you know, my name is Len. I am an Invasive Radiologist from Tampa. I am thirty-six years old. I have taught medicine in Europe and currently am head of radiology in a hospital in Tampa. I love Beatle memorabilia, Cuban cigars, and bike riding the Pinellas Trail on weekends. Meet me for a drink, and let's get to know each other. Len

This Len guy must have been on the site when she sent her response note to him. She was not expecting an email so fast. It was great he lived in Tampa; it was only an hour north of Bradenton Beach. And he said he was a radiologist. Giggling, the word radiologist reminded her of that old black and white comic on TV, where the guy kept getting shocked and looked like a skeleton. For some reason, the word radiologist sounded funny. Sick, but funny! It was good he had a well-paying job. His hand wouldn't be out looking for handouts. And being a radiologist, he probably didn't have the long on-call hours, like a physician practicing family health or cardiac medicine.

She kind of wrinkled her nose when she read he loved *The Beatles* stuff. She was sure Len was proud of his Beatles collection. Keira loved music but not the tchotchke and dust collecting stuff associated with the group. Whenever she saw clips of the live Beatle concerts, she never understood the women in those 1960s videos. They were screaming and fainting while *The Beatles* sang their songs. What was that all about? Maybe it was that generation, but it didn't make sense. She didn't understand his fixation with a group of musicians who were now in their eighties. And as far as Cuban cigar smoke, some of the guys at work smoked cigars during lunch. Those things had a nasty smell on a good day.

Dear Len,

Thank you for the interesting note. When did you decide you wanted to go into medicine as a career? You said you taught medicine in Europe. Did you earn your degree in Europe and then continue to live there for an extended time? How did you get from the European medical theater to Tampa? Sorry for all the questions, I was fascinated with the jump from European medicine to American medicine and the differences in style and techniques used. Tell me more, Mistress of Palms

Keira, knowing it was late, needed to be asleep. When the alarm chimed in the morning, she would regret staying up so long. But, for some reason, it felt like there was a need to scan through some of the men. She came across one guy. He was fifty years old. Too old for her, but he had such a kind-looking face she could tell he had experienced much in his life. His blue eyes were mesmerizing. She noticed a green dot by his name, meaning he was actually on the website, and she could talk with him in the message box.

"Hi"

"Hi yourself"

"Your sign-on name is JFlounderGig. What does that mean?"

"My name is Jimmy, and I gig flounder."

"Hi Jimmy, I'm new on here. I have never heard the term gig flounder, explain please?"

"Gigging a flounder means you stab it with a trident-like pole rather than catch it with a fishhook."

"Oh, that's different. I see you live in Maine. I thought flounders were warm-water fish. Do you gig them that far north?"

"Yes, we have flounder up here, but they like sandy outlet streams rather than the rocky shallows of the shores here. I saw your picture for the first time earlier today. You have a very nice profile. I am sure you have received a lot of hits, haven't you?"

"Thank you for the neat information on flounder. As you can see, I am not a fisherman. Yes, I have several emails." Keira typed.

"Please, be careful. There are many men and also women who will try to scam you."

"Why do they scam people? I don't understand." Keira asked, tilting her head in confusion.

"I don't know why; I am not a scammer. However, they scam because they want something from you, like parting with your money. I have had women who ask for gift cards and plane flights across the country or to exotic vacation spots – with or without me."

"Oh, that sounds evil."

"Just be warned. Sorry, it is late, and I need to go to bed. It was nice talking to you. Good night."

Keira, too, realized it was way past her bedtime. She closed down her laptop and slid under the covers. Sleep was slow in coming while she thought about what the Jimmy person said about scammers.

In the landscape company world, she had run across many people who wanted their yards beautiful but didn't want to pay for the artistry. She had learned very early on to charge people to have a blueprint drawn up with the stipulation; the cost would later be applied to the contract price if signed on by the client. There was too many who loved her architectural designs. They would then copy them. Putting in many hours designing something unique for their green space and then financially out for all those creative hours spent. Keira punched her pillow and rolled on her side. She knew the weeds from the flowers! Drifting off to sleep, she smiled and decided that would be a great marketing slogan.

Chapter 3
♥♥♥♥♥♥♥♥♥♥♥♥♥

Keira sent a message to Kraig, her foreman, letting him know she would be at the job site after lunch. He knew her specified schedule and timeline to get the contract done. She relied on him to make sure the day-to-day operations went smoothly. Kraig was someone with strong leadership qualities. He knew when to take control and make decisions. His instincts lead him to notify her of issues she, as the boss, should handle.

She remembered when she hired him on. Peter, her lovely husband at the time, hated Kraig. He didn't want Kraig hired; they even had a heated discussion over him. Maybe it was because Kraig was a hard worker from day one. Unlike Peter, he had no design on her landscape business other than being the best he could be for the company. Unfortunately, she recalled the devastating day on the Weinsworth Mansion project. She found out Peter had been having sex with Mrs. Weinsworth. Kraig stepped up to the plate, so to speak, and took charge; while she filed for divorce and then fell apart.

What made her think of those dark days? She finished dressing in a brightly colored sundress and sandals rather than her usual khaki shorts and uniform logo shirt. She let her hair hang loose and headed off the gangplank.

As Keira walked across the parking lot, she swore someone was watching her. She hoped it was Micah. But knowing her luck, it was probably that crazy pelican that was in love with the weather vane eagle. The enamored bird once brought a large dead fish and laid it on the peak of the steel roof. The weather vane eagle caught wind and turned the other way, poor pelican. It was all good until the very dead and stinky fish slid down the metal roof and landed with a splat at the feet of some snooty rich yacht person. The always drunk guys on pier 4 spent a whole week raising their glasses and made salutes to big billed bird friends. Of course, with a couple of drinks, the toasting slowly and very loudly slurred into big busted broads. It was funny how even the smallest of things made them laugh. By Memorial Day, they had returned to toasting Bacchus. He was the god of wine, and they always paid tribute to him – a lot. It was about the same time Keira started working late at the office for some reason.

"Good Morning Keira, how can I help you?" Marla, the marina's secretary, and Micah Andreas' right-hand person asked as Keira walked into the office. She ran the place with an iron fist, just ask the always drunk guys.

"I have my dock space rent check for you. Marla, I took your advice and wrote up a profile for that dating site. What do you think?" Keira said, anxious for her friend to see what she had written and posted to the site.

"Here is your receipt. Oh my, Keira, this is yummy." Marla gushed as she read over the paper.

The phone rang, and knowing Marla was busy, Keira waved and walked out the door. Slipping on her sunglasses, she headed for her Jeep.

"She isn't terminating her lease agreement, is she?" Micah asked as he saw Keira walked out into the bright morning sun. He had walked up behind his secretary, picked up the paper from Marla's desk, and scanned it.

"No, that is her profile bio for one of the dating websites. I think it sounds great."

"Why is she wasting time and money on this crap?" Micah grumbled, still looking at the words Keira had written.

"Look at her Micah; she is gorgeous, young, well established, and I think she needs a man in her life. So I encouraged her."

"Marla, those sites are full of scammers."

"Then, you could always, I don't know, maybe ask her out."

"Didn't Nicola do enough damage to my life? Why would I put myself through that again? I'm jaded. It would never work."

Driving her Jeep up the street from the marina, Keira parked in front of The Wet T-Shirt shop.

"Sorry, we aren't open quite yet. Oh hi, Keira, come on in," Petra said as she walked out of the stock room.

"I wanted to drop off my advertisement banner for the Wet T-Shirt contest, and here is my sponsor check. How are things coming along? "Keira said as she handed over her company's promotional sign and banknote.

"I have ordered all the T-shirts, several store owners have agreed to assist sponsoring the event, three food trucks have signed up, and I am working on a DJ or sound system," Petra stated as she counted them off her fingers.

"Oh Petra, I need to buy this mermaid sitting on a swing held up by a palm tree t-shirt."

"For you, it is on the house. You have done so much for my business. You order all your workers' t-shirts through me. You always support my business whenever you can. Nope, it's yours."

"Thank you. I love it." Keira said, holding the t-shirt up against her chest. "Just let me know if there is anything else I can help you with."

Keira was still smiling when she slipped on her sunglasses and headed toward doors down to The Crystal Corner Gem Shop. She didn't want to be rude to Summer Catori, the owner of The Pet Shop, but she didn't need any pet-related items right now. Where would she put them on her boat if she bought anything, she wondered? Space was limited, and for safety reasons, things needed to be bolted down.

Keira remembered the story she heard several years ago of a sailboat that got caught in a sudden squall. The boat rolled and knocked out the owner when a cooking pot hit him in the head. From that time on, she locked everything away when she sailed anywhere. And besides, today, she was on a mission.

"Good Morning, you always remind me of moss agate," Susyn Blair-Hunt, the owner of the gem shop, greeting Keira, as she opened the glass door to The Crystal Corner Gem Shop.

Keira looked at Susyn rather oddly. "I look like a dense clump of cells?" Keira questioned.

"No, Keira St Cloud, you are confident, creative, and inspire plants to thrive." Susyn laughed, raising her hands to the heavens. "Those are some of the properties of moss agate. I was paying you a compliment. What may I help you with?"

As usual, every time Keira entered the gem shop, a relaxed calmness came over her. It was the same sort of therapeutic energy she felt when she dug in fresh sun-kissed warm soil. Instead of the gem shop being cold and sterile looking, like clear quartz crystals, Susyn had created a sunny, bright, and warm fire opal and Larimar type atmosphere. It took her a moment to remember why she came in. Oh yes, "I have a question for you. Are there gems that are specific to certain countries, you know, like Turkey?"

"Let see, diaspore, which is an aluminum hydrogen oxide mineral. It has several trade names, such as Zultanite. Then, there is blue chalcedony found around Istanbul and agates and obsidian from the ancient lava beds. Also, there is pink tourmaline and purple jade. Are you looking for one of these specifically because I do have pink tourmaline in earrings and purple jade in a ring?" Susyn asked as she pulled out a couple of trays of semi-precious gems from the Eastern European area.

"The purple jade reminds me of Easter. And the pink tourmaline is too pink, girlie girl for me. Oh, I like that purple in the white gold." Keira said, pointing to a beautifully set gem ring.

Susyn lifted the amethyst ring from its cushioned box and handed it to Keira. "This amethyst is a deep purple and was mined in Uruguay. However, these amethysts were mined in Arizona." Susyn said as she pointed to a few semi-precious gems in the middle of the box. "And let me see, this one is from Pennsylvania. You know, amethyst is very calming; it helps you feel less scattered. And in your line of work, it blocks negative environmental energies. It is interesting, you asked about it. Are you having an issue with a landscape project?"

"No, someone was talking about amethyst the other day, and I wanted your expert knowledge on it."

"I want to show you something." Susyn reached into a closed container and pulled out a tissue-wrapped envelope. After unwrapping it, she laid it on the glass counter. "This is why I said you remind me of moss agate."

"This is moss agate? It's beautiful. It looks like an aerial view of a dense forest with all those medium and dark green colors. Now, I understand the comparison. You envision me in a forest of green trees and spruce. It would be the perfect Christmas gift for my foreman. Do you have a more masculine chain?"

"Keira, it is summer. Are you already buying Christmas gifts?"

"I realized a long time ago if you see something you think you might want to buy. You better buy it immediately; because it won't be there if you decide to come back for it later."

"Wise woman."

It was after eleven when Keira walked out of the gem shop with her early Christmas package. As she climbed in her Jeep, she waved at Brian driving down the street. He was the proprietor of The Dive Bar, across the parking lot from the marina. Brian also owned an identical Jeep as her. She thought about the one night he had tried to drive her jeep home instead of his own. It had become the standard joke of 'I'll take yours; it's cleaner.'

As Keira drove south on Gulf Drive towards Longboat Key, she smiled and thought how much she loved the small village-type community, the shops, and the marina had. The owners and locals pretty much knew each other and waved in passing. Traffic was light this time of day as she drove along Coquina Beach. The drive over Longboat Pass Bridge, the water was a beautiful turquoise blue when she looked out over the gulf. She wished she could be out on her boat enjoying the day, even though there was no breeze whatsoever.

The information Susyn had given her on amethyst was incredible. She almost laughed when Susyn asked if there was an issue with a landscaping project. The company was running smoothly at the moment. Keira looked around at the homes as she drove the two-lane road through Longboat key. Her mission was to scout out potential landscaping needs or issues she may be able to address. Most of the properties were well taken care of by landscape companies hired by the property management company of many of the out-of-state owners. But maybe she could give them a better deal. Well, that was her excuse for her drive on such a beautiful day. It was the privilege of owning her own company; she could justify her time management. And, using this time as she was at the moment, she kept her balance and creativity working for her.

She heard a ping from her phone. Since she was driving, it would have to wait until she could find a place to pull over. She knew it wasn't Kraig. The ringtone set up for him was a truck horn.

"I love when you pretend to play hard to get. It makes me so horny. I am hard thinking how wet you were last time we were together. Text me! Scott"

Keira pulled over at the marine dry storage site, which also just happened to be one of her favorite restaurants. She loved the Dry Dock Restaurant. Their food never ceased to amaze her at how delicious and well prepared their selections were. She had never had a bad meal. She looked at her cell text. What was with that Scott guy, she thought. His text was a more provocative text a bit ago than his last text. She checked back, and she had sent a message stating, he had sent his message to the wrong number, and here he was again. It wasn't funny anymore; it bordered on annoying. Keira decided to block him. That would put an end to that.

Later that evening, Keira was lying in bed. She stared at the moon shining through the open hatch door. Ever since buying her sailboat, it had been her dream of anchoring her boat offshore on a calm night. She wanted to lie in the arms of someone who loved her, always and forever, while watching the moon rise in the night sky. She wasn't sure that would ever happen. Her thoughts then reflected on the conversation she had with Susyn. Why would Wildman – Matt tell her he was excavating amethyst in Turkey, but Susyn said it was dug or found in parts of the United States and

Uruguay? She never mentioned anything about Europe. Maybe the amethyst found in the caves of Turkey was an unexpected discovery and scientific to the gem community. Matt could get kudos for his achievement.

Keira's eyes were heavy, but she realized she hadn't been on the website all day. She could have a potential lover waiting to hear from her. Funny how that thought woke her up a bit. Grinning, she turned on her side and pressed the on-button to start her laptop. She would give herself ten minutes to find her true love and then call it a night. Sure enough, there were some messages.

Rad & Sexy- Len

My Dearest Keira,

May call you Keira, correct? I must confess; one of my only flaws may be my lack of patience at times. I always have been one of those who must learn everything about whatever I happen upon immediately. I have little tolerance for people who waste time with idle chitchat. I want to yell, 'get to the point'. It is how I have always been; it has helped me in my specialized field of medicine.

You asked if I earned my degree in Europe. In the short version of the story, I received my undergraduate education at Harvard. A few of us decided to take a couple of weeks and see the sights of England, Scotland, and Wales before hitting the books hard in our advanced medical education. One night while drinking more than we should have, a wager was made among my friends and me. The bet was that I couldn't get accepted and obtain my medical degree in England. I did and ended up staying and becoming a professor for a few years before returning home.

One last thing I would like to share with you before I close this note, did I tell you I collect The

Beatles' memorabilia? I acquired the love of The
Beatles while in England. Over the years, I have
gained an extensive collection of some of their
highly sought-after belongings. Oh no, two flaws
you now have learned about me. Len

Keira bunched her pillows up under her head and neck. This Len guy had now mentioned in two letters that he loved The Beatles' memorabilia. So, it must be important to him, or he was impressed with his collection. There was very little she knew about the early 1960s rock band. Her computer search engine revealed the band was at the top of the music charts the same time her parents were born. As she scanned some of *The Beatles* songs, she noticed one titled 'The Long and Winding Road.' The lyrics were beautiful.

How could Len love The Beatles' music? Yet he admits he doesn't have any patience with people slowly telling of their personal experiences? The pitfalls and wrong turns in someone's arduous life journey are like a metaphor of the long road back to someone's door, The Beatles' song sang about.

Keira was puzzled. Didn't Len realize love takes time to develop? Yes, there are those people who fall in love at first sight. She thought of KC Bradlow, her attorney. During a conversation at a charity event, she had learned he had fallen in love with romance author Lea Finn the first night they had gone to dinner. But that sort of thing doesn't happen every day.

When Keira closed her eyes, she could see a long and winding road in her mind, like in *the Beatles*' song. It passed through a dark forest, a beautiful meadow, and then, bam, hurricane-force winds, and rain and the road washed away. That was like relationships in some ways. The journey was long, and though sometimes fun, the road became difficult to navigate through at times. The idle chit chat, as he called it, was necessary to help during the rough times. And even though she didn't want to think about her marriage, it might have been salvaged, with a little more, ok, ok, a lot more chit chat.

Dear Len,

Maybe it is the romantic in me, but I feel it takes time to develop feelings about someone. So, to get to know you better, tell me more about you.   Keira

As she flipped through the pictures, a profile popped up of a guy waterboarding on what looked like to be Lake Mead or maybe Lake Mohave. His face clearly showed someone enjoying his day on the water.

ExtremeLover
Anna Maria Island, FL
Age 32
Height 5'9"
About me: I am most passionate about my family and friends, extreme sports and am in search of a good woman...

Dear ExtremeLover,
    I enjoyed reading your extended profile. I, too, am looking for that unique man to share special moments. You mentioned you are passionate about extreme sports, as in participating or watching?
                                            Mistress of Palms

She didn't want to mention, hey, we live on the same island; you might live right down the street from me. What if he was a jerk? Or worse, he was a stalker or a scammer, like those, Jimmy from Maine warned her. They both lived on the same island; he could find her in a heartbeat, especially since she had a profile picture. Maybe she shouldn't have sent a message to someone who lived so close. Wait a minute, she thought, that was the whole idea behind signing up for this dating website. If she was going to become paranoid because Jimmy from Maine told her about scammers, she should just delete her account. Frowning, she paused for a second and drummed her fingers on the mattress. Keira wanted to feel the thrill of someone caring about her. She wanted to have the butterfly feeling in her stomach when she thought of someone. And she wanted to be with someone who made her toes curl and her heart race, yep, lots of passion.

It was the quiet ding of the flag from the website that pulled Keira from her lusty thoughts.

Cooleduardo
36 years old
Miami, FL
Latino/Hispanic
5' 9' brown eyes
In a Nutshell: Athletic, responsible, romantic

> *Dear Mistress of Palms,*
> *I know, I live a distance from you, but when I came across your photo, I paused. You may be a mistress of palms, but you are a goddess to me. You are one hot lady. I am sure every male on this dating site seeks to caress your silky smooth skin and taste your lovely lips. When I close my eyes, my desire is to learn the curves of your body and dream of tropical nights of passion with you. I will not apologize for my provocative thoughts; I am a red- blooded Hispanic who appreciates beauty.*
> *Eduardo Luise*

Keira's mouth fell open, and her fingers stopped mid-drumming when she read the email from Eduardo Luise. Oh my, she thought, she didn't want to encourage the guy's horniness or respond to him if he only thought of women as play toys to stroke his libido. She had worked with many Latino men on her crews over the years. Some of them were extremely red hot-blooded Hispanics with an appreciation for sex. They expressed themselves explicitly, more than what she was used to, this wasn't wrong, just somewhat uncomfortable for her.

Here she was, just minutes ago wanting steamy red hot passionate lovemaking and now? She giggled; Eduardo Luise from Miami, was someone who was practically throwing himself at her.

Even his name radiated hot sex. And she was acting like a blushing virgin. Was it because he was saying exactly what he wanted before getting to know her? But, what exactly were her expectations in a relationship?

Dear Eduardo Luise,

Thank you for your interesting email. I was surprised how much "vision" you received looking at my profile and picture. I would love to be able to have hot steamy sex. To be a red-blooded female with burning emotion coursing through my veins, but then my conscience would kick in. I cannot be the wild and free sexy type of woman and respect myself in the morning. I wasn't raised that way.

To make love to someone, I want to love that someone for the rest of my life. I don't think I could mentally handle mindless sex, all for the sake of satisfying an urge. Don't get me wrong, I have strong desires and would love to give that someone pure, mind-melting, pleasurable love. I am not trying to insult anyone and the passion they choose to give to someone; it just has to have a long-term meaning to me. I don't want to be cast aside when the novelty of sex runs out or someone younger and perkier shows up.

Mistress of Palms

As she was about to send the note to Eduardo Luise, a letter from **Rad and Sexy – Len** showed up. She felt like a zombie and needed to get to sleep. Her eyes were starting to blur; ok, one more email and then sleep.

> Dear Keira,
>
> Why don't we meet maybe Wednesday night or Thursday evening for dinner? We could go to the Columbia Restaurant on Sand Key, drink champagne Sangria, and get to know each other?
>
> Len

Oh, man…

Dear Len,

I am sorry I really can't make it during the week right now. As much as I would love to have dinner with you on Thursday night, I am on a critical time restraint to complete a project. I have to make my deadline or else.

Can we make it on the weekend?   Keira

Keira looked at the time on her computer; it was after midnight. If Len sent another letter, she would have to answer it tomorrow. She just couldn't haggle over when to meet for dinner.

Thank goodness she brushed her teeth before she climbed into bed. Yawning a couple of times, Keira couldn't remember if she had set the security alarm. She had tapped in the code so many times, it had become a habit. Tomorrow would be, for sure, a double coffee morning. She closed her laptop and pushed it out of her way. Pulling the blanket over her shoulders, Keira's eyes slid shut.

?

Chapter 4
♥♥♥♥♥♥♥♥♥♥♥♥♥

It was late, but Keira hadn't heard the old clock in the tower chime the hour. Or maybe it was very early as a fishing trawler headed for the open water. The gentle rocking of her boat lulled her back to sleep. He had been such a fantastic lover, whispering words of endearment in her ear. His lips kissed his way down her neck, and softly he slid her breast in his mouth. She arched her back at the exquisite feeling of his tongue caressing her nipple. As he pulled her pelvis against his firm shaft, she couldn't remember feeling this aroused. His fingers skimmed down her flat abdomen before dipping between her legs. She was so ready for him. All she wanted was to feel him inside her. She was impatient; why was he teasing her? Finally he… Keira sat straight up in bed. She pushed her hair out of her eyes. Her arms had a thin layer of perspiration across them, and her bed sheets were damp. Her heart was still racing. Taking a deep breath, all she could think was WOW.

Climbing out of bed, she headed for the shower. Her mind was still in total wonderment of the dream she just had. It had to be because of the email she received from Eduardo Luise. Yet, she didn't remember seeing his face in her dream. The dark hair beneath her fingers was curly and long, not short and straight like Eduardo's picture. She was puzzled as she lathered shampoo into her hair.

Keira realized as she toweled off, it was only four thirty in the morning. So, she crawled back into her bed, curled up under a fresh blanket, and went back to sleep.

The sun was shining when Keira once again sat up in her bed with a start.

"Oh crap, it's nine a.m.!" Keira jumped out of bed and scrambled to throw her khaki shorts, T-shirt, and work boots on. As she ran across the parking lot, she tied her hair in a ponytail. She saw Micah watching her, but she was late for work. Nope, no stopping for coffee now either.

Kraig, Keira's foreman, had the work site running smoothly, when she slammed her Jeep door closed. In fact, with the delivery of the pool part already in place, they were ahead of schedule. Keira confirmed, at this point, the next job was ready to start on Monday as planned. She told him about the potential clients she had talked with. Keira expressed her excitement about the possible design she planned to sit down and work on to present to them.

"Keira, have you thought about what we are going to do for the crew on Independence Day? Last year you rented the pavilion at the beach. But they are probably already booked solid." Kraig asked as he walked the pool perimeter and gardens they had been working on.

"Oh, no, that is next month, isn't it? It completely slipped my mind." Keira said.

"I was thinking. I could have it at my house. I live across the Manatee River in Palmetto, on the water. The crew and their families could swim in the pool and play volleyball. We could grill out and the dock is big enough for several of the guys to fish. It is just an idea." Kraig suggested.

"You wouldn't mind? Because I love the idea! I would furnish all the food. The crew and their families could bring their drinks, towels, and pool attire." Keira exclaimed excitedly.

"We could have it around four in the afternoon. Then, those who want to stay; will be able to watch the green bridge fireworks later in the evening."

"That sounds like a wonderful idea. I will put a note in the envelopes with their paychecks. And I have a month to get the food together." Keira pointed out.

She heard her phone ping. Since she was talking with Kraig and she had blocked that creep Scott guy, it was probably just a telemarketer wanting to tell her about her car warranty about to expire, for the tenth time this month.

At the office, Keira sat at the design table working on a landscape idea for the St Dominic Care Facility contract presentation. There were some fine details she still wanted to add. Her shoulders ached. But, since she was late getting to work this morning, she decided to work for a couple more hours. She heard someone punching in the code for the back door lock and turned around.

"I figured you probably haven't eaten all day, so I bought you a Philly cheesesteak with extra provolone and onions, no green peppers," Kraig said as he set a fountain drink and the bag of food on the table.

"Awww. Thank you. How did you know?" Keira said as she pulled the sandwich from the bag.

"Keira, I have worked with you; how long? I know when you are focused on something, you lose track of time." Kraig said, as he watched her take a bite of the Philly cheese steak. "So, how is the blueprint coming along?"

"Yummm, thank you so much, this is incredibly good." Keira rolled her eyes and plopped back down on the stool.

"I like that you are getting rid of those huge boulders from the back. And making a succulent garden out of that old fountain is a great idea." Kraig said, looking over the blueprints sitting on the desk. "Are you going to be heading home soon?" Kraig asked as he turned to look at Keira.

"No, I want to get it finished, so I'll be here for a couple more hours."

"What do you need me to do to help so you can get this done faster?" Kraig asked, folding his arms over his chest.

"Nothing, I just have to finish it off, and then I'm out of here."

"Fine," Kraig settled. "But, I don't want you at work until noon tomorrow. No discussion."

"But..."

"No, you don't take any time off; you haven't had a vacation in years. You need a break, boss lady." Kraig said firmly.

"We will cut back in July and August when it gets too hot to work. I will go on vacation then." Keira reasoned.

"Noon and not before," Kraig said as he folded Keira in his arms and hugged her. He kissed her forehead before he turned and walked out the door.

Keira stared at the door as it quietly shut. Kraig had never hugged her, even when she crashed after her divorce. Why now? Her thoughts whirled around the last couple of years of working with Kraig. He was hard working and strong. His work ethic was one the other crew members looked up to and admired. There was such respect for him on the job sites. She had never heard Kraig trash talk about any of the guys. Come to think about it; she never heard him talk of his family either. He, too, had been married, but if she remembered correctly, little Mike had once joked, saying good thing Kraig never put his wife's name on his house deed or a tattoo on his arm.

Shaking her head, clearly she wasn't going to get any more work done here at the office. She remembered the text on her phone.

"Blocking me, so I had to go buy a prepaid mobile phone only gave me more of a hard-on. Come on, my beautiful bitch, call me. Scott"

Keira gritted her teeth together. This jerk was, as the guys would say, pissing me off. She didn't want to talk to him; it would only encourage him. She didn't under-stand why he was targeting her phone. She blocked him once already. Well, she was going to keep blocking him. He could buy stock in burner phones for all she cared. He was going to be buying a lot of prepaid phones if he continued. Besides, she thoroughly hated when guys called women a dog in heat. It was rude and disrespectful unless, of course, it was that time of the month, and they were acting like a dog.

She rolled the blueprints and placed them in the cylinder canister, grabbed her backpack, and locked the door. But on the way home, Keira's thoughts were too scattered. She thought about the dating website and wondered if it was a mistake to continue, would she find love reading guys' profiles? She thought about Eduardo's letter and the passion in her heart and soul, it stirred. Although the dream from earlier this morning had faded from her thoughts, her quest to find true love was still a dream worth pursuing. Was it right in front of her, and she needed to stop and look around? Or was this entire idea silliness? Maybe her marriage to Peter had been her one chance at love.

Keira pulled into the parking lot by the beach. Grabbing the blanket she always kept in the back of her jeep, she walked to the soft, still warm sand away from the late afternoon beach crowd. She always liked sitting high up on the dune by the sea oats so she could stare out along the horizon. Closing her eyes to the sun's brightness, she felt the wind pick up. She could almost feel the mainsail spring to life and her boat picking up speed. The salt spray caressing washer face as the hull rode the waves energized her. Just as she was enjoying her imaginary sail against the setting of the sun, Micah Andreas's jet boat skimmed along the water, leaving a silvery wake in his path. She knew it was his boat by the painted detailing on the side of his craft. Once again, shaking her head, she decided to head for home. First Kraig and now Micah, even the sanctity of the beach couldn't ignore the male testosterone interwoven in her life at the moment.

Later that evening, she finally finished the blueprint for the proposed landscape contract while sitting at her chart table. She walked out to catch a breath of fresh air and stretch when she saw Micah pulling into his dock space. Even though it was almost dark, she could see his profile. She studied his sleekness; he was trim and had lean muscle mass to his arms and legs, not the huge bulky ones. His hair was probably shoulder length or a little longer. He kept it tied at the base of his neck. Maybe, the always drunk guys had him figured out. With his build and coloring, Micah could be some Greek shipping tycoon's offspring. He handled boats with the ease of being on the water his entire life. Not having the energy to get into a conversation with him, she turned, ducked down into her cabin, and closed the hatch.

Keira sat back down at her chart table, opened her laptop; the flag sprang up, noting there was mail to be read. Taking a deep breath, she decided she should deal with **Rad & Sexy – Len** first.

Dear Keira,
   What do you mean you are on a critical time
restraint? What do you do for a living? Len

Keira thought about the Riverview Blvd job they were to start on Monday. She took it on because it was a two-week project. One of those re-landscapes and job completed, done, and everyone is happy, kind of projects. She felt that those sites were the ones that kept the morale of the guys up. They could see completion, which gave them satisfaction quickly. The longer the contracts were, the men got tired of the day-to-day routine, and sometimes sloppiness and accidents started occurring.

Dear Len,
   I am a landscape architect, and the project deadline is due in two weeks. If I am late in completing the contract, I lose 25% of the revenue per day. That is critical.   Keira

She was sure Len's ego didn't like the fact that she was altering his plans. But, if he cared about her, he was altering his plans. But, if he cared about her, he would respect her work ethic. As if he, like most men, would care about her desires over his. She almost laughed out loud at that idea. Many guys didn't think beyond their own wants. Yes, granted, there was a small percentage that did pay attention to their partner's needs. But most didn't. She sent a wish to heaven, hoping the small percentage guy might live near; so she could find him.

Keira looked to the next email:

ExtremeLover

Dear Mistress of Palms,
   I loved your photo and your sign-on name. Tell me
how you came up with that one. I am looking for
someone who wants to be treated as a lady. I have old-
school values and in caring. I still like opening doors for

my special person. I believe that no one should be alone. Life is too short. You should enjoy and share each day with someone you love. I am looking for a wonderful woman interested in a long-term relationship, hopefully, one that will last a lifetime. In enjoying life to the fullest, I love the thrill of extreme sports. No, not watching it on TV but feeling the adrenaline rush of being part of the sport.   *Michael*

Dear Michael,

Thank you for your note. The meaning behind my sign-on name is simply about my love of palm trees. Take a walk through a grassy meadow full of palm trees with a gentle breeze whispering through the fronds and the sound of the surf rolling in on the beach. There is nothing extreme about it, just total contentment.

What are some of the sports that stimulate your adrenalin?

            Keira

Keira knew, the moment she sent the note; she could be opening up a can of worms so to speak. The always drunk guys would answer the 'what simulates your Adrenalin' with some sexual connotation. Hopefully, this man has more class than that sort of behavior. She truly wanted to know what extreme and probably dangerous sport revved up his senses and caused his heart to race. She had seen some television shows on death-defying sports. She didn't understand the need to physically push her own body to its limits. The entire concept intrigued her, though. What if he didn't respond? She would never know the sport that caused him to walk the fine line between life and accidental death. Hmmm, she thought, did she even want to get involved with someone who needed that type of stimulation to be satisfied? Man, the bar was set high for failure with this guy.

When Keira started to open the next email, she noticed there was already another note from:

Rad & Sexy – Len.

> *Keira,*
>
> *Are you a landscaper? Do you trim bushes and plant trees? Maybe you could give me some suggestions for my beach house lawn; it's in horrible condition. As much as I hate going out on the weekends because of the tourists, I guess we could meet at the Columbia Restaurant on Sand Key, Saturday night at seven pm?   Len*

Keira couldn't believe what she was reading, 'you could give me some suggestions,' and 'I guess we could meet' sure sounded like he was doing her a favor. His opinion of himself may be high, but his attitude wasn't making any romantic points with her. It was time for her to close her computer and take a break.

Changing out of her work clothes, she pulled on a short top which showed off her flat midriff and her favorite jean skirt. Looking in the bathroom mirror, she added mascara to her lashes to bring out the blueness of her eyes and combed out her hair. A tiny bit of blush to her cheeks, a spritz of tropical cologne behind her ears and on her blouse, and off the boat she went.

It was only a short walk across the parking lot to The Dive Bar. Keira always thought it was funny that Brian, the owner of the little pub, couldn't have come up with a better name for his bar. But, he had once explained the word dive referred to a little dingy hole in the wall type of bar. It had sticky floors, great appetizer-type foods, and questionable writings on the bathroom walls. It was usually frequented by local residents letting off steam after work. And that it did. But during tourist season, out-of-towners realized how great the cuisine was and visited also.

As she looked up the street, the quirkiness of each of the shops along Marina Street had funky names. The Sand Pile Mini Golf Course was next door to the bar. After a few rounds on the course of crazy sandcastles and mounds of sand, you needed a drink, Steve, the owner, always joked. Petra owned The Wet T-Shirt Shop, next door to the mini-golf course. She was in the process of hosting a wet t-shirt contest and festival at Coquina Beach during the 4th of July festivities week. Summer Catori owned The Pet Shop that didn't sell any pets, but rather animal-related items and houseware. If you wanted a monkey chandelier for your tropical dining room, that was the place to go. And Susyn, although she owned The Crystal Corner Gem Shop, her horoscopes and natal chart readings after hours were the best! Next to the marina was the Azul Del Mar Dive Shop, which Keira thought Markos owned since he was always there selling wetsuits and chartering scuba excursions. Keira was excited; coming soon was the Mermaid Isle Beach Restaurant. It would be across the street from The Crystal Corner Gem Shop and next door to the dive shop. Chef Zac Karas was not only the owner of the new restaurant but also, The Mermaid Isle, downtown Sarasota. His food was fantastic.

Keira walked in and waved to Petra and Susyn sitting at one of the round tables sipping white wine. There were quite a few people drinking and visiting; the guitar player hadn't even started playing yet. Some were familiar faces, and some had to be tourists. She saw Marla at the bar.

"Mind if I join you?" Keira asked Micah's secretary, Marla, a good friend of hers.

"Sure, I didn't think I would see you here in the middle of the week."

"What can I get you, Keira?" Brian asked from behind the bar.

"I will have what she's drinking," Keira said, pointing to Marla's drink.

"Rum Runner."

"Ooo yes, for sure, thanks," Keira said as she slid onto the bar stool.

"So, tell me, how is the manhunt going?' Marla asked.

"Ha, I knew you were dying to ask. It's going well; I have talked to some very interesting guys." Keira said as Brian set her drink in front of her. "Thanks, Brian."

"Hey, if you are looking for an interesting guy, I'm your man." Brian grinned.

"Excuse me, Brian; you will say anything to get my clean Jeep."
"Busted, dang!"

Each time Keira went to the little pub, she thought the side entrance leading out to the wood deck overlooking the waterway was beautiful. On nights like tonight, with the doors open, twinkle lights in the trees, and a slight breeze, it was perfect. A man sitting on a stool had just started strumming his guitar. Judging by his tip brandy snifter, he must be good. And just like that, he began singing a Jimmy Buffett song. Keira sat listening, deep in thought. It brought back so many memories of her childhood. She would sit on the outside curb humming his songs while her parents played his music on their cassette player. She remembered wanting to be a pirate on the high seas. Oh, and she reminded her parents every night at dinner since they lived in paradise, they should eat cheeseburgers. There were always rumors on Duval Street of when Jimmy would show up and sing.

"Care to dance?"

Keira glanced up to see a tall man with pink skin standing with his hand outstretched. She looked at Marla, who had raised her eyebrows, and smiled. Sure, she thought. It was time to start stepping out of her comfort zone. She stood and followed the, had to be a tourist with pink skin, to the parquet floor. Keira smiled up at the guy as he took her in his arms to dance to one of Jimmy's more nostalgic songs. She decided he would be hurting in the morning with the amount of sunburned skin he had at the moment.

"What's your name?"

"Keira and you are..."

"Carl, Carl Mrzyglod."

"Are you here on vacation?" Keira asked, trying to keep from having close body contact with the guy.

"No, I am a doctor in Bradenton and Sarasota. I just bought a boat from the owner of the marina. I spent the day getting familiar with the instrument panel. I am taking her tomorrow morning to my private dock at my home in Sarasota. I thought I would stop here for a drink, you know, in celebration before I drive home. "

"You're a doctor. What is your specialty?" Keira asked. She was becoming annoyed. This so-called doctor kept trying to pull her close to him. Maybe she should step on his foot accidentally but not. It would be her luck; he was a podiatrist and wore expensive insoles because he knew better.

"I am in family practice, but I can hold my own in cardiac emergencies and trauma."

Keira picked up rather quickly the self-importance in the tone of his voice. Now she understood why she didn't frequent bars. She glanced at the door just as Micah Andreas came in and walked between the tables. He took a seat next to Marla. She saw Brian hand him a bottle of beer.

"This place really fits its name. What a dive."

"Hey Keira, your car has its headlights on," Micah called out to Keira.

"It serves its purpose for the locals." Keira said and turned to walk back to her seat.

"But the song hasn't ended."

"I'm not a very good dancer," Keira stated, looking at the guy's hand on her arm.

"Thanks for the dance. Be careful driving home." Keira said sweetly. She hoped his skin would peel from the sunburn. She tugged her arm free and walked back to the bar. "Thanks, Micah. I owe you." Pulling a twenty-dollar bill out of her pocket, she laid it under her drink.

"It's on the house. Go turn off the headlights on 'my' car," Brian said and winked at her.

"Talk to you soon," Keira said as she touched Marla's shoulder. She turned and walked out into the humid night air. Why did the Mrzy-whatever guy, have to spoil her evening? She just wanted to enjoy some music. No, she wasn't going to let him stomp on her pleasure. She turned and walked over to the outside seating area. She chose a table out of sight from the bar's doors. If the guy walked out, he wouldn't see her at first glance.

Keira settled down and listened to a rendition of *Savage Garden*'s song 'I Knew I Loved You.' The guy on guitar was good; his rendition was smooth, gentle, and dreamy. It was romantic. He sang it how she wanted love to be.

A rum runner was set in front of her on the table, scaring the heck out of her. "Crap, Micah, do you enjoy sneaking up on me?" Keira cried.

Laughing, Micah sat down, "care if I join you?" He set his bottle of beer on the table next to her drink.

"Stop laughing. You are getting dang good at creeping up on me," Keira said as she took a sip of her rum runner. Oh, so good and icy cold at that, she thought.

"I take it; you were not enamored with the good doctor?"

"He had the audacity to call our little pub a dive!" Keira frowned. Micah loved the fierceness of Keira's loyalty. "Well, it is called The Dive Bar."

Keira sat sipping her drink, looking out over the water. She loved the calmness of the night. It was peaceful listening to the music playing in the background. Even if Jimmy did step on a pop-top and blew out his flip flop, life was good. "You know doc boy is going to be in a world of hurt with that sunburn."

"Yes, he was 'testing' his new play toy all day."

"He said he was going to drive it down to Sarasota tomorrow to his private dock," Keira said, looking at Micah.

"Good luck with that. I hope his dock space isn't in shallow water. That boat has a deep draft."

"So, tell me, how did you come about owning a marina?" Keira asked.

"I was looking for a new business venture. The opportunity to purchase the marina presented itself to me. The dry storage building looked like it would cave in, and the docks were in poor condition. A little work here and there; I hired a great crew of mechanics, and with satisfied customer's word of mouth, the business took off." Micah said with a shrug of his shoulders.

Grinning, Keira decided to tease him a little bit, "all you need now is some palm trees and good landscaping!"

"I heard one of the boat owners is a landscape architect. Maybe we could barter a couple of palm trees for dock space rent. I will have to make a stipulation, though."

"Oh, and what is that?"

"The landscape blueprint will have to include all the potholes to be removed from the parking lot. I don't want any of my renters to break a leg when they sprint across it." Micah joked, as he took a swig of his beer.

"Ah, you saw that, yes, one of my more graceful moves," Keira whispered and smiled. She liked the comfortable conversation they had been having up to her late for work jog to her car earlier in the morning. "I better get home; I don't want to be late for work two days in a row."

"Man, you have crummy working conditions when the boss can't even be late for work! I will walk you back to your boat." Micah stood and extended his hand. "I don't want the Doc to harass you on your way home."

Later that evening, once again, Keira sat in bed with her laptop open. She was still thinking about Micah walking her back to her dock. His excuse was under the guise of protecting her, which was sweet. He hadn't seemed in any hurry to leave when she stepped onto her gangplank on pier 6. Maybe he was waiting for an invite for a nightcap. Or gee, she could have asked him if he wanted to see her "artwork." Laughing at that thought, she clicked on a note from **Cooleduardo**, her hot Latin lover.

> *Dear Mistress of Palms,*
>
> *Where have you been hiding? I feel my search for the perfect woman is over. You are the one. You have waited to give your love to the man; you will be with for the rest of your life. You are the kind of woman who does not flounce her inner beauty, but with the right man, her passion heats up the night. I am sure we could light a fire between us. I want to take you. I want to rock you. I wonder if you scream when you climax. Tell me; I need to know. Mistress of Palms, I want to dream of you even when you are*

next to me in bed.
Please say yes, Eduardo Luise

OK, it was one thing to joke about this Eduardo guy being a hot Latin lover, but his assumption of sexual bliss was a little unnerving. He knew nothing about her other than he wanted to go to bed with her. There was no point in even responding to him. If he wrote sensual notes like that to her, how many other women on the dating site got the same line? He seemed like he was very proficient at copying and pasting sexy emails.

She sent Rad & Sexy - Len a quick note confirming she would meet him at the Columbia Restaurant on Sand Key at seven pm on Saturday night. She was having second thoughts on him. He was showing signs of arrogance in his emails. But then again, was she just being over-sensitive about her work? It was best to keep her notes to him simple right now. She would be able to judge his true character in person.

Peter Flynn
26 years of age
Brandon, FL
Scorpio
Hazel eyes

Dear Mistress of Palms,
Where do I start? My name is not Peter Flynn. He is a friend and business associate of mine. He asked me to get on his computer while he drove to get his car washed this afternoon and order a pizza. He would pick it up on the way home. When I got on his computer, it was sitting idle on the dating website. I came across your profile and fell in love with you. I hope you don't mind, but I had to write you a quick note. Oh by the way, what toppings do you like on your pizza?

Dear Peter Flynn's Friend,

Whoever you are, thank you for the funny note; I like chicken and bacon on my pizza.   Mistress of Palms

Mentioning pizza, Keira decided she was hungry. She had only eaten half the sandwich Kraig brought her at the office this afternoon. Sliding out of bed, she walked into the galley kitchen and pulled from the refrigerator the Philly cheesesteak on crusty bread. The crust wasn't so crusty anymore, but that was ok. As she wandered out on her deck, she saw the good doc climbing aboard his new boat. Guess he wasn't driving back to Sarasota tonight. If he drove his boat home, how would he get his car home? Deciding it wasn't her problem, she instead studied his boat. It sure was a nice cruiser; big, somewhat cumbersome in the water, but still, very nice. It was funny how people with money had to have the biggest and the best boats. They usually didn't know how to handle them, though. His boat would probably sit in the water at his Sarasota Bay home, like a trophy. It would collect barnacles and slowly wither away in the sun, poor boat.

Keira watched a late evening fishing boat; it was lit up like a Christmas tree, return to the dock across the Intracoastal Waterway by the *Star Fish Company* seafood market. It was a late haul; must have been a slim catch, so they stayed out until they got their haul. After finishing her sandwich, she wandered back down to her bunk. There were still a few emails to read.

Peter Flynn

> *Dear Mistress of Palms,*
> *My name is Basil Simons. I currently live in Georgetown, Washington, D.C. I came down to Florida to visit Peter while wait to see if a contract; that I bid on would win. This is such a lovely area. I have decided to relocate here, and luckily for me, Peter is a real estate agent. He has been showing*

me places for sale.

I seriously hope that I did not offend you. I was taken away by the beauty of your photo. And I love the uniqueness of the sign-on name of Mistress of Palms. Does that have some special meaning? Are you an Egyptian princess from the Bahariya Oasis?

Basil

Keira had never heard of a place called the Bahariya Oasis in Egypt. She used her search engine and was impressed with the mass of palm trees the pictures showed. In the middle of the desert, there was a huge grove of date palms and a couple of buildings. She wondered how Basil knew the oasis, maybe he was a National Geographic buff.

Dear Basil,

Buying a home can be a long and tiring process. In this home, every wall is wall-papered, or the bathrooms need updating and that home has a confusing layout. Yep, I have been there and done that.

You did not offend me with your email. My sign-on name is Mistress of Palms because I love palm trees. It is that simple. I have never heard of the Bahariya oasis. I had to look up the place. All those beautiful date palms sitting in the middle of the desert were absolutely beautiful.   Mistress of Palms

Keira wasn't sure why but she didn't feel the need to give out too much information to this Basil guy. He lived in Georgetown, Washington D.C. He could be looking at homes to pass the time of day during his vacation. She had heard some tourists do that, wasting realtors' time knowing they had no intention of buying a parcel of land or home. They were looking at what was on the market; the same with going on someone else's website to look for women; that was dishonest, for sure. He hadn't paid his fees or been vetted to verify it was really him.

Time for bed...

Chapter 5
♥♥♥♥♥♥♥♥♥♥♥♥♥♥

Keira was amazed at how fast the week flew by after her evening drink at The Dive Bar. Friday evening, she dropped her laptop on her chart table and flopped down on her bed. The plan was to only sleep a few minutes before a shower and dinner, but Keira slept through until five am on Saturday morning. Oh man, she must have been tired and hadn't realized it. She had pushed herself and her crew the last couple of days to get the contract done on time. Minutes before the end of the workday on Friday evening, the client signed the completed contract and handed Keira the check, payment in full. He was satisfied, and the crew was relieved. Monday morning, their next project would start on Riverview Blvd.

Before she started her Saturday list of things to do, she grabbed her purse and drove down to the convenience store for a cup of coffee. On the way back to the marina, she realized she hadn't seen Micah since Wednesday evening - not that she was watching for him. She had left for work every day before eight am when the marina opened. Her days were long and divided between designing landscape blueprints, the job site work, and the lawn service her company provided. The marina was closed for business by the time she walked across the parking lot in the evenings.

Taking a sip of coffee, she sat down at the chart table and opened her laptop. Sure enough, there were way too many emails to read; thankfully Keira had gotten a large cup of Joe. She was going to need it. There was an email from Cooleduardo, which she decided to delete. She wasn't interested in a long distance relationship. Besides, a connection based on sex would burn itself out. If she wanted a quickie, she wouldn't have to look far. She could walk two piers over, and the always drunk guys would be more than happy to oblige.

ExtremeLover - Michael

Dear Keira,

During the winter I love heli-skiing. The regular trails feel like bunny runs to me; they are not challenging at all. Skiing uncharted virgin snow is the absolute best. It is a rush knowing you are the first one down the mountain. All of your senses are alert and sometimes on overdrive since any misjudgments; there is no calling 911. Drifted over cliffs, avalanches, snow-covered boulders, taking a wrong turn and getting lost in the trees or even hitting a tree, so much can happen. When you remain upright and survive until the end of the trail, it is a buzz like no other. The adrenaline coursing through your veins is an exhilarating feeling.

Since I live on the beach here in Florida, I love everything to do with water. I love kite surfing, big wave surfing, and scuba diving with trimix breathing gas. What are some sports you enjoy participating in?
Michael

Dropping out of a helicopter to ski down a mountain that hadn't been inspected and monitored for loose snow, hidden boulders, or dangerous blind spots like drifted over cliffs was extreme skiing. It wasn't for the weak or average skier. Keira wished she could ski like that, to have the guts to do something completely, off the charts, extreme. She grew up in the tropics. Ice was for cocktail drinks, and snow usually meant cocaine, and that was a bad word for her as a little kid.

Dear Michael,
I love sailing, scuba diving, and mast painting.
Keira

Peter Flynn's friend (Basil)

Dear Mistress of Palms,

Please, may I have your name? I was surprised you didn't sign your name at the end of your note to me. You have not asked anything about me. I fear you do not care to continue with our conversation while I am here in Florida. Or is it you know I am leaving soon and do not want to become involved with someone who lives out of state?

As far as the house-hunting search goes, I found a perfect place in Brandon that I plan to bid on, the more I think about it. It has four bedrooms and four bathrooms. The place is move-in ready. I seriously do not have time to remodel or change things to make it more like a home for my daughter. And what I like about it the most is, between the main house and the garage is a mother-in- law suite which would be perfect for my daughter's nanny. Oh yes, it also has a heated caged pool overlooking a pond. Oh wait, peter told me it is a lake, not a pond, even though it is the size of a pond. It is a 'Florida lake.'

Basil

Lake Superior, Lake Michigan, Lake Erie, Lake Ontario, and Lake Huron were great bodies of water; hence the name The Great Lakes. Lake Okeechobee is a large lake. Even the little over-flow retention ponds sometimes are classified as lakes in Florida. Keira giggled. What a great real estate marketing strategy; advertising ponds as lakefront property to out-of-state home buyers.

As Keira re-read Basil's email, she still did not feel comfortable giving him her real name. There was this nagging feeling she didn't know who he was. If she told him her real name; and that she was the proprietor of a landscape service, he could search for her company. She didn't want to be fearful of being stalked at her place of business. If she quit talking to him, he could, out of anger, smear her company. Or, what if he tried to blackmail her company to keep his mouth shut about any lie he wanted to make up? One bad review of malice, even if it wasn't true, could bankrupt a business. She wasn't trying to be paranoid, just cautious. The dating website hadn't cleared him.

In the meantime, she decided instead of telling him her name was Keira, which was short for Keira Leighanna, her Christian name, she would change her name just a bit.

Dear Basil,

My name is K Lee. You can thank my lovely mother for my strange name spelling. As you can tell, I said that with much sarcasm in my writing.

Now, for inquiring minds, have you placed a contract on the house you were looking at with Peter? Tell me about your daughter. What kind of work do you do for a living? Tell me about the bid for work; you put in. What is the time frame before they post who won the bid? I hope you have a good day. K Lee

Maelstrom
26 years of age
Tampa
6'0" Brown eyes

"A HONEST, SINCERE, GENUINE, REAL, NICE, TRUTHFUL, CANDID, RESPECTFUL, MAN, GUY, FELLOW, GENTLEMAN, DUDE, SEARCHING, LOOKING, HUNTING, INQUIRING, SEEKING, PURSUING, WOMAN, LADY, FEMALE, GIRL, LASSIE, DAME, MAIDEN, DAMSEL, CHICK, SWEETHEART, TO SHARE, ALLOCATE, DISPENSE, AWARD, EXPLORE, APPROPRIATE, LIFE EXPERIENCES, ADVENTURES, ESCAPADES, INTERLUDES, ROMANCES, FLINGS, STUNTS, CAPERS, ANTICS, EVENTS, WILL NOT REVEAL, SHARE, SHOW, TELL, DIVULGE, DISCLOSE, PROVIDE, SCAMMERS, CRIMINALS, SWINDLERS, COMPUTER-GENERATED BOTS, ROBOTS, CON ARTISTS, DIRT BAGS HACKERS, SCUM, SNAKES, PHONIES, FRAUDS, FAKES, PRIVATE, PERSONAL, PHYSICAL HISTORY, PHOTOS, SOCIAL SECURITY, DRIVERS LICENSE NUMBERS, FINANCIAL ASSETS, EMPLOYMENT STATUS OR HEALTH INFORMATION; WHEN INTELLIGENT, SMART; BRIGHT, EDUCATED,

SEEMINGLY NICE WOMAN, SHARES, ALLOCATE, DISPENSE, LIFE EXPERIENCES, ADVENTURES, ESCAPADES, ROMANCES, FLINGS, STUNTS, FLINGS, STUNTS, CAPERS, ANTICS, THIS HONEST, SINCERE, GENUINE, REAL, NICE, TRUTHFUL, RESPECTFUL GENTLEMAN, WILL DO THE SAME."

After reading this person's profile, Keira was one hundred percent baffled. His sign-on name was perfect for what he wrote. His words seemed like an array of jumbled words in the hope to cause a whirlwind of chaos. Keira thought maybe he had been previously hacked, scammed, or his credit cards stolen. But thinking about it, there was possibility that the person was a paranoid schizophrenic. The paranoia was most definitely right there waving a red flag. The schizophrenic part, from what she recalled from her university psych class days, there was a fine line between delusional and the real world. A paranoid schizophrenic person sometimes spoke in confusing ways, she remembered.

While she was trying to decipher the weirdness of this individual, a message came across in her message box.

"HI"

It was from him. That was strange. Should she answer him, or ignore him and turn off her computer? That seemed rude; besides, she always wanted to give people the benefit of the doubt. She could practically hear her mother say, 'Keir darling, you never know the circumstances that cause that person to be that way.' Of course, she and her family lived in Key West when she was growing up, and back then, most, not all, but most everyone was a fruitcake there.

"Hi"

"SINCE THERE ARE MANY, SCAMMERS, CRIMINALS, SWINDLERS, COMPUTER-GENERATED BOTS, ROBOTS, CON ARTISTS, DIRTBAGS, HACKERS, SCUM, SNAKES, PHONIES, FRAUDS, CHEATERS, LIARS ON CYBERSPACE, INTERNET, COMPUTER, DATING WEBSITES, I WONDER, QUESTION, INQUIRE WHAT YOU ARE SEARCHING, SEEKING, HUNTING, LOOKING FOR?"

"I am, like most females on this dating website, looking for that special someone for me."

"SINCE THERE ARE MANY, SCAMMERS, CRIMINALS, SWINDLERS, COMPUTER-GENERATED BOTS, ROBOTS, CON ARTISTS, DIRTBAGS, HACKERS, SCUM, SNAKES, PHONIES, FRAUDS, CHEATERS, LIARS ON CYBERSPACE, INTERNET, COMPUTER, DATING WEBSITES, I WONDER, QUESTION, INQUIRE WHAT YOU ARE SEARCHING, SEEKING, HUNTING, LOOKING FOR?"

"I just told you, I am looking for that perfect someone for me."

"SINCE THERE ARE MANY, SCAMMERS, CRIMINALS, SWINDLERS, COMPUTER-GENERATED BOTS, ROBOTS, CON ARTISTS, DIRTBAGS, HACKERS, SCUM, SNAKES, PHONIES, FRAUDS, CHEATERS, LIARS ON CYBERSPACE, INTERNET, COMPUTER, DATING WEBSITES, I WONDER, QUESTION, INQUIRE WHAT YOU ARE SEARCHING, SEEKING, HUNTING, LOOKING FOR?"

Keira decided another approach was needed. "I am not any of the above adjectives. Tell me a little bit about who you are?"

"A HONEST, SINCERE, GENUINE, REAL, NICE, TRUTHFUL, CANDID, RESPECTFUL, MAN, GUY, FELLOW, GENTLEMAN, DUD, SEARCHING, LOOKING, HUNTING, INQUIRING, SEEKING, PURSUING, WOMAN, LADY, FEMALE, GIRL, LASSIE, DAME, MAIDEN, DAMSEL, SWEETHEART, CHICK, TO SHARE, ALLOCATE, DISPENSE, AWARD, EXPLORE, APPROPRIATE, LIFE EXPERIENCES, ADVENTURES, ESCAPADES, INTERLUDES, ROMANCES, FLINGS, STUNTS, CAPERS, ANTICS, EVENTS, WILL NOT REVEAL, SHARE, SHOW, TELL, DIVULGE, DISCLOSE, DISCUSS, PROVIDE, SCAMMERS, CRIMINALS, SWINDLERS, COMPUTER-GENERATED BOTS, ROBOTS, CON ARTISTS, DIRT BAGS, HACKERS, SCUM, SNAKES, PHONIES, FRAUDS, FAKES, PRIVATE, PERSONAL, PHYSICAL HISTORY, PHOTOS, SOCIAL SECURITY, DRIVERS LICENSE NUMBERS, FINANCIAL ASSETS, EMPLOYMENT STATUS OR HEALTH INFORMATION; WHEN INTELLIGENT, SMART, BRIGHT, EDUCATED, SEEMINGLY NICE WOMAN, SHARES, ALLOCATE, DISPENSE, LIFE EXPERIENCES, ADVENTURES, ESCAPADES, ROMANCES, FLINGS, STUNTS, CAPERS, ANTICS, THIS HONEST, SINCERE, GENUINE, REAL, NICE, TRUTHFUL, RESPECTFUL GENTLEMAN, WILL DO THE SAME."

"If you do not divulge any information about yourself, why are you on here?"

"A HONEST, SINCERE, GENUINE, REAL, NICE, TRUTHFUL, CANDID, RESPECTFUL, MAN, GUY, FELLOW, GENTLEMAN, DUDE, SEARCHING, LOOKING, HUNTING, INQUIRING, SEEKING, PURSUING, WOMAN, LADY, FEMALE, GIRL, LASSIE, DAME, MAIDEN, DAMSEL, SWEETHEART, CHICK, TO SHARE, ALLOCATE, DISPENSE, AWARD, EXPLORE, APPROPRIATE, LIFE EXPERIENCES, ADVENTURES, ESCAPADES, INTERLUDES, ROMANCES, FLINGS, STUNTS, CAPERS, ANTICS, EVENTS, WILL NOT REVEAL, SHARE, SHOW, TELL, DIVULGE, DISCLOSE, DISCUSS, PROVIDE, SCAMMERS, CRIMINALS, SWINDLERS, COMPUTER-GENERATED BOTS, ROBOTS, CON ARTISTS, DIRT BAGS, HACKERS, SCUM, SNAKES, PHONIES, FRAUDS, FAKES, PRIVATE, PERSONAL, PHYSICAL HISTORY, PHOTOS, SOCIAL SECURITY, DRIVERS LICENSE NUMBERS, FINANCIAL ASSETS, EMPLOYMENT STATUS OR HEALTH INFORMATION; WHEN INTELLIGENT, SMART, BRIGHT, EDUCATED, SEEMINGLY NICE WOMAN, SHARES, ALLOCATE, DISPENSE, LIFE EXPERIENCES, ADVENTURES, ESCAPADES, ROMANCES, FLINGS, STUNTS, CAPERS, ANTICS, THIS HONEST, SINCERE, GENUINE, REAL, NICE, TRUTHFUL, RESPECTFUL GENTLEMAN, WILL DO THE SAME."

Keira was getting fed up with this stupid game, one last try. "Are you angry? Why do you type in Caps? Stop yelling at me!"

"THIS HONEST, SINCERE, TRUE, GENUINE GENTLEMAN TYPES IN CAPS DUE TO EYESIGHT BEING EXTREMELY, VERY, HIGHLY FARSIGHTED; NOT BLIND; FARSIGHTED; NOT HOLLERING, SCREAMING, YELLING AT YOU BY TYPING IN CAPS"

"Are you married?" Keira typed and then wondered, would he be on the website if he were married? Hmm, there were a lot of guys who needed an ego booster during their boring marriage and tried to hit on single females. She had seen it at The Dive Bar.

"SINGLE, ALONE, SOLO, UNACCOMPANIED, MARRIAGE WITHIN 2 YEARS UPON GRADUATING UNIVERSITY, SHORT 2 YEAR MARRIAGE; FOR LAST 3 YEARS BEEN BY SELF, SOLO, SOLITARY, UNATTACHED, AVAILABLE, THIS HONEST, SINCERE, GENUINE, REAL, TRUTHFUL, RESPECTFUL, MAN, GUY, FELLOW, GENTLEMAN WILL ONE DAY MARRY, LIVE WITH, COHABITATE, COMMON LAW MARRIAGE WITH SOMEONE, SOMEBODY, ANYONE, NEW ACQUAINTANCE, GIRL-

FRIEND, NEIGHBOR, FRIEND, BECOME ACQUAINTED WITH; WILL COURT, STEADY, DATE, FLIRT, BECOME INVOLVED, COPULATE, SLEEP TOGETHER, MATE, FOR CONTINUOUS, PERMANENT RELATIONSHIP."

Keira started laughing. From what she could piece together after he got divorced, he had lived like a monk. That could sure explain the entire thesaurus-driven word game. Part of her was having fun figuring out the word puzzle. She sort of felt sorry for him, but it was her day off, and she had lots to get done this morning. Besides, the more she thought about it, he hadn't been hacked in the past to become the paranoid person she first thought he was; he had to be a hacker. He was playing on her sympathies in his last statement. He was creepy. How else would he have known she was reading on his profile page? She didn't want to be any part of that. So, using logic and not trying to make him mad so he would hack into her account.

"Maelstrom, it has been nice talking with you; thank you. I have many tasks to complete today, on my day off, so I will have to close. Have a good afternoon. Bye."

Keira closed the message box and turned off her computer. But having second thoughts, she turned the button back on and went to her profile, and changed her password. Scrolling through the main screen of the website, Keira changed the password questions and answers. After closing out of the website, she went to her email account and changed her password. Before signing off her computer, she changed her password to log onto her computer also. She had always heard on social media if someone hacked your account, change your password and or notify support. She wished she was more computer savvy. Palm trees, yes, ask her anything, computers, not so much.

No matter how large a storage unit is, whatever Keira needed was never easy to find. Why was that, she wondered? That was the case as she rummaged through the storage space under the main deck of her sailboat. Oh yeah, she had replaced the spinnaker sleeve the other day just moments before a downpour swept in off the gulf.

Shoving the old sock in the storage unit in the rush; her toolbox had gotten pushed to the hull wall.

She carried her chest of tools out to the deck. It was time to get some much-needed projects done. The morning air wasn't hot or humid yet. So, it would be a good day to change the lights on the masthead, check the radio antenna, check and oil the wind speed meter and attach the new bird deterrent. She was sick of sea gulls, sitting up there dropping poop on her clean mahogany flooring. She strapped her tool belt around her waist and added the extra stuff she needed to the pockets. Next, she fitted the harness between her legs and clipped the ascender to the hoist line. She had been taught at an early age how to climb to the top of the mast. The mast ladder was convenient, but the mast climbing harness was an added safety measure. Most people didn't use both. However, since she was working alone, safety came first. Many guys would shake their heads, but that was why women lived longer!

It was slow going up the mast, step by step until she reached the top. The view was, as always, breathtaking. Stop sightseeing and get to work, she thought. Keira set to work on the task of the morning. The wind-speed meter was working fine, but she lubricated the spin bearings anyway. The salt air was so corrosive. The lightning dissipator looked in good condition. After all of her inspections, she replaced the light. It was a law to have lights on top of the mast when sailing. She knew if she didn't replace the light right now, in two evenings, the bulb would go dead and she would be spending another morning climbing the mast. Dang, as she was tightening down the last screw; the screwdriver slipped out of her hand and dropped to the deck. She started laughing. Usually, she would curse when that happened. But since it had become an unfortunate habit, why, waste a good swear word? She had learned the hard way; to always carry a couple of extra items she would need for just such happenings. Some cute guy had just docked his boat next to hers and heard the tool hit the wood floor. He looked around with a puzzled look on his face and then up and waved to her.

Lastly, she was sick of the birdie droppings hitting her deck. She pulled from the side pouch of her belt what looked like an umbrella without the material covering. Very carefully using the battery-operated drill, she had strapped to a cord around her neck, drilled holes in the mast, and bolted down the device. She had to stop a couple of times when her arm muscles were about to give out. Nothing was ever easy as the directions made out to be. Finally, the install was complete. She was rather proud of herself. It looked great, and hopefully, the seagulls would get the hint and go elsewhere. While she was figuratively patting herself on the back, she noticed security cameras mounted on the light post along the piers. Hmm, that added another layer of protection to living on her boat. But she wondered how long they had been there. She hadn't seen them before. Of course, she hadn't been at topmast in several months seeing things from a different angle.

After inching down the mast, it seemed Keira had a following. Several of the weekend boat owners had stopped what they were doing to watch. The new guy in the cabin cruiser cleated next to her boat had also paused to watch. When she stepped back on deck, they started clapping. The always drunk guys toasted and whistled.

"Nice repelling. Oh, I'm Jack. Can I offer you a beer?"

"Hi, I'm Keira. Thanks, but no, if I drink a beer now, I will need a nap." Keira grinned.

"It is Saturday, time for some fun." The guy said with a shrug.

As Keira took her tools and put them back in the storage unit behind the stairs, she decided she was hungry. Grabbing her laptop bag and purse, she headed for her car, waving to the always drunk guys. Keira decided it was time for some Wicked Cantina tacos; they were the best. It was only noon, and if she ate now, she wouldn't ruin her dinner date meal at seven, with Len.

Having dinner and getting to know Len as a person; was going to be interesting. She knew what he looked like unless that was an old picture of him. She found a couple of guys on the site who said they were in their forties. Either they had bad genes, or they looked like mature adults in their senior high school picture. Anyway, she hoped he wasn't as arrogant as he wrote.

Keira didn't need to study the menu at the Wicked Cantina once she was seated. But she did chant in her head over and over, to eat light. It was hard because she loved pretty much everything they created. Their chefs had been with the restaurant for several years and were extremely good at what they cooked. She couldn't remember when the place wasn't busy, especially during the winter season, when there was a wait time just to get in the door.

"Are you going to order your usual or confuse me and order something different?" The server grinned.

"I wouldn't want to make your day difficult; I'll order my favorite wicked brisket tacos and a side salad with ranch dressing, please." Keira smiled.

While she waited for her food to be grilled and plated, she opened her laptop. She grinned as she ate some chips and salsa....a note from Michael.

ExtremeLover - Michael

> *Dear Keira,*
>
> *You had me for a moment when you said you love mast painting. I thought, what the hell is that? And then I realized you paint the mainsail mast.*
>
> *Yes, that could be very challenging, especially if you have a fear of heights. How did you get into doing that sort of thing? You said you love diving. What are some of your favorite dive sites?*
>
> *Michael*

Dear Michael,

When I was a kid, I loved being around the boat docks. One fishing charter boat captain paid me to chum the water for his deep-sea fishermen excursions. I realized if I ate breakfast; there was usually more chum than if I didn't. That was a smelly job, but hey, I was young. I also did the touch-up painting of chipped areas on masts for yacht owners. To a fourteen-year-old, that was extreme! My friends thought I was crazy. But I wanted to learn how to dive. Saving money for lessons for the junior diver certification was my goal. And being on the water all the time was a bonus.

I noticed, in your last letter you said you used tri-mix when diving. OK, you have had more than just recreational diving training; you are doing some deep dives with that combination of gasses. So, tell me, what type of exploring of the deep have you done?

I love diving in Cozumel, but many dive companies do not like to give tours through shipwrecks. The dive shop I frequented by the center pier of San Miguel always said, 'they do not like to promote junk in the water'. But for me, reef after reef, although they are beautiful, became boring after so many dives. I have dove Aruba, drift diving in Bonaire, Jamaica, and the Bahamas. Where are your favorite dive sites?

Surfing and kite surfing both look like so much fun, but here on the west coast of Florida, we have to practically wait for a hurricane in the gulf to get any size waves. Do you head to the east coast, or do you do Hawaii and Pacific surfing? Keira

She was just about to open the last email when the server set her brisket tacos and tossed salad in front of her. The aroma was fantastic.

"Is there anything else you need right now?"

"May I have some extra napkins, please?" Keira asked.

She couldn't wait to take a bite; the tacos looked delicious. She was starving. The more she thought about it, the last time she had eaten was the day before, at noon. No wonder she was hungry.

"Do you mind if I join you?"

Keira looked up to see Micah standing with his hand on the chair across from her. This time he hadn't startled her. However, she did have her mouth full of brisket and hot sauce. Her food went down the wrong pipe, and the hot sauce stuck in her throat. She started coughing, and tears came to her eyes. Trying to take a sip of water didn't help; it just made things worse. Finally taking a few very shallow breaths, she dabbed her tearful eyes with the only napkin on the table. After coughing several more times, like someone with a very nasty lung infection, she was able to speak.

"Yes, have a seat." Keira croaked.

The server came back with the extra napkins Keira had thankfully requested earlier. She also brought a fresh glass of ice water. "Sir, what can I get for you?"

"I will have the cowboy tacos with the refried beans and rice; and whatever you have on tap."

"Were you at the office today?" Keira asked as she continued to take small sips of water to clear her throat.

"No, I have been out of town and just got back. I live down Gulf Drive, closer to Holmes Beach, and decided I needed some tacos."

"Marla put a cabin cruiser next to my slip. He pulled in this morning; he seems nice. I think I scared him when I dropped a screwdriver from the top of the mast." Keira said as she once again took a bite from her brisket taco. It was heavenly. She hoped Micah didn't see her eyes roll.

"You were at the top this morning?" Micah scowled.

"Yes, I changed the light and added a bird deflector. I also oiled the wind meter and made sure everything was in working order." Keira answered.

"Why didn't you bring your boat over to maintenance? They would have taken care of it." Micah again scowled just as his beer was placed in front of him, followed by his plate of food. "It's dangerous for you to go up by yourself and with no one around."

"Never thought of it, oh well, I got the job done. I have a dent in the mahogany floor, that's all." Keira shrugged and continued to enjoy her tacos. "What do you have planned for the rest of your day?" She definitely could see Micah wanted to say more about the dangers of her climbing the mast to change the light. It was a nice feeling to know someone worried. However, he hadn't any idea that she had been climbing masts since she was fourteen. And she didn't take chances.

"I need to pressure wash my driveway."

"Ahh... your honey-do list," Keira joked.

"I don't understand. What is a honey-do list?"

"You know, a list of weekend projects your wife wants you to do instead of relaxing," Keira said as she wiped her fingers on her napkin and pushed her plate aside.

"The only problem with that is, I don't have a wife." Micah grinned.

"Oh." Keira felt dumb, but at the same time, her stomach did a little flip flop and not because of the spicy brisket. When Micah grinned, his features were beautiful. Holy crap! He had black curly hair with touches of gray at his temples. With his hair tied in a ponytail at the base of his neck, it brought out his piercing bluish-gray eyes.

The server came and took their plates from the table and asked if there was anything else she could get them. Micah looked up and shook his head. He sat back in his chair and glanced out over the gulf. "I never tire of the view of the turquoise water and blue sky."

"The other day, I stopped at the beach on the way home from work. The gulf was dead calm. But when I closed my eyes, I could feel the hull riding the waves and the salt air touching my face. I love the sound of the sails expanding as the wind slams against them. The white sand beach in the distance and the horizon beckoning me; it was magical. " Keira felt like she had a grip on her boat's wheel rather than holding her beverage glass. She stared across the horizon.

Micah listened to the quietness of Keira's voice as he watched her describing her love of sailing. He smiled. Looking up, he handed the server his credit card without saying a word. It was the first time he found someone who expressed their reverence for the sea so beautifully. He wondered when her passion for the open water began.

Keira blinked a couple of times. She was embarrassed when she realized she had shown her one true weakness – sailing. Her parents had dismissed her love of the sea with a wave of their hands. They attributed it to her listening to pirate folklore on the docks. Her childhood friends were more focused on boys rather than exploring the beyond with her. And her ex-husband thought bobbing around on a boat in shark-infested waters was crazy.

"I'm sorry, I need to leave." She said to Micah as she turned to look for the server to pay her bill.

"I took care of the check; I enjoyed lunch, thank you," Micah said as he stood to leave. "Enjoy your weekend."

Keira sat there and watched Micah as he walked across the parking lot and slipped into his sports car. Confused over what had just transpired, it took her a moment to gather her laptop and purse to leave. Why did she confess her feelings? Most people could never comprehend the freedom she felt at sea. Micah owned a jet boat; he was into power, speed, and conquering the sea. How could he understand the beauty of waltzing with the waves?

Now, how did Micah pay for the check when the server hadn't placed their bills on the table? Once again, Micah Andreas was sneaky! She looked at her phone and realized she needed to hurry to the grocery store. She had just enough time to get there and back home to shower before her drive to Sand Key and Len.

Thinking back as she dressed for her dinner date. Len had attempted to make some endearing comments in his emails as if he was trying to be patient with 'mundane conversations'. During one discussion, she finally understood his somewhat condescending attitude. He had explained he was the chief radiologist at one of the local hospitals near his home on Clearwater Beach. He mentioned several times he was the youngest, at thirty-six, to be appointed head of the entire department. Although there was no excuse for his patronizing behavior, it made sense. He emphasized he was a 'doctor' and more important than some of us who played in the dirt. It will be interesting to see how he acts in person, Keira said to the mirror as she dabbed some perfume behind her ears.

Keira glanced at her watch as she crossed the bridge from Anna Maria Island onto the mainland, heading north towards Clearwater. She was on schedule. Her cell rang while driving through town. She never used her cell phone while in her car. It was just too dangerous. Luckily driving through town late in the afternoon, she was able to find an empty parallel parking space. After glancing at the caller, she answered the call.

"Keira, I am sorry to call you, but I am going to have to cancel dinner this evening. I have one doctor on vacation and another one called in sick. I think he has that damn flu. The director of ER called me; there was a multi-car accident with victims coming in. I will be spending this evening reading trauma x-rays. I'm sorry; I was looking forward to meeting you in person and having a nice dinner. We will get together soon. I promise. Gotta run. Bye."

Keira sat staring out the windshield. She never got a word in edgewise. Len called, stated he couldn't make it, and hung up. Now what? Well, she decided she was all dressed up and nowhere to go. She had been looking forward to a great Italian meal, the Columbia restaurant was known for. Heck with it, Keira thought as she pulled back into traffic; she was going to stop at one of the high-end restaurants along the Manatee River. Now where to eat?

She thought about going to *Mattison's Riverwalk grille* or *Pier 22*; both were great places to eat. The river-scape from the waterfront tables was spectacular. But at the last minute, she decided to stop at the *Oak and Stone* restaurant. She could get a couple of slices of their fantastic pizza, sip wine from their rooftop seating area and enjoy the view from high above the Manatee River.

The hostess who greeted her at the door asked if she wanted the rooftop or the street-level bar. Of course, Keira wanted the rooftop

"It may be a bit loud as we are experimenting with a Saturday evening twilight band." The hostess in black explained.

"Who is playing?"

"T De Novo, you know, the all attorney band. They will start playing in a while. I hope you will enjoy them.". The hostess beamed.

Keira took the elevator to the top floor. She was seated at a table in the corner overlooking the Manatee River and the marina across the street. The water was a sparkling liquid golden color as the sun began its' descend. The server immediately asked for her drink order.

Just as she looked up from the menu, KC Bradlow, Lea Finn, and KC's sister, Kristianna Romanoff walked towards her.

"Keira, are you here alone?" KC Bradlow asked.

"Hi, yes, my date had an emergency and had to bail. Do you care to join me?"

"I think you met Lea at a charity event last fall, and you know my little sister and law partner, Kristi." KC joked.

"I heard you are singing tonight."

"Yes, I have to help set up. So, if you will excuse me, I will talk with you later."

The three women ordered drinks and within minutes were chatting. Keira expressed her excitement that Chef Karas was opening The Mermaid Isle Beach Restaurant on Bradenton Beach. She could tell Kristi was dying to talk about the grand opening. Kristi let them know the staff was in training at The Mermaid Isle Sarasota Restaurant at the moment.

"Keira owns The Landscape Architect and Lawn Care Service Company. She lives on a yacht at the marina, down the street from Zac's soon-to-be-opened restaurant," Kristi explained to Lea.

"Oh." Lea looked at Kristi, then Keira. "It's your company that did the fantastic landscaping on Kai's yard and keeps it looking so beautiful."

Keira accepted the praise with grace but inwardly she was ecstatic that Lea Finn, the local bestselling author enjoyed her creation at KC Bradlow's lavish home and lawn. That property had the most beautiful and healthy palm trees Keira had seen in a long while.

Lea pointed out Kristi's engagement ring for Keira to admire.

"Yes, I was just looking at the elegant diamond on your finger. It's a striking design." Keira said as she admired Kristi's ring.

They listened, while sipping their drinks as Kristi told of the chaotic Christmas morning engagement proposal.

Lea asked if Keira was familiar with The Crystal Corner Gem Shop. When Keira said yes, Lea explained how her memory finally returned after the New Year's Eve accident. Susyn Blair-Hunt had given her protective gems earlier in December that may have saved her and Kai's life that night. Keira smiled and knew Susyn was very good at sharing her knowledge of beautiful gemstones in helping people. The details of Lea and KC's accident survival on New Year's Eve were an excellent example of the gem's powers.

It was interesting how the three of them had found so much in common in such a short time, Keira thought. And then, as they ate their dinners, T De Novo band lead vocal, KC Bradlow, began to sing. It was such a beautiful evening to be sitting out while listening to KC and his band. A large number of people had gathered to listen to the early evening music. The rooftop was crowded but being open- air, it didn't seem like it at all.

The clock tower on the City Pier chimed the late hour as Keira walked the plank to her boat. Jack, her new dock mate, was sitting out on the deck of his cabin cruiser watching a movie on TV.

"Care to join me for a drink?"

"Thanks, but I have more than enough to drink this evening."

"Then, how about I get you a bottle of water? Please, keep hydrated or you will have a nasty hangover in the morning," Jack suggested.

"Sure, let me change out of my shoes and turn on my air conditioner for the night. I will be right over."

Keira spent the next hour learning about the new guy on the dock. His name was Jack. He lost his house in the divorce but, he got his thirty-seven-foot cabin cruiser which he planned to live on for the time being. She laughed when Jack had said he had already met the always drunk guy and decided the name she gave them was perfect. She had the feeling he only owned the cruiser as a showpiece and was not an avid boater. Living on a boat was not for everyone. When she asked what his profession was, he quietly said he was a hospital administrator. She respected his desire to keep a low profile about his line of work. She just wanted to be known as someone who enjoyed living on her boat, not a landscaper or business owner. After enough time had passed, Keira graciously thanked him for the bottle of water and bid him a good night.

After she returned to her cabin, she didn't have the energy to open her laptop. She had a fantastic evening listening to the T De Novo band at the *Oak and Stone* Restaurant. With the two rum runner drinks, plus waking up early this morning, Keira was exhausted. She changed into her nightshirt, forced herself to drink a large glass of water, before crawling into her bunk.

Chapter 6
♥♥♥♥♥♥♥♥♥♥♥♥♥

It was after eight when Keira woke up. She listened to the muffled conversations on the docks and decided she could lounge in bed for a while longer. It was Sunday. There was nothing that demanded her attention at the moment. The phone was silent, no client questions, absolutely nothing that needed her focus. Jack, the hospital administrator, the next berth over must have met Mr. Benson. The older gentleman was explaining the different baits used for the array of fish he liked to catch. She smiled.

Thinking back over the last twelve hours, even though Len had canceled their dinner date, she enjoyed her evening out. She couldn't believe she had accidentally met KC Bradlow, her attorney, his girlfriend Lea Finn, and his sister Kristianna Romanoff at the Oak and Stone rooftop bar and grill. She had forgotten KC was part of the all attorney band, T De Novo. They listened to his music while nibbling on their meals. The group had exceptional sound and sang great songs. When KC was on break, he told Lea how Keira's landscape company had removed all the shrubs and straggly plants in his yard when he moved in. He dramatically threw his hands up and repeated, 'I want them all gone.'

"So that is how his lawn of palm trees came about. It is so simple but strikingly beautiful. And the fact, you kept some of the stone paths." Lea had gushed.

"You know Keira redesigned that small patio off the living room facing the canal. She brought out the beauty of the palladium windows across the entire back of the house and increased the outdoor space at least three times its area. We still enjoy sitting out there." KC had pointed out.

"I love how you created a seating area with a fire pit. Oh, and the huge hammock between palms in the backyard. Can you pencil me in to design the lot that Zac and I are building a house on? We will be living down the street from Lea and KC." Kristi had asked.

"I would love to create something special for your new home's lawn," Keira remembered saying.

"You guys, thank you. I had heard rumors before I started your landscape project; you were into details and difficult to work with." Keira teased. Yes, KC Bradlow was meticulous. But, she knew, her vision for his lawn would complimented the beauty of his home. She would never forget the look on his face on the day of completion. For being a sophisticated attorney, he was like a happy little kid.

The easy bantering and laughter continued even after the band's gig ended, and KC joined them for one last drink.

Keira wandered into the galley. Instead of driving to the convenience store for a cup of coffee, she decided to pull out her coffee pot that someone gave her as a gag gift for Christmas one year. She found the gift of coffee grounds, the person had added. Mrs. Claus's secret blend of ground coffee beans; wonder what her secret was, Keira thought. She looked at the expiration date and decided the classified mixture was still safe. While the coffee was brewing, Keira sat at her chart table. She noticed a missed call and a text from last evening on her cell phone.

"I just got word; there is trouble with the design. I'm flying back to Singapore tomorrow night. I want to see you before I leave. Scott"

Does this jerk never give up? Keira thought. She had blocked him, and he had continued to persist! Since the jerk was leaving the country, maybe he would realize, whoever he was trying to get in touch with, didn't care. Shaking her head, she pushed the on button and her laptop lit up.

Instead of opening up the notes from men who had been seeking her out, she wanted to find someone who had characteristics she wanted in a man. She scanned the profiles of a couple of guys but nothing was exciting about them. Then, a profile popped up that practically hit her in the face. She had never seen this one before.

Theseus
34 years of age
Tampa, FL
Gemini
6′2″

The extended profile was a very interesting read. Keira studied the attached photos. There were two of the back of a man's head in cruise ship captain attire with a view of the bridge and the windows overlooking the sea. In one of the pictures, the man held a glass with a Greek anchor, trident, and cross etched in the stemware. It dawned on her; Theseus was a Greek god or son of a king or something like that from mythology. After using her search engine, giggling, she started typing...

Dear Theseus,
It seems you have had a very colorful life. You defeated the Minotaur, son of the Cretan Queen Pasiphae, and a white bull. I won't get into the creepiness of that union. I do congratulate you on your successful conquer! You became a hero in Greek mythology. I still, though, do not understand how you had two fathers, but, hey, it's none of my business, right?
So, now you show up on a dating website as a sea captain for Royal Caribbean and a part-time gig doing dive charters out of Tampa. It is very suspicious that you had close ties with Poseidon, god of the sea, and now you are a sea captain.
Other than the Greek god thing, when did you decide you wanted to sail the seas? I see you have a master's degree in marine engineering, and you served in the Navy with command of your own vessel. Being the captain of the ship, would it be faster to explain where you haven't sailed? I question this because I am intrigued by your past. And I, too, love the wind in my hair and the scent of salty sea air.
I feel at home on the water, even if I am the Mistress of Palms.

After she sent the email to Theseus, she reread it and giggled some more. She would love to see the look on the guy's face when he read it. Or, was he used to other women sending him quirky notes? Was that how some chicks got the attention of guys? Keira never played those kind of games' her emails were usually straightforward. It wasn't her style to send off the wall notes like this one. But there was something about his profile that made her want to act crazy for a change. Maybe it was the straight-laced military uniform sea captain photos. Whatever it was, she felt like a pirate wanting to go after some booty.

There was a note from **ExtremeLover – Michael.** He, too, was interesting, yet she was fearful she could not keep up with his extreme love. The water had finally dripped into the glass coffee pot, so while she read Michael's letter, she sipped on the weird flavored coffee.

> *Dear Keira,*
> *I can't believe you would have done almost anything in exchange for dive time. You must have loved diving very much. Most kids would never consider doing such things, especially the chumming of water on commercial fishing boats. With the number of shark attacks, is that even legal anymore? Also, to paint yacht masts was pretty ambitious for a kid; and kind of dangerous. I can see the owners of the marinas around here, seeing a girl monkey climb up a mast to paint it. They would go ballistic these days, not to mention their liability; insurance would go through the roof!*
> *You asked about some of the places I have dived. A fun dive was in Hawaii. Doing a night dive with manta rays was stunningly beautiful. They were everywhere. I have done Cozumel reefs and the great blue hole in Belize, which was incredible. A bunch of us traveled to Australia for some exciting*

dives. I have also dived some of the reefs in
Indonesia and up through Malaysia. Of course, I
have done the ABC islands and all of the Caribbean.
     I received a call to do some surfing in Australia for
a couple of weeks; I will know more about it in a few
days.   Michael

Dear Michael,

Reading your email brought back memories of when I hung out at the marina near where I lived as a child. I would pitch in and help hose down the docks after the fish hauls were brought in or help out wherever possible, even though they paid me only a small token of a wage. I saved all of it for dive lessons. Maybe it was a sense of belonging.

I always felt at home at the water's edge. Anyway when the owner of the marina died, in his will, he left me money to put towards my first boat. An attorney summoned me to his office. He told me the owner had thought of me over the years as one of his grandchildren. It was such an honor to hear that, especially when he had always been so stern. He had demanded much of me, and then I understood why, I was like family.

Yesterday, I spend the morning changing the light on the mast top and added a bird deflector to my sailboat. Funny that you mentioned marina owners and the dangers of, as you say, monkey climbing masts. The marina's owner found out I did exactly that, and sure enough, he was not happy with me. Oh well, it was a beautiful view from up there.

The dive sites you mentioned in your email sounded so cool. I would love to visit some of them, but I am afraid I am only a recreational diver. You would probably be bored with me tagging along, even if my dive logbook is extensive.   Keira

By the time she got done writing and sending the letter to Michael, she still wasn't sure what was in Mrs. Claus's secret blend of coffee. It tasted a bit like peppermint mud with a hint of dish soap, very strange and not one to be tried again. As she poured the concoction down the sink drain, a marine forecast came across her phone. There was a wind advisory for later this afternoon, up to twenty-five knots. She quickly washed her coffee mug and headed up on deck to check out the weather.

"Hi, Mr. Benson."

"Good Morning Keira, it looks like it is going to be a great day for a sail." Mr. Benson said as he cast his fishing line into the water.

"Yes, it is." Keira smiled. She headed back to the galley to secure all of her belongings. It was indeed a great day for a sail, as Mr. Benson had said.

Keira had a fantastic day sailing along the coast, heading north towards the Sunshine Skyway Bridge. The breeze had kicked up, and her boat handled the wind with style and grace. With a burst of speed, she would ride a wave exquisitely, dipping and turning with the elegance of a dancer. Black Beauty, the name of the boat, followed Keira's commands from the helm without resistance or difficulty. There were very few sailboats out on the water for some reason. But, never the less, it had been an invigorating run.

With reluctance and sadness in her heart, Keira turned her craft south and headed for home. The sun had begun its descent towards the sea. Keira feared the strong winds would soon settle down. She remembered the one time she was way out in the Straits of Florida, halfway between Key West and Cuba. The zephyr had died down and she feared the currents were going to pull her towards the forbidden island. She had never worked so hard in her life watching for traces of winds, trying to catch the slightest to drive the sails home.

Once in the sound, she slowly motored her way back to the dock. Watching Jack clumsily jump off his cruiser, he grabbed her boat's railing and held it steady against the pier.

"Thanks."

"The wind was so strong; I called Micah to take his towboat out to look for you," Jack said as he watched her throw the bumpers over the side and threaded the ropes from her boat through the cleats.

"You did WHAT? Why?" Keira almost shouted.

"There are small craft warnings out; I heard the warnings beep across the marine weather station. I feared you got caught out there and were in danger." Jack pleaded his fears. "Oh, here comes Micah, now."

Keira wanted to scream and stomp her feet; she was ready to throw a temper tantrum. Just because she was a woman didn't mean she couldn't handle her sailboat. Keira wasn't reckless. She had more sailing hours than most of the people on the docks put together and knew what the sails on her boat could withstand. Calm down, she thought. Laugh it off. You have to live here; don't say something you can't take back, she chanted in her head.

"Thank you for coming, the weather was getting worse, and Keira was still out there when I called you. She just got in now." Jack told Micah as he walked onto the gangplank.

"I watched you sail past my house. You have the only black sailboat with a pirate with dreadlocks on the mainsail. You handled her very well; she rides nicely in the water. I'm glad you got back safe. I have to check on some docks that let loose. Jack, Keira." With a nod, Micah walked away.

Talk about knocking the wind out of your sails, Keira thought. She was all ready to verbally slam anyone who questioned her sailing skills. What did Micah do? He said she handled her boat really well.

"Thanks for your concern Jack, I appreciate it. I'm going to call it a day. I need to tie down the sails and hose down the deck. Tomorrow, I have a full day scheduled, night." Keira said.

"Keira...I'm sorry I overreacted. I'm new at this boat stuff." "Not a problem."

Keira spent the next couple of hours covering the sails, swabbing the deck, and cleaning her home. She glanced up once from her tasks to see Micah securing one of the docks. Another time he was talking with one of the yacht owners several piers over. It was interesting to see him working on a Sunday. She wondered if he labored and helped out on the docks during the week as he was this evening.

Micah and the Sunday evening dock work were forgotten when

her stomach started growling. All she had eaten since breakfast was, oh wait, she only drank that nasty coffee. It was time for dinner. Grilled scallops and a salad sounded like an excellent choice for dinner.

With her dinner dishes cleared away, it was time to plan how to tackle the Riverview Blvd project starting Monday morning. However, she opened her laptop. There was a letter from Cooleduardo which she thought about opening but decided to delete without looking at it. She opened the next note:

Rad & Sexy - Len

> *Dear Keira,*
>
> *I'm sorry we were unable to have dinner Saturday evening. I worked half of the night reading stat x-rays for the large number of trauma victims brought in. It was a horrible evening. I hope your weekend was better than mine.*
>
> *Why don't you come over to my house on Saturday at About two p.m.? You could take a look at my yard and give me some suggestions, and then, we could go to lunch at one of the beach cafes. I will text you the directions later in the week.*
>
> *Len*

Keira thought about Len's second attempt to get together. Although it wasn't his fault that he had to go to work, it was the apathy in his voice when he called, and now again, his note was very generic. There wasn't anything inspiring in his words about getting together with her on Saturday. The phrases, looking forward to seeing you or can't wait to have you come to my home wasn't in the note. Keira frowned. Maybe he was just tired. But, their relationship was new; it should be exciting. And then, the bit about her looking at his yard; it seemed more like a work proposal about to be contracted out, if and only if Mr. Doctor approved.

Dear Len,

Thank you for the lunch invitation for next Saturday. Two in the afternoon sounds like a good time to relax and enjoy a bite to eat. I am sad that you had such a tough weekend. Does it weigh heavily on your heart when you see so many broken bones and damaged people? How do you mentally handle the trauma that you work with, especially during the winter season when there is an overabundance of tourist traffic on the road and accidents occurring?

My Saturday evening turned out to be unexpectedly fun. I went to one of the rooftop restaurants downtown Bradenton called Oak and Stone Bar and Grill. The place was experimenting with having what they called a twilight band come in to play. It is a smart marketing strategy; since the drinking and party crowd usually doesn't start before ten in the evening. It's a great way to pull in early evening patrons. While I was there having dinner, my attorney, his girlfriend, and his sister came in. He just happened to be the lead singer of the band, T De Novo, and was scheduled to sing that evening. His sister and girlfriend ended up sitting and had dinner with me.

Today the marine forecast predicted small craft warnings. So I took my sailboat out and had a fantastic time sailing. Now I am exhausted and ready for bed. I hope you have a good evening.

Keira

Keira heard footsteps on the narrow planks between hers and jack's boat. She wasn't used to the sound. Since many cabin cruisers didn't need a deep water docking space, like her boat; there were few boats near hers. Most boats had either outboard propellers that could be raised or had a shallower draft and didn't need the deeper bottom. She hadn't turned on her cabin lights and had mentioned to Jack; she was making it an early night. So, she pretty much didn't know of anyone who would be visiting her. She heard Jack ask the person to come aboard his boat and then offered the person a beer. The other voice was soft-spoken and said little. Then it dawned on Keira; it was Micah. She was surprised. It was a Sunday evening, and he was hanging out on the docks, which she had never seen him do before.

She could hear her name come up a couple of times. Jack asked questions like, if she was seeing anyone, how long had she lived on her boat, and then he changed the subject. Micah's responses were hard to hear. His voice, when he did talk, was rich in tone and soothing. She felt guilty listening to their conversation, even though she wasn't eavesdropping.

Keira took her laptop and crawled into bed. She fluffed her pillows to get comfortable and clicked on an email from **Wildman - Matt**. She hadn't heard from him in several days.

> *Dear Keira,*
>
> *Thank you for finally telling me your name. I can now put a name on the beautiful profile picture I have of you.*
>
> *I broke down and gave the long weekend off that I had been contemplating. I think I said something to you about them needing a weekend to spend time with their families. Anyway, it was good for them, and I, too, needed the break. I spent Saturday morning up-dating permits with the local government and completing payroll and paperwork for the day. Around noon, I set off to explore the town. The marketplace ...*

Oh... Jack said something funny. Keira wondered what it was because she could hear the sound of Micah chuckling. Stop it, she thought. Now, where was she? Oh, yeah, Matt.

> *The marketplace was magnificent. The spice vendors and silk shops were interesting to see. I would have loved to wrap you in scarves of the finest threads of silk. I am sure you would have loved the feel of the cloth against your skin. I saw so many handmade rugs, some of which would look great in my home in Florida. There were baskets hanging from the ceilings in several of the ceiling in several of*

the shops. Local women make them while their
husbands are away, either fishing or working the
fields. I did purchase some homemade loaves of
bread. I could not pass up purchasing a beautiful
Cabernet Sauvignon wine, also made locally. It will
be nice to sit out and have a glass of wine while
watching the sunset. I will toast to your beauty, my
love, Matt.

Dear Matt,

I have seen travel brochures of Istanbul's Grand Bazaar. It would be a fantastic adventure to browse through one of the oldest and most beautiful marketplaces in the world. Did you buy anything other than the wine and loaves of bread? Is the Mediterranean Sea with its turquoise water and the rocky and rugged terrain all around Turkey as beautiful as the pictures? I am glad you were able to take some time off to enjoy your surroundings. Were the men refreshed when they returned to work?

I am working on a new contract across town starting tomorrow morning. I am looking forward to tackling this project. The results will be so beautiful when completed.

Stay safe. Keira

Keira slid out of bed to get a glass of something to drink. While she was pouring some wine, she noticed Micah's legs. The galley windows looked out over the gangplank. It wasn't as if she was spying; or anything. He just happened to climb off Jack's boat as she was looking out. Nice thighs. Quit with the surveillance, she thought. He is off-limits, even if he is single. Taking her glass, she climbed back into bed and opened a new note from **Theseus.**

Dear Mistress of Palms,
I enjoyed the humor of your email. It was a
breath of fresh air. Yes, we do not usually discuss
the family tree much, you know, ancient history. I
noticed you said you love salty sea air. In my sailing

adventures, I have seen coconuts floating on the tropical currents. I have heard they can survive for long periods of time in the water. Being the Mistress of Palms and feeling at home with wet feet, you must have family ties with the coconut palm.

I have sailed six of the seven seas. During my naval days, I crossed the equator several times and have been around Cape Hope and Cape Horn. The Arctic Ocean is the only body of water I have not spent any time in the vicinity of. Remember, I am of Greek heritage, not the indigenous people, who are native to the Arctic. Do you sail?

Tell me how you have come to be known as the Mistress of Palms?   *Theseus*

Dear Theseus,

I, too, will not discuss my family of coconuts! Although, I will say the life span of a coconut palm is about 80 years. With good nutrition and not too many hurricanes in a season, I will not suffer root rot or fungal diseases!! The old man palm, no disrespect to my grandfather, is a slow grower. It takes about ten years to grow a mere five inches. And his beard becomes very thick with a layer of fibers that looks like wool. Oh wait, I promised not to talk about my family.

I love to sail. I got my first job when I was ten. Dumping fish guts into the water for deep sea fishing charter vessels. Believe it or not, it was my job. I couldn't believe someone would pay me to be out on the water every day. I learned; never to eat breakfast before chumming. There was more chum, if I did. I hosed down docks after trawlers brought in their hauls. I saved all the money I made on odd jobs I did hanging around the marina. From the docks, I watched vacation-type people take beginner sailing lessons. After the classes, it was my job to rinse down the sunfish sailboats. I would ask a ton of questions until they finally gave in and taught me how to sail. I bought a used catamaran when I was fifteen. And that is how it began.

My sign-on name is Mistress of Palms because I love a forest of palm trees, with a balmy breeze teasing their branches. I am the owner of an architectural design, landscaping and lawn care company. I love caring for palm trees. They are majestic, and most will sway but remain proudly standing during a hurricane.

Mistress of Palms

As Keira pressed send, she realized she talked of her youth learning to dive and sail with ExtremeLover – Michael and Theseus. She was attracted to two different men, both drawn to the sea. Michael, with his continued seeking of pleasure, turned into an enterprise. Theseus' duty to his country, joining the Navy, turned into a career. ExtremeLover's passion for seeking the ultimate rush of adrenaline was a bit intimidating. Maybe it was because she understood her limitations but always wished for more guts. And Theseus, already there was something about him she felt comfortable enough to show a side of herself, she usually kept hidden. She wanted to find if he had pirate blood or was he one hundred percent Navy? Either way, he had extreme respect for the sea.

Peter Flynn's Friend – Basil

> *Dear K Lee,*
> *I love your name; it is unique like you. And now, I have the name of the woman I dream of at night. Thank you.*
> *Yes, I put a bid on the house that I was impressed with here in Brandon. I am hoping to hear back from the other Realtor tomorrow.*
> *Yes, I put a bid on the house that I was impressed with here in Brandon. I am hoping to hear back from the other Realtor tomorrow morning. The reason the place is perfect for me, is the in-law suite. As you know, I live in Washington D.C. My now ex-wife ran*

off with an ambassador from the Mideast. He
promised her gold and riches. As devastating as it
seems, the silver lining is that her ambassador lover
refused to take our ten-year- old daughter with
them when they left the country. So, I have sole
custody of her. However, the problem is, there are
times when I have to be out of the country to check
on my projects overseas. I build large industrial
warehouses for companies around the world.

By having a live-in nanny, who cares for my
daughter, there is no disruption of care or sleeping
arrangements when I am away. Although my
parents live over the state line in Virginia, they are
elderly and cannot care for a spirited ten year old for
more than a few hours at a time.

I must close for now; I have overseas calls to
make. Until we speak again, Love, Basil

Dear Basil,

I hope you hear back shortly from the real estate agent letting you know your bid for the house; is yours. It would solve so many of your concerns, I am sure.

It must have been devastating for you and your daughter when your wife left with the ambassador of another country. It is a low blow to our egos and painful to our hearts, but to children, it is catastrophic. Their whole world revolves around family. I'm sorry; you don't need to hear that from me. You have lived through it, but my heart does go out to you and your daughter.

Thank you for telling me about your need for a nanny for your daughter. The in-law suite sounds perfect for your situation.

You never told me; did you get the bid on the job you were hoping to get? K Lee

Keira closed her laptop and took it out to the chart table so she wouldn't forget it in the morning. She climbed back into bed and curled up on her side. Thoughts of the pleasure of sailing earlier in the day came to her mind. She had been filled with such reverence when she spotted a dolphin playing in the waves alongside her boat. It looked like it was having fun jumping from wave to wave. And then it disappeared. She wondered where it went. Did it return to its pod? She remembered the first time she saw a mamma dolphin teaching her baby how to breach. With her nose, she had pushed the baby's fluke out of the water. It was the perfect "10" if she would have judged the breach.

She wondered if ExtremeLover – Michael would have enjoyed sailing with her. The adrenaline-junkie part of him probably would have hung over the side to feel the salt spray against his face. That made her smile. And then, she thought of Micah's praise for her sailing skills. That was a surprise to hear. She wondered where he lived that he could have watched her sail by. She bet his homes in one of those huge houses on the north end of Anna Maria Island. Or maybe he was a beach shack kind of guy, although he didn't look like it. *Jimmy Buffett*, when he lived in the keys dressed like a beach bum and sometimes a tourist, and he was rich. So, it was possible, Micah could live like a hermit crab in a cozy little shell of a house.

Chapter 7
♥♥♥♥♥♥♥♥♥♥♥♥♥

Monday morning was the start of the Riverview Blvd project. Keira pulled into the driveway next door to the yard her crew was to begin working on. She hoped, judging by the flooded street, it wasn't going to be a Murphy's Law type of day. After talking to the foreman of the street department, Keira found out in the wee small hours of the morning, for unknown reasons, a water main broke, flooding the entire area. That wasn't the way she wanted to start a Monday, but the city's DOT crew was at least working to repair the damage with their equipment.

Keira walked the property with Kraig to determine how to alter their project construction plan to prevent delays in the completion time. Keira radioed Chuck and told him to cancel bringing the mini-dozer from the warehouse. Kraig set a crew of 4 to begin clearing the river's edge of debris, even if it would be slower without the bulldozer to clear out the roots. Jack could continue with the staking of where the cement retaining wall would be. And she made a point of welcoming Marcus back. With the game plan in place, Keira walked with her can of spray paint, marking the bushes for removal later.

By lunchtime, although the residents of the landscape project were not around to hear, Keira was fed up with the razzing to Marcus. His manly ego was taking a severe beating. It was his new wife, who was caught in the next room, having sex with some guy. Throughout the morning, many of the crew continued to barrage Marcus about his Vegas wedding and annulment – two days later.

Keira gathered, none of the guys had liked Marcus's girl even when they dated. So the 'I told ya so' kept being said in both English and Spanish.

"Kraig, can we talk about some alterations I have made?" Keira said to her foreman as she walked to the soon-to-be-demolished patio with blueprints in hand.

As they stood by the empty pool, out of earshot of the other workers, Kraig asked, "Ok, what's up? You never make changes to the blueprint."

"And I am not this time either. Look, I never interfere with how you handle the crew, well, almost, never. But I am rather sick of..."

"I know, I will say something."

"Thanks."

Keira spent midday prying the old wood stairs and decrepit cement out of the ground. The pickax and jackhammer were painfully giving her muscles a work-out. However, there was no way she could lug the chunks of cement across a quarter of an acre of mud to the back of her work truck. Driving across the still soggy front lawn without getting her truck stuck up to its' doors was out of the question.

When Keira took a water break, a couple of the guys teased her about having sore muscles tomorrow. She showed them her biceps, which gave them all a laugh. A couple of the guys enthusiastically gave her a thumbs-up gesture. Out of the corner of her eye, she saw Kraig running towards her and the joking crew.

"Keira, you need to get to the hospital. One of the lawn crew, I think it was Dante, got cut really bad by debris he hit while mowing, that ricocheted off a tree."

As Keira drove down Manatee Avenue towards the hospital, she wiped down her arms with wet cloths she kept in the truck. She was sure she smelled of sweat and dirt.

Her company logo on her shirt explained why she was filthy; project sites were not the cleanest of jobs. For some reason, it was ok for guys to smell of body odor and look like they had been rutting around in the dirt, but not so much for women. Ignoring the unfairness of the double standard, she needed to check on her injured lawn mowing crew person, immediately. As Keira drove across Wares Creek, a low flying pelican hit her windshield. It took her completely by surprise; she swerved a bit out of her lane. With her heart pounding against her rib cage Keira thought, crap, that was close. Thank goodness no one was traveling right next to her. Keira would have side-swiped them for sure. It not only scared the heck out of her, but smashed her company truck's windshield. But, with afternoon traffic, there was no place to pull over. Keira had to keep driving until she got to the hospital.

The hospital's emergency department was busy with trauma victims arriving by ambulance. Several people were sitting on vinyl chairs waiting to have their broken bones set, cuts stitched up, or x-rays taken after their falls. Dante, an employee of The Landscape Architect and Lawn Care Service, received several layers of stitches. Lawn mowing was potentially a dangerous job if and when the blades hit something sharp. Dante was walking out of the curtained cubicle just as Keira rushed through the double doors of the ER Department.

"Dante, how are you doing? Hello Mrs. Sebastian, I am glad you were with him when he got his arm cleaned, stitched, and bandaged." Keira said as she guided them to the sitting area against the wall.

"No thanks to you." Mrs. Sebastian grumbled. "Now he will be off work, an emergency room bill, an ambulance bill, and no money coming in."

"Gloria, mantenerse al margen de esta!" Dante scolded his wife.

"Mrs. Sebastian, I assure you, the company will handle the medical bills. Dante, how did it happen? How long did the doctor say you should be off work? Keira asked.

"I didn't see the beer bottle in the grass. The mower blades hit and shattered the glass. Part of the bottle hit a tree I was mowing around and cut through my shirt and arm. The doc said two days, but I will be back tomorrow. I am fine. He did a good job of stitching up my arm."

"No! Dos days, Dante."

"GLORIA!"

"Dante, I will leave that decision up to you. Now, let me go and settle the bill. Be careful going home and call me if you need anything."

"Si and gracias, Miss Keira," Dante nodded.

A Bradenton Police officer was standing by Keira's work truck when she walked out of the emergency department exit doors.

"Miss, is this your truck?"

"Yes, a pelican hit my windshield while I was rushing to get here," Keira said. She noticed the officer glanced down at the medical bill paperwork she had in her hand.

"I'm sorry if you had an emergency, but I can't let you drive that truck on the road with the windshield like that. It is unsafe for you and other drivers if it would completely break free."

By that, the hospital security officer on a golf cart rolled to a stop in front of Keira's truck. "I'm sorry, miss, it is against hospital policy to have windshields repaired in the hospital parking lot."

"What?"

"Windshield companies could drop glass particles on the ground. It could become a hazard and liability for the hospital."

"Fine, I will call my insurance company and have my truck towed to a shop to have it fixed."

Keira thanked the officer for what; she didn't know, but it was wise to keep good relations with the police department. Her company logo was on the side of the truck. Rolling her eyes, she pulled her phone from her satchel and called her insurance for the tow and repair.

While she waited, she called Kraig and told him the whole unbelievable story. He, of course, asked if she wanted him to pick her up, as if it was just a routine day at work.

"Yes, I would appreciate you picking me up after work. The auto repair shop said they couldn't fix the damaged windshield until tomorrow morning," Keira explained.

Her jeep was at the office. But she didn't feel comfortable leaving all the equipment in the back of her truck in an unsecured lot overnight. She figured she and Kraig could unload the stuff and take it back in her Jeep to the warehouse behind the office.

Two hours later, Kraig helped her unload the generator and chests of tools from the bed of the work truck into Kraig's truck. She picked up the last toolbox and dropped it. Keira fell to her knees. Pain shot through her finger and up her arm. She somehow had broken the blood vessel in her ring finger. The pain was so intense; she applied pressure to the spot hoping the throbbing would stop. Tears came to her eyes. She didn't want to act like a baby. But damn, it hurt badly. She, for sure couldn't let Kraig hear the nasty vocabulary words she thought about and wanted to scream.

Kraig kneeled down. He grabbed Keira's shoulders and questioned, "Keira, are you ok? Do you need to go back to the emergency room?"

"No, I just blew a blood vessel in my finger. I knew I strained my fingers when I picked up the box wrong. It will be OK, but it hurts like hell." Keira tried to laugh. She could see the concern for her written all across Kraig's face. It was overwhelming to see the fear he was showing. She had never seen that type of emotion in him before.

It took a while to unload the equipment at the office. Keira felt like a one-handed wallpaper hanger – completely helpless. She was exhausted. The muscles the guys had teased her about earlier in the day were now starting to tighten up.

"Keira, do you want to grab something to eat before you head for home? You haven't eaten today, again."

Looking down at her work shorts and shirt, she felt so gritty, and her finger hurt. She wanted to say no, but she was hungry. "Let's go somewhere close; I will follow you in my jeep."

Kraig took Keira to one of the little cafés downtown with outdoor seating. She didn't feel quite so out of place in her somewhat smelly work clothes. Kraig ordered a beer, while Keira decided on only a lemon-lime for herself. If she had anything with alcohol in it, she would face plant the table.

When the server placed the heaping plate of hot wings and celery on the little table between them, Keira thought she had gone to heaven. The aroma was tantalizing. "Oh. My. Gosh." was all Keira could say.

"You know I would have liked to take you somewhere nicer."

"No, this is perfect. I have never been here. And these wings are probably the best I have had in a while." Keira said as she reached for another wing.

"Well, well, well, now I understand why you wanted to hire Kraig and why you always stuck up for him. You were probably fucking him while I was preoccupied with the play toys you bought me." Peter, Keira's ex-husband, said with his hands on his hips.

"Excuse me?"

"I think you should leave."

"No, it's a damn good reason why I should stay!" Peter growled as he threw his beer bottle towards the mesh trash bin and missed.

A big burly man who looked like someone Keira would want on her team charged out of the pub, just as the three biker guys sitting at a table near the street, stood.

"You heard these people, leave!" snarled one of the biker guys.

"Get the hell out of my pub. You're drunk. I shoulda kicked ya out hours ago. Git before I call the cops."

Keira saw Peter as he glared at her for a minute or two. He must have decided it was best not to argue when outnumbered; he turned and stumbled off.

"Thanks, Skip."

"You folks enjoy your meal. I got your bill."

Keira had lost her appetite when Peter showed up. But she didn't want Kraig to know how shook up she was, pretended to be full.

"I don't think I can eat another wing. They were so good. Thank you for bringing me here. The live band a couple of doors down, the street tables, a slight breeze, and drunken comedy entertainment, this was nice." Keira laughed. "I need to get home. Tomorrow has to be better than today, right?"

When Kraig opened Keira's jeep door for her, he hugged her and whispered, "I'm crazy about you."

Keira stepped out of his embrace and shook her head, "shhh, don't say that. I enjoy working with you and don't want to complicate things." She turned and slid into the driver's seat. She started her car and glanced one more time at Kraig before driving away.

Halfway home, the tears started flowing down Keira's face. Gripping the steering wheel, she realized Peter's unexpected arrival at the pub downtown hit her last nerve. Kraig's continued attempt to smother her with hugs, felt unprofessional. The blown blood vessel in her finger still throbbed. The shattered windshield could have cause a serious multi car accident downtown. She kind of felt bad for the dead pelican and its poor judgment. Well, maybe not that bad with the amount of damage it caused. But then again, why would a bird do a low fly by in traffic? And then, Dante's arm gushing blood and needing a zillion stitches, minus a hundred million or so. His wife's accusing eyes, as if she was a slasher, were scary. To think, an early morning broken water main slowing the project down started all the chaos. All she needed now was Eduardo Luise's sweaty, horny body lounging on her clean bed sheets. With that last thought, she hiccupped, sniffed, and kept driving across the bridge to the marina.

Later that evening, Keira stood under the shower and let the water run down her body. She knew she shouldn't be wasting water, but tonight she needed it. Closing her eyes, Keira leaned against the shower wall and let the steam surround her. Within seconds, she quickly came to attention when she realized the bilge pump was sounding and acting funny. Please don't go out, please don't go out. Or, at least not till Saturday, Keira prayed. But when she looked down at her feet, the water was draining well, so was it her imagination? She turned off the water and wrapped herself in a towel. She had had enough for one day. It was time to climb into bed. But even walking the few feet to her bunk seemed like miles away.

She wondered if there were any happy notes from her men...

Peter Flynn's Friend - Basil

> *Dear K Lee,*
> *I am going to be extremely busy for a while. First,*

I was able to obtain the house in Brandon. So, inspections and transfer of ownership are in the works. Secondly, I won the bid I put in on. The contract is to build a large warehouse, office space, and housing development for an oil refinery company in Cape Town, South Africa.

I am on a flight back to Washington right now. I have an early morning meeting set up with the Ministry of Works in South Africa. We need to move forward quickly on getting the permits and materials to get this project underway as soon as possible. The clock is ticking. I will be trying to spend as much time with my daughter as possible since I will have to go to Cape Town from time to time to keep the project on schedule.

Love to you, my dear, Basil.

Dear Basil,

Congratulations on buying a new home here in Florida. It will be exciting for your daughter to move here. She will make new friends in the neighborhood over the summer before starting school in the fall.

Also, the contract bid you won sounds like a massive project. It seems like such a large undertaking. What is your timeline for completion? Are you going to bring in your supervisors and work with a locally-based crew? Do you have to contend with the union there? Oh my, I am overwhelmed just thinking of all the red tape to work around. Best of luck!   K Lee

"THIS HONEST, SINCERE, GENUINE, REAL, NICE, TRUTHFUL, CANDID, RESPECTFUL, MAN, GUY, FELLOW, GENTLEMAN, DUDE, SEARCHING, LOOKING, HUNTING, INQUIRING, SEEKING, PURSUINGWOMAN, LADY, FEMALE, GIRL, LASSIE, DAME, MAIDEN, DAMSEL, SWEETHEART, CHICK, TO SHARE, ALLOCATE, DISPENSE, AWARD, EXPLORE, APPROPRIATE, LIFE EXPERIENCES, ADVENTURES, ESCAPADES, INTERLUDES, ROMANCES, FLINGS, STUNTS, CAPERS,

ANTICS, EVENTS, WILL NOT REVEAL, SHARE, SHOW, TELL, DIVULGE, DISCLOSE, DISCUSS, PROVIDE, SCAMMERS, CRIMINALS, SWINDLERS, COMPUTER-GENERATED BOTS, ROBOTS, CON ARTISTS, DIRT BAGS, HACKERS, SCUM, SNAKES, PHONIES, FRAUDS, FAKES, PRIVATE, PERSONAL, PHYSICAL HISTORY, PHOTOS, SOCIAL SECURITY, DRIVERS LICENSE NUMBERS, FINANCIAL ASSETS, EMPLOYMENT STATUS OR HEALTH INFORMATION; WHEN INTELLIGENT, SMART, BRIGHT, EDUCATED, SEEMINGLY NICE WOMAN, SHARES, ALLOCATE, DISPENSE, LIFE EXPERIENCES, ADVENTURES, ESCAPADES, ROMANCES, FLINGS, STUNTS, CAPERS, ANTICS, THIS HONEST, SINCERE, GENUINE, REAL, NICE, TRUTHFUL, RESPECTFUL GENTLEMAN, WILL DO THE SAME."

Another long note came across Keira's message box from Maelstrom. She wasn't up to word games with this weirdo, not tonight, she thought. She wanted to think of happy thoughts. So, ignoring it, she went onto another email.

Wildman - Matt

Dear Keira...

"THIS HONEST, SINCERE, GENUINE, REAL, NICE, TRUTHFUL, CANDID, RESPECTFUL, MAN, GUY, FELLOW, GENTLEMAN, DUDE, SEARCHING, LOOKING, HUNTING, INQUIRING, SEEKING, PURSUING, WOMAN, LADY, FEMALE, GIRL, LASSIE, DAME, MAIDEN, DAMSEL, SWEETHEART, CHICK, TO SHARE, ALLOCATE, DISPENSE, AWARD, EXPLORE, APPROPRIATE, LIFE EXPERIENCES, ADVENTURES, ESCAPADES, INTERLUDES, ROMANCES, FLINGS, STUNTS, CAPERS, ANTICS, EVENTS, WILL NOT REVEAL, SHARE, SHOW, TELL, DIVULGE, DISCLOSE, DISCUSS, PROVIDE, SCAMMERS, CRIMINALS, SWINDLERS, COMPUTER GENERATED BOTS, ROBOTS, CON ARTISTS, DIRT BAGS, HACKERS, SCUM, SNAKES, PHONIES, FRAUDS, FAKES, PRIVATE, PERSONAL, PHYSICAL HISTORY, PHOTOS, SOCIAL SECURITY, DRIVERS LICENSE NUMBERS, FINANCIAL ASSETS, EMPLOYMENT STATUS OR HEALTH INFORMATION; WHEN INTELLIGENT, SMART, BRIGHT,

EDUCATED, SEEMINGLY NICE WOMAN, SHARES, ALLOCATE, DISPENSE, LIFE EXPERIENCES, ADVENTURES, ESCAPADES, ROMANCES, FLINGS, STUNTS, CAPERS, ANTICS, THIS HONEST, SINCERE, GENUINE, REAL, NICE, TRUTHFUL, RESPECTFUL GENTLEMAN, WILL DO THE SAME."

Oh please, this is so 'grade school', Keira thought. Nope, she wasn't going to play his game. She wasn't going to answer his message.

> Dear Keira,
> Yes, the men did enjoy their time away from work. One evening while sitting around a fire, a few men spoke of heavy rains and landslides. The stories they told were frightful. I am not sure if the torrential downpours they talked of were a one- time thing or a seasonal occurrence. It was troubling to hear. Problematic weather conditions could slow the timeline of the project. I will have to look further into it. Maybe even a trip into town for a visit to the local government building. I may have the crews working more hours before the rains come, if their stories are correct.
> We are working quite deep in one of the forks of the cave. There is a small lake with many different rock formations around it. I am not sure how deep the water is, but it is fresh water and very cold. The men became fearful when the lights flickered. They felt it was a bad omen and we should not disturb the cavern. I let them know it was the generator probably running low on fuel. Fears and phobias can sabotage a worksite here.   Matt

"WHY, HOW COME, MYSTIFIED, PUZZLED, WOMAN, LADY, FEMALE, GIRL, LASSIE, DAME, MAIDEN, DAMSEL, SWEETHEART, CHICK, NOT WRITING, ANSWERING, TYPING, TALKING, MAKING

STATEMENT TO HONEST, SINCERE, GENUINE, REAL, NICE, CANDID, TRUTHFUL, RESPECTFUL, MAN, GUY, FELLOW, DUDE GENTLEMAN, SEARCHING, LOOKING, HUNTING, INQUIRING, PURSUING, SEEKING, WOMAN, LADY, FEMALE, GIRL, LASSIE, DAME, MAIDEN, DAMSEL, SWEETHEART, CHICK, TO SHARE, ALLOCATE, DISPENSE, AWARD, EXPLORE, APPROPRIATE, LIFE EXPERIENCES, ADVENTURES, ESCAPADES, INTERLUDES, ROMANCES, FLINGS, STUNTS, CAPERS, ANTICS, EVENTS WITH?"

Grrr, she was not going to respond. Instead, she looked up local weather conditions for Turkey. The seven-day forecast revealed occasional showers with intermittent sun. Why was Matt so concerned?

Dear Matt,
    After reading your letter, I was troubled by your concerns over the rains and weather conditions in the mountains region of Turkey. Where there are large bodies of water, such as the Mediterranean Sea, there will always be storms coming in off the water, striking the land. It is not unusual for the elders of a village to speak of events or periods in time when disasters have occurred. They sometimes remember their grand-parent's stories and repeat them. Were the men sitting around the campfire just remembering the past, or were they trying to scare you? I have seen times when one drink leads to another, and the stories become stretched. Legends become larger than life. And the folklore of the mighty storms and floods the elements took on human traits. Although the elders may have put fear in the young, folk tales were used to teach respect for nature.
    When I was in southern Mexico one time, it was after dark, and we were all gathered around a campfire. The local people talked of times before electricity. They spoke of their fears of hurricane-force winds and rains. They told of their elders running through the jungle to alert members of their village, of invasions. When asked how they could see to run in the darkness, they spoke of shells bleached white by the sun made into paths. Each of those stories talked of the trials of the past. They taught respect for their elder's way and how to

deal with life in the future.

There is much history, legends, and mysteries in the old world of the European nations. Fears and superstitions run deep in the villages. I am sure you will keep a level head and remember there usually are logical explanations like the flickering lights in the cave.

Take care, Keira

Smiling, Keira remembered when she was just starting the company. The older workers loved to weave quite the story of how to do things. Yes, they were the elders and were due respect for their knowledge and wisdom. But they also had the gift of pranking well established under their belts.

"WHY, HOW COME, MYSTIFIED, PUZZLED, WOMAN, LADY, FEMALE, GIRL, LASSIE, DAME, MAIDEN, DAMSEL, SWEETHEART, CHICK, NOT WRITING, ANSWERING, TYPING, TALKING, MAKING STATEMENT TO HONEST, SINCERE, GENUINE, REAL, NICE, TRUTHFUL, CANDID, RESPECTFUL, MAN, GUY, FELLOW, GENTLEMAN, DUDE, SEARCHING, LOOKING, HUNTING, INQUIRING, SEEKING, PURSUING, WOMAN, LADY, FEMALE, GIRL, LASSIE, DAME, MAIDEN, DAMSEL, SWEETHEART, CHICK, TO SHARE, ALLOCATE, DISPENSE, AWARD, EXPLORE, APPROPRIATE, LIFE EXPERIENCES, ADVENTURES, ESCAPADES, INTERLUDES, ROMANCES, FLINGS, STUNTS, CAPERS, ANTICS, EVENTS WITH?

Nope, you can waste your time typing your thesaurus of words all you want. I'm not going to answer you, Keira decided.

ExtremeLover – Michael

> *Dear Keira,*
> *Thank you for the story of your hanging out at*
> *the local marina. Memories are what make us who*
> *we are today. I'm sure some of the memories were*
> *bittersweet since the marina owner has passed.*
> *Please do not feel as if your recreational diving is*

inferior to my extreme diving. I was a 'just for fun' diver when I was in high school. The only problem was, my sometimes stupid and wild stunts back then turned into a lucrative career. I am an extreme sports photojournalist.

I, without a doubt, enjoy what I do. It does, at times, promote dangerous situations for some people who do not have the experience to handle such sports. I can add disclaimers at the end of my camera footage. But there are always a few individuals who do not know their limitations.

Michael

Dear Michael,

Have you heard when you will be going south of the equator for some surfing? It seems funny that as we are moving into the summer solstice, they are smack dab in their winter and perfect surfing weather. I am sure it is very frustrating for you unable to surf the gulf when it is so calm you can see the bottom at thirty feet.

I have to tell you. On Sunday, when the small gale sprung up, I went out and sailed almost to Egmont Key and back was a fantastic ride, and as always, my sailboat handled it well. One of the new guys, living on his boat temporarily, had a panic attack over me being out in the 25-knot winds. He called the marina's towboat to come search for me. I know he was concerned, but it was downright frustrating that he didn't think I could handle the wind. I believe that he would have thought nothing of you out sailing in a storm or any other man.

Why is it, so many men do not think women are capable of having boating skills?   Keira

Extremelover – Michael

Dear Keira,

The guy who called the rescue towboat in the wind squall that popped up on Sunday was concerned for your welfare. And I am sure after you thought about it a while, you realized he was just

worried about you. And that was a good thing, even if he is a toad. Not all women can do some of the things you do with ease and style. Please, don't set the women's brigade on me; many women in the workforce want to be equal or superior to men but won't or can't do the job, the minute things become tough going. It is expected for a guy to take over or take pity. I don't see it as much in surfing or skiing because those sports are individuals against nature, other than the flirty chicks asking if I will carry their surfboards or ski equipment for them! But in the corporate world, many women don't work that hard. I am sure you have seen it in your field. Do I sound like a chauvinistic male?   Michael

Keira sat up in bed abruptly. Michael was online; he read her email right after she sent it. Looking at the ceiling, dreamily she thought, he is somewhere on Anna Maria Island thinking about me. Keira looked down and realized the towel she had wrapped up in earlier had slipped to her waist. She quickly reached across the bed and grabbed her old ratty nightshirt, pulling it down over her head and naked breast. Still blushing, she laughed thinking and who would have seen her bare chest? No one.

Keira needed to stretch her stiff muscles. After peaking out the portal window, to make sure Jack's lights were off, she walked out on the deck with her glass of wine. The mugginess had decreased a little; it was a nice late night. She wondered if Michael was thinking of her. Would he be an extreme lover like his profile name? The thought of him being her lover made her toes curl and put a smile on her face.

"Nice night, isn't it?"

"Oh crap, you scared me," Keira exclaimed as she whirled around to see Jack sitting on the dock with his legs hanging over the edge.

"I'm not used to boats down here at my end. I have gotten accustom to being here alone." Keira rolled her eyes in the darkness, knowing she just opened a can of worms with that statement.

"Doesn't it bother you being alone?"

"Sometimes, but mostly it's a frame of mind. As the saying goes, you can be alone in a crowd." Keira shrugged, taking a sip of wine. Keira watched as Jack stood up and walked down the gangplank. He sat down between their boats.

"Are you divorced, or have you never been married?"

Here we go, Keira thought. If she was never married, it was because she was temperamental or no one wanted her. If she was divorced, someone was better, cuter, and sexier than she was. She took a sip of wine and said, "Divorced."

"Since you know I lost everything but my boat in my divorce, can you tell me about yours?"

Hmm, she thought, she could be funny and say, yeah, see me living on my boat? Or she could rant and scream and pull her hair out at the injustice of her divorce. She could confide in him telling him how Peter was screwing not only some guy's wife but her employer's at the moment.

"You know, it is too nice of a night for that kind of discussion." Besides, Keira thought, she was leaning against the railing in nothing but a ratty old nightshirt, no bra, no underpants, just a mid- thigh T-shirt. Come to think of it. The shirt could have been Peter's.

"So, what do you do as a hospital administrator?"

"Do you like living on your boat?" Jack asked as he polished off the last of his beer.

"I guess it is too nice of a night to talk about job requisites. Yes, I enjoy living on my boat. I love the water, so it seemed reasonable when the opportunity to purchase it arose.

"You're lucky. I miss my home, the pool, and especially the hot tub on chilly nights."

"And your children?"

"I miss them the most. But the constant arguing got to the point; I enjoyed working longer and longer hours not to come home. Do you have children?"

"No. Well, it's late. Nice talking with you, night." Keira walked back down into the galley and rinsed out her wine glass. After turning on the alarm, she crawled back in bed with her laptop. Jack seemed to be so lost. Being a rebound lover was not what she wanted to be. Those romances seldom lasted. He needed to find himself, learn who he was, and begin to like himself before he dove headfirst into his next love. Those steps took time.

Keira clicked open the website and was dumb-founded.

"WHY, HOW COME, MYSTIFIED, PUZZLED, WOMAN, LADY, FEMALE, GIRL, LASSIE, DAME, MAIDEN, DAMSEL, SWEETHEART, CHICK, NOT WRITING, ANSWERING, TYPING, TALKING, MAKING STATEMENT TO HONEST, SINCERE, GENUINE, REAL, NICE, CANDID, TRUTHFUL, RESPECTFUL, MAN, GUY, FELLOW, GENTLEMAN, DUDE SEARCHING, LOOKING, HUNTING, INQUIRING, SEEKING, PURSUING, WOMAN, LADY, FEMALE, GIRL, LASSIE, DAME, MAIDEN, DAMSEL, SWEETHEART, CHICK, TO SHARE, ALLOCATE, DISPENSE, AWARD, EXPLORE, APPROPRIATE, LIFE EXPERIENCES, ADVENTURES, ESCAPADES, INTERLUDES, ROMANCES, FLINGS, STUNTS, CAPERS, ANTICS, EVENTS WITH?"

"WHY, HOW COME, MYSTIFIED, PUZZLED, WOMAN, LADY, GIRL, FEMALE, LASSIE, DAME, MAIDEN, DAMSEL, SWEETHEART, CHICK, NOT WRITING, ANSWERING, TYPING, TALKING, MAKING STATE-MENT TO HONEST, SINCERE, GENUINE, REAL, NICE, CANDID, TRUTHFUL, RESPECTFUL, MAN, GUY, FELLOW, GENTLEMAN, DUDE, SEARCHING, LOOKING, HUNTING, INQUIRING, SEEKING, PURSUING, WOMAN, LADY, FEMALE, GIRL, LASSIE, DAME, MAIDEN, DAMSEL, SWEETHEART, CHICK, TO SHARE, ALLOCATE, DISPENSE, AWARD, EXPLORE,APPROPRIATE, LIFE EXPERIENCES, ADVENTURES, ESCAPADES, NTERLUDES, ROMANCES, FLINGS, STUNTS, CAPERS ANTICS, EVENTS WITH?"

"WHY, HOW COME, MYSTIFIED, PUZZLED, WOMAN, LADY, FEMALE, GIRL, LASSIE, DAME, MAIDEN, DAMSEL, SWEETHEART, CHICK, NOT WRITING, ANSWERING, TYPING, TALKING, MAKING STATEMENT TO HONEST, SINCERE, GENUINE, REAL, NICE, CANDID, TRUTHFUL, RESPECTFUL, MAN, GUY, FELLOW, GENTLEMAN, DUDE, SEARCHING, LOOKING, HUNTING, INQUIRING, SEEKING, PURSUING, WOMAN, LADY, FEMALE, GIRL, LASSIE, DAME, MAIDEN, DAMSEL, SWEETHEART, CHICK, TO SHARE, ALLOCATE , DISPENSE, AWARD,

EXPLORE, APPROPRIATE, LIFE EXPERIENCES, ADVENTURES, ESCAPADES, INTERLUDES, ROMANCES, FLINGS, STUNTS, CAPERS, ANTICS, EVENTS WITH?"

What was that guy's problem? Why wouldn't he get the message when she didn't answer back that maybe, just maybe, she didn't want to talk to him? There was one last email she wanted to read before she went to sleep.

Theseus

> *Dear Mistress of Palms,*
> *I welcomed and appreciated your sense of humor this evening when I sat down to read your note. It has been one heck of a day. We set sail this afternoon for a four day cruise to Mexico. Usually, it is an uneventful journey. A man had a heart attack and needed to be transported by helicopter off the ship. His wife was not only hysterical, but obnoxiously inebriated. One of the main freezers broke down. While I talked with some guests after dinner, their child decided to vomit the Chilean sea bass he just ate down my leg. Not cool, you know? And it is entirely your fault since you mentioned chum earlier!*
> *It is a breathtakingly beautiful night for a cruise; the moon is not quite yet full. The reflection on the water never gets old. I wonder what you see when you look out your window?*
> *Tomorrow we will cruise and dock Wednesday at Cozumel for the day. Do you dive? There are some fantastic reefs to dive within twenty minutes in any direction of the island. Or would you like to browse the shops in San Miguel? So many questions I wonder about you.   Theseus*

Dear Theseus,

Oh my, I thought I had a bad day, but congratulations, you get the trophy. I can't imagine having to airlift someone off a ship. Yet, if he is in a health crisis, beyond the capability of your cruise physician, it would be your only choice, I guess. And as for the child vomiting down your leg, that had to be a rather nasty smelling. I hope you brought extra uniforms along. Tell me more about some of the crazy things that have happened to you while being Captain of the ship.

I sat out this evening on my boat; just before I read your email. The humidity dropped when the sun went down, so the air was balmy with a slight breeze. I did not see the beauty that you saw from the helm as you sailed south. I saw the lights glistening off the water along the Cortez Bridge and the mainland. It always gives me comfort, like a night light guiding the way home for some.

Yes, I have logged many dive hours exploring the reefs around Cozumel. And although the coral beds and walls are beautiful, I much prefer shipwrecks. Sorry, I don't mean to sound callous or insensitive since you are sailing a ship at the moment. When I dive and touch a vessel that has sunk, I wonder about the tale behind the wreck. Were there survivors; what was their story? And the ship, lying broken and abandoned on the sea's floor. Did it struggle to stay afloat? There are so many connections I feel when I dive around a shipwreck.

As for browsing the streets and shops of San Miguel, yes, I enjoy looking at the wares from the people who labored over their creations. I love listening to people speaking Spanish. It is different than the Cuban Spanish that I grew up hearing or the Tex-Mex Spanish of some of the crew members of my company. My favorite place in Cozumel is Casa Mission Restaurant. It has an old-world charm, with gardens all around the building, full of exotic flowers and trees. The mingling of flavors wafting through the open-air rooms as they prepare and serve the meals is tantalizing. The dim lighting is romantic. And the most enchanting moment is when they turn off all the lights. One of the specially trained servers creates and pours a Sexy Mayan coffee. The blue flames from the alcohol, when poured from one pot to the next, are dazzling. I hope, while you are there, you will take a cab to Casa Mission Restaurant for a meal. Tell me about your visit. Stay safe until we speak again, Keira

Keira closed her laptop just as another message came across from Maelstrom. She laughed, thinking the guy would never give up. As she pulled the blanket over her shoulders and closed her eyes, she thought of a romantic stroll through the gardens of Casa Mission with Theseus. He would embrace and kiss her by the fountain before they casually walked into the dining area. The flicker of candles on the white linen table cloths set the mood for the evening. Black iron chandeliers hanging from the ceiling cast a dim light, creating an intimate setting for the table overlooking the torch-lit gardens. And Theseus, well, he only had eyes for her...

Chapter 8
♥♥♥♥♥♥♥♥♥♥♥♥♥

Usually, Keira was excited to start each day. She loved creating beautiful landscapes for others to look upon when they gazed across their yards. It didn't matter if it was an estate or a tiny parcel of green space if it brought joy. However, yesterday had one obstacle after another. She had survived the day with the help of Kraig until his whispered words, 'I'm crazy about you,' caught her totally off guard. She relied on him, respected him, and enjoyed her work relationship with him. She had made the mistake of mixing her professional and personal life one other time. And we all know what happened there, she thought.

She had tried tricking her brain into relaxing for the night by reading Theseus's email last. She found his profile captivating and wanted to learn more about him. And he hadn't let her down. She remembered as she was falling asleep; how he was sailing his plotted course to Cozumel by the light of the almost full moon. It sounded so enchanting to cruise towards Cozumel under a blanket of stars. But her sleep had been interrupted when Peter invaded her dreams by throwing a beer bottle on the instrument panels on the bridge of Theseus's ship. Shorting out the electronic navigational system on the cruise liner, it was drifting somewhere in the Gulf of Mexico, lost. Kraig was driving the mini bulldozer trying to help Keira plow a path through the water to the ship. And Dante's wife was yelling at Keira that it was all her fault. What an exhausting night.

She was just about to climb off her boat when Kraig called, "the ground is dry enough; do you want Chuck to bring the mini dozer over from the warehouse?"

"Yes. Have you heard from Dante?"

"He showed up for work and has already begun mowing

Bayshores' Seagull Villa complex," Kraig said as he whistled to get the attention of one of the crew.

"Oh my ear, I think you broke my eardrum. I am going to head over to check on Dante before I come to the Riverview project."

"Keira?"

Keira leaned against the side of her boat; she closed her eyes. Here it comes, she thought, words from his heart to back up what he said about being crazy about her. What was there to talk about at the moment? She didn't want complications in her work relationship with him.

"Yeah?"

"Can you stop off at the donut shop on the way here and bring us a couple of boxes of donuts? Sometime during the night, a large stingray beached itself and died. A couple of the guys thought it might have happened because we cleared all the underbrush away from the shoreline yesterday. They have been remorseful and quiet since they found it."

Dante appreciated Keira stopping at the Seagull Villa complex to check on him. He tried to apologize for his wife's anger at the hospital. Keira shrugged it off by telling him, his wife loved him and was worried about him.

When Keira pulled into the Riverview Blvd work site, she took a deep breath and carried the donuts and coffee over to the soon-to-be-demolished patio.

Gather around, guys. I am sorry my muscles were too sore from yesterday's workout to cook you omelets and egg sandwiches. Please don't let the boss know I was late." Keira said as she offered the boxes of donuts to the crew.

The mood turned upbeat as the men grabbed donuts and coffee and joked about sore muscles. Keira made arrangements with Kraig to pick up the work truck from the automotive shop after work. She left soon after that, letting Kraig know she was heading back to the office. She needed to take one last look at the blueprints before giving her presentation to the Board of Directors for the St Dominic Care Facility. She was excited to show how she planned to give the residents more outdoor seating areas and less maintenance for their lawn crew.

It was after six in the evening when Keira dropped her work satchel on the chart table and flopped down on her bed. She was exhausted but at least the day went by without any major drama. In celebration, she had stopped off at Publix and bought two lobster tails. Maybe she would grill them; yes, that sounded like a great idea.

While she prepared her dinner, she thought, Kraig hadn't brought up his feelings for her today. That was a good thing. The Board of Directors at St Dominic's Care Facility approved her blueprints without a hitch. And lastly, the work truck was back in the warehouse, the damaged windshield repaired and looking like new. It was a good day indeed.

It was almost nine when she opened up her laptop to check in with her men...

Wildman - Matt

Dear Keira,

I am glad I listened to the elders at the campfire the other night. The rains have started. It is dark and feels like the heavens have opened up. I underestimated the amount of rainfall that could occur over a short amount of time here. The men were accurate in their fears of mudslides. I keep an eye on the cave opening and mountain above for any signs of loose rock movement. I fear, if there are heavy rains for any length of time, the generator will not be able to pump water from the dig site plus keep the lights on. I must search around for a second generator to help maintain the workload.

Please write soon, my lobe. The dreary weather makes me downcast. Hearing from you warms my heart.   Matt

Keira wondered if she was overly tired and sensitive. She had noticed a trait in many of the guys who emailed her. Their focus, while writing to her, was all about them. Granted, the potential for a mudslide or a deluge of rain was a worrisome concern for Matt. She understood that. Nevertheless, he could at least have asked how her day was or show some interest in what was happening in her life. The conversations were becoming very one-sided.

Dear Matt,

I am sorry the rains have slowed progress. It is a worry to me that there could be possible mudslides or cave-ins. Should you stop mining and shut down the operation? I mean, for the safety of your men, it would only be for a short time. Or, were you able to locate a second generator?

I have been busy here also. The latest job site had a water-main rupture that slowed progress. The property we are currently working on looks like an island in the middle of a lake. Then, one of my lawn crew members working on another job site got hit with debris and had to go to the emergency department at the local hospital. While I was driving there to make sure he was ok, a pelican hit my windshield. Because it was damaged so severely, I had to have the work truck towed. The police would not let me drive to the automotive garage to have it repaired. I had to have it towed. Thank goodness today was a better day.

I hope the rains settle down and you can get back to beautiful gem mining.   Keira

ExtremeLover – Michael

Dear Keira,

In my note to you last night, I have a feeling I came across as a male chauvinistic pig when you never answered back. I am sorry if I touched on a sore spot about women pulling their weight in the workplace. Hey, forgive me; it was a male perspective. You can blame it on testosterone levels

or something like that laughing, I just thought about
my high school years wanting to have muscles and
doing weight training in the workout room after
school. Many of the guys in the locker room drank
muscle-enhancing powdered drinks. When I read up
on all the damage those types of enhancers could do
to your brain and the rest of your organs, I thought
no way.

The point of my note was not to offend but to let
you know the guy was concerned for your welfare.
However, he probably is a non-prince type toad, so
don't kiss him!   *Michael*

Dear Michael,

I have to tell you I loved your letter that I just received. I remember my mother calling men on TV, male chauvinistic pigs. My father would run around the house pretending to be a pig, making snorting sounds. And you wonder why I climbed sailboat masts?

Anyway, I am sorry I did not answer back on your last night's letter. Yesterday was one drama after another; I was undeniably exhausted. I closed my eyes for a second after reading your note and fell asleep. No, it wasn't because the letter was boring; fatigue overcame me and zzzzzzzzz.

I did understand what you were saying in your message. I should be grateful the neighbor guy was concerned for my safety. He wanted to send out the search and rescue boat before I became a search and recovery victim. The guy is recently divorced. He seems adrift. He is missing his family life and needed to worry about someone. Sorry, I refuse to be a rebound lover, nope, no way.

I was thinking, do you realize, while surfing, you ride on a board on a wave? I am not as brave; I ride the waves on several boards!!

Wannabe Confucius, Keira

Laughing at her use of idioms, Keira pressed send and went to her galley refrigerator for something to nibble on. She saw Jack through the window, climbing onto his boat carrying a 24 pack of beer and his briefcase. Either he has a lot of burning the midnight oil paperwork to finish, or he was having a bad work week. Maybe she should pay Susyn, at The Crystal Corner Gem Shop, a visit to see how the stars and planet were aligned. Some of them may have collided because so far, this week hasn't been good. Today was ok except for the beached and very dead stingray.

ExtremeLover - Michael

> *Keira,*
> *You have my curiosity up. Tell me what happened yesterday that made your day so horrible.*
> *Wannabe Shrink Michael*

Dear Wannabe Shrink Michael,
How much do you charge? Is it by the hour or by the written word? Are you a scammer shrink? Hmm, you couldn't exploit me in the media because I am a 'nobody.' And by the end of next week, I could be bankrupt, so there goes the money thing. Do you still want to hear about it?

Monday morning was the start of a new job site project. My crew and I got there, right off the bat, a water main had broken. The area looked like a lake with a house on an island. I refigured my work plan since each contract has a completion date clause written in it, even though this wasn't my fault. I couldn't bring in my mini bulldozer and couldn't haul away the broken-up cement. Midday, one of my lawn-crew hit a piece of glass; it cut his arm which required lots of stitches. His wife accused me, saying it was my fault. The evil look she gave me, I wouldn't doubt she tried to put a curse on me.

On the drive to the hospital to check on the crew member, a low flying pelican hit my windshield. It splintered the glass. The police wouldn't let me drive on the road. He feared the windshield would fly apart, hurting me or someone else. The hospital grounds' security wouldn't let a windshield repair company fix it in the parking lot for fear the repair people would leave behind glass bits on the parking lot. Hospital liability if someone got hurt later sort of thing. I had to call my insurance for a tow. The repair, unfortunately, couldn't be done until the next day because of the late hour in the day it came in. The auto body repair shop did not have a secure overnight parking area. My foreman and I lugged all the equipment from the work truck into his truck. I blew a blood vessel in my finger, lifting some of the tool chests. We decided to stop and eat downtown at an outdoor café, since I didn't think many restaurants would have served us smelling like dirt and, well, other stuff. While we ate, we had a run-in with a disgruntled and drunken ex-employee. A couple of biker guys showed off their muscles and teeth, growling at the guy. The owner of the pub ranted and kicked the guy away from his establishment. That all happened before six p.m.

When I got home and took a shower, I think the bilge pump might be going out in my shower. Although it was draining partially well, it was making some weird sounds. I never thought about it, but getting electrocuted by shower water would have been a perfect finale to the day. Replacing the bilge pump may be a Saturday project. I am exhausted just typing the entire saga.

Bet that is the last time you ever ask anyone to tell you about their bad day.   Bad Luck Babe

ExtremeLover - Michael

> Bad Luck Babe,
>   I would never scam anyone. There have been several people who have tried to scam me. It is a difficult situation; you have to keep focused on logic, not emotions.
>   You seriously had one heck of a day. But I am sure you handled each situation as it hit you, with class and poise. I think the worst part was the broken blood vessel in your finger. Because it bleeds into the muscle and stretches the fibers, it naturally does hurt like hell. With all that happened, think of it this way, by the number of weird stuff that transpired all in one day, I would have to say

your run of bad luck has ended for the year, if not longer!!!

I guess I missed it, I knew you owned a boat, but I didn't realize you live on it. That is extreme! I am proud to say I know you.

I wanted to ask if you wanted to have dinner with me on Friday night, maybe at Sandbar down the road. But I just got off the phone. My mother is having emergency surgery in a few minutes. I'm leaving as soon as I close this note and drive up to the hospital in Orlando. My sister can't take care of her right now as she just had a new baby. So, I am elected. I will talk with you when I can. Stay sweet, my lovely Keira. Michael

Dear Michael,

I am not sure when you will have a chance to read this note. I feel sad for your mom; I am sure she is frightened. It is good of you to be there for her when she gets out of surgery. I am sending prayers her way for a speedy recovery. Keep me posted!

Hugs to you, Keira

SonicMusicMix
30 years of age
Tampa, FL
Aquarius
5'9" Brown eyes

Dear Mistress of Palms,

I enjoyed reading over your profile. You seem level- headed and down-to-earth. So many women on this dating site are expecting larger-than- life love affairs with bottomless credit card accounts. They want to fly to exotic locations, all expenses paid for by none other than me. It is very disheartening. I joined this program to find a friendship that would maybe turn into a relationship and possibly more. What have I found? So far, octopus tentacle women have been trying to grab hold of me or anyone who will support their wants. Sadly, this has been only week two. Please tell me you hate saltwater and live far inland!

Tell me a little bit more about you. Me? I own an audio-production company here in Tampa. I create soundtracks for major shorts teams, elevator music for corporations, dance recital music tracks, and much more. My world is full of music on any given day. I hope to hear back from you.   Storm

Wow, Keira thought, he sounded so um upbeat. She laughed at her pun. Thinking about a day full of music, it would be like heaven. Oh, come to think of it, the Christmas music at department stores starts right after Halloween and lasts through December. She had heard employees grumbling and threatening to strangle anyone remotely into the holiday jingle by the beginning of December.

Dear Storm,

Thank you for responding to my profile. What an unusual name, Storm. I am sure you hear that all the time, but I think it is a unique first name. I am sorry to hear there are so many women with expectations of being wined and dined. It would be nice to be kept in a lifestyle way beyond my expectations. The price to pay for that type of life is way too high for me. Anyway, I am not an octopus, but I love saltwater. And there is a small detail that I have to let you know, I live on a sailboat, yep, floating in the Intracoastal Waterway between Anna Maria Island and the mainland. I am not landlocked as you were hoping!!!

Owning an audio-production company surrounded by music all day seems like the ideal career. It would be a fun and enjoyable way of making a living. Well, maybe not elevator music; it would be easy to nod off to sleep after more than a fifteen-minute track. How did you get started? Come on, do tell...

I am a landscape architect. My company creates rolling greens for golf courses; I design landscapes for new construction communities and put life back into dead-looking yards for people. So essentially, I spend my day playing in the dirt. And, I love all things Palm Trees.

Keira

"A HONEST, SINCERE, GENUINE, REAL, NICE, TRUTHFUL, CANDID, RESPECTFUL, MAN, GUY, FELLOW, GENTLEMAN, DUDE, SEARCHING, LOOKING, HUNTING, INQUIRING, SEEKING, PURSUING, WOMAN, LADY, FEMALE, GIRL, LASSIE, DAME, MAIDEN, DAMSEL, CHICK, SWEETHEART, TO SHARE, ALLOCATE, DISPENSE, AWARD, EXPLORE, APPROPRIATE, LIFE EXPERIENCES, ADVENTURES, ESCAPADES, INTERLUDES, ROMANCES, FLINGS, STUNTS, CAPERS, ANTICS, EVENTS, WILL NOT REVEAL, SHARE, SHOW, TELL, DIVULGE, DISCLOSE, DISCUSS, PROVIDE, SCAMMERS, CRIMINALS, SWINDLERS, COMPUTER GENERATED BOTS, ROBOTS, CON ARTISTS, DIRT BAGS, HACKERS, SCUM, SNAKES, PHONIES, FRAUDS, FAKES, PRIVATE, PERSONAL, PHYSICAL HISTORY, PHOTOS, SOCIAL SECURITY, DRIVERS LICENSE NUMBERS, FINANCIAL ASSETS, EMPLOYMENT STATUS OR HEALTH INFORMATION, WHEN INTELLIGENT, SMART, BRIGHT, EDUCATED, SEEMINGLY NICE WOMAN, SHARES, ALLOCATE, DISPENSE, LIFE EXPERIENCES, ADVENTURES, ESCAPADES, ROMANCES, FLINGS, STUNTS STUNTS,CAPERS, ANTICS, THIS HONEST, SINCERE, GENUINE, REAL, NICE, TRUTHFUL, RESPECTFUL GENTLEMAN, WILL DO THE SAME."

"Maelstrom, I beg of you. Please stop messaging me. I have found someone I am genuinely interested in. I would like to focus on getting to know this person better. So out of respect for me, please stop?" Keira typed.

Peter Flynn - Basil

> *My Dearest K Lee,*
> *It seems like a lifetime ago since I have talked*
> *with you. Everything with the South African project*

feels like it is at warp speed. At the very moment, I just boarded the red-eye flight en route to Texas for a meeting with my financial backers in the morning. I was hoping we could have dealt with all the paperwork over the computer, but policies are policies, and they need to see my financial plan for the expenditure of funds in person.

As I fly across the night sky, I have been thinking about our feelings for each other. I honestly believe we have a great understanding of what it takes to make a good relationship work. Neither of us is right out of university with our heads in the clouds. Due to or because of past experiences, I now know how to treat my woman with respect and integrity. I know how important it is to become best friends and share the good, along with the unpleasant things. And I know that you are supportive of my endeavors. We must promise to trust each other with our hearts. It is my prayer for our relationship.

I think once you have seen the house I purchased in Brandon, you will love it. I hope you will enjoy decorating it to your liking. I trust your judgment in creating a home for us. I have already talked with my daughter. Although she was a little bit reluctant at first, she has now warmed up to the idea of you becoming a part of our family. I think it would be wise to keep the nanny on in a supportive role since I would never ask you to give up your career.

I saw that your area of the country was getting a bad storm. I hope that you were able to stay dry and were safe from the brutal weather. The airline server just placed my meal in front of me. After I finish, I hope to get a few minutes of sleep. I love you with all my heart, Basil

Keira was utterly shocked by the words of endearment Basil

assumed. His audacity was beyond contempt. He believed they had a great understanding of what it took to make a good relationship work. First, you had to be in a relationship to make it work. They had not gotten to that point yet. Giving her information about his family life, buying a home, and working out of the country didn't constitute a relationship. As far as she was concerned, they were barely acquaintances. She didn't even know if he was who he said he was.

What angered her most was how he wrote out the terms of a relationship like it was a written legally binding document. We will be best friends; you will be supportive of me. You will decorate my house, and I will let you have a career. Um, not your decisions, bud, Keira thought.

And what inclement weather was he talking about? It had been sunny and breezy, not a cloud in the sky. Keira decided he must be writing to a couple of women and one of them lived in an area where the weather conditions were not good. What else could it be?

Theseus

Dear Keira,

I saw you had sent an email to me, but I have been on duty all day. It was cruising day, and our entire crew was on deck, making sure all the guests were enjoying their day at sea. There were tours of the bridge. I can always spot a Navy veteran during those visits. They have a glazed look in their eyes as if they remember their glory days. The pool was jam-packed, and of course, the bars were busy. I wonder what you would enjoy doing on a cruise? Are you a gambling lady? There are lots of shops to browse, the spa, sauna, & exercise room, rock climbing, cooking demonstrations, you name it. Tell me, how would you spend your day on a cruise?

You mentioned you were familiar with Cuban Spanish speaking people from your childhood. Are you of Cuban descent? Once again, there is so much

I would like to learn about you. Until we speak again,
Theseus

Keira sat holding her laptop. There was something about Theseus that made her smile. She didn't know what it was and then it dawned on her; she chose him. The two guys, ExtremeLover - Michael and Theseus, were the two she had initiated her correspondence with first. They were the ones she wanted to get to know better.

Dear Theseus,
Exploring the ship all day would give me great pleasure. If I took the tour of the bridge, I would probably get kicked out. I would ask so many questions, you know, like, have you ever been attacked by pirates, how many millions of gallons of fuel do you carry, what is your cruising speed, can I drive the boat, I mean ship? Being in an overcrowded, standing room only, pool, and holding a beer is not my idea of a fun day. And since the water is cold saltwater drawn in from the ocean, I would look funny standing in my wetsuit. So, I am going to leave the saltwater pool for the tourists. I can swim in the nice warm water of the Gulf of Mexico any time I want.

I have never been one to primp and pamper myself, so enjoying the spa would be a vacation experience I haven't tried before. I don't think I need to spend time rock climbing since I already climb masts. I suppose I would enjoy watching the sea. I could be like Miss Daisy while you drive. But, I am sure I would always point out where the wind was and miss watching the sails.

You asked if I was of Cuban descent. No, I grew up in Key West. Many of the workers were from Cuba. I loved to listen to the lyrical tone of their language dialect. It was soft and romantic I can think of nothing more sensual than a romantic Spanish love song sung by a Cuban singer holding a guitar. OK, I have said romantic twice in a matter of a few words. Enough!

Life seems so complicated at times. Your questions reminded me of that easy-going life of long ago. Oh, to be carefree again, sailing with the wind in my hair and not worrying about workers comp, new while re-landscaping someone's backyard.

Oh, my, gosh, I have written a short novel. Please forgive me for causing you to go blind trying to read this letter.

While you sail your ship south towards Cozumel, I will be resting on the soft roll of the waves beneath my boat.   Keira

Chapter 9
♥♥♥♥♥♥♥♥♥♥♥♥♥♥

Keira's work crew seemed to settle into a smooth rhythm once the city repaired the water main. She continued to rely on Kraig as her foreman at the job site while she worked to bring in new clients. He was focused and took over removing the deteriorating cement patio but kept the pool foundation unharmed, which saved considerable costs. The crew stepped up their pace trimming back and removing the bushes Keira had marked on Monday. Keira didn't want to jinx the project, but it looked like the Riverview Blvd project would come in under budget and on time.

She realized her reputation, not only as a landscape designer, continued to soar; her lawn service part of the business was growing. Keira frequently drove to the contract sites after the mowing was complete. It was the little details that mattered. Making sure the sidewalks had been cleared of grass clippings; there were no un-mowed areas and no clumps of sheared grass, ruining the sculpted lawns. It was time to create a lawn care foreman position to oversee that aspect of her business.

A frantic call came over Keira's phone. Hector, one of the most reliable of the lawn crew, was in a panic.

"Miss Keira, Miss Keira, while I was edging along da sidewalk, a homeless person took one of the riding mowers out of the trailer. He stole it. I ran after him, but he was too fast for me."

"Oh my God, which lawn site are you at? Have you called the police?"

"Si. They are what you call it, canvasing the hood. Oh, Policeman wants to talk to you." Hector said.

Keira grabbed the office phone and called Kraig. While she talked to the police, Kraig heard the information, as the policeman reported it to her. Another officer was searching the subdivision. They would keep her informed.

After the officer hung up his phone from the briefing, Kraig took his truck, and Keira jumped in her jeep. They met up with Hector and Eddy at the lawn care site where they had been mowing.

"Did you have the chains locked on the trailer while you were trimming?" Kraig demanded.

"Si, Eddy was blowing the grass from da driveway. I heard the chains hit the side of the trailer as the guy drove the mower off. Here, look at the lock, is broken."

"He climbed over the side of the trailer. I saw him earlier sitting under that tree on the corner of la street." Eddy pointed down the road.

"I told all this to da cop," Hector said.

Kraig decided to search, street by street, for their stolen property. Keira was heading south towards the road out of the subdivision; when one of the police officers drove up in his car.

"Are you Keira St Cloud, the owner of this lawn care service?"

"Yes, I'm Keira."

"We caught the person who took your mower out for a joyride. He ran off the sidewalk, rolled the mower down the embankment and into the lake. He was crawling out of the water. The mower is on its side, half-submerged in the lake at the end of the subdivision. Do you want to press charges?"

"Yes."

"Very well, I will take care of the paperwork. We will impound your mower as evidence at this time."

"We understand. Thank you, Officer."

Keira met Kraig back at the office for a quick meeting. They reviewed the standard policy for securing equipment when not in use at the job sites. Keira called the company's insurance, and Kraig returned to the landscape work site to keep the guys on schedule there.

While she was waiting on return calls, Keira put an ad on one of the top online employment recruitment websites. She urgently needed to interview secretaries. Up until this time, she was able to handle all the incoming calls. The logbook of potential clients, both on the landscaping design projects and on the upkeep of lawn care services her company provided, was up to date. However after the situation today, she most definitely needed someone at the office to take incoming calls or help with fielding problems. Also, as Kraig had said, she hadn't had a vacation in almost forever and needed one. If she had reliable backup people in place, she could soon anticipate fun away from her business.

Lastly, Keira contacted her attorney. She needed to set up an appointment.

"Yes, Kraig, what do you need?" Keira answered when she saw Kraig was calling her.

"Tell me again why we are filing charges against the homeless guy? Isn't that bad for company publicity?"

"If he tries to file a claim against the company saying he got hurt, he could have a case against us. However, there is a case on file that he stole our property first and then got hurt, does he have a claim? I'm not sure. I am hoping his charge against us would be dropped since he stole the mower. I phoned my attorney's office to find out." Keira explained.

Wildman - Matt

> Dear Keira,
> The rains continue. Due to all the overtime that I had to pay to hurry along the production, money is running short. I cannot afford to buy a second generator. I am not sure how long the first one can hold out. I have contacted my investors. I am asking if they would advance me on the payment owed to for the amethyst. After all, I have already sent it to the market. I have not heard back from them and do not know what else to do.
> I am very concerned. I fear for my team. I don't know how I am going to cover the costs of expense

and pay the men. I would never, at any other time, ask anything of you, my love. But I am in dire straits so to speak. Is there any way you could float me a loan for five thousand? I would pay you back with interest. It would only be for a matter of a couple of weeks. I will pay you back by the first of next month. The next installment check of the contract will be deposited into my bank account at the end of the month. I only ask this of you because the crew needs to feed their families. I know you love me and will help me in my time of need; just as I would assist you and help you if ever you asked. Please, I need your help desperately,

Matt

Keira was glad she was sitting down when she read Matt's email. However, she stood up and paced back and forth across the galley floor. If a friend required physical help moving to a new home or out of state, a helping hand would be there. If friends were sick or had a family member pass on, sending a meal or assist, without question, would be done. She had learned the hard way when it came to money: never give cash or 'lend' financial support. Many who did, never again saw their money when providing that kind of assistance. It caused long-term hard feelings.

She was so angry, how dare he ask her for money? 'I would never, at any other time, ask anything of you, my love,' she mimicked. Screaming, 'my love, seriously' could be heard on the docks. Never having met face to face and then asking for five thousand dollars from someone he barely knew was damn ballsy, she thought. It was ok to float him a loan to pay his workers but did he care about where or how she would come up with the five thousand? What about putting food on her plate? What about paying her bills? I don't think so, Keira thought.

Taking a deep breath, Keira pressed the message box open, "Hi Jimmy, glad you are on tonight."

"Hi, I haven't talked to you in a while. How are you doing?"

"Have you found the love of your life yet?" Keira asked JFlounderGig – Jimmy, trying to ignore her anger.

"No, have you?"

"No, we are a sorry bunch, you know?"

"I'm selective, and with your looks, so should you be."

"Aww, thanks. Jimmy, some guy tried to scam me tonight. I just wanted to say thanks to you; I was semi-prepared."

"Semi-prepared?"

"You told me about scammers the first time I talked to you. So, I was on the lookout for some sort of scam. Even though your brain tells you, scam, scam, scam, it still hurts. I have invested time and energy in getting to know this someone. And then it still took me by surprise. I just didn't want to think of him as a scammer." Keira confessed.

"Don't let it get you down. Scamming is a business. Scammers make up a scenario and slowly draw you in with terms of endearment. Then boom, something happens and all of a sudden, they need money for some crisis. A couple of thousand for a two-week cut and paste of enchanting and enticing words, yep, that is mighty fine earnings. They don't even claim it as income on their taxes!"

"You are correct. Thank you again, Jimmy. Keep in touch."

"Night"

Keira started at the dark TV screen above her chart table. If she was in some sort of situation or a desperate need of money to pull her company through until a completion check on a contract came through, she sure hoped someone would help her. What if a piece of equipment broke needed to finish a job and they were down to the wire on the contract deadline; she firmly believed someone would help her out. Lending a hand to other construction companies in a pinch, Keira had built a network of go-to businesses that would help each other out. But, it was crucial for any business; to develop a reserve fund for emergencies.

Keira turned off her computer, slipped on her flip-flops, and headed across the parking lot to The Dive Bar. It would be funny to tell about the joyriding homeless man, but not until the guy was convicted.

"Hey Keira, what'll ya have?" Brian asked from behind the bar.

"Rum runner to go, please."

"Where ya been? Micah is out of town, and I haven't seen you in almost a week. Dang." Marla said as she offered Keira some of her hot-out-of-the-oven pizza bombs.

Keira tilted her head, "Where is Micah?"

"Umm, I can't remember where he said he was going. But he is gone. You abandoned me. I'm all alone." Marla shook her head slowly.

"Brian, how much has Marla drank?"

"One experimental Curacao, strawberry and banana Margarita"

"Does that make me a lab rat?" Marla slurred.

"No, that makes you drunk. You need to come and spend the night on my boat. In the morning, you can walk across the parking lot to work." Keira reasoned.

"No, I get seasick on boats."

"My boat is tied to the dock; it isn't moving."

"Hey Bobby, you will walk me home, right?" Marla yelled down the bar to one of the locals.

Keira slowly walked back to her boat, sipping her icy cold rum runner and laughing over Marla's confession of getting seasick. She was second in command at the marina, but gets seasick, which sounded ironic and funny to Keira. The antics at the bar helped improve her mood.

Tripping over a rut in the parking lot, Keira decided she definitely needed to draw a blueprint for Micah. It would not only enhance the beauty of the marina but also fix the uneven back lot. Didn't Micah say something similar not long ago? Speaking of Micah, Marla had mentioned he was gone. Wondering how long he had been away, but then again, she usually didn't see him much during the week. Heading out early to job sites or working late, Keira saw little activities happening at the marina.

As she got closer to the steps leading to the dock, it would be nice if there was a note from ExtremeLover – Michael or Theseus. What was Theseus's real name? Was it George, Dimitri, or Homer? No, it couldn't be Homer, he was a Greek Poet. Poets didn't kill a Minotaur and then; write a poem about it. Unless, of course, he wrote Greek tragedies, na, from the pictures she remembered seeing, Homer looked wimpy. Climbing over the rail and onto her boat, she saw Jack inside his cabin, talking loudly on his cell phone. Keira quickly slipped down the steps into the galley and shut the hatch. Taking another sip of her drink, she opened her laptop.

Rad and Sexy - Len

> *Dear Keira,*
> *Sorry, I haven't talked with you. I have been at Jacksonville at a Radiology conference for the last couple of days. I will be heading home on Thursday. But I just wanted to check in with you to make sure we are still on for lunch on Saturday, at two in the afternoon. I am anxious to hear what you have to say about my lawn.*
> *Enclosed are directions to my house. You have my cell phone number if anything should come up, otherwise, I will see you than.*   *Len*

Dear Len,
    Thanks for sending the directions to your house. I know you are busy with the conference. So, I will see you on Saturday at two-ish.
Keira

SonicMusicMix - Storm

> *Dear Keira,*
> *Finally, I have found someone who doesn't expect to be flown to the Bahamas for a walk on the beach and a night of drinking and wild sex. Don't get me wrong, all three are my idea of great things to*

do, but!

I have never known of anyone who lives on a sailboat. Talk about a unique home. I mean, I have heard of the houseboats on the river in Portland, Oregon. And at one time weren't there houseboat docks in Key West? But I have never known of someone who actually lived on one. Please tell me, what made you decide you wanted to live on the water.

As far as developing an audio production company, it started with my little sister needing a soundtrack for her gymnastics competition. She couldn't find any music that she felt comfortable doing her routine to and was four minutes long. My sister's gymnastic association liked what they heard for her routine song and contacted me to do more. I found I loved creating sound bites for people. And one thing led to another, and my studio evolved into a career.

I have to tell you, I just signed a contract to be the DJ at the Coquina Beach Wet T-Shirt contest in a couple of weeks. Maybe you have seen the advertisements for it? If it isn't far from where you live, perhaps we could get together afterward for drinks. No pressure.   Storm

Dear Storm,

Your opening paragraph was excellent, especially the but... Identifying and establishing boundaries in any relationship is probably rule number one. It develops trust and a lasting connection. So with that said, it is difficult to walk down the beach thinking about wild sex after a night of drinking.

I grew up loving the ocean and being around boats. The opportunity to buy the sailboat of my dreams presented itself to me; I couldn't resist and purchased it. It is a minimalist way of living. Having artwork and special treasures sitting around is difficult when every square inch of space has to be utilized carefully. Not to mention owning a sailboat, I live for the wind. Having tchotchkes sitting here and there can be dangerous. Yes, Key West used to have houseboat row. It was very 'Key West' back in the day, but an embarrassment and controversial subject to some islanders in later years.

I am excited to hear you picked up the contract as DJ for the Wet T-Shirt Contest. Petra – the host of the festivities has several different types of food trucks scheduled for each day. And trolley pickup points, off the island, so people do not have to worry about parking. She has done an excellent job of setting up the entire event. She had to jump through a lot of hoops with the local city council. It was probably her amazing organizational skills that got the festival approved. I think all of her hard work is going to pay off extremely well. My company is one of the sponsors for the festival. It will be a fun Fourth of July weekend for the people who visit our beaches. I don't know how exhausted you will be after a day of being a DJ, but yes celebrating your success after the festival would be fun.

Keira

Keira couldn't wait to check in with Petra at The Wet T-Shirt Shop. Last week when she took her sponsorship check over to the store, Petra was stressing. She was worried about finding a good DJ; someone who would play the kind of music that would be enjoyed by the young. But with the elderly populations, who would be sitting anywhere along the shore, they would enjoy the music as well. Keira knew Petra was into detail; that was what would make the festival a success or not.

Peter Flynn – Basil

Dearest K Lee,
I have not heard from you. I saw severe storms were in your area. They probably knocked out your electricity. I do hope, although you are without power, you are safe. I am sure you will be ecstatic

when your area resumes normalcy. You shall find
you have all these emails from me. You will then
have much catching up to do.

I know you are interested in what went on in my
meetings in Texas. I signed the last documents for
financing the Southern Africa ware-house project. I
ordered all the equipment I needed for the
construction of the parcel of land. The surveyors are
on the job site as we speak. I hope within a matter
of days, the footers are formed out, and concrete
laid. This project has to get underway. My foreman
will keep me updated. However I have to fly over
soon to make sure everything is running smoothly
and satisfactorily to my liking.

Do take care of yourself; I do not want you to
take ill.   *All my love, Basil*

Keira started laughing; he hadn't heard from her because she thought it was weird that he thought severe weather was in her area. All Basil had to do was check his search engine to see the local climate conditions of Anna Maria Island. Since he was buying a home in Brandon, an hour north of Bradenton, wouldn't he be concerned with his investment? Shouldn't Basil be watching to make sure there wasn't any flooding in his area? Did he realize, even though it was early in the season for a hurricane to hit the local area, if Brandon was in the path of a hurricane, there would be no closing on his home until it passed. Oh well, it was something his real estate friend, Peter Flynn should have discussed if Basil was truly concerned about the weather conditions.

After drinking the last of the rum runner, Keira carried her laptop and set it on her bed. Her to-do list was long for the next couple of days. But, she was anxious to open the letter from Theseus. She could wait on brushing her teeth and changing into her nightshirt.

Theseus

Dear Keira,

I would never go blind reading your emails. I have begun looking forward to them; they are refreshing and I would never go blind reading your emails. I have begun looking forward to them; they are refreshing and give me a deeper understanding of your personality.

Last night after the change of duty, I looked out over the sea and thought of your email. When you said you would get kicked off the bridge for asking too many questions, I had to smile. Most people are overwhelmed when taking our tour of the bridge. Seeing all the monitors beeping and instrument panel lights, they don't ask many questions. They merely nod their heads as we explain the different areas. BTW, this cruise ship carries four million gallons of fuel; in response to your earlier question.

I was moved by the email you sent talking about exploring Cozumel. After securing the ship in port this morning and finishing the ship's port documents, I decided to take shore leave. It surprised my second-in- command since I seldom do so. I decided to stir their interests even more by inquiring where to find the nearest jeep rental agency. Having already searched and found one nearby, it was fun seeing the intrigue in their eyes.

One of my shipmates decided to tease me about having a secret rendezvous with a beautiful senorita in San Miguel. They thought they had it all figured out.

I browsed some of the streets and shops of San Miguel as you described. In every storefront full of trinkets, many, if not all of the shop owners, wanted to make a deal. I listened to their voice patterns and realized you were correct, they pronounce some words differently than in Florida. I would not have *thought anything of it until you mentioned it.*

In my four-speed glow-in-the-dark green Jeep with no doors, I followed the poorly drawn map that I created to get to Casa Mission Restaurant. It is a distance from town, as you said. Some areas I drove through were not the safest of neighborhoods for a nonresident to walk through. The Casa Mission was exactly how you described it, with old world charm and beautiful gardens. Of course, you would notice the landscaping! Since it was a little after two in the afternoon, I decided I would have lunch there. It would have been so much more enjoyable if you were sitting across from me sharing my meal. With a light breeze coming in through the open doors, the tantalizing aroma of our meals, and the quiet conversation between myself and the beautiful Mistress of Palms, it would be the perfect afternoon.

I must close this note. We leave port at ten this evening for our return journey home tomorrow. I wish you a good evening.   *Theseus*

Keira leaned back against the pillows on her bed. She tried to imagine being held by Theseus through the night. What kind of lover would he be? Some of the words he wrote in his letter, he had to be romantic. Who wanders around San Miguel and visits her favorite restaurant just because she told him it was special? Would she ever get the chance to stroll the gardens of Casa Mission in the early evening with him? In her mind's eye, she saw dimly lit black iron chandelier lights hanging from the rafters and the side doors open to let in the cooler evening air. The red glazed tiles were warm to her toes as she slipped her feet out of her sandals. A platter of parrillada de carne was placed in front of them; the aroma of the seasoned meats wafting through the air. And later, as the sea glistened in the light of the moon, he slowly passionately explored her body.

Looking at Theseus's profile pictures, she wished he would have turned around so she could have seen his face. What color were his eyes? Was he divorced or had his wife passed away, or maybe he was never married, the sea being his mistress? She wondered why that part of his profile was left blank. As she thought about it, there were very few facts she did know of him.

Dear Theseus,

You intrigued me. Tell me more of this secret rendezvous you had with the beautiful senorita in San Miguel? But first, explain how you made her acquaintance? Is here a special place you two meet when you take leave from your voyage? In the secluded shadows of the lighthouse at Parque Punta Sur would you make love to her?

And after a magical afternoon, you regretfully return to the ship that keeps you from her until you can again slip away. Maybe you should have never mentioned her, to begin with, then, I could not question your relationship with her. But now, I am drawn to your story of your enchanting secret lover. I can't wait to hear more.

Keira

It was after two in the afternoon the next day. Keira was still sitting at her office desk, reading resume after resume for the secretary position she had posted. She heard a ping on her computer, signaling she had yet another message. Eager to see if it was from Theseus or ExtremeLover – Michael, letting her know his mother was resting at home in Orlando and doing well. She still needed to order the food for the company Fourth of July picnic. Number three on the list was reading through the lawn crews' files. Determining if any of the guys were qualified for a supervisory position with the company was time consuming.

Hearing the warehouse garage doors opening, she realized the lawn crew had finished for the day. She would give them a few minutes to shut down their equipment. It would be interesting to see if they cleaned the grass from the mowers and inspected the blades if they needed sharpening. Did they need to be told or were they motivated to take the initiative on their own?

"Check the blades on mower two."

"Yeah, the center blade was not giving an even cut. I swear I mowed half of Tinsley's backyard twice."

"Hey, is there a new drive belt in the cabinet, no left of the cans of oil? Yeah, that one, can you bring it over here? This belt looks like it's about to fray."

"Can't we let it wait until tomorrow when it is cooler here in the shop?"

"No, do it now, or it will be forgotten until it breaks down in the middle of a job."

"When did you change the oil on mower three..."

The chatter in the garage continued on, some whining, but the stronger crew made sure repairs to the equipment were made. Keira was please thought that the crew, pretty much, answered her question. She would have to take the files home and read them over tonight.

"Keira, the cement truck will pour the retaining wall and the slab for the new deck in the morning. The guys have it all formed out. The cement is scheduled for 7:30. Chip and Marcus agreed to come in at seven instead of eight." Kraig said as he walked into Keira's office.

"And are the homeowners ok with the seven am schedule change?" Keira asked

"The homeowners are on board with that. They expressed their pleasure with the speed at which we are progressing," Kraig said as he plopped down in the chair across from her.

"Keira..."

"I ordered all the food for the fourth. Carlos said he could get about twenty-five chairs and a few tables from his church's fellowship hall Sunday after the morning service. I need to stop after work at a couple of different places and see if I can rent or borrow some coolers to hold the meat in until we can grill it. Is there anything else we need for the party?" Keira ignored her gut feeling of what Kraig wanted to discuss and listed all she had gotten accomplished to him. "Oh, I was going to buy some sparklers and other low-grade fireworks, but I decided against it. I wouldn't want you as a homeowner or my business liable if anyone got hurt with the sparklers."

"No, I think you have it all covered. I will be at the job site at seven tomorrow. Good night."

Keira watched as Kraig got up slowly and walked out the door. She was sure he wanted to talk about his feelings for her. It was cowardly to give him all the information about the party. After all, the fourth of Jul was three weeks away. Addressing the possibility of the relationship he would like to have with her; would mean she had to consider or admit to having feelings for him. Drumming her fingers on her desk and staring out the office window, she realized she didn't know how she felt about Kraig. He was her employee. She would not let her feelings develop beyond her professional position. What would happen to her credibility with the other employees if she developed a relationship with him? It happened with Peter, and she had gotten burned. It was Kraig who picked up the pieces of her at that time. She remembered when he finally told her the guys had walked around her on tiptoes fearing they might trigger her wrath. Thankfully she functioned professionally at work and cried, screamed, and raged her anger privately. Wouldn't he, of all people, understand why she couldn't let it happen again?

It was interesting to see the marina parking lot full of cars when Keira parked and headed towards her boat. Even Marla was still in the office. That was different, but she decided it was none of her business. Once inside the galley of her boat, Keira pulled off her work clothes and put on a tank top and shorts.

While she was eating a huge wedge of lettuce, bacon, and tomato salad for dinner, she heard footsteps walking the plank at the same time as a ping came across her phone.

"Hey darling, I need ten thousand dollars. I got in a jam over here, and the government is holding my passport until I turn over twelve thousand in fees on the bridge project. You know I will pay you back. I know you have the money since I saw your bank statement lying on the coffee table the evening we screwed the night away. Call me when you wire the money to me. Thanks. Love you, Scott"

Keira read the text and laughed. Where was the guy, Singapore?

Keira read the text and laughed. Where was the guy, Singapore? Good luck with that, Keira thought and turned off her phone.

"Hey Micah, come aboard. You are just in time for some fresh grilled yellowtail," Jack suggested.

"That looks good enough to eat. I have the P.I. report you were waiting for." Micah said as he climbed onto Jack's boat.

The voices became muffled, and Keira went back to eating. Somehow her meal looked puny compared to hearing of Jack's grilled yellowtail snapper. Yes, she could have stopped at the fish market and picked out a perfect fresh catch for dinner, but she would have to eat fish for the next couple of days. Frowning, Keira opened her laptop. While she waited for her website to boot up, she wondered if the private investigator's report Jack was expecting was dirt on his ex-wife. She recalled him saying he had missed his home and family. Maybe the end of his exile was coming soon.

Wildman – Matt

> Dear Keira,
>
> I am so hurt. I have not heard back from you. I thought you loved me and would be supportive of me in my time of need. I can't believe you will not help me. My men are desperate to feed their families. I need to get a second generator to keep the caves from flooding. You are my only hope until the end of the month. Please, Keira, I have not given up on our love. I promise to pay you back.
>
> Matt

Keira shook her head as she looked at the weather forecast for the next seven days in Turkey. There was a chance of showers but only a 30% probability on Monday of next week. If the sea coast there was anything like the gulf coast here, such a low percentage meant slim to no rain at all. Why would someone try to say the weather was nasty when anyone could check it out for themselves, on the internet? Did he think she was that gullible?

Dear Matt,

I am sorry to hear you are still having difficulties with your generator during the monsoon season there in Turkey. I do not have the cash to send you. I feel bad, but I am barely making ends meet myself. Why do you think I put in long hours working each day? I have a mortgage and utilities required to pay each month. It is difficult making ends meet for me, living by myself. I can't help you.

Keira

Theseus

Dear Keira,

I was sitting out on my deck reading your email while he pool service was cleaning the pool. The guy almost fell in while testing the chemical balance of the water. I, seriously, didn't mean to scare the guy by abruptly walking into the house. He must have thought I was crazy. Your email of passionate encounter at the old lighthouse, at the north point of the island, was great.

Now about my secret meeting with the beautiful senorita, I assure you there would be nothing covert about walking with her down the middle of the street full of tourists in San Miguel. I would be proud to hold the hand of my lady, with shining dark hair and striking blue eyes. Yes, it would be seductive to have a so-called secret tryst. However, it would not be necessary on my part as I am not married. Are you?

Your email sounded like a turn of the century, no not this century but the last one, the high seas tale of secret romance with a pirate. What is the name of your ship, my lady? How did you come about owning her? Was she part of the bounty you pillaged across the Caribbean? Your turn, do tell...

Theseus

Keira thought she died and had gone to heaven. She bit her lip and smiled as she reread his email. If her mind wandered just a bit, imagine having hot sex with Theseus. She started laughing, thinking, now she sounded just like what's his name, Eduardo Luise. Pushing her laptop aside, Keira opened her top hatch and peaked out to see if Jack was sitting out on his deck. With no sound coming from his boat, she climbed out the hatch and hopped onto the dock. Keira wasn't in the mood to walk over to The Dive Bar. Wandering down the pier, walking past the gas pumps, she headed for the farthest point and sat down on the wood planks at the edge. Looking down into the dark water, she thought about the sea horses she had seen with their tails wrapped around a root of some dead plant. Or the mussels busy at work, filtering the bacteria and other pollutants from the water.

"Care if I join you?" Micah asked as he sat down next to her.

"You do have a way of sneaking up on me." Keira said, somewhat sarcastically.

Micah was the only one who could quietly walk his docks, blindfolded. "You are here late."

"There is rumored to be a turf war down the beach the next couple of nights. I thought I would keep an eye out and patrol the marina."

"Micah, you have potholes, gravel, and sand, no turf. I know turf; nope, you only have some weeds that do not constitute grass or a lawn." Keira said as she looked at Micah, trying to keep from laughing at her pun.

"Yeah, the landscape designer hasn't drawn up any plans for my marina yet," Micah said as he watched the Cortez bridge guard gate slowly descend.

"Fire that designer and hire me." Keira joked.

"I heard you aren't cheap." Micah grinned in the dark.

"That's a good thing." Keira laughed. She watched as the bridge slowly opened to let a night fishing trawler pass on its way out to the gulf.

"Why did you pick my marina to dock your boat?"

"Of all the marinas around, I felt yours would be the safest with a direct hit hurricane. The barrier island would take the beating. Across the Intracoastal, the boats take the head-on winds and then the mainland."

"Not many people think about stuff like that. Brian or someone at The Dive Bar once said you brought your boat up from the keys. Did you buy it down there?" Micah asked as he watched the trawler's small waves rock some of the boats docked in deeper water.

"You heard right. I bought it several years ago at a seized property police auction in Key West. It was a drug-smuggling boat between Jamaica and Key West," Keira said, trying to touch the water with her toes.

"Are you afraid the smugglers will come after your boat?"

"No, I was told they were killed in the gun battle. All the mahogany flooring had to be replaced; because of the stench from the dried blood on the deck."

Keira remembered the gory shape her boat was in when she bought it. Gunshot holes had riddled one side of the fiberglass hull. The entire seating area was shredded in the search for hidden drugs. Her heart hurt and she felt pain for the boat that sat in the marina bruised and battered nearly to death.

"Did you change the name on the boat to Black Beauty?" Micah asked quietly.

"No, you know it is bad luck to change the name of a boat." "That boat had bad luck."

"Her bad luck days of drug-running ended in Key West. She is free now to dance proudly on the waves," Keira smiled at Micah.

She felt his warm moist lips slide effortlessly against hers. There was nothing forced or rushed, just the exploring of her lips. When he helped her to her feet, he looked into her eyes as he kissed her hand.

"Night, Micah," Keira whispered before she turned and slowly walked back towards her boat.

Chapter 10
♥♥♥♥♥♥♥♥♥♥♥♥♥

Saturday morning dawned sunny and not a bit of breeze. Keira waited until seven before walking over to Azul del Mar Dive Shop.

"Morning Markos, would you fill up my dive tank please," Keira asked as she set the aluminum cylinder by the side of the counter.

"Going diving in search of sunken treasures?" "No, it's barnacle scraping day," Keira explained.

"Why don't you let the crew at the marina put your boat on the lift and scrape them off?" Markos asked.

"Maybe next month, but I don't mind spending the time making sure the bottom is in good condition."

Keira hauled her filled air tank back to her boat. She thought about the time; she watched the marina in Key West put a sailboat on the marine travel lift and accidentally dropped it. When the boat hit the cement, the rudder snapped off; and the keel underneath the boat shattered. It was horrifying to watch, even though no one got hurt. Sure it was a long time ago, and the lifts have improved immensely over the years, but it still left her feeling uneasy. Maybe next month, she would have the marina pressure wash and apply antifouling boat bottom paint to the hull. But for now, she would manually scrape.

"Hey, are you going diving by yourself?" Jack asked as Keira strapped the air tank to the holder at the back of her boat. "I heard that isn't safe."

"Morning Jack, I anchor my boat just left of Beer Can Island. It's time to scrub the barnacles off her bottom. Tell you what; I will only be out there a couple of hours. Come anchor your boat off mine and help me scrape," Keira challenged.

Jack was a hospital administrator. She knew he would never help her. They hired people to do the manual labor type stuff. It wasn't that she was putting him down, but he was a land lover. His boat was only for show; she would almost bet the ranch on it. Oh wait, she didn't own a ranch.

"Well, maybe I will drive my boat out and guard your boat as you dive under."

"Sure, see you in a while," Keira said as she threw her tether lines on the dock and pushed the hull away from its mooring. It felt good to motor her boat down the Intracoastal Waterway towards the Longboat Key Bridge. She planned to anchor at the twenty-five feet depth.

She only had a few hours to scrape, so anchoring and tossing the dive flag out, Keira had to work rapidly. She had on a t-shirt over her bathing suit. Keira suited into her dive Buoyancy Control Device otherwise known as a BCD, with her air tank strapped to her back. With her regulator in between her teeth, she stepped off the side of her boat. The water was warm. Quickly she got started removing the barnacles. She always questioned if she had body odor from the work-out of scraping; would anyone notice the smell? Grinning at how she could entertain herself, she kept working. Shoving the scraper along the bottom of the hull, Keira wondered if that Scott guy figured it out yet, that no one was sending him ten thousand dollars. She dropped the scraper and cursed as she watched the tool drift down to the sand bottom. Bending, Keira dove after the knife; it felt good to stretch and swim. She picked up a couple of black sand dollars off the gulf floor. Flipping them over in her hand, they looked healthy. She hated when people searching for shells kept live sand dollars. It was illegal. They filter the sand and are part of the food chain. Setting them on the sand, she retrieved her scraper and headed back to the hull.

That if the Scott guy made the entire story up, pretending to be calling the wrong number? As she scraped, what if he was a scammer? What if she would have carried on a conversation with him, asking him what number was he trying to reach. Or I think you put the wrong number in your phone; he would have tried to sweet-talk her. Then hit her up for ten grand, and when she said no, he continued on with his scam trying to put a guilt trip on her. Oh, help me; I'm trapped in Singapore, so sad too bad, Scotty boy, Keira giggled, sending extra bubbles to the surface.

She thought about Micah's kiss on Thursday night. It took her totally by surprise. There wasn't any urgency in his lips when they met hers, just a gentle kiss. And then, after he helped her to her feet, he kissed her hand. Simple as it was, there was something so gallant about the way he kissed her hand. Ok, ok, she was putting too much thought into it. One and one-half kisses didn't mean anything to a guy; they did things on a whim, just because it felt right, at the moment. Micah probably impulsively kissed her, never to be repeated. As depressing as that sounded, she didn't care; his lips tasted sooo good. She wanted more.

Keira got most of the barnacles removed by eleven am, even if she never focused on inspecting the hull like she was supposed to. With the number of laughter bubbles, if someone noticed them while boating by, they could have easily thought she was in trouble. Yeah, mentally, that is. She was in sad shape when she was so easily entertained, by herself. It was time to head back.

As she pulled in her dive flag and lifted the anchor over the side, she felt like someone was watching her. She scanned the horizon. There were several boats out in deeper water with guys fishing off the swim platform. The speedboat from across the bay that ran the para-sailing operation was a distance away. She didn't see any drones or people on the beach with binoculars. She just couldn't shake the creepy feeling that someone was following her every move.

Good planning, Keira thought; she got back to the dock by eleven-thirty. Sure enough, Jack was talking on his cell phone as she tied her boat to the cleats. Hearing him saying something about keeping surveillance, she wondered if he was keeping track of his ex-wife's activities. Keira decided he had an obsessive hang-up with her. It seemed like he couldn't let go, or was he trying to catch her in the act of something. It was all so cloak-and-dagger. She had to smile, knowing he wouldn't have shown up to watch her scrub the bottom of her boat. It would have been a great bet. She would have gotten the ranch.

Looking at her watch, if she showered and took a bit of time sort of primping, she could be on the road by twelve-thirty and at Len's house by two, providing she didn't get lost.

It was five minutes to two when Keira pulled into Len's beach house driveway. So, this was where he lived. Len's house was large, with a basic coastal structural design. The front lawn was mostly sand, with a few plugs of grass, here and there. The bushes were overgrown and out of shape. When she stood at the front door, the wood trim was in poor condition. She hoped he had forgotten about his want of her landscape assessment.

Over the years, she had seen what salt air and humidity could do to a brand new home. Wood rot and bleached white from the rays of the sun, wood trim took a beating. She rang the doorbell a second time and checked Len's address on her phone. Yep, she had the correct house number. While she held her phone, she called him.

"Hey Keira, see the gate by the garage? Come around to the back of the house. I'm in the pool."

So much for being ready to go to lunch, Keira thought. Oh well, it was his day off. So as directed, she walked the sandy path to the backyard.

"Hey baby, take your clothes off and come on in; the water is great," Len called from the deep end of the pool.

"No thanks. I was scuba diving all morning. I am pretty water-logged; besides, I didn't bring a bathing suit." Keira pointed out. She told him she was scuba diving rather than scrubbing crap off the bottom of her boat, because well, it sounded better.

Keira watched as Len climbed out of the pool, totally naked. His body wasn't as great as he appeared to think it was. Yes, one part was standing at attention, so to speak, but that wasn't even impressive. He walked over to her and kissed her, attempting to shove his tongue into her mouth. At the same time, he slid his hand under the hem of her sundress and pushed her thong aside. He was just about to ram his fingers into her vagina when she stepped away from him.

"Baby, let's go in the house. I am sure you could use a cool drink right about now. How was the drive up here?" Len said as he grabbed her hand and pulled her towards the patio sliding glass door.

Once in the kitchen, naked Len walked to the refrigerator and reached in for a bottle of vodka and cranberry juice. Keira glanced around the house quickly. He was right; The Beatles' memorabilia was everywhere she looked. On the walls, there were concert posters. Bobble-heads of each member of the band sat on the dining room table along with commemorative pictures and plaques. Beatles-themed blankets were draped over the sofa and chairs. It was claustrophobic. The house looked like a normally overpriced beach house, but the clutter poorly devalued the place. He walked up to her and pressed the glass of vodka and cranberry juice in her hand. She hated the concoction but took a sip anyway. She hated it even more afterward.

Naked Len put his head between her neck and shoulder and attempted to kiss her or maybe nibble on her earlobe. It felt awkward. Keira couldn't decide if she was angry or becoming freaked out by the entire situation.

"God, your body is hot. I am so horny. I want to fuck you. Come on, take your clothes off. Can't you see my dick is so stiff, it's painful? I can go as deep as you want. Hey baby, where are you going?"

"Go put on some damn clothes," Keira said as she headed for the front door. She unlocked it and hurried to her Jeep, slamming the door hard. Once in the car, her fingers were shaking so badly, it was hard to lock the door and push the ignition to start the engine. She would worry about her seat belt as soon as she got farther away. What a jerk, she thought as she stepped on the gas to distance herself from his home. She pulled to the side of the road a couple of miles off the beach road. Quickly she turned on her phone and pulled up the dating website. Keira found Len's profile and blocked it. Thank goodness all his emails came through the dating service and not her private email address. She also blocked his number from her phone.

On the drive back to the island, Keira stopped at the rest area before driving over the Sunshine Skyway Bridge. Once parked, she walked to the restroom to freshen up. Feeling dingy after being pawed by Len in his lack of attire, Keira looked at her reflection in the mirror. Maybe she should thank the stars she had not gotten emotionally attached to him. All Keira could see in her mind's eye was him walking toward her naked. Or, when he thought he could touch her intimately without her consent. Cringing, she dried her hands and walked out to the row of vending machines. Dropping some money into the slot, she selected an icy cold bottle of water.

Leisurely she walked along the small beach shaded by pine trees and beautiful palms. The water sparkling in the sun, the sound of boats, and the laughter of kids across the small bay calmed her anger. She sat down near the water's edge on one of the boulders. Glancing down she saw a fiddler crab scurrying in and out of his home with bits of something in his claw. It seemed like a lot of work for such a little guy.

Keira should have trusted her instincts when she thought Len was arrogant and condescending. She could now add horny pervert to his list of attributes. He strutted around his pool deck; for his neighbors and anyone else to see, which was disgusting. If he had a tall barrier fence so no one could see in, what he chose to do in the privacy of his backyard was his choice. She remembered swimming naked in her family pool in Key West with her friends on extremely hot days. Her parents hadn't been home. She and her friends thought they were so cool at twelve. It was fun; she loved the water against her skin, usually not exposed. It made her feel risky and a rebel. Of course, there was so much tropical foliage between the houses; lizards had a hard time going from one yard to another. Anyway, she was a kid back then, not even a teenager yet. Len was an adult. Didn't he care about his reputation? Or was this just a show for her? Either way, he was not her first choice candidate for a relationship, not now or ever.

When Keira pulled into the parking lot, she saw Micah walking towards the office from one of the piers. She had never seen him look so tired or dirty. Even his hair was dusty, almost white instead of the rich dark black. Where had he been, rutting around the underbelly of some old boats? She thought of his kiss as she grabbed her purse and walked the plank to her home on the water. She sighed, thinking; Len would have stuck his tongue down her throat if she would have let him. He was a jerk; she wanted no part of him. Micah's kiss was fleeting, and all she could think about was exploring his kisses a bit more. She was about to kick off her shoes and change out of her sundress, yet she felt restless. It was almost Saturday evening, and she didn't want to be on her boat. It wasn't as if she wanted to go out bar hopping or socializing. She just didn't want to be sitting around thinking about Micah's kiss. She opened her laptop and used her search engine to find a hotel on the beach anywhere between Bradenton Beach and Venice. There it was. Keira stared at her computer screen, a hotel with a balcony view of the gulf just down the road a few miles, on Lido Beach. She booked a room for the night, specifying what she wanted. It was pricey, but it wasn't like she blew through money every day. She never bought herself anything. So this was a justified mini-vaca. She placed her laptop, a fresh set of clothes, her good bathing suit, and her best silk night-gown in her backpack. As she set the security alarm on her boat, she saw Micah at the other end of the docks.

"Guard the fort." She told Jack as she walked the plank heading for the small path along the property line to her Jeep.

"Hey, where are you going..."

Keira pretended not to hear Jack calling after her. Out of the corner of her eye, she saw Micah stop walking and watched her start her car. It would have been fun to snatch him from the dock and take him to the hotel with her. She would have her wicked way with Micah Andreas all night and into the early morning hours. No consequences or questions would be asked of her behavior, just a night of pleasurable passion. Oh well, she was not Eduardo Luise and it was not to be. But she would have fun; just as soon as she stopped at the grocery store and picked up some wine.

It was just after five when she checked in at the hotel on Lido beach. The view from her room was spectacular. Her balcony looked down over the pools and out over the gulf and vast horizon, just what she wanted. She put the wine, shrimp, and fruits in the mini frig and dropped her backpack on the king-size bed. Yes, she could have used room service to order what she wanted to eat, but she really didn't want to interact with anyone, just enjoy her evening stress-free. And it all started now. Heading out the door and down the elevator, she walked across the little bridge as instructed. With the lounge chairs facing the water and late afternoon sun, her sunglasses in place, she stretched out on one of the loungers and closed her eyes.

Nope, she wasn't going to think about anything. Stop, she paid too much for the room with a view of the beautiful gulf to think about weirdo-naked guys. Ninety-nine bottles of beer on the wall, ninety-nine bottles of beer, take one...please mind, stop thinking. And then, of course, the phone rang.

"Hi, Marla."

"Come over to The Dive Bar for a drink."

Keira knew the gang was probably all standing there listening in on the conversation. So she whispered, "I'll talk to you on Monday." She turned her cell phone off. Smiling, she should have whispered, I can't talk, and with passion in her voice, say, oh baby yes, yes, yes...and then dropped her phone on the floor. It would have been perfect letting Marla and the eavesdroppers think she was having wild sex. Dang, she didn't think fast enough. Giving up on relaxing on the beach, she walked back to her room.

Taking her shrimp cocktail and the glass of wine out to the balcony, she set her laptop on the glass tabletop and connected using the hotel WIFI. The breeze off the gulf kept the temperature comfortable.

Wildman – Matt

Dear Keira,
*   I can't believe you would not help someone you*
love. I know you love me. How can you be so

heartless? Haven't you ever needed help? Please
can you at least send me a couple of thousand
dollars? It would help my men put food on their
tables. Matt

Matt,

I am sorry. You are breaking my heart. I wish I could help you, but I seriously do not have the financial means to assist you.

Keira

There that sounded sincere. She pressed send and knew as she took a sip of wine; the email was on its way to some scammer in Turkey or wherever. He was not going to be happy after spending time and energy with no return profit. 'I know you love me' and then, trying to play the guilt game, didn't work. She knew better and wasn't buying it at all. In fact, she had some questions for JFlounderGig - Jimmy about scammers, but it didn't look like he was on the website at the moment. Oh well, maybe later, she thought.

ExtremeLover – Michael

Dear Keira,
Thank you for your prayers for my mother. That
was very kind of you. Due to the lateness of her
surgery, she stayed the night and was able to be
discharged the following morning. She was doing
well, she sat in the recliner, and we talked about my
sister and my childhood. So many memories,
remembering the funny stunts we tried to pull. But
as the day wore on, she was looking paler and paler.
I called her physician and explained my concerns. As
we talked, my mother quit breathing. I called 911
and ended up initiating CPR until they got there. I
have never been so afraid in all my life.
They found out she had internal bleeding around
the surgical area and went into shock due to blood

loss. Maybe if she had been in rehab, they would have found the bleeding earlier. Part of me is angry that the hospitals, these days, release patients the same day as surgery or within 23 hours. I guess it is all about the money. So, now I am sitting here in the family room of the ICU. They will keep a closer eye on her in here for the next couple of days. When she started perking up, she told me to go home and sleep. My mother is so fearful she will be a burden to me.

I have to tell you when I started this journey on the dating website; my goal was to find a long-term relationship. I don't think I seriously understood what that meant. I talked to several women. They too, were looking for love. It was fun talking to them and learning what they liked. I loved the attention. But then I met you. Their personalities seemed shallow in comparison to the things we talked about from letter to letter. You teased and made me laugh, but more importantly, your caring comes through in each note. And I thank you for that. You are on the edge of my mind all the time. It is a fantastic feeling, as an extreme addiction, in a good way. Love, Michael

Keira took a drink from her wine glass. Her heart went out to Michael. In the last couple of days, not only had his mother gone through major surgery, she then went into shock from blood loss. All he could do was sit back helplessly, fearing for her life. She thought about Matt, who was trying to scam her in a bogus drama. And then there was Michael and his mother, who were going through a real-life and death crisis.

Dear Michael,

Thank you so much for dropping me a quick note. I know you have more important things to worry about than letter writing. I feel so sad to hear of your mother's near-death experience. I know it must have been terrifying for you. I wish I could have been with you, to support you and encourage you. I am glad she is now stabilized and will be in ICU for a bit of time. I pray that the worst is behind her and she is now on the mend.

I am awestruck by the words you have used to describe your thoughts on how our relationship is progressing. You also hold a special place in my heart. My fear is, are you real or a dream? Once your mother is stable and able to be on her own, I wish to spend some one-on-one time getting to know you better. I hope that doesn't sound selfish of me. Hugs to you, Keira

Tears were rolling down her face as she typed her note to Michael. There were so many emotions running through her mind at the moment. She was happy by his feelings for her. Yet, she also feared she was creating this larger-than-life image of Michael in her head. What if she fell head over heels in love with him, only to find out he was like Len, a real-life jerk? Or, worse, he was sitting at a desk, in front of a computer saying he was into extreme sports and really not. In reality, he was a con-man or scammer, like Matt. He could have stolen someone's identity and made up the entire story of his mother being rushed to the hospital, to build sympathy. Keira was dumbfounded and frustrated by the waste of energy by evil people doing bad things to good people.

The sun was beginning to dip beyond the Gulf of Mexico. The sky was painted in red, orange, and yellow hues, causing the water to sparkle like thousands and thousands of fiery diamonds. Keira sat back in the deck chair. She closed her eyes and transported herself and a lover, of course, to the edge of the horizon. They would be sitting on her boat, sipping wine while watching the sun in all its beautiful colors moving through the heavens.

Wiping the almost dry tears from her face with the back of her hand, she dredged a jumbo shrimp through the spicy cocktail sauce she had bought. Although jumbo shrimp was a conflict of terms, they were so good to nibble on. She opened a note from:

SonicMusicMix. – Storm.

Dear Keira,

I should have known the community of Bradenton Beach would be a tight-knit group of people, and you would know them. Petra was like a whirlwind when I talked to her. She has more energy in her little finger than most people have in their entire bodies. She was professional yet so personable. I think I will enjoy working with her.

I hope you are having fun this weekend. Dawn, my sister was in a wedding last night. She didn't want her best friend sitting by herself, so being the nice guy that I am; I went to the reception with her. We listened to a band from the Bradenton area. I am not sure if you have heard of them, but their sound was great – T De Novo. Are you familiar with them? I guess they are attorneys by day and do band gigs on weekends and special events. I either wish I was a lawyer or could sing like their lead singer. They were impressive.

Are you doing anything special this weekend?

Storm

Dear Storm,

It was so sweet of you to take your sister's friend to the wedding. But I'm not buying it. You took her because you wanted to eat the wedding cake, right? Did you dance to the chicken song, flapping your arms and bending your knees in a funky way?

Yes, I know the band called T De Novo. They have a great sound like you said. Actually, the lead singer is my attorney! I sat at the Oak and Stone Rooftop Grill and listened to them do a concert, a couple of weeks ago. It was a fun evening.

This weekend started as planned. I took my boat out and scrubbed the barnacles off the hull. Don't say it. I know, I know, I could have taken it to the marina, and they can take the barnacles off, faster and easier than me. But it was a fun excuse to take my boat out, anchor it offshore, and put on my scuba gear. I had made plans to look at a doctor's yard for a possible landscape design up in Clearwater. That turned into a fiasco I will not discuss. I was frustrated that I had wasted a couple of hours of drive time. I needed to do something fun and different. So I rented a suite at a very expensive hotel in Sarasota overlooking the gulf. I planned on jumping on the king-size bed, using all the hot water just because I could, soak in the jetted tub, and leave all the lights on all night. As stupid as it sounds, I don't have a king-size bed on my boat and there is only a shower stall. I am not doing those things, but I may soak in the tub for an hour or so. Now, if you will excuse me, I am going to eat my jumbo shrimp. I would have purchased caviar, but Publix didn't have any. I sure hope you aren't trying to live vicariously through me, because this is just a onetime thing! Keira

Keira was still laughing about the silly email she sent to Storm when her cell rang. She seldom had phone calls; please don't be that Scott guy. Her parents only called when something normal happened in the keys. And that was next to never.

"Hello?"

"Keira, this is Kraig. I hope I'm not disturbing you." "Is something wrong? Did one of the guys get hurt?"

"No, it's nothing about the company. I just wanted to talk with you."

Keira closed her eyes. She didn't want to have this discussion this evening with him, especially over the phone. This night was to be her special fun night. It may not make sense to anyone else, but she needed to be away from the boat and her life, just one damn night. "I can't talk right now. Please can we talk on Monday?"

"Sure."

Keira looked at her phone. Kraig had hung up. Great, now she had to worry if Kraig was unstable and about to harm himself. No, he wasn't that kind of guy. He was level-headed. But, she led him to believe she wasn't alone. Maybe it seemed unfair. She wasn't sure of her feelings for him. Nevertheless, she needed to think things through before she talked with him.

Peter Flynn's Friend -Basil

My lovely K Lee,

I was anxious to make sure my foreman and his men were up to speed on the project. The footers for the foundation went in as planned. But still, I have invested so much of my personal finances. If one aspect of this job site is out of sync, the entire contract could crash. I have had nightmares thinking about how much is on the line. So, I hopped on the flight out of Washington set for South Africa. Sweetheart, please pray for my strength to fulfill this contract on time.

I want to have trust in you and me. There may be many trustworthy people, but only a few are worth trusting with your heart; choose wisely. To be trusted is a greater compliment than to be loved, for you can love many but without trust you have nothing. The heart already knows what the mind can only dream of. Trust your heart. The distance cannot and will not hurt a bond between two people that is based on mutual respect, trust, commitment, and love. Jealousy is not a sign of true love; it's the insecurities that come in the way because love has just one important ingredient: Trust.

I believe by the time we both agree and accept that the word Trust is very much important in our relationship; then we are going to live a peaceful and prosperous life together with our family to come.

I will text you when I finally arrive in South Africa. I have a layover in New York before landing in Johannesburg. I then have to wait and take a next-day flight to Cape Town. I love you Baby, Basil

Dear Basil,

I was so surprised when I read in your email that you took a flight out of Washington for South Africa. You barely returned home from Texas to say hi to your daughter, and then you were gone again. However, I understand the need to keep the forward momentum going on a contracted job site. Having a trusted foreman, who knows the strengths and weaknesses of their crew, is crucial in running any business. But I don't have to tell you that.

I would enjoy seeing pictures as the work progresses. Not to mention, I have heard South Africa and Cape Town have beautiful beaches and extreme mountain ranges.

Stop and smell the roses, K Lee

The sun had set. There were only a few lovers walking hand in hand along the edge of the water. Looking down, there were still a couple of diehard children splashing in the pool and bored parents stuck there watching them. Keira picked up her laptop and walked into her suite. The evening breeze off the water kept the room cool. What was she going to say in an email to Basil? In his last note, he was in Texas and worried about some storm that never hit Florida. Now he was emailing he was on a flight to Africa and rambled on, declaring everything in a relationship is all about trust. She set her laptop down on the kitchenette bar and wandered into the bathroom. Basil's flight across the continent was not her top concern at the moment. Smiling, she turned on the hot water for a bath. It had been a while since she had a long luxurious soak in a whirlpool tub. And she was going to take advantage of it until she pruned beyond recognition! Grabbing the last of the wine she brought with her, she climbed into the hot swirling water and almost purred. It was fantastic.

Laughing, Keira wondered if Jack had called out the National Guard to find her since she wasn't home yet. Or maybe he only called Micah. And Micah had gone to The Dive Bar to get the low down from Marla on her whereabouts. Marla must have been extremely disappointed when she refused to give out any information. It was funny but sad how Marla hated not being in the know of everything.

She inspected her toes, peeking out through the soap bubbles. If she got a pedicure, what color would she have her toes painted? Pink was too girly-girl. Purple was not her color, and black looked dirty. White would soon look black and dirty; why waste time doing that color? Red, with a wicked grin, Keira realized red would be so provocative. Who would think to hide siren red toenails in work boots? Palm tree caregiver wields a jackhammer by day and calls to the ship captains out at sea during the night. Hmmm, would Theseus be tempted by her toes? She sure hoped so, but she hadn't heard from him in two days.

Thinking back, she had read his letter. He had asked a couple of questions about her boat and said he would be proud to hold hands with the lady with dark hair and blue eyes. She hoped he was talking about her. But then, come to think of it, she had slipped out her top hatch and taken a walk. Micah had kissed her later that night. She never wrote back to Theseus.

Leaning her head on the cool sidewall of the tub, she decided she had polished off the entire bottle of wine. Being near to possibly drunk, she couldn't email him tonight. For sure, she would confess her undying love to him. That would never work. She was not her parents. She sat up in the bathtub, sloshing water over the side, and wondered if she was adopted. She couldn't be their daughter. Her parents acted like newlyweds since the day they got married; even though she hadn't been born yet, they had sex all the time. She couldn't remember a time when they weren't touching each other. Dinner was always late because mixing meat for meatloaf was a visual turn-on to them. Rinsing the vegetables caused a need to take a shower together. It was so embarrassing. And here she was alone, possibly drunk in a bathtub, in a seven hundred dollar-a- night, out of season, hotel suite.

Keira woke up to the sound of waves washing ashore and the fragrant scent of salty air. What time was it? She hadn't heard old Mr. Benson's walk to the end of the pier to cast his Sunday ritual fishing line into the water. And then she remembered, she had been sleeping in the super large, very comfortable king-size bed in the middle of the suite she rented yesterday afternoon. The bed was the epitome of comfort. She could almost give up her sailboat for it. Stretching, Keira smiled at the luxurious feeling of lying in amongst the silky sheets. It was a sinfully wicked feeling.

She had crawled into bed naked after her bubble bath and unfortunately, alone. I'm not going to dwell on the 'alone' part, Keira thought. She stretched again and rolled over, hugging the mound of pillows that had not fallen off the bed during the night. There was nothing like feeling refreshed and ready to take on the world once again. She grabbed the grapes from the mini fridge she had bought the day before and opened her laptop. There was a note from Theseus.

Dear Keira,

I was a bit concerned when I didn't hear back from you. I reread the email I sent to you to see if I somehow had insulted you. It was not my intention, and I apologize if I did. I questioned if I have scared you away due to my extended time at sea. I assure you, I have cut back. I usually do not discuss my personal life with many people. After all, it is my life story and possibly boring to others. Yet, to develop a relationship on this unorthodox dating system is a, some-what, necessary evil.

While I was in the Navy, one of my brothers was visiting relatives in Santorini. A bad storm came up abruptly, killing him. It was months before my family could get word to me as my ship was at sea on a radio silence mission. When my parents needed me the most, I was not there for them. And that is why I retired from the Navy. Yes, I am loyal to my country. The death of my oldest brother and the deterioration of my marriage afterward had me rethinking my priorities.

My position with the cruise line is part-time. I fill

*in if one of the captains becomes ill or requests time
off. It gives me my sailing fix to keep me balanced. I
also enjoy doing dive charters as a side job for the
fun of being on the water.*

  *As I sit here looking out to sea from the balcony
of my home, I wonder where you are. Are you sailing
and out of range for your laptop? Have you found
someone and do not care to correspond with me any
further? Theseus*

Keira read Theseus's note a couple of times. She could feel the sadness throughout the letter. As if he was tired and needed her arms around him. Her feelings for him were puzzling at the moment. She would have loved to have a face to put with his name. There was something special about him. She felt calm when she read his words. He was someone whom she would love to wake up next to in the mornings. To know he would guard and protect her through the night would be heaven. Being there for her when she couldn't be strong and holding her, just because, would be a dream comes true. Yet it was all so confusing since she had never met him. To tell anyone how she felt, they would laugh and call her crazy for sure.

As luxurious as the bed was with all the pillows and expensive thread count bed linens, it was time to get up. She spent time putting on the red and white sundress she brought with her the day before. If only her toenails were painted red! It was nice not bumping her arms on the door or her knees on the toilet like she did while dressing on her boat. She could see her entire outfit in the mirror, not small sections at a time. Maybe this hotel stay was not a good idea; in less than twenty-four hours, she has become spoiled with the luxuries she didn't have.

She walked to the Drift Kitchen and Bar on the eighth floor for breakfast. The view was again positively breathtaking of the gulf. Theseus was still on her mind.

She hadn't written him back yet; she needed to choose her words wisely. Besides, she was still on her mini-vacation from reality. Wait, Theseus was a mythological warrior-type person and not truly real.

"May I take your order, please?"

Keira looked up. She had been deep within her thoughts, "um, I would like the Eggs Benedict, please."

"How would you like the eggs cooked?"

"Very lightly poached, and may I have a mimosa, please?"

While she sat looking out over the water and sipping her breakfast champagne cocktail, she decided she needed to go shopping. She could add a bit of flair to her bunk with beautiful bed linens and several more pillows. Adding a couple of coats of paint to lighten the interior of the hull of her boat and maybe some new tiles for the shower would spruce up the bathroom. She would hire it out rather than doing it all herself.

When her breakfast arrived, she was excited about her plan to spruce up her boat.

"Would you like another mimosa?"

"No, may I have a glass of grapefruit juice; it is fresh-squeezed, correct?" Keira asked.

"Yes, I will get it right out to you. Enjoy your breakfast."

After her fantastic breakfast, Keira walked along the beach for a few minutes. The water was warm against her feet. She would have loved to take a quick plunge into the sea, but the plan in her head was more important. When Keira returned to her suite, she sat down and opened her laptop.

Dear Theseus,

I am here. I have not left you. Please, there is no need for apologies.

Thank you for telling me of your brother's death. I am sure it was difficult to discuss the feelings we try to hide because of the pain it causes. Sometimes telling a stranger is easier. We can step outside the expected emotions connected to our grief. We can rant, scream, be angry, even throw things without pity or repercussions that loved ones would possibly give. I wish I could have been that stranger so I could have hugged you to ease your distress.

I, too, have looked out to sea most of the weekend. I have searched the horizon for answers.   Keira

Keira closed her laptop after sending the email to Theseus. She still had so many questions to ask of him. First and foremost, what was his name? The inquiring would have to wait. With her plan in place for the rest of the day, she placed her laptop in her backpack. Walking out of the beautiful suite; the night at the resort had served its purpose. It refreshed and revitalized her, even if it dented her credit card a bit.

It was after six in the evening when Keira returned to her boat. The weekend parties had wound down as the last sunburned people headed for home. It took several trips to and from her Jeep to carry all the pillows, bed linens, and new outfits she had purchased earlier in the afternoon. But it would all be worth it.

She was surprised and yet, glad Jack was not sitting out on his boat. It was nice not having to explain her weekend away. Nor did she have to justify her spending spree to anyone. Although the galley hatch was closed, she had yet to turn on her cabin lights when she heard Jack walk the plank to his boat. Sitting at her chart table, she ate a couple of pieces of crispy chicken she had purchased at Publix on the way home. She had been too exhausted to think about cooking and rationalized it as the last indulgence of her mini vacation.

When Keira climbed into bed, she laughed; it sure wasn't the king-size bed like last night, but it was her bed, and she loved it all the same. It had been a bit of a disappointment after realizing she would be spending time at the laundromat before she could sleep on her expensive and new sheets. Not caring, Keira puffed up the brand-new pillows, without cases, behind her head and opened her laptop. Ignoring all the emails waiting to be opened, she zeroed in on the note from **Theseus.**

My Dearest Keira,
   Thank you for your email. It warmed my heart to know you would have wanted to be with me after my brother's passing.

I do not know the reasons for your silence the last few days. I am sure when you are ready, and you trust me, you will explain. Just know I am here for you. But tell me, when you searched the horizon, did you find the answers, your heart questioned?

Theos

Chapter 11
♥♥♥♥♥♥♥♥♥♥♥♥♥

The sky was turning pink when Keira stretched. She needed to get a move on before the marina came alive with scuba excursions, fishing boats needing fuel, and the office opened. With regret, Keira quickly got out of her bed and dressed. She grabbed a notepad, pencil, and her camera and slowly walked the perimeter of the marina, measuring the distance. After gathering enough photos and measurements, Keira headed back to her boat. She saw Micah's sports car pull in next to the office. She was happy he hadn't seen what she had been doing.

Line one of her to-do list completed. Reaching for her phone from the charging station on the chart table, she texted Kraig.

"Business meeting at noon, meet me at the office. Bring casual, not work clothes attire for the meeting. Please, make sure the crew understands what needs to be completed by the end of the day. Keira"

Keira quickly took a shower after sending the text. Although the day was young, she still had much to do. Keira decided while showering she didn't want to spend her next off day sitting at the laundromat while her clothes washed.

On the way to her first appointment, she pulled into George's Full-Service Dry Cleaning & Laundromat. The bell tinkled when she opened the door. Mr. Wu was so caring and a real sweetheart.

"Miss Keira, you dirty clothes quickly?"

"George, may I please have these items cleaned and pressed? And these just washed, dried, and folded?" Keira asked.

"I like watching you sit looking bored on Saturday. Other ladies fat and ugly, you pretty to my eyes." George confessed, blushing to his ears.

"Aww, George, I love you."

"You no tell wife. She make me sleep on lumpy sofa again and again and again." George laughed.

Keira chuckled over her conversation with George on her drive to the Bradlow and Bradlow Attorneys' office. She had been surprised to secure an early morning appointment with KC Bradlow. Betsy, his secretary, had informed Keira he was in court almost every Monday. But a new attorney was taking KC's court case today. Once seated in front of KC's desk, she explained the changes she wanted to make to her Landscape Architect and Lawn Care Service Company. He gave her advice on what to do and not to do, to protect her assets. He had Betsy draw up temporary forms for Keira until they could have the formal legal documents ready for signing. At the end of her meeting, Keira was pleased with the outcome and advice KC always gave her. He was knowledgeable and cared about what his clients needed.

Confused to the name change from Bradlow and Gresheim to Bradlow and Bradlow Attorney's office, Keira wondered if something had happened to Attorney Gresheim? She had met him only once but he had left a caring impression never the less. KC let her know Mr. Gresheim had traded his office for an Arizona golf community. How could Arizona be better than Florida???

Right before she left KC's office, but after her formal meeting was over, KC had suggested some Saturday she should meet Kristi and Zac, and him and Lea on their boats at Egmont Key with her sailboat. He explained Zac Karas had his sailboat tied to the pier at Marina Jack's marina. Keira loved the idea and told him to let her know when they were all sailing to the small island in the gulf.

As she drove to the office, she thought how much fun it would be to hang out on a Saturday with KC and Lea, the famous local romance author at Egmont Key. Kristi, KC Bradlow's sister, was engaged to Zac Karas, owner of The Mermaid Isle in Sarasota. KC had mentioned Zac also had a sailboat, so they too would be there. When she parked next to the office back door, her happy feeling about the possible adventure faded to nothing. She would be the fifth person out; two beautiful couples and herself. Although it was her own choice not to have a guy, a companion, a lover, whatever she wanted to call him, she still was alone. Couples had special bonds, quiet nods, secret and personal body movements that they shared. A single person wasn't privy to the body language. It was as if most of the group's gathering was fun and laughter, but a sheer curtain was always present. She was there at the edge, enjoying the friendship but not the private jokes. Most times, she ignored her awareness of it, but there were moments when the invisible barrier hurt.

The office was still as Keira brewed a pot of coffee. The phone sat on her desk, quiet. All the client follow-up calls were completed and filed. She had the perfect people in place, and the business was running smoothly. She had an hour before Kraig was to meet her for their business meeting. She poured a cup of coffee and sat down at her drafting table. It was time to create a beautiful landscape for Micah's marina. She drew the perimeter lines of the area that needed to be revitalized. She sketched in palm trees and seating areas for the weekend boaters to gather. She looked at the photos she had taken earlier in the morning. Behind the warehouse, where the old boats and engine parts sat deteriorating, needed to be rejuvenated. And, she still couldn't decide what to do with that area behind the office? She drew and redrew different ways to camouflage the eyesores. Her coffee sat untouched and cold as she sketched the parking area minus the potholes.

"I have watched you on many occasions drawing up blueprints for a client." Kraig said as he slowly walked across the office.

"Oh...I'm sorry, I didn't hear you come in." Keira said, dropping her pencil. It rolled off the drafting table.

"It has always amazed me how completely focused you are. It is as if you are standing in the middle of the paper drawing, moving bushes and boulders, or throwing something off the edge of the design. I have wished many times you would have given me even one iota of your attention that you give to designing lawns." Kraig quietly said walking up to her and kissed her neck.

Keira swiveled on her chair to face him and ignored the kiss. "How is the Riverview project progressing?"

Kraig gave her a quick rundown on what the guys had completed and still needed to finish on the worksite. He let her know they were right on schedule.

"Do you want to change out of your work clothing? " Keira asked Kraig. She wished she could have taken a picture of his startled facial expression. "Come with me, I will show you where you can change."

After seeing the full three-piece bathroom that he always thought was a closet off Keira's office, he pulled Keira to him and slowly kissed her.

Keira enjoyed the softness of Kraig's lips. She wanted to explore them a little longer but stepped back from him and said, "I will let you change clothes. We have a meeting to go to," and walked back to her drafting table.

Carefully she slid the blueprints inside her cylinder transport container. Grabbing her cold cup of coffee, she walked to the compact kitchen, turned off the coffee pot, and rinsed out her cup. When she turned around, he was leaning against the door frame.

"You are beautiful even when you are cleaning up the kitchen and doing domestic chores."

"Careful, the feminist will attack you for that kind of statement." Keira grinned. She grabbed her satchel and blueprint canister and walked out of the office towards her Jeep.

As Kraig slid in the passenger seat, he asked, "Where is the business meeting located? Do I need to present anything?"

Keira smiled without giving any hints of the meeting's agenda. The drive downtown to the river was short; sitting at *Pier 22* Restaurant overlooking the water would be a treat. Only a few people would want to dine out in the heat of the day. Pulling into valet parking, she handed her keys to the parking attendant. With the soft breeze off the Manatee River, she chose to be seated on the patio. It was almost one in the afternoon, and as she predicted, there were only a few couples sitting on the patio sipping drinks. It would give them the privacy they needed for their discussion.

"May I take your drink order?"

"I would like a white wine, please." Keira requested. She could see Kraig was still confused about the business part of the meeting. She saw him look around for suit-type people to show up.

"Bourbon and Coke, please," Kraig stated.

After the server walked away from the table, Keira began to explain her proposal to Kraig. She pushed the prospectus, as prepared by her attorney, towards him. Before he could say anything, she began to explain her deal. Kraig had the option to purchase half of the Landscape Architect and Lawn Care Service. Otherwise, she would continue her control of the financial side and any decisions, but he would have a say in the contracts and businesses they conducted. Keira explained that if he decided against the purchase aspect of the deal, she requested in writing what he would bring to the business table. She outlined the business holdings and her vision for future company growth. At this point, there was no disclosure of the financial reports. If he asked, she had certifications of sound financial business practices and no outstanding long-term debts.

She expressed her desire to promote one of the lawn crew members to a supervisor position. However, it was only if one of the crew met the expectations of the supervisory job description she wanted to create. Lastly, she explained, she had already initiated the search for a full-time secretary with one of the top employment websites.

"May I take your orders?"

"I would like the grouper piccata," Keira said as she handed the server her menu.

"I will take the fresh catch."

"Our fresh catch is grilled yellowtail snapper with mango salsa. Is that ok with you, sir?"

"Yes."

Once the server left, Keira could see how overwhelmed Kraig was. He sat looking out over the Manatee River as if he had never seen it before. Running his thumb around the rim of the cocktail glass sitting in front of him; Kraig continued to ponder all that Keira had said. He looked at her as she sat waiting as he absorbed the magnitude of what she had moments ago proposed to him. She watched him take a deep breath.

"When you texted me saying we were going to a business meeting, I thought you were giving a presentation and needed my knowledge on certain aspects of the fieldwork. You have completely blown my mind. Is this why you would not talk to me on Saturday night?"

"Partially," Keira smiled.

"Why are you doing this?" Kraig asked, staring at Keira.

"Sir, your yellowtail snapper and for you, Miss, grouper piccata; I will check back in a few minutes to see if you need anything."

Keira cut into her grouper and tasted it. She thought she had gone to heaven. The flavor was spot on; it was excellent. Taking a sip of wine, she knew Kraig was trying to work things out in his head. Taking a deep breath, she looked over the water. Theseus sitting on his deck looking across the water came to mind. She wanted to find her 'someone.' She set her fork down.

"A while back, you said I hadn't had a vacation in a long time, if ever. I enjoy the business that I have created. But you were right; I need time off from time to time. Let me ask you. Who taught the lawn crew how to check and repair our equipment after finishing assigned lawns? Why did you ask me to bring in donuts the other day? It is hard to develop pride in the work the guys do, but you have done it. Who volunteered his house for our July 4th celebration? Who knows the ground and fieldwork better than you? You have spotted ground irrigation problems that would have caused root rot in our trees that are guaranteed once we plant them. Who was here for me when Peter was sleeping with Mrs. Weinsworth? Shall I go on?" Keira questioned as she took a sip of wine.

"Again, why are you doing this? You could just give me a raise."

"Kraig, don't underestimate yourself; you are good. You love my business as much as I do. I think with your knowledge base and work ethic, you are a great leader. And I love you for that."

Keira watched as Kraig picked up his fork and ate. There was no further discussion on the proposal she had made. The server came and refilled their ice water. Still, he said nothing.

The server returned and removed their plates. She suggested an after-meal coffee with a slice of amaretto cheesecake with a gingerbread crust and almond garnish. Kraig shook his head, not wanting either.

"As I have said, I was caught off guard by your proposal. I am honored you are giving me this opportunity. I have several ideas that I believe will expand your business. Thank you. I will not let you down." Kraig said, extending his hand, which Keira shook.

Keira dropped Kraig at the office after explaining she was heading back to the marina to see what she still needed to add to the blueprint drawings of a proposal she wanted to make. She wasn't used to explaining her every move pertaining to the company. There were times she liked to sit in her boat and work on drawings. The water and the rocking of her boat gave her inspiration.

As she headed towards home, she realized she was mentally exhausted. It had taken her a while to let go of part of her company to anyone. Never, during her marriage to Peter, had she wanted to sign over half of her business to him. His constant wish to blow through her money had nixed that notion from the start. But Kraig was different. He had shown dedication in his job and every opportunity to better her company without asking for anything. She believed in her heart, she made the right decision

.

Seeing Petra was still at The Wet T-Shirt Shop, Keira pulled into the parking spot right outside the entrance.

"Keira, I am glad you stopped in. I have so much to tell you; oh my gosh, that dress is beautiful on you. Where have you been?" Petra gushed.

"I had a business meeting. Do you need any help with the contest preparations?"

"Come with me; I have to stock the back shelf with the new T-shirt inventory from Hawaii. Everything is coming together perfectly. But," Petra said, lowering her voice to a whisper. "This man walked into my shop this morning. He was absolutely, positively, and utterly the dreamiest guy I have ever seen. He wore skin-tight man jeans and a t-shirt with music notes coming through a sonic boom across the front. I have never seen a t-shirt like that. Underneath the picture were the words Sonic Music Mix. He was Storm Griffin, the DJ I hired for the festival. He was eye candy, for sure." Petra said as she looked to heaven.

"Why was he here?"

"He wanted to 'check out the area', was what he told me. I was completely speechless. You would have loved him immediately. But I want him. I think I am in love!" Petra giggled.

Keira had never seen her friend so animated over a guy before. Markos, the owner of Azul Del Mar Dive Shop, bought his entire stock of dive t-shirts from Petra just to see her, a couple of times a week. She never drooled over him, and Keira had thought he was cute. There was no way she was going to mention she had been talking to Storm on her dating website.

"Petra, that is so cool. Was he impressed with the shop, your ideas for the festival, tell me everything!"

"He thought the beach area was perfect. He let me hear, on his phone, some of the songs he plans for my event. He uses his hands to describe things, oh his hands. One touch and I would have melted right here on the wood floor, into a pool of goo."

Laughing, Keira waved to her friend as she walked out the door. She was seriously worried about going into a diabetic coma with all the sugar-sweet talk from Petra. She drove down the street and into the marina parking lot. Once out of the car, she walked to the junk piled behind the office and tried to decide how to either relocate it somewhere else or hide it. And then she had a great idea. She whirled around to head for her boat to work on changing part of the blueprint and ran into the toned body of Micah.

"Oh"

"Hi," Micah said as he stepped back from her.

"I ... I um, was just looking at your pile of junk," Keira said as she pointed to the mound behind her.

"You mean like my junk could be your up-cycled treasures sort of thing?"

"Um, well yes, exactly," Keira agreed. She wanted to kick herself. She was always tongue-tied when she was around him.

"You are dressed too nice to be rutting around engine parts. I am just heading out for something to eat. Would you like to have dinner with me?" Micah asked as he twirled his keyring around his finger.

"Sure, that would be nice." Keira decided. She saw the moment of surprise in his facial expression, and then it was gone. He must have thought she would have turned him down.

"Do you mind if I put my stuff in the back of your car rather than running it down to the boat?"

Micah held the passenger door for Keira to slide into his car. Carefully he set her work satchel and cylinder canister on the back seat. He drove slowly out of the parking lot and headed south along Gulf of Mexico Drive, over the Longboat Pass Bridge.

"I take it you are working on some blueprints for an upcoming project? I can't believe you are bypassing my pothole parking lot project. I'm hurt." Micah teased. His pouting look never really reached his eyes.

Keira just smiled. If he only knew, or should she tell him that she was working on it? She watched as he pulled his sports car into *Mar Vista Dockside Restaurant*. She loved this restaurant. The shaded eating area along the water created a relaxing dining experience. Most people wrinkle their noses over the heavy smell of brine and fish at certain times of the year. But it reminded Keira of hot steamy evenings in the keys and home.

With menus in hand, the hostess guided them to a table near the Intracoastal Waterway edge. It was a balmy evening, not too hot or humid, perfect for eating outside. "What may I get you from the bar?"

"A glass of ice water and a rum-runner, please," Keira stated.

"I will have a rum and Coke," Micah said.

After the hostess walked away, he looked at Keira and said, "And is this your new work attire?"

"No, I had meetings all day, so I had to look professional for a change."

"It's a good look on you."

After drinks were served, they decided against appetizers. Keira ordered scallops rumaki while Micah ordered the baked seafood medley. Since she had eaten a large meal at lunch, she was happy with the smaller appetizer portion of scallops. She watched the server place the overloaded plate of shrimp, scallops, and crab served over rice and vegetables in front of Micah. Figuring he may not have eaten all day, or like her, sometimes things came up at the office, and eating lunch was a bite here and there. Micah smiled with pleasure as he started eating.

Their food was delicious. And, the conversation, a light bantering, for the rest of the evening, was enjoyable. Micah had a witty sense of humor once the defensive wall came down that he, she was sure, used to protect himself. Keira remembered the drunken ladies from the stranded boat. Micah probably had women throwing themselves at him all the time. His good looks and the fact that he owned a well-established business were important factors to many women. The question was, were they important to her?

Honestly, yes, looks and financial stability was important to her. Her ex-husband had all the right moves and had been very attractive. Many women had taken a double look at Peter when they had gone to dinner engagements or out places together. He had loved the female attention he had received at fundraisers and business banquets they had gone to. It didn't seem to matter to the bold and unashamed women that there was a shiny wedding ring on his fourth finger on his left hand.

Peter was the most financially unstable person she knew, but it didn't stop him from flashing Keira's wealth around. He dressed well, thanks to her. The sports car driven by Peter all around town was not purchased by Santa or his faerie godmother but by Keira. And he used his Christmas gift of a Jaguar to pick up chicks while she worked. So, yes, looks and financial stability were things Keira had set as a top priority to be suspicious of.

Did Micah love the attention women gave him?

"You seem very reflective all of a sudden. Is something wrong?" Micah asked as he pushed his plate aside.

"The wealth on this island is staggering, yet this place has a rustic charm among the mangroves."

"Yes, that is true. On Saturday, a while back, I was hauling old engine parts to the dumpster. I saw you on your knees with a spade, removing grass and weeds around what looked like another weed. And now, I have a small palmetto palm. You even put stakes around it so the lawn service wouldn't mow over it. That fascinated me," Micah couldn't believe he was telling Keira he had watched her pulling weeds.

"I'm sorry; I had no right to stake a palm on your property. I can't seem to help myself when it comes to palm trees."

As Micah drove over the Longboat Key Bridge, Keira looked to the west across the open water, "Oh, what a beautiful night."

Keira was surprised when Micah turned on the side road of Coquina Beach Park. She watched as he parked his car at one of the parking spaces in front of the tiny beach along the pass. Micah got out of the car and grabbed Keira's hand. They both slipped out of their shoes and stood at the edge of the water. Micah slowly pulled Keira into his arms and kissed her with the lights along the bridge reflecting on the dark water as a backdrop.

Keira felt a wave of energy flowing between herself and Micah like she had never experienced with anyone else. Was it the enchanting lights shimmering on the water or the warm sea lapping at their ankles? It was an indescribably wonderful feeling, whatever it was. How could it be that kissing Micah felt magical and way to short? It had been so long since she felt anything remotely exciting.

When Micah ended the kiss, she saw a deep-searching look in his eyes. Did he feel the same electrical current flow between them? She didn't know, but the drive back to the marina was too short. And when Micah parked his car by the property line path to her boat, he again leaned over and slowly kissed her.

"Thank you for dinner. I enjoyed the evening." Keira pressed her hands to the sides of his face. Looking into his eyes, she wished their evening together wasn't over. She climbed out of his car.

"Night."

"Keira? I'm heading over to Miami tomorrow to look at a boat."

Micah said as he stood watching her walk towards her boat.

When Keira saw Jack sitting on his deck, she was glad Micah hadn't walked her to the gangplank. She wasn't sure how chatty Jack had gotten with the always drunk guys. Being the topic of conversations for the entire marina would have made Keira cringe. Having dinner with the owner of the marina would be like a tsunami hitting the coast. The entire world would know. He was off- limits for that specific reason. Men gossiped more than women and the always drunk guys, definitely had loose lips, no filters whatsoever.

"Geeze, you are getting home late," Jack observed as Keira climbed on board her boat and unlocked her hatch.

"Yeah, you know how long and boring business meetings are. Night."

Keira hated to change out of her dress. Today and this evening, she felt beautifully feminine. Windblown and dirt-smudged was her usual look. Instead of putting on her usual nightshirt, she chose the satin nightgown she had taken on her mini-vacation Saturday night. She wanted to feel sexy just a little longer. She was about to brush her teeth when she heard a quiet knock on her cabin hatch door.

"Micah?"

"Here are your landscape blueprints and satchel," Micah said as he held out her forgotten things from his car.

Keira saw his mouth fall open when he looked at her low-cut satin dressing gown. She realized the marina's lamp post lights caused an iridescent shimmer to the material. A fleeting look of something Keira hoped was awe passed over his eyes. But the enchantment was broken when Jack said "hi" from his boat.

Micah tilted his head and bid her a shy goodnight.

Seeing the look on Micah's face when he looked down at her nightgown was sheer lust; Keira was sure of it. Her gown bodice hugged the curve of her breasts perfectly. She wondered if his imagination had run wild as he drove home. Had she known he was at her galley hatch, she would have pulled on a t-shirt. It was rather embarrassing. At the same time, she was excited that he found her appealing. The thought gave her a warm fuzzy feeling.

There was no way she was going to sleep after seeing the desire in Micah's eyes. She sat down at her chart table and unrolled the marina blueprints. She tried to focus on making the changes she had thought of when Micah had caught her snooping around. Her mind kept finding a way back to the sensation of Micah's kiss. The deep-water inlet of Longboat Key pass was the perfect setting for him to pull her close. It was like the passage to the open sea could be a metaphor like the beginning of something with him. Oh, stop it, she thought. Guys do not waste time thinking like that. He wanted to kiss her. There was no way he could kiss and drive at the same time, so he pulled over, end of the story. His reaction to her nightgown was sheer lust. If she had big boobs he would have found a way to fall between them or drop something to get a better look during dinner. She worked with guys; it was that simple, that was how they thought. But it did boost her self-esteem when she saw him looking at her nightgown. Ok enough.

She rolled up the blueprint and slid it back in the canister. Micah mentioned he was going to Miami for a couple of days. There was no longer the urgency to complete the drawings for him. So, she opened her laptop to the website.

Wildman – Matt

> *Keira,*
> *You are one heartless bitch.*

The note from Matt was a surprise but not. She was so glad she didn't fall for his scam. She wondered how much money he had made, pleading some story about needing to feed his workers or some other line of B.S. to kind-hearted women. There should be a law against his type of behavior. But because women voluntarily gave scammers, like him, money, the lawyers are unable to prosecute.

SonicMusicMix – Storm

Dear Keira,

I laughed reading the email you sent me. Going to the wedding with my sister's friend, I had no vested interest in her. She was fun and cute but never-the-less dancing with her was like clowning with one of my cousins. However, the cake was fantastic.

Driving three hours somewhere on your day off for a potential job and the possible client that doesn't take you or your business seriously would get my ire up. It is one thing to take a drive for the fun of going somewhere unique or exploring some out-of-the-way place. But to spend time and energy on game players is another. I am glad you were able to salvage the weekend with the use of your credit card!

I drove down to Bradenton Beach this morning. I didn't have any clients booked and wanted to get a feel for the area I was going to DJ at. You understand the importance of prep work. The beach area is perfect for what Petra has planned. The space is large and will be able to handle a lot of people without feeling crammed together. I will need to bring more speakers than I had originally anticipated. Not to worry though, I have it covered. I am just glad I recognized the need upfront.

I stopped in to see Petra at her shop. She is a natural for owning a T-shirt shop. She was mesmerized by my company logo shirt. I don't think she took her eyes off my shirt for more than a few minutes. Her personality is perfect for her business; she is very enthusiastic.

I was hoping while I walked from her shop down to The Dive Bar for a bite to eat before I headed home, I was hoping I would have run into you somehow. I know it was a Monday and all, but it would have been worth the drive down to meet you.

Sometimes planned first meetings are awkward. Maybe we can get together before the upcoming holiday. Take care, Storm

Dear Storm,

I knew it; I knew that cake was your downfall!!!! That was a smart move to walk the area where you will be playing your music for the July third festivities. It is such a major project for our little community. If it is a success this year, next year there will be a larger crowd. This could drum up so much business for you, no pun intended! I am not sure who all is sponsoring this event, but big businesses always are looking for great music for their private or corporate parties. It would have been nice to run into you today. I laugh because I was surprisingly dressed in nice attire due to meetings all day. Usually, I wear khaki shorts, a polo shirt with my business logo on it, and work boots. Within an hour after starting the workday, I look like a dusty rag-a-muffin; yes, I have been called that. Hey, when you plant trees and move shrubs, manicures and cute white sports outfits, however fashionable, are not realistic accoutre.

It is late, and I still have a blueprint to work on, for a landscape presentation later this week. I wish you a great night's sleep.

Keira

"Babe, please, I need your help. I don't want to be stuck in this god-forsaken country. I sold my watch and my leather coat. Please, I beg of you, can you send me eight thousand? I'm desperate. Scott"

Keira couldn't help but grin at the persistence of the phone stalker, Scott. Oh well, there was no way she would send him a thing. She did notice after she sent Storm the email, JFlounderGig - Jimmy was on the website.

"Jimmy, how are you doing?"

"It may be June, but it is cold out tonight, even by Maine's standards."

"Oh no, that sure makes for a short summer for you." "Our summer usually doesn't start until the 4th of July."

"I have a question for you… do scammers work together, you know, like sit in a warehouse and develop a database that they share? Or, are these guys, Individuals, who one day decided they could get rich preying on unsuspected generally nice people?" Keira asked.

"I don't know for sure, but I think both. The copy and paste emails from several different individuals have the same words that play on the emotions of their subjects. One person who was talking to me was nice one minute and an hour later, rude and sarcastic. When I repeated a statement that I had said earlier in the conversation, the person typed, well, you are going to tell me anyway, right? It was almost as if she was tag-teaming me or had just come on her shift." Jimmy explained.

"I had a person who said they were working in Turkey excavating amethyst from mines in the mountains. He said they were having heavy rains and landslides and needed money because his generator couldn't keep up, his men were overworked, and he couldn't make payroll. He asked me for five thousand. I checked the weather forecast, and it showed mild temps with only a small percentage of rain. And by the way, amethyst is not mined in Turkey."

"The guy must have been a rookie!! Oh yes, when they talk to you for a couple of days and then all of a sudden they have an out- of-country job, I guarantee they are a scammer. Oh, there is a new husband and wife scam team going on right now."

"Are you kidding me? Tell me, what they do?"

"For women, a guy shows you some pictures of himself as a nice looking guy sitting on a zebra print sofa or some exotic looking chair. The pictures get racier He talks to you for a day or so. Then, all of a sudden, there are pictures of a woman sitting on the same chair striking a provocative pose. The woman from the chair pose, breaks into the conversation and tells you the guy will tell you someone hacked his account, and that is how the woman's pictures got posted. But she will tell you not to talk to the guy because he is her ex-husband and a hacker or scammer. She tells you how horrid he is blah, blah, blah. She talks and confides in you, telling you 'secrets of him' or that he loves kinky sex. All of a sudden, she needs your help because he is threatening her or blackmailing her with some very dirty poses far worse than the pictures of her that you have seen. She needs your help to go into hiding...a mere five thousand would help her get lost, with the promise to repay you when she feels safe somewhere."

"Has this happened to you?" Keira asked, mortified of such evil behavior.

"No, but a neighbor of mine down the road came over for coffee one morning and showed me the play-by-play emails and pictures."

"Thank you for telling me. I feel like I have become suspicious of everyone I have talked to until proven innocent. That upsets me. I cannot be myself or enjoy the conversation as part of getting to know someone. Thanks Jimmy."

"Just do not give out too much personal information; this especially pertains to birthmarks, tattoos, and nicknames. However, I was a real asshole one night."

"Oh no, do tell."

"This woman started talking to me. It was an on-again-off-again chat. She told me she had been in the military during the Iraq War. She talked about some of her experiences while out there. It seemed interesting, but, most people do not talk about their time in the service with civilians. She talked of taking leave time and traveling to the marketplace for a day of shopping. She said someone slipped her some rare gold jewelry. Fearful of taking it out of the country at the time, she put it in a bank vault. Now she wants to go back and retrieve it. But of course, she doesn't have enough money for the flights. So she asked me if she could get a loan from me. She told me she would pay me back as soon as she sells the jewels on the auction block in New York. Yeah, right, so I asked her how much she needed. Then I said I would have to get a loan, putting my car up as collateral. I kept giving her excuses for the delays. Finally, I told her the loan came through. The money had to clear the bank. I asked her where I should send the money. I kept stalling. She gave me the address of some apartment in downtown Atlanta in a very shady neighborhood. But she had told me she lived in upstate New York. When she grew tired of my excuses, she called me every name in the book, words that would never get her through the pearly gates of heaven for sure. I just laughed and finally had her blocked."

"You are so good. I would be afraid those types of people would come after me."

"When you play at their game, you are playing with fire. That's a fact. Take care, Keira."

"Thanks once again for the information."

Keira snuggled against her new pillows and thought about what Jimmy had told her. Around the world, there were people willing to fleece someone without any guilt or remorse. That was so upsetting. She never wished harm on anyone but scammers; they would be the exception to her rule. The damage that any scammer did to other, she hoped, would come to haunt them tenfold. Was it wrong to think that way? Probably, but if it eliminated those kinds of people, the world would become a better place to live.

It was late. About to turn off her laptop for the night, she noticed a new message from someone. It was from
Theseus - Theos:

> *My Dearest Keira,*
>
> *Being Monday, I am sure you were extremely busy with your business. I had the local marina pressure wash the bottom of my boat today. There is a new type of anti-fouling paint that just came out on the market. It is supposed to prevent the buildup of algae and debris on the lower hull, for a longer amount of time. The manufacturer guarantees it will keep the boat cleaner longer. It was a bit pricey, but I decided to give it a try.*
>
> *While I was waiting on the painting of my boat's lower hull, I decided I would spend some time painting the interior walls of my house. Yes, I could hire it out, but I figured I had time to do the painting and make any repairs to the drywall if needed. I moved the furniture and was about to crack open*

the pain can when I got a phone call from the cruise
liner's main office. The ship's master captain, out of
Cape Canaveral, has taken ill midway through his
tour.

Thank goodness tomorrow is their day in port. I
will report for duty at zero six hundred hours and
bring the cruise ship home from the Bahamas. I fly
out in the next hour. So much for painting, you know?

Anyway does my secret mistress have any
romantic spots for me to visit in Key West? Theos

Keira thought about a cruise from Cape Canaveral to the Bahamas and back. She had heard the men at work talk about taking their girlfriends and wives on those cruises. They called them the booze-cruises. They were a short run from Miami or Cape Canaveral to the Bahamas and back, or they would stop in Grand Bahama and Key West for a day. She had read Lea Finn's novel After Midnight Excursions and thought she would prefer an Alaskan cruise more than a cruise to the Bahamas. With all the port stops and so many excursions, she would never want to sit drinking on a cruise ship or spend the entire time gambling. Going to Ketchikan for a day or taking a half-day train trip up into the Yukon sounded fun. The helicopter excursion of walking on a glacier would, for sure, be an adventure in itself. Maybe she wasn't interested in the Bahamas cruise because she had sailed to the islands several times. There was always something to explore, but she would like some new and different places to travel. Sailing through the Panama Canal would be the adventure of a lifetime, but she had heard going through the locks were very expensive.

Dear Theos,

Thank you again for trusting me by telling me your name. I am not sure if I could handle your life. Being called up to take a last-minute cruise assignment, never knowing your day-to-day schedule, would be unsettling. How do you follow a routine? Gee, I am sounding so predictable and boring. But I think it would be difficult to make plans and then have to cancel. Or, as you were just getting started with the prep work before painting your house, you are motivated. And now, with everything covered, ready to paint, you leave.

When I get home from a vacation, my motivation level is almost non-existent. Dropping my suitcase out of the pathway between the living room sofa and my bed is ambitious. Oh wait; I can't remember the last time I was on vacation. Ok, now I am depressed.

Romantic spots to visit while in Key West are hard to come by because of the volume of people touring the islands on any given day. The large hotel chains have beautiful views of the water and sunsets. Some of the bed and breakfast inns have very secluded gardens with small pools. They may stimulate a seductive and passionate night. The bars and restaurants are sometimes standing room only and have loud music. And the wild antics of the tourists after consuming large amounts of alcohol always make for memorable moments on their vacation. There are sunset cruises people can take with live music and hors d' oeuvres. Those are all nice but not too private. I would have to say, sailing my boat to the Dry Tortugas and spending the night anchored just off the island would be romantic. The day ferry returns people to Key West around five in the afternoon. The people, who camp on the island, usually pitch their tents and socialize with other campers around their fires. So, as the darkness of night closes in, the gentle waves soothe the restless soul, and romance stirs the air.

I wonder if you are now aboard ship. Take care, Keira

Theseus – Theos

Dear Keira,

I made it safely to the ship. Rather than waiting for morning to take charge, I relieved the second in command immediately. The helicopter I flew in on airlifted the gravely ill Captain to the nearest hospital.

From the bridge, all is quiet, ten knots wind speed, partly cloudy, a nice night to sail. The casino and bars are the places to be this evening. All is orderly for the time being, but the night is young. As I look out over the sea, once again, I think of you. With your love of sailing, it is as if you are with me, guiding me back to port.

I sense a change in your writing since your last email. I am not sure if you are tired from an exhausting day and your need sleep. From some of the things you have written, owning your own company is far from easy. Is it taking its toll on you? When you said you haven't had a vacation in a long time, I wonder...shall I be the pirate that kidnaps you? I will sequester you on my fully equipped yacht, making sure you have everything you could possibly need, so you can relax and once again enjoy life. Or, have found someone who has melted your heart and curled your toes? The very thought of that causes me grief.

While I am on board the ship, I look forward to your emails. Your words carry me through the night, and it seems, found a place in my heart. I would have never believed when I joined the dating website it was possible to develop such feelings as I have for you. Every email you write shows me a different facet of your personality. With you, I could see a lifetime of adventure and love. Maybe I should not have bared my heart like this, yet you are special to me. I do not want to lose you. Please remain in my heart, sail with me. My love, Theos

Keira read Theos's email twice. It was beautifully penned and so full of heart. She wondered how difficult it must have been for him to reveal his feelings. He expressed his pain if she had found love with someone else, yet he strived to explain how he could spend a lifetime getting to know her. He simply stated what his heart felt.

Matt had called her a heartless bitch a few minutes ago in an email. He hadn't gotten what he wanted. Yet, here was Theos, expressing his love even though he feared he could have already lost her love. There was no malice in his words; he could have voiced his displeasure quite firmly, but he didn't. Keira looked at the stars through the hatch. If he only knew how confused she was; she wanted to love him. He was a romantic sea captain searching for love. Two ships in the...

Keira sat up in bed. Her mouth fell open. She remembered when she was growing up. She fantasized about a pirate stealing her away from Key West. He took her to the outer reaches of the Caribbean Sea, where she had never been. St Lucia, Barbados, Trinidad, and all the places she had seen on sailing charts were too far south for her little sailboat but not pirate ships. And didn't Theos just suggest he be the pirate who would kidnap her? Of course, he was making a joke to make her smile when she read the email, but was he her childhood wish? Nonsense, the whole thing was nonsense, she thought. But the fantasy of Theos, her mysterious secret pirate lover, lingered in her mind.

What about Michael? He was fascinating to email with, and he, too, had expressed his amazement at finding her. Two men, one a sea captain and the other a photojournalist who lived life on the edge, she found both enchanting. Was she trying to escape normalcy? Or, was she fantasizing about a grandeur romance? Was her life really that bad? She had worked so hard to establish her landscape business as one of the top around. And now she still wasn't happy? Keira rolled on her side. Tears slowly slid onto one of her new pillows. Her thoughts were scattered and jumbled as she drifted into a restless sleep.

Chapter 12
♥♥♥♥♥♥♥♥♥♥♥♥♥

Keira woke several times during the night. She had wicked dreams of being kidnapped by a pirate in the image of Theseus the statue, only when she looked closer, it was Len, and he was still naked. With his proudly displayed penis, he had grabbed her and set sail in the middle of a hurricane on a boat he didn't know how to sail. He kept saying, 'Arrr you be drinkin cranberry vodka cuz I be all outa rum' and tried to force her to take the pewter mug from his hand. She remembered threatening to vomit the nasty drink onto his penis. Every time lightning streaked across the black sky, Keira's cream colored satin nightgown glowed iridescently. Barracudas with their vicious teeth were like flying fish, chasing her across the wet wood floor of the ship. Michael standing in his scuba gear kept telling her, rule one, Barracudas will attack anything shiny. And Len repeatedly told her to take off her clothes.

  She paced the galley floor, trying to shake the dream from her thoughts. So tired, she thought she was going to vomit. But, her eyes were on guard duty, forcing her not to sleep. Finally wearing herself out, Keira grabbed her pillow and crawled onto the deck bench to sleep under the stars. She hoped she was looking at the same calm night sky as Theos. Slowly drifting off to sleep, Keira knew he would protect her while he steered the ship through the night. She dreamed of him sounding the distress horn on Micah's work tug that belched diesel smoke across the water. Why was Theos on Micah's tug boat? He tossed her a life ring from the ship and told her she couldn't float on a pillow full of salty tears; she would drown. Wobbly, she finally stood holding the anchor from Micah's work tug. But his tug was now nowhere to be seen. Finally, she yelled to Storm to stop playing the song twinkle, twinkle little star on his phone, It was crazy.

Keira had no idea where those dreams manifested. There wasn't a full moon yet. She had been eating healthy foods, nothing weird that she could justifiably blame on her strange dreams. Afraid to try and go back to sleep, Keira decided it was almost time to get up anyway. She showered and drove to the office to finish Micah's parking lot and landscape design.

"I just came in to pick up the payroll checks," Kraig said as he walked up to the drafting table to see how the design was coming along. "What is that?"

"A rusty boat engine picnic table," Keira said, tilting her head to look at the funky table from a different angle.

"Are you ok? You look tired." Kraig whispered, as he pulled her to his chest and held her there.

"I had the weirdest dreams last night. You know how nasty-looking barracuda's teeth are, right? Well, I was standing on a boat in a hurricane, and barracudas were like flying fish trying to eat me." Keira said. She didn't want to explain who all the men were in the dream. And how do you explain, a naked physician tried to force her to drink vodka and cranberry juice?

"Why don't you finish up the blueprint and then go home and sleep?" Kraig said, still holding her close.

"I have to go over the files for the lawn crew to see who we can promote to a supervisory position. Also, we need to find someone to take your position now that you are the boss man." Keira grinned and pulled away from him. "Don't forget we need an office secretary."

"Tell you what; let's continue as we are now. I will oversee everything as I have been; you design and make presentations to possible clients. I made a list of possible new contracts we may be able to pull in. When someone stands out who has strong leadership qualities, we will promote them. How does that sound? A secretary would free up some of your time. Have you seen any good applicants from the website?"

"I would like to set up an interview with a couple of qualified potentials," Keira said, drumming her thumb on the drafting table.

"That sounds good. I'm heading over to check on the final stage of the Riverview Blvd job. Why don't you finish up and go home? You can schedule interviews tomorrow morning when you are fresh." Kraig said firmly.

"Oh, the St Dominic project may be set back a week to ten days. They have state inspections next week and do not want their landscape torn up. However, I may have a quick parking lot project that will take less than a week. We could schedule it for next week. I will know more when I finalize the prints with the owner.

Keira stood by her Jeep and inspected the property line of the marina. Glancing at the blueprint of the marina's green space, she needed to take one last look to see if she missed anything. Since Micah was out of town, Keira walked the parking lot to the back of the dry storage bay that housed the boats off the water. The gas pumps and dock piers she had walked many times, but this was with a different and critical eye, she viewed them. Satisfied with what Keira saw, in correlation to the changes she had drawn up, she was positive Micah would like it. She stood looking over the beautiful motor and sailboats tethered to the docks; she loved the marina just as she had loved the wood pier jutting out into the Straits of Florida growing up.

"What are you doing here in the middle of the day?" Marla asked as she walked towards her.

"I am playing hooky this afternoon. Have you eaten lunch?"

"I have to kind of hang around the office since Micah isn't here. What did you have in mind?"

"Why don't I run down to Smoqehouse and grab some Cuban sandwiches or whatever you want to eat, and we can eat here?" Keira asked.

"That sounds like a perfect plan."

Thirty minutes later, Keira could almost hear Marla purring as she ate her Islander sandwich. She kept saying she couldn't understand how the grilled pineapple and pepper jack cheese tasted so good on the ham and smoked chicken. Even the bun was toasted to perfection. However they did it, Marla loved her sandwich.

Marla had never had poutine. Keira insisted she needed to try it. She watched Marla roll her eyes and declared it was her new go- to side dish. Keira enjoyed the Cuban sandwich and had purchased a second one for a late-night snack.

"So tell me about your secret Saturday night. I couldn't believe you refused to talk when I called to get you to come over to The Dive Bar." Marla frowned as she looked across the boat docks instead of Keira.

Keira told her the naked truth behind her never gotten lunch date with Len. Just like guy locker-room smut talk, they laughed over the teeny weenie syndrome. She told Marla about some of the other guys she had talked online to. The beautiful mind of Theos and extreme sports-loving Michael were easy to describe. But, she opted to omit any discussion on the audio-production company owner, Storm.

She wasn't sure if Petra had talked to Marla about the dreamy DJ she hired. Music was music to Marla. She would immediately connect the audio-production company owner from Clearwater and Dreamy DJ from Clearwater. Others wouldn't, but she would. Keira explained the weirdness of how she met Basil and the Latin lover Eduardo Luise's lusty want of sex-capades.

"So, who do you like the most?" Marla asked.

"That's just it; I could love a couple of them," Keira said, feeling uncomfortable and not sure of her feelings. She glanced at Micah's jet boat and decided to change the subject. She chose what she was about to say next carefully. "You know, it is rather interesting. Micah is so reserved. He could be cocky with all the women on the docks constantly flirting with him." She watched Marla take a drink of her diet soda. It was as if she was debating what she should or could say about her boss.

"Keira, you own your own business. You understand professionalism. You are probably my best friend ever. I trust you and know you would never harm anyone knowingly. I need you to promise never to repeat what I am going to tell you." Marla said solemnly.

"I would never hurt Micah. I am just trying to understand his quietness."

"I have known him most of my life. He is like one of my brothers. He was, at one time, married to a woman who practically destroyed him." Marla frowned, looking across the parking lot.

"How?"

"Micah was a blast to be around, growing up. He led us kids on many adventures. However, he was also very loyal to his family. Mama Andreas wanted him to settle down and marry, probably to anchor his feet in the earth like his brothers. His parents were very old world when it came to marriage.

"You will probably never hear Micah mention Nicola. His parents deemed her the perfect wife material. She was beautiful. With her looks, she and Micah would create beautiful babies together. And so they married. Little did his parents know, her antics made Micah look like a saint. She blew through his money like water, demanding bigger and better of everything. Nicola had affairs; she may have had an abortion. It was hush-hush and only mentioned one time. Having the perfect body was high on Nic's list of priorities. Being pregnant would ruin her self-image of a desirable body. I'm not sure if it was Micah's child or someone else's. She taunted and embarrassed Micah on many occasions. She made his life miserable. However, he stayed faithful to his marriage vows. She finally ran off with some ugly but very rich Swiss guy with a title. What is sad is, she had all that and more with Micah."

"How did Micah's parents know Nicola?" Keira asked as she sipped on her no longer iced tea.

"Nicola was the daughter of Micah's father's best friend."

There was so much more Keira wanted to ask about Micah. She wondered about all the rumors discussed by the always drunk guys. But Keira didn't want Marla to think she was interested in him. Marla was one of those people; when she got an idea in her head, she was like a dog with a bone. She spent all her energy trying to make things work, no matter if the thought was or was not a good idea.

"That is a sad story. I feel bad for Micah, even though it isn't any of my business. I promise, what you have told me will go no farther than this table." Keira declared.

They talked a bit more before Keira said she had to get back to work, and Marla agreed, saying the same.

"Oh, Marla, when did you say Micah would be back in the office?"

"He will be home on Thursday afternoon. I am not sure if he will be at the marina until Friday."

"Can you set up a business meeting for me with him either Thursday afternoon or Friday morning, please?" Keira didn't want to discuss the basis of the requested meeting. She wanted to see the surprise look on Micah's face.

"I'll text you the time. Talk with you later." Marla smiled and walked towards the office.

"Marla. Call one of your dock workers! I think that cruisers over there got loose from its moorings. It is drifting towards the bridge." Keira yelled to her friend.

The current was strong under the bridge with the changing tide; she had learned that the first time she had motored under the Cortez Bridge. It would be horrifying to notify someone; their beloved boat hit the pilings and has large gouges in its hull. She watched as two guys in a nearby dingy, rowing towards the renegade boat. One of Micah's crew still needed to go after the escapee boat; she didn't think the rowers could bring it in against the tidal current.

With the blueprint of the marina to Keira's satisfaction she decided she needed to check out some of the local landscape. Heading down to the lower deck storage unit, Keira found her old beach chair. Quickly putting a towel, a bottle of water, and a very outdated magazine in her backpack, she headed for Coquina Beach.

It would not be wise to get sunburned while playing hooky from work. Keira set her chair in the shade of a cluster of tall pine trees.

It was finally time to read her two-year-old magazine, once and for all. She sat with her toes in the warm sand and thought about the conversation she had with Marla. She hadn't turned a page of the out-of-date publication. So many questions whirled around in her head.

Poor Micah, it sounded like he was married to someone who never respected him. But one thought kept nagging at her. What did Marla mean when she said that Nicola ran off with some titled very rich but ugly Swiss guy when she had all that and more with Micah?

She didn't understand. How was Micah titled? Where was he from, and how rich was he? Wiggling her toes in the sand, none of it made sense, and the more she rehashed Marla's words in her mind, the more tired she got. Reclining her chair back so she could see the passing clouds, the soothing rhythmic sound of the waves gently washing ashore caused her eyes to grow heavy and close.

It was good to get back to her boat before Jack got home from wherever he worked. It was nice not having to dodge his fifty questions on how her day was. It was exhausting rehashing every iota of the last eight hours. He wasn't a bad guy, just overzealous. Thinking about it, he would have interrogated her on why she was clean, not dirty, and had on a bathing suit. Laughing, she stripped the linens from her bed and replaced them with the newly washed, expensive sheet she bought last weekend. Mr. Wu was very insistent she would be missed on Saturday. She fluffed the extra pillows. The tiny LED lights along the ceiling gave a romantic touch to the once dark forward cabin, and now the beautiful linens and pillows added to the ambiance. Her bed looked almost like the seven hundred dollar-a-night suites. Too bad she wasn't tired at the moment or had a sexy guy to share her inviting bed.

Her thoughts returned to Micah and his ill-fated marriage. Micah and Nicola Andreas – their names together sounded pretty. Just how beautiful was his wife? Was Marla secretly envious of Micah and Nicola? Maybe Micah was horrible in bed or had a Len size penis. Oh good grief, stop the nonsense. There were three sides to every story, his side, her side and the truth. And none of which were her business, and neither was Micah. He was her landlord and, therefore, off-limits.

SonicMusicMix - Storm

Dear Keira,

I hope you got your blueprint for the presentation done and have successfully acquired the contract for all your hard work on the design.

I was thinking, no, no, it didn't hurt! I guess I am showing my age, right? Anyway, on the way home from visiting Coquina Beach the other day, I saw a little shack of a restaurant called the Sea Hut. It was on the left side of US 19 before I headed over the Skyway Bridge. I am not sure if you know the place. I was wondering, would you like to meet me there Saturday night for dinner around six in the evening?

Again, I was thinking, over-exercising my brain just a little, I was thinking with all the people at the third of July wet T-Shirt Contest milling around, it might be hard talking with you – getting to know you. So, what do you think? This way, we can talk uninterrupted. I know this is short notice and if you have other plans already, I understand. Just let me know.   *Storm*

Dear Storm,

I think you are absolutely correct. The third of July could be very chaotic, especially for you. You will have all of those groupie-type women trying to get your attention. The swooning and fainting chicks all over the place would be rather cumbersome to climb over. So yes, I would like to meet you at six-ish for dinner on Saturday night. I have been to the Sea Hut a couple of times, and the food was flavorful in the past.

Yes, I have the blueprints completed. I have to set up an appointment with the owner to give my presentation. I am excited about what this design has to offer. It will be unique to the possible client's business. My aim is that he sees the vision as I do.

I hope you have a good evening and I will see you on Saturday.

Keira

Peter Flynn's Friend - Basil

Dear K Lee,

I am in Johannesburg, awaiting my flight to Cape Town. I am rather frustrated; I wanted to fly from Texas after the financial meeting to Brandon. I was anxious to start making changes to the new house with you. I can't stand the awful beige paint on all the walls. I figure you have more insight into what color palate would fit the style of our house. However, I had to fly back to Washington, and then after seeing my daughter, I, yet again, was on a plane to South Africa. So the house in Brandon and paint colors will have to wait.

There are some concerns with the metalworker's union. I have been in constant contact with our labor relations team. We have a meeting set up for the day after tomorrow, so I am in a rush to get there. I hope there are no breakdowns or delays in the flights. Oh, speaking of which, they just called my flight, sorry love, I have to close. I will be out of contact with you for a few days.

Don't forget how much I love you. Hugs and kisses, Basil.

Dear Basil,

It sounds like you will have a full schedule with all the meetings the minute your feet touch the ground of Cape Town. I am sure there is much your supervisors need to get you up to speed on. I fear you took on too much. You are in the process of buying a house in Brandon, which is a huge undertaking in itself. You also have a contract underway in South Africa. And the welfare of your daughter is a top priority on your list. I don't know how you are managing all of this. My head is spinning thinking about it all.

By the time you read this, you probably have had the metalworker's union meeting. How did it go? With the cultural differences and the language barriers, things can become dicey rather quickly.

I hope you slept on your flights, so you don't have to fight jet lag and long-drawn-out meetings. Nothing is worse than face-planting during an important meeting.   K Lee

Keira almost forgot to sign her name K Lee. After talking with Jimmy, she was so glad she decided not to tell Basil her real name. He was very self-assured in his thinking. Why would she be readily available to drop everything for him? How did she know what paint colors he wanted on his walls? It all made her very suspicious. His arrogance, she understood. She had encountered many professional men over the years who thought they were God's gift to woman-kind. She still didn't understand; what gave Basil the idea she was there for his every asking?

Keira could feel the night settling in. The birds had headed inland, the breeze calmed, and the water was like glass. Not even a fish dared to breach. She walked outside to stretch. Dang, she thought, why she hadn't checked to see if Jack was sitting out.

"Hi neighbor, care for a beer?" Jack asked.

"Hi Jack, no thanks, I'm good."

"Have you heard? There is a possibility of drugs coming in around the Fourth of July holiday?" Jack mentioned.

"No, I hadn't heard that, but I'm not into that stuff, so it doesn't interest me. It is probably frustrating for you since you are a hospital administrator." Keira said, thinking of the drugs that floated in on the Atlantic side of Key West when she was a kid.

"Yeah, I have seen kids in the intensive care unit brain dead on ventilators. Parents were swearing up and down their kid has never done drugs. However, the doctor has the blood analysis of their teenager's drug screening in his hand. It's sad." Jack shook his head.

"I can't imagine," Keira said as she decided the conversation with Jack was depressing. "Oh well, have a good evening Jack."

"Keira, do you ever get lonely living on your boat by yourself?"

"No, can't say that I do. Don't stay out too late; it's a work day tomorrow!" Sounding like a parent, Keira laughed and climbed the steps back down into her boat.

She wasn't sure what Jack was trying to say to her. Why was he making conversation about the drug thing? Was Jack thinking about his kids and concerned with possible drug use now that he wasn't around them as much? And why did he ask her if she was lonely living alone? Was he looking for someone to spoon with in the middle of the night? Or, was she just overanalyzing the conversation and that was all it was, conversation? Geeze, maybe she was lonely and hadn't figured it out yet.

Dear Theos,

Thank you for telling me you are back on board the ship. It sounded so high class to fly by helicopter to meet the cruise liner. Of course, it makes sense. The captain needed to be air-lifted to the nearest hospital. The helicopter ambulance crew had to get to the ship to pick him up, and you needed to get there to take command. As you can tell, I have been planting palm trees too long and do not get out of the forest much!! Sorry for the lack of sophistication on my part.

This evening, I had the weirdest conversation with my neighbor. His name is Jack. He is a nice enough guy. I fear, since his divorce, he has been lonely. Anyway, he mentioned there is a possibility of illegal drugs coming into the area over the fourth of July. I guess it makes sense since all the festivities, going on soon. Have you ever seen high-speed drug boats while you are out in open water? I have seen jet boats racing each other but never have I sensed danger where I have sailed. Of course, since I am a woman sailing alone, I am careful where my boat goes. I usually hug the coastline for my safety. Then I think, my boat used to be a drug-smuggling boat. Do other boat owners see mine and wonder if I am a drug runner?

In my moment of reflecting, I finally realized the depth of love and passion I have in my heart. To recognize the capability of giving of myself that I have within me was staggering. You see, for so many years, I thought I had my one chance at love, and I let it slip through my fingers. I had mentally built a wall around my heart after that. And now, I have slowly taken down those barriers. I have freed my innerself to be who I have always been but have been afraid to let show.

As you wrote, you wondered if you should not have bared so much of your heart to me. You are special to me, and I have no regrets of what I have whispered back to you.

So as the sun touches the horizon, look, and you will see, I am sailing with you.   Keira

After Keira pressed send, she wondered if Theos was on his voyage home. She slipped into a pair of sandals and locked her cabin door. Walking to The Dive Bar, Keira thought, what would it be like to be with a sea captain? Would she eventually become bitter of his need to sail? It was a hobby and her love to sail, but if she had children, would that change? Of course, it would change things; soccer games, neighborhood birthday parties were all events more important than sailing.

"Whadaya have Keira?"

"May I have a Pina colada, please?" Keira asked as she looked across the bar. Marla was chit-chatting with some guy. Jack was hitting on some busty chick she had seen a couple of times. She smiled at that.

"What? No rum runner?"

"I can't be a pirate every day!" Keira laughed. She decided to sit out on the deck; she could listen to the guitar player without feeling like she had to make small talk with some nearly drunk guy.

"Hey Keira, Micah asked me to..." "Here's your Pina colada."

"Thanks, Brian, Markos, what did Micah ask you to do?" Keira asked. She saw Brian shake his head and glare at Markos. She wasn't sure what that was all about.

"Um, oh yeah, he wanted me to make sure the garbage was emptied by your dock space; while he is gone." Markos stammered. Keira wondered what he was going to say about Micah before Brian cut him off. It was interesting; seldom did she see Markos at The Dive Bar. There was a cute skinny young thing seen kissing him many times in the parking lot. She wondered if they had broken up. Geeze, it was becoming a soap opera in the hood.

There were no nightmares that night, and when morning came, Keira was ready to take on the world. At the office, she set up appointments with three women for the secretary position. Ordering office furniture for the soon-to-be office secretary was high on her list. Checking off one more thing on her to-do list, Keira called the phone carrier to order additional wiring for a second phone line. It was time-consuming to look through each of the landscape employee files for a potential supervisor candidate. But it had to be done. Keira wrote an informational manual for Kraig during her lunch break. She listed all her 'go-to' people in case of any breakdowns or malfunctions in equipment with a deadline looming. It was important to list all the companies Keira would help if they needed anything from her shop. There were a few businesses she had helped, and they had burned her in the process.

One time, she had lent out her heavy duty equipment and some of her crew to help a company meet its deadline. There was no reimbursement for her crew's labor, not even a thank-you Keira for, in a pinch, helping them.

Marla returned Keira's call and professionally announced Micah would be available to see her at three pm on Thursday. Marla inquired about the nature of the meeting, but Keira quickly said she had a call she had to take and hung up. Keira laughed at Marla's persistence. She wanted to keep the meeting a surprise.

By the end of the workday, Keira was proud of all she had accomplished. Now, if her love life could be so promising...

?

Chapter 13
♥♥♥♥♥♥♥♥♥♥♥♥♥

Peter Flynn – Basil

K Lee Dearest,

Oh, thank God, you have finally written to me. I was so concerned about your well-being. You are in my heart and on my mind throughout the day. I wondered if you had found someone else on that silly dating website. I would suffer immensely if some character stole your heart. I sincerely hope, since our love is so strong, that you will cancel your membership. I do not want to think that you may be corresponding with someone other than me. I am sure you do not have time to waste being on hold on their helpline, whose representative doesn't even speak English. I could not bear it if they stressed you with their rude customer service. Just send me your password, and I will handle terminating your membership. Those dating websites try to keep your membership money or charge you cancellation fees. I know how to deal with them.

The meeting with the labor union and our management team went well. It was touch and go there for a while, but everything worked out. We had a feast afterward. I wish you could have seen the banquet table full of food; it was fit for the gods. I sent some pictures of the people involved in the negotiations. I am the cute guy in the middle. The

*woman on my left is the liaison between me and
the South African team. And the guy on the right is
my chief manager of operations. The other pictures
are of me and my view of the ocean while thinking
of you.*

*My lodging is very accommodating here. Looking
out my balcony doors is utterly breathtaking. I see
the South Atlantic Ocean. Of course, that view
comes at a hefty fee. So, to keep within budget, I
will move out in the next day or two and move into
a weekly rental unit. I will also have to rent a car as
the taxi services can be expensive. They have the
reputation of taking the longest routes for more
money with tourists. I will let you know when I
make these changes. I must rest now, it is late, and
I have much to accomplish here tomorrow. I trust
you love me as I do you. All my love, Basil*

Keira laughed and thought; yeah, I trust that you are pulling my leg. Of course, he would ask for her password to the website. Basil was smooth and full of finesse in the way he offhandedly wanted to prevent her from having to deal with out-of-country non-English speaking customer service personnel. He gets her password, all her credit card numbers, her address, and personal information to do with it, what he wishes. He could scam people with her photos of herself, not to mention damage her professional life and everything she had ever worked to achieve. The thought made her shutter. To think there were people out in the world who would do such things.

Dear Basil,
Thank you so much for your thoughtfulness and concern with the dating website canceling process. I have been too busy to be bothered with the silly boys on that site. But as you say, I will lose the money I have invested in the service, no worries though; I will just let my membership lag.
I am glad the leadership meetings went well. Sometimes

negotiations can be rather spirited, to put it nicely. Thank you for sending me pictures of you and the team you are working with daily. It gives me a better idea of who everyone is when you mention names. Also, the view from your hotel room is spectacular. I am sure you spend your free time looking from your balcony across the water. I was not expecting to see a couple of pictures of your penis. That was mighty bold of you. I would have been so worried someone would hack into the account and later exploit those pictures of your um hard-on. K Lee

Still laughing, Keira examined the pictures of Basil's penis. He hadn't sent just one, but several. Did he want to prove to her it was standing on its own merit and not propped up? Oh darn, the perfect sarcastic comeback would have been, next time, could you put a measuring tape next to your penis to prove how large it is. That comment would have been so deflating. As much fun as she was having, making fun of his penis, she deleted the pictures. It wasn't that she hated male genitalia; there was a time and place for everything. She didn't want those kinds of photos on her computer.

ExtremeLover – Michael

> *Dear Keira*
> *Sorry I have not written back in a while. My mother was released from the hospital. I have been taking care of her at her home. I had asked if she could go to rehab for further strengthening after nearly dying and then being in ICU. Her case manager felt she was strong enough to go home with a home health person coming in a couple of times a week for physical therapy.*
> *I now understand how angry people are with health care as a whole. What if my mother had no one to look after her at all? As you can tell, I am very frustrated with the lack of extended care she is getting. My sister is not helping. Since she has her*

new baby, she has politely said I need to take care of our mother; she is busy. So, I will be here a while longer. However, the company I work for is getting worried. Their peak wave season in Australia is now. They are not sure how much longer they can wait on me.

I think of you often in the middle of the night when I know I should be sleeping. My frustration gets the better of me. I am sure if your arms were around me, I would know, all would work out the way it is supposed to be. Sorry, I am venting to you. Please forgive me. Love, Michael

Dear Michael,

I feel bad that you have to deal with the lack of quality extended care your mother needs. I understand the frustration you must feel with your job on the line and your mother's poor health. I am unsure how I can help other than to give you venting support. Sometimes during a rant and yelling fit, it all comes clear what you need to do. Keep the faith.   Love, Keira

What a great week it had been, Keira thought as she dressed for her date with Storm. She had interviewed three different women for the secretary position. The first candidate, Kraig, and she both agreed was entirely too fussy. One didn't have the skillset to answer the phone and keep a list of appointments straight. And then there was Tina. She could type a form letter. She had experienced in advertising, and she had a pleasing personality. Tina could easily charm a client waiting at the front desk. Kraig had seemed VERY interested in her.

When Keira gave him a questioning look, his comeback was, 'Tina had bigger breasts than she had.' Some of the guys she employed had bigger breasts than she did, which was all she could think to retort.

Working with the crew all day, almost every day, she had learned early on that farting meant they had drunk too much coffee and needed an early break in the morning. Belching was acceptable behavior when the lunch special was good. She had heard, women usually discussed manicures, fingernail polish colors, and other women. Men's discussions brought a whole new meaning to the words bodily functions.

Keira looked at her breasts in the bathroom mirror. Nope, they weren't big, but she wasn't exactly flat chested either. She slipped her favorite short-sleeve plaid shirt over a white tank top and jean skirt. The Sea Hut was a great seafood restaurant but laid back. Her outfit was perfect for dinner with Storm.

She thought about the meeting she had on Thursday afternoon with Micah. She had brought a stand-up easel and the proposed blueprints of the marina. He had asked why she was placing artificial grass in areas shaded with palm trees. She had smiled and counter-asked if he had time to water and mow the small grassy spaces. The life span of the alternate turf was ten years. It would look great and hold up well, she had explained. He pointed and had questioned her about the picnic tables. She remembered grinning and told him they were boat engines and parts she had found behind the dry storage building. All she needed to add was a tabletop. He had smiled at that idea. His last question was about the timeline for work completion and price. She told him there was a delay in the next project, and she could have a crew working on his project starting Monday morning. As for the cost of the project, all she asked was for him to pay for the blacktopping of the parking lot.

She had called in a favor. The asphalt paving firm was reputable and could start on Monday. She just needed approval from Micah. They would complete the paving in two phases; as not to interrupt the day-to-day routines of Micah's business. His only question at that point was the cost of the labor of her crew. She smiled and reminded him of the free dock space rental for a month agreement in exchange.

Micah had loved the entire project presentation after she explained all the questionable areas he had concerns over. He had called Marla into his office to show her the work planned. She, too, marveled at how beautifully the landscape blueprints were show-the marina. Micah was about to sign the contract when Keira made one last stipulation while they were all together.

"I try very hard to keep my professional life and my private life separate. I request when the project gets started, there is no mention from any of your employees, I live on my sailboat. None of my crew needs to know I have any affiliate with the marina other than a contract to fulfill. The financial terms of the contract are not to be discussed with my business partner if the discussion would come up. This contract is between Micah's business and me."

"So, what you are saying is, you are financing the project, other than the resurfacing of the parking lot, on your own." Micah had stated. And she had agreed.

As she thought back to his statement, Micah had given her an almost quizzical look at the time. She had hoped it was a look of professional respect. Pausing mid-search for her favorite sandals, the look on his face was something more... There was something hidden or maybe guarded, like a secret he was keeping. Oh, good grief, he has mesmerizing eyes, period. Now, if she could find her lost sandals, she would be all set.

With a few minutes to spare before leaving for the restaurant, Keira decided she needed to check her emails to see if Storm had canceled at the last minute. There were two notes from Theos. She hadn't heard from him in a day or so, but figured he was still on his way home from the cruise. Before she opened them, she was happy to see Storm had not bailed on her.

Theseus – Theos

> *My Keira,*
> *I just returned home from my cruise to the Bahamas. Thank goodness it was an uneventful return trip. The crew was ever so happy to see their home port. Because the captain had taken ill on board the ship, they were almost fearful something else would happen.*

I loved reading your long letter. It was as if you were talking to me over a cup of coffee. First, you wrote of my emergency helicopter flight to the ship. I could feel the awe in your writing and could imagine the look on your face. However, I was surprised when you said you were unsophisticated. Never put yourself down. I have seen some very cultured and aristocratic individuals pull some very unrefined stunts and hurtful deeds.

Second, you described Jack like some guy standing at the fence between neighboring yards chit chatting. It made me smile.

In his discussion of drugs coming in through the waterways, there are always the dreaded drug smugglers on the high seas. I am glad that you are aware they are out there and take precautions when you sail. Since your boat has been out of the business for such a long while; I am sure it is no longer on the radar as a drug-smuggling vessel.

I am glad you have come to realize just how special you are. I read it in your letters and fall deeper in love with you. The softness of your heart, the beauty of your soul, yet you are strong and determined. All noble qualities, some titled kings and queens, have never been able to achieve. Never change, my beautiful Keira.   Love, Theos

Dear Keira,

I noticed I hadn't heard back from you. When I checked, my email from two days ago was never delivered; until thirty minutes ago. Sometimes, I curse the dropped signals across the sky.

I am standing on my balcony looking out to sea. I wonder if you need to feel the water beneath your feet, as I? I think of you and I, as one with the ocean, you with salt in your hair, and me with the wind in *my face, Love Theos*

As Keira read the letters from Theos, her eyes misted, and she feared she would mess up her makeup. The notes were once again beautifully written. Any fears she had about anything seemed to float away.

Her cell phone rang.

"Keira, this is Storm. I am going to be a little late. There were a couple of cars that decided to exchange paint colors on highway 19 coming south."

"Are you ok?"

"Yes, I am sitting in the traffic jam waiting for the police to clean up the debris from the road so we can all pass. I sure hope the food at the restaurant is good because I am starving. See you soon."

Keira closed her laptop, grabbed her purse, and headed off her sailboat towards her car. She saw Micah standing in the parking lot talking with one of the weekend boaters. She waved to him as she unlocked her Jeep.

"Hey Keira, wait," Micah called to her.

She watched him jog across the parking lot. A perfect specimen of a man, without a doubt, Keira confirmed once again.

"I wanted to talk with you away from Marla. Please, let me pay for your crews' labor."

"Micah, the contract is signed. We agreed on the terms. Do you want me to close the parking lot Sunday evening, or are you going to?" Keira asked.

"I will."

"Ok, see you early Monday morning. My crew will be here at seven a.m. or shortly afterward with the mini bulldozer. The palm trees come between nine and ten."

"You own a mini dozer?" Micah asked incredulously.

"Yeah, but since my business partner found out I was having too much fun driving it, he limits my playtime on our equipment. You should see me with the jackhammer. The guys call me Rosita the Riveter. Most of them are Hispanic; they think it's funny. You know, Rosie from the 1940's poster – Rosetta. Get it?" Keira shook her head; realizing being Greek, Micah might not have understood the World War Two female, Rosie, the factory poster women who was trying to boost morale in the workforce. "Oh well, I will talk with you on Monday."

"Keira…" Micah hesitated, and then said, "You look nice, have a good evening."

"Thanks." Keira started her Jeep's engine and knew he paused to say something and then thought against it.

She drove out of the parking lot and down the street. Parking in front of The Crystal Corner Gem Shop, Keira got out of her car and walked into the shop.

"Keira, it is always good to see you." Susyn welcomed her.

"I wasn't expecting to see you at this time of the afternoon on a Saturday."

"I give readings some evenings. Oh, here is Lea now. Lea Finn, do you know Keira St Cloud?" Susyn asked as she welcomed Lea into the shop.

"Yes, hi Keira, you have to come for dinner one evening. You must see how much we love your design of our backyard. Kai will grill steaks while we lounge in the pool." Lea joked.

"I would love to see how you have it set up. KC has my number." Keira smiled.

"Keira, here is a Fuchsite charm. I put it on a gold serpentine bracelet. This stone will help you understand the man standing between two worlds. It will heighten your ability to use logic and the emotions of your heart to comprehend him. He is one of the few, who is born under the charming and clever sign of Gemini. His moon is also in Gemini. He is a Gemini male through and through. Both he and his twin will give you more than your heart has ever asked for." Susyn said as she placed the bracelet around Keira's left wrist.

"Thank you. It is funny; I did come in for some special gem to wear this evening. You knew what I needed." Keira said as she looked first at Susyn, then Lea, and smiled.

She handed Susyn her credit card so she could be on her way. She didn't want to infringe on Lea's reading time. It would be interesting to schedule a reading some evening. What would the Spirits want to say to her?

Lea hugged Keira and let her know she would call to set up a dinner date soon.

Keira was in a happy frame of mind as she headed north towards the Sunshine Skyway Bridge. She was puzzled by the statements Susyn had made. She didn't know too much about moon signs, but she did know, the sun sign was her birth month. She was never interested in astrology growing up. Her mother was always quoting her horoscope for the day. She would encourage Keira to know what sign a guy was before she went out with him. If they were the wrong sign, not compatible with hers when it came to love and marriage, don't bother, dump him, she would say. Obviously, Keira hadn't listened because she had married Peter. He was a cancer birth sign, and that sure didn't work out.

The restaurant was on the edge of the Terra Ceia Bay and about two miles from the Sunshine Skyway Bridge. She drove into the parking lot and wondered if Storm had arrived yet. She pulled down her visor to look at her makeup when there was a knock on her window. There stood Storm. Petra was right; he was dreamy looking, more so than in his pictures. She stepped out of her Jeep.

"Keira, finally, I get to meet you." Storm said, wrapping his arms around her in a hug.

"I'm sorry, have you been waiting long?" Keira asked as she stepped out of his hug.

"No, I just got here but come, I'm starving." Storm said, tugging on her hand.

They were seated on the patio overlooking the inlet leading out to Terra Ceia Bay. It was a warm, humid night and so quiet; she could hear the sounds of mosquitoes all around. But none seemed to be biting them. Ahhh, Keira thought, citronella plants were sitting all around the deck. A bug light was hanging at the farthest end of the terrace, and she noticed a bat house above the tree line. As creepy as bats were, they sure kept the mosquito population down.

"What would you like from the bar?" The server asked.

"I would like a white wine spritzer, please," Keira stated while Storm asked what local brews they carried.

"For someone who said they were a landscaper, you sure do not meet the description I had in my head." Storm laughed.

Thank goodness Keira wasn't taking a sip of water; it would have come out of her nose. "Did you expect some burly muscled woman who never shaved her legs?" Keira laughed.

"Nooo, well, yeah."

And that was how the conversation continued all night, a light banter of joking and teasing and exploring each other's personality. The meal might have been superb, but their continued topic hopping kept them focused on each other. Keira had become so relaxed talk to Storm; she had slipped out of her sandals and sat Indian style in her chair. Sipping on her third spritzer, she listened to something Storm was trying to describe. But her mind wandered; Storm was fascinating, witty, so very personable, and easy on the eyes.

"Excuse me, would you like anything more from the bar? It is the last call for drinks."

"Oh, we are sorry, time got away from us. Thank you, we will be leaving shortly." Storm informed the server.

"No, I am glad you felt comfortable staying after dining with us this evening."

Keira could tell Storm had enjoyed their conversations as much as she had. They stood leaning against their cars and continued chatting once out in the parking lot. It was as if they were long-lost friends catching up; their discussions bounced from one subject to another. The technical side of Storm's audio production company was fascinating. And who would have thought he wanted to know the differences in all the palm trees or was he just being kind? She felt he was genuinely sincere.

"Storm, as much as I love talking with you, the mosquitoes are more savage here than on the inland; they are eating me alive."

"I'm sorry. It is late, and you have a long drive back to the island. I have enjoyed meeting you. I would like to see you again. May I call you?"

"Yes, I would enjoy seeing you again also. Of course, I will see you next Saturday. I can't believe it is almost July." Keira said as he leaned in towards her and kissed her lips.

"I would like to say one last thing before you head home. I know I'm not an engineer, but the gravel in this parking lot is substandard. I'm sure Keira's company would not include it in her landscape designs." Storm grinned.

Keira burst out laughing. Storm pulled her to him, and right there in the middle of the gravel parking lot, not blacktopped, but gravel, he kissed her again. The embrace kind of elevated the grit to pebbles, not gemstones, just pebbles. The kiss was endearing all the same, Keira thought. And then the servers and kitchen staff barged out through the front doors laughing. That was the end of that kiss. Storm bid her a good night shortly afterward. He watched as Keira started her Jeep and drove out of the parking lot.

Keira hummed to her favorite playlist of songs on her radio all the way home. It had been a great dinner date. Storm was fascinating, and she enjoyed her evening with him. Even Cortez Bridge lights seemed prettier this evening.

As she headed onto the island, she saw a flash out of the corner of her eye. It wasn't from the headlights of an oncoming car hitting her mirror. She wasn't sure if one of the electrical transformers had blown out or if there was an explosion somewhere. She hadn't heard any boom connected with the flash. However, when she pulled into the entrance of the marina parking lot, she could easily see the light from a fire on the water. There was smoke billowing from one of the boats.

Parking at the corner of the lot, Keira walked over to one of the lamp posts. She stood out of the way to watch the chaos down by the dock. Micah and another person she didn't know threw anchor lines from his work tug onto the deck of the inflamed boat. She guessed he was going to pull the burning vessel away from the other boats mooring at the docks.

Marla came running up to her, "I was at the pub when I heard an explosion. What happened?"

"I don't know. I was on the bridge coming home when I saw a flash, but didn't know what it was until I parked."

"Oh my God," Marla screamed. "Look, a guy just ran from the burning cabin. He is on fire."

Everything was happening so fast. Micah was able to angle the blazing boat with his tug, so the firemen were in a better position to fight the flames. Tears ran down Keira's face as she watched the firemen aim their water hoses towards the burning boat. The guy who had been on the tug with Micah jumped in the water. It looked like he was attempting to pull the inflamed victim to the shore. She wasn't sure how they could see anything between the darkness and the dark water. The emergency medical team was able to wade into the shallower water with a canvas stretcher. Marla and Keira watched as the guy slowly swam with the motionless person in tow, towards the paramedics. Keira knew if the guy didn't die from the smoke inhalation, the burns to his body from running through the fire would.

"Oh, look, the local news team is here to put their spin on the fire." Marla pointed out. "They will speculate it was a meth lab or drug-related. Nothing as simple as a propane leak or fire due to smoking ever happens anymore."

"I'm going to bed, night Marla."

"You don't want to walk back to the Dive Bar with me?"

"No, everyone will be speculating on the fire," Keira uttered.

The evening with Storm had been such a fun night; she didn't want to hear depressing or negative talk right now. After Marla started walking toward the bar; Keira headed to her part of the dock. Watching the, now, smoldering boat, she heard one of the always drunk guys adamantly stating that Micah was the most proficient boat handler around. She had to agree. He worked the marina's tugboat with ease. Instead of going to bed, Keira sat down on the end of the dock and watched as the fire crew broke down the flames until there was only acrid smelling smoke, and the skeleton hull remained.

It was late when Keira climbed into bed. She turned on her laptop, a note from Storm popped up.

SonicMusicMix – Storm

> *Dear Keira,*
> *Thank you for a great evening. I enjoyed our*
> *dinner together. I can't wait to see you again.*
>
> *Storm*

Dear Storm,

I, too, enjoyed our dinner together. I haven't laughed and talked so much in a long while.

I am looking forward to seeing you when you come to Coquina Beach to DJ. However, I am sure you are going to have many adoring fans. Would you be embarrassed if I was one of your groupies?

On a sad note, you would not believe what happened. There was a boat fire when I got home. A man was inside the burning cabin cruiser; he was on fire when he jumped off the side of the boat. I haven't heard yet if he is still alive. The entire scene was unbelievably sad. But, I am still smiling over meeting you.

Thank you again for a great dinner and visit.   Keira

Keira rolled on her side and studied the fuchsite charm Susyn had given her. She had said it would help her understand the man coming into her life. Was there someone new entering her life? Susyn mentioned twins. Thinking, thinking, hmmm, the only twins she knew was from grade school, and Miss Bessie and Bonnie. They were the ninety-something-year-old elders who lived two streets over in one of the beach bungalows. They rode their three-wheel bikes every Sunday morning on the side of the narrow main street, slowing beach traffic down horribly. Mr. Benson called them the damn idiot twins.

A minor explosion rocked the boats tied to the docks. Keira sat up and ran out on deck to see what was happening. Jack was standing on top of his engine cover seats.

"Can you see any fires? Do you know what direction the blast came from?" Keira asked. She turned and again saw people running towards the marina from the little pub. She was sure many local friends and neighbors were on edge after seeing the boat fire and the man engulfed in flames as he ran from the boat cabin.

"Oh look, another boat fire. The flames are coming from a boat anchored by those condominiums on the other side of the bridge. Come stand over here; you can see it better." Jack exclaimed.

"Thanks, but no, thanks. Two boat fires in one evening; what is going on?"

"It is almost the holiday; didn't I tell you drug dealers were possibly coming in?" Jack replied.

Keira could hear the frustration in Jack's voice. She kneeled on the cushioned back seat of her boat and watched as the fire engines arrived. Firemen were scrambling with their hoses to douse the fire from above the boat. The police had blocked the flow of traffic. It was interesting to see the number of people getting out of their cars at the entrance onto the bridge, for a closer look.

"Hey, guys, are you watching the show?" Micah asked.

Keira looked towards him, standing on the gangplank. In the light of the lamp post, his clothes were filthy, and his hair hung down his back in what looked like wet ringlets. She hadn't realized his hair was so long. Nevertheless, she could see the fatigue in his body by the way he stood on the wood planking. His shoulders were drooping, and his hands could have been a bit burnt under all the grime.

"Hey Micah, do you need a beer or two?" Jack asked as he opened the mini frig under the steering counsel.

"Yeah, it is going to be a long night."

"Do they know what caused the fire on the boat earlier this evening?" Keira asked as she watched Micah sit down on the gangplank.

"Possibly arson."

"Micah, come sit down where it is a little more comfortable." Jack offered as he handed Micah a bottle of beer.

"When you fall asleep, should I wrap a bungee cord around you so you don't fall off the plank?" Keira giggled.

"Oh, that's cold." Keira pulled away from leaning against the railing when Micah tapped her arm with the wet beer bottle.

"Are you spending the night here?" Jack asked as he sat down in his captains' chair.

"Yeah, I have to guard the place."

"You know the owner may consider you're sleeping on the dock as loitering. He may call the Bradenton Beach Police Department." Keira teased.

"How much have you had to drink tonight?"

"Three wine spritzers three hours ago, so I'm good." Keira shot back.

"Children, stop bickering. Don't make me call your fathers." Jack teased.

"My father is in Greece, good luck with that," Micah mentioned as he took a swig of beer from the bottle.

"My father doesn't even know I am out this late."

Jack rolled his eyes and threw his arms to heaven. "Damn kids, ya'll are delinquents."

Sliding off the cushioned seat, Keira walked to the side of her boat. Very gently, she leaned over to Micah and kissed his cheek, "goodnight, boys."

"Aren't you going to kiss me goodnight?" Jack whined.

"Two seconds ago, you were about to call my dad, and now you expect me to kiss you goodnight? Um, no way, Narc."

Laughing out loud and almost unable to speak, Micah said between gasps, "Keira, I'm going to fall off the dock."

"Ask the narc guy, right there, to call for an ambulance and the emergency medical team before you drown." Keira nodded before heading into the galley of her boat.

Chapter 14
♥♥♥♥♥♥♥♥♥♥♥♥♥

Monday morning, just as Keira promised, her landscape crew showed up with the mini bulldozer at the marina. While they unloaded the equipment and moved the flatbed off the island, she and Kraig discussed the timeline to get the project completed. The asphalt company foreman arrived and walked over to confer with Keira and Kraig. Before long, the blacktopping company crew had started breaking down the gravel and uneven parking lot. The day couldn't have been any hotter or more humid; sweat trickled down the men's backs. The dust from the gravel clung to the workers' damp skin and clothing. Keira provided energy drinks and water under the shade of one of the only trees on the property line to prevent heat-stroke. She had learned a long ago that a couple of cases of hydrating drinks were cheaper than men with dehydration, heat exhaustion, and off of work with sick days.

Kraig got on the mini dozer and moved the oddly shaped, heavy boat engines to be pressure washed and painted. He dug holes in the ground for the palm trees Keira had ordered. Keira oversaw the asphalt grading and leveling of the parking lot.

"So you didn't get to play on the bulldozer today." Micah grinned as he teased Keira.

"Kraig was fearful I would pop a wheelie on the boat ramp slope and roll into the water. Imagine that?" Keira laughed.

"The asphalt company will be leveling the entire lot. They will be paving this section today." Keira pointed to the flagged area. "It will remain closed this evening. Tomorrow they will finish up with the other section, to the lot line. They will strike the white lines next week. Oh yes, I forgot, the gradient for the runoff will be towards the grassy area to the south and east towards the water. Any pollutants from the parked cars will be filtered through the turf and sand before reaching water, except for torrential downpours from tropical storms and hurricanes. Then, it's an act of God; extreme runoffs are above my pay grade!"

"Keira, you are thorough." Micah smiled. "It's my job but thank you."

"Micah, I have the proposals you wanted me to get for you," Marla said as she walked towards them. "Do you want me to put them on your desk?"

Keira left midday to get the St Dominic contract signed and the project date slotted on the calendar. When she returned to check on the progress, it was almost three in the afternoon. The men were exhausted and almost close enough to the end of the day to go home. However, one of her beloved windmill palm trees was lying on the cement. She had hand-picked them out for the marina, and now one was snapped in two. Walking over, Keira knelt on the ground and inspected it closer.

"Don't get between Keira and her palm trees. She will eat you alive." Kraig whispered to Micah.

"Hot temper," Micah asked.

"No, not really; very slow to anger, but don't mess with her palm trees. When it comes to her palms and she gets pissed, run. I have seen it only twice,"

Micah steered Kraig towards the newly laid blacktop. "So what happened?"

"One I will not discuss, and the other, someone cut down a very healthy forty-foot bottle palm. The guy who killed the palm, he quit. He knew he had let her down and couldn't deal with it. It sounds silly and dramatic but the men are very loyal to her. They know her love of palm trees." Taking a deep breath, Kraig said, "I better go deal with her before she throws one of those boat engines at the bridge."

Micah smiled and walked back to the office.

"Explain," Keira demanded as she touched one of the other newly planted palms. She knew it was stressed and would take a couple of days to strengthen back up.

"We planted the tree. The guys were staking her up while I was moving the dozer. The palm fell over the blade." Kraig retold the event quietly.

"Did you order another one?"

"It will be here on Wednesday."

Keira was fuming. She knew all eyes were on her, but she couldn't help but be mad. The crew was waiting to see what she would do.

In the past, they had used the bulldozer's blade to hold a palm in place. Usually, Keira held her hands around the middle of the palm; while two of the guys would shore up the trunk. She couldn't be in two places at once and was frustrated when careless behavior occurred.

"I want it here tomorrow, even if you have to go and pick it up yourself." Keira glared at Kraig. She looked up and saw Micah watching the interaction between them from his second-floor office window. Knowing it would be unprofessional to let a client see how angry she was, she turned and walked off the worksite.

Keira slammed the door of her Jeep and started her engine. She wasn't about to go back to the office. She would end up screaming at Kraig when he showed up after work. She couldn't go home, because well, she was home. Hopping on her boat and removing the ropes from the cleats was out of the question. She had made a big deal about not letting the crew know where she lived. She was already hot; going to the beach would not cool her down. Drinking would not settle her anger, just dilute it.

The best way to calm down was with ice cream. Keira stopped and grabbed stressed-out Petra from The Wet T-Shirt Shop. She told Petra's assistant to handle the customers; they would be back.

"How did you know I was about to kill someone?" Petra asked as she licked her rocky road ice cream cone.

"Because I was about to strangle Kraig," Keira retorted. "That's bad. Wow. What happened?"

"You know how I love palm trees. Well, one fell during planting and it snapped in two. It wasn't anyone's fault. There were two boat explosions over the weekend, which was unsettling. I went out for a date on Saturday night with someone, a single guy; I really liked him. If a relationship develops, it could hurt a close friend. What do you do, you know? I didn't ask Susyn to come along with us because, I guess, I don't want to feel her calming presence right now. I want to be angry. I'm frustrated and have no reason to be, but I am. Crap, I'm doomed; I'm going to hell for sure." Keira complained.

Laughing, Petra said, "You aren't going to hell. I love Susyn, but every once in a while, she needs to tell me what I want to hear rather than what I need to hear. If someone damaged an entire case of my beloved specially designed T-shirts, it could result in murder. So, I get it about the palm tree. And if you find love with someone special and he isn't married or gay, you have to grab him! Your friend, if she loves you, will understand."

"May I have a scoop of coconut and one of butter pecan, please?"

"Oh no, I guess I made things worse if you are ordering a second ice cream cone." Petra cried.

"Naaa, I didn't eat breakfast. Now tell me who and why are you were going to kill someone."

When Keira dropped Petra back off at The Wet T-Shirt shop, they both were no longer feeling like they could, should, or would murder someone. Quite possibly, they were on a sugar buzz and slap happy. Keira giggled and wanted to throw her padded bra at Kraig's face. He was always making fun of her flat chest. And Petra no longer cared if her new assistant didn't know how to steam the wrinkles out of T-shirts. She would throw water on them that would get the wrinkles out. Everything was funny until Petra told Keira she was going to have sex with Storm because she loved him. Keira sobered up like someone slapped her in the face.

"I think I need a nap," Keira said, trying to cover her feelings.

"Thanks for a great ice cream run. I needed that. See you Saturday." Petra said as she got out of Keira's Jeep.

Thank God all the workers had gone home for the day. Keira parked her Jeep on the grass by The Dive Bar. She made sure not one iota of her rear tire or the shadow of her Jeep bumper was on the street. She wasn't about to pay a parking fine for that infraction. There was only one sign posted on the bridge pertaining to parking.

Damn, Micah and Jack were sitting having a beer and grilling hamburgers on Jack's grill. Not fair, Keira thought as she tripped on the loose board, walking the dock to her boat. She felt like that one idiot guy on Sunday who always tripped and cursed.

"Are you drunk?" Jack asked as he watched her climb aboard hers.

"That question was asked last night; while you all were holding beers. And again, you ask if I'm drunk, but you are the ones drinking beer. The answer was no then and still is no." Keira retorted and slammed her galley door.

She had no business taking her frustrations out on the guys. She kinda felt bad, but not really. Her sugar buzz hadn't faded. She just didn't appreciate being asked if she was drunk. She had never been one to drink to excess, and she wasn't going to start now. Ok, ok, she did drink the entire bottle of wine a couple of weeks ago at the very elite resort. It was on her mini-vacation. She was only there one night and had to drink it all. It would be wasteful to dump half a bottle of good wine down the drain, she justified. Thinking about Petra and her declaration of love for Storm, how was she going to deal with that?

"Why is it, when you have an itch in your panties, I am good enough to stroke and cream you? But now, I am in need of funds, and you are off humpin some dipstick. Fuck you. I will find my own way back to the states. Be gone when I get home."

Keira started laughing; she wondered how many temporary phones he had purchased. The idiot will return home to nothing or a total trashed place. Again, it was not her problem, Delete.

Peter Flynn – Basil

My future wife, K Lee,
*   I have been working side by side with my main*
foreman to make sure everything is running

smoothly. The office space design is coming along quite well. The interior designer has chosen modest but quality furniture, flooring, and lighting. I will be approving the ordering in the next day or two.

I wish you were here with me. I would escape and take you to some of the street markets and flea markets. There are some awesome shops I know you would adore. You would have to bring an extra suitcase for all the things I have seen and would love to buy for you. And then there are also several national parks that you would love to hike while taking pictures. Maybe on my next trip down here, you could accompany me. In the evening, I would make passionate love to you. I would not have to send pictures of my body to prove how much I love you. I would make it evident over and over again; by taking you, in every room in the apartment. I would love to hear you scream my name. I know sex with me would be so pleasurable for you.

I had dinner with several local government officials this evening. They each brought their wives. I felt like the extra wheel, but next time you will be here with me. The food was superb. I had the barbecue lamb and chakalaka, which was a spicy vegetable relish over corn porridge. We toasted and drank far too much.

So I must close as it is late and I am very tired. But I wanted to get a note off to you. I didn't want you to pout. All my love, sweet-heart.

I miss you much, Basil

Keira scrunched up her face thinking about the pictures he had sent her of his penis and now assuming she would enjoy having sex with him. The thought of his hot and sweaty body pressing down on her made her stomach lurch. She refused to call it making love. It would be sex and nothing more, and not going to happen in this lifetime. She would only make love to someone whom she loved and wanted to share her passion. Laughing, she decided Eduardo Luise, the hot Latino from Miami, would be a better sexual lover than Basil.

Dear Basil,

I am glad you are settling in well in South Africa. It sounds like the construction site is progressing well. I am sure, now that you are starting to see headway, you can relax and enjoy your stay there.

I have never thought about visiting South Africa. You will have to send me pictures so I can see the different terrain of the country-side.

This week there was news of two different sets of arson near where I live. It is a rumor it may be drug-related, with the Fourth of July holiday coming soon. It is a shame people try to destroy each other and their property. I will keep you posted. You may need to check with your friend in Brandon to increase security on your new home since it is vacant.   Be safe. K Lee

After she sent the letter to Basil, she felt like taking a walk. Letters from him tended to frustrate her with his words assuming she would be his wife. She noticed that Micah had left the gangplank between her boat and Jack's. Either that, or he fell in the water, she grinned. The drapes in Jack's boat windows were thin enough to see he was watching TV. She walked towards the newly paved parking lot. It will be nice when the blacktopping is completed. There wouldn't be any low spots or holes to worry about while she trekked over to The Dive Bar or when she was late for work and ran to her car. She walked across the parking lot to inspect another one of the newly planted palm trees.

"You really do love palm trees, don't you?" Micah said as he patted the trunk.

"Crap, you scared me. I am used to hearing footsteps on the gravel. The asphalt is quiet. Yes, I love palm trees." Keira whispered.

"I take it no one is getting fired over the damaged palm tree."

"They got the message I was not happy; that was enough. I am a woman in a man's work territory; I have to demand perfection.

There are landscapers and lawn care companies a dime a dozen around here. So I have to make sure my company stands out as being the best." Keira said as she walked over to the sand-blasted boat engine waiting to be painted.

"I admire your strength and determination."

"Some days, I don't feel so strong."

Micah tilted her chin as his lips met hers, his tongue coaxing her mouth open. Keira felt his arm slide around her waist and eased her to his chest. Usually, she instinctively pressed her hand against a guy's chest or stepped out of the embrace, feeling trapped. But with Micah, Keira rested her palm against his heart, wanting to feel the rhythmic pulse. It could have only been a moment or a few minutes at best, yet when he released her, she wanted more. Running her hands along his jaw, she kissed his lips again.

"Night, Micah."

Back in her bed, Keira looked at all the romantic pillows and low lights. Would she ever share the soft sheets and scent of the night's steamy air with someone special? Maybe if she would have ogled over Zac Efron and NSYNC pictures with her friends when she was younger, she'd be over that phase now! Hugging her pillow, she wondered if Zac Efron kissed like Micah Andreas.

Every morning Keira had made a mad dash to hide her car a couple of streets over and walked back to the marina. So far, no one had blown her home cover, but she wasn't taking any chances. She ate lunch with Susyn, from the Crystal Corner Gem Shop, or Summer, the owner of The Pet Shop. Summer was a very unobtrusive person. She was hard to get to know, but once Summer trusted her, they had become close friends. Staying clear of The Dive Bar, so some of the locals would not forget and tease her about some of the goofy stuff that occurred at the pub was difficult.

She always had fun there, even though Brian would never make his mortgage payments with the little bit she contributed by way of drinking. Marla kept a close ear out and intercepted any hint of conversations about her.

One day during the workweek, Keira was on her hands and knees anchoring the artificial grass along the entrance to the office area. If the turf was installed correctly, with silica sand to keep the fibers standing, it would be difficult to see the difference between high-grade artificial and real grass. She watched a man slowly backing his boat trailer down the ramp to launch his vessel. He was midway to the water when the trailer let go from the hitch ball at the back of his car bumper. As it hit the ground, it made a grating sound trying to grab hold of the cement. The front wheel of the boat trailer started bouncing and skipping, twisting until the boat trailer turned on its side, rolling the boat over and over down the slope. Keira heard the fiberglass hull fracturing and splintering. The demolished boat finally came to rest halfway submerged at the waters' edge on its side.

The man had gotten out of his car, watched in horror as his beloved vessel took the tumble. He sat down in the middle of the boat ramp with his head in his hands. Keira's heart went out to him. Micah ran from the office to make sure the man was ok, and no one else had been in the way of the runaway boat. She saw one of the dockworkers walk over to the overhead boat carriers. After the insurance company was called, they would be lifting the broken boat from blocking the ramp. What a nightmare for sure.

What had Susyn called it? Mercury was in retrograde. It seemed as if something weird was going to happen badly; it did during the retro. There must be something to it, Keira decided. A palm had fallen over and snapped in half. Why hadn't it just fallen to the ground? Nope, it broke in two when it hit the mini dozer. Now, the boat trailer had let loose from the hitch. The boat fell off the trailer as the front wheel had turned and rolled the trailer.

What were the odds of that happening?

It was hot and muggy even after the sun had gone down. Unfortunately, the last afternoon showers hadn't given any relief for even a short bit of time. This evening the air was still. The Gulf of Mexico was like bathwater at ninety degrees. With the gulf water that warm, hurricanes soon would be brewing in the south

Caribbean, for sure. Keira had turned the air conditioner to a low setting. She was bone tired but too hot to go to sleep until the cabin had cooled down. She put on a tank top and shorts and walked over to the pub. None of the workers would be there at this time of night.

Micah, Markos, and Marla were sitting out on the patio drinking beer and laughing over a loaded plate of nachos. Keira knew they had been long-time friends.

"Hey Brian, how are you doing? May I have a rum runner, please?"

"The marina is looking good. Your workers love your creativity with the engine tables. I wonder what you could repurpose around here." Brian said as he pushed the icy rum runner towards her.

"Just say the word, my friend, and you will find out!" Keira grinned.

"Keira, you gonna be a snob, or are you going to join us?" Markos walked up behind Keira and asked.

Keira smiled at Brian before following Markos back to the table of friends. It was unusual to see him at the pub. She wondered if he was without a girlfriend at the moment. She watched him set three more bottles of beer on the table. It seemed they were several drinks ahead of her.

"Hi, Keira. Now, tell me who really stole the bottle of ouzo that night?" Marla asked, drumming her fingers on the table and looking from Markos to Micah.

"It was Markos. I would never do such a thing." Micah laughed.

"What? You were the leader of our band of thieves' capers."

"Here is the story. Markos stole…"

"Borrowed".

"Ok, Markos took the bottle of ouzo off a café table on the beach. Wasn't it Armeni Beach? Anyway, Papa Andreas and o kalyteros filos sat down not ten minutes later and talked half the night. We had to sleep in that little boat in the harbor, so we wouldn't get caught, remember? Thank God for the tarp. I was so cold." Marla complained.

"We got in trouble for staying out all night. Plus, I think Papa knew we were in the boat. That is why he too stayed out so late."

Markos explained to Keira.

"Remember when Nina lost her bathing suit jumping off the cliff?" Micah grinned.

"Who is Nina?" Keira asked as she took a sip of her rum runner.

"My sister, yes, we told her to hold on to her top." Micah laughed.

"Whatever happened to Vinny?" Markos asked, shaking his head.

"You mean Vinny, who knocked over the headstone marker at Oia Cemetery? We had to sweep, clean, and scrub that place while he vacationed in Italy all summer." Marla complained.

"I hope he is sweeping floors for a living." Markos laughed.

Keira laughed along with them even though she didn't know the people they were talking about. The friends' storytelling and reminiscing of their antics of years ago was funny. Taking a drink of her rum runner; the icy liquid slid down her hot throat. She could hear the guy who sat in the corner by the bar, strumming his guitar. It was a romantic ballad. Oh, to be loved like the lyrics of the song.

"IT SMELLS LIKE DEAD FISH IN HERE."

"Oh, oh, tourists in Hawaiian shirts, this can't be good," Marla stated as they all looked in the direction of the booming voice.

"I'm sorry, we are on the waterway, and when the tide is low, sometimes it smells like brine and fish. What can I get you boys to drink?" Brian asked, trying to make light of the humid night air.

"WHAT DO YOU HAVE?"

Keira listened as Brian named the IPA, bottled and on tap beers he sold. For some reason, the out-of-towners were being rude. Maybe they had been trolley hopping the bars up and down the island.

"WHAT KIND OF FUCKING PLACE IS THIS? YOU DON'T EVEN HAVE DECENT FUCKING BEER!"

"Brian here sells what us locals like to drink. There are some fine restaurants along Gulf Drive that have better stock," stated one of the fishermen sitting at the bar.

"I DIDN'T ASK YOU, GROUPER HUMPER."

"Marla, call the police, and then you two leave. It's going to get ugly," Micah stated quietly and looked at Keira.

"I'm sorry none of my drinks interest you tonight," Brian said. He took the empty beer bottle from Markos and dropped it in the recycle bin.

"YOU'VE BEEN DRINKING THAT PUSSY BEER? THOSE STONE CRABS MUST HAVE PINCHED OFF YOUR DICK, PRETTY BOY".

"I think it is time for you to leave," Markos said quietly.

"I THINK NOT."

As Keira stood to leave, she heard the sound of chair legs scraping the old wood planked floor and getting pushed out of the way. One of the out-of-towners swung his arm back to punch Markos. Micah grabbed his fisted hand. Some of the regulars were getting out of the line of punches. While the tourist clashed with the hardier locals, some beer bottles crashed, hitting the floor. A few bottles just rolled towards the door dribbling beer along their way.

Great, Keira thought, another night of Mercury in retrograde. She saw the local police pull up just as Brian and two other men hauled two of the three out-of-towners to the street, holding their arms behind their backs.

Sitting down at her chart table, Keira opened her laptop. She hadn't heard from Theos in a while. Having read his last letter right before she left to see Storm for dinner, oops she never wrote him back.

Dear Theos,

I am sorry I have not written back to you. Your two letters came at the same time. Yes, you are correct; the dropped connections are almost as frustrating as the slowness of regular mail.

I feel the gentle rocking of the hull of my sailboat, which I am very comfortable with. It is easy to associate the rhythm of the waves caressing the side of my boat as if you were touching my face with your hand. Calmness comes over me when I think of you. I think of fresh air with the tang of salt and blue sky. I want to play in the sea on the other side of the island of Cozumel. To look across the trench to see the evening lights of Playa Del Carmen while holding your hand would be the perfect ending to a vacation day with you.

It would be fun to take a day, rent a car and journey inland to

Coba. Or, we could drive towards Belize; while I take pictures of you enjoying life and listening to Spanish songs on the radio.

On days when there are difficulties at work, having you hold me through the night would make the next day easier.

Smiling and thinking of you, Keira

SonicMusicMix – Storm

Dear Keira,

I hope your week is going well. Mine is not so good. Some of my equipment got damaged when one of the sprinklers' heads in the ceiling sprung a leak. You know electrical equipment does not like to take showers. I can joke about it now. But at the time, I was ready to pull my hair out.

A high-profile artist had scheduled time in the largest of the recording rooms. He was coming in less than twelve hours. The studio he booked to cut his songs in was almost a kiddie wading pool. Well, he was ok with using a smaller room. And I feel the acoustics were, in truth, better for his singing style in the other room. It all worked out, but I, without a doubt, was sweating there for a while. I have a contractor coming tomorrow. Hopefully, he can do the repairs and beef up the soundproofing in the main recording studio immediately.

I had a very interesting day today. I got a call from Petra. She was in the area and wanted to get together up here for lunch. My assistant could handle a couple of hours without me, so I agreed to meet her at a pasta bar down the street. Does her energy ever ebb? The food was good, and our conversation flowed. But no carbo crash afterward for Petra. She wanted to come to see my studio. I always love to show off my workplace, so what the heck.

I didn't think she had too much to drink during lunch, a glass of red wine or maybe two. But at the office, she was overly aggressive. I made an excuse; I had an appointment coming in that I couldn't pass onto my assistant.

Keira, I know you and Petra are friends. I only tell you this because I don't want you to hear an exaggerated story. I hope she didn't feel I was being mean when I practically pushed her out the door. I really would have enjoyed spending my lunch time with you at the pasta bar. See you Saturday.

Your, Storm

So, she did it, Keira thought. Petra had said she wanted to have sex with Storm. Geeze, how could Petra do it in the middle of the day, nothing romantic, no foreplay between him and her, just heavy breathing, a bit of kissing, and sweaty sex? Did they really go all the way? Or was Storm just saying Petra made a play for him, and he was fearful she would tell her about it? Either way, she had to decide where she stood with her friend and Storm. Saturday was only a day away.

ExtremeLover – Michael

Dear Keira,

You are not going to believe what I am about to tell you. I sure hope you are sitting down. I had a heated discussion over the phone with the people I have a contract with down in Australia. They were demanding I come immediately or else they are going to sue me for breach of contract. I get it, but I have been stalling with the care of my mother as my excuse. They understood up until a lull in the weather causes them to panic. They are desperate for the pictures I am under contract to provide. If the weather calms and the waves diminish, they could lose millions of dollars.

When I got off the phone, my mother asked me to go to her "favorite" pizza parlor across town and buy her a pizza. So, I did as she asked. You know we can never deny our parents anything. When I returned, an ambulance was at her home. They said she slipped and fell.

She told the doctors she had slipped in the bathroom the day before, which was the first I had heard of it. The doctors conferred and deemed her unfit to return to her home. They only found bruising and said she was very lucky. They are placing her in assisted living.

She will settle in the rehab and progressive stage assisted living facility near my sister's home tomorrow. She demanded I call the firm and tell them I will be on the first flight out on Saturday. My mother must have overheard my original phone conversation. I swear she was ecstatic when I told her of all the arrangements made. As I was about to leave the hospital to drive back to her home, she instructed me to close down her house. She said to call her when I finished the task.

So this evening, after washing bed linens, throwing food out of the pantry, scrubbing the bathrooms, and bringing in her patio furniture, I called her. She told me to go home and get my stuf together to fly out. She said Chloe could come to take care of her, other people have babies, and their lives do not stop. She loved me but I needed to get my ass on the plane, quoted from my mother. I had to laugh; she only talked like that when she was very determined or sassing back to my father. So, I am in a mad dash to tie up all the loose ends here, and I will be on the Friday afternoon flight out of Tampa International. I wanted to see you before I leave, but

I don't know how I could fit in everything. I am sorry if that sounds cold, there is no easy way of saying it. I guess we will have to email for another month before I return.

You know you have been my strength though all of my mother's health issues. Without you, I do not know what I would have done. You are in a special place in my heart. I will try and text you between flights. I am so glad you are firmly in my heart.

Love, Michael

Keira sat on the edge of her chair and decided she needed a drink and a stiff one at that. Michael's plans had changed. He was leaving in less than twenty-four hours. Yes, she hadn't opened any of her emails in two days. She had been extremely busy, but Michael was leaving for Australia tomorrow afternoon. Tears rolled down her face. She wanted to meet him, touch him and make sure he was real. She was falling in love with him, but what if it was all an illusion? What if he was like the others and is a scammer. As Jimmy said, Michael plans to leave the country and then has some unbelievable dyer issue come up and needs money. Just another friggin scammer and what does she get, her heart broken.

Keira stood and paced her little galley walkway. If ever her thirty-eight–foot sailboat was too small, it was right about now. She needed space, but where could she go? It was too late to walk the beach. If she went outside, Jack would ask her fifty questions like a grade-schooler. She could go to the office where she secretly had a Murphy bed built into the wall in case of a hurricane. She lived in a mandatory evacuation zone, and the office was in a no evac zone. No, that was stupid; she had to be back at the marina for a final walk around for the final inspection before her company signed off on the project in the morning.

Dear Michael,

This is the first time I have had all week to sit down and read your email. Tears are running down my face. I am sad your mother fell. It is a good thing she is going to assisted living for therapy. She will finally receive the proper therapy. It is what you said she needed all along.

I am sad that you are leaving so soon. I know you are rushing to get everything accomplished before you go. There are always so many loose ends that have to be closed. But did I hear correctly, you are only going to be gone a month. That isn't so long. I have catsup in the refrigerator older than that. I wanted to meet you before you leave. And for that, I am broken-hearted. So many things can happen in a month. You could get a fantastic next assignment that will take you to Indonesia or some other exotic place. You could meet some lovely Australian girl and never return.

I would ask you to postpone your flight time for just one more day, but I know that would be asking too much. And I know the contract is on the line. So, I will say, have a safe trip. Email me when you can and send pictures to me. I would love to see your action shots. How about, I count down the days until you come home to me. It will be much more fun, we can make it... extremely fun when you get home...get it extreme? Hint! Hint! Hint! Take care. Hugs and kisses to you. Remember my love.   Safe travels, Keira

Keira closed her laptop, turned off the pale blue ambient lights around her bed, and crawled between the sheets. Michael had to fulfill his contract with the company. Although she was upset, Keira hoped she sounded positive rather than whiney in the letter she just sent. If he turned out to be a scammer, what would she do? Staring at the bow hatch, please, please, be a genuinely real and loving person, she prayed. With sadness, she welcomed her bunk shrouded in darkness. It engulfed her and mirrored her depressed feelings at the same time.

Chapter 15

♥♥♥♥♥♥♥♥♥♥♥♥♥

Keira walked down to the convenience store for a cup of coffee. She didn't have to hurry today since it was the final inspection of the marina before signing off on the project. None of the crew would be there. All the equipment was back at the warehouse. The guys were either helping the lawn crew finish up all the lawns before the long Fourth of July holiday weekend or were cleaning equipment behind the office.

"Keira, can I walk with you? I have so much to tell you," Petra said as she joined Keira on her trek back to the marina.

"Sure, what's up?" Keira asked, taking a sip of her hot coffee. She pretty much knew what Petra was about to tell her.

"I am ready for the festival tomorrow, I think. It is so exciting. Everything is turning out perfectly. The food trucks, the vendors for the farmers market, and a cotton candy truck, that I persuaded at the last minute, are all set. There will not be any balloons. It has been proven they will harm the fish if the latex goes down over the water. And, there is no rain in the forecast either." Petra said without taking a breath.

"Is there anything I can do to help?"

"I went up to Clearwater to see Storm and took him out to lunch. I would love to have his children; they would be so pretty. I was going to have sex with him. But, I think he is seeing someone else. He was polite, but he just wasn't into me. I was so disappointed; I cried all the way home." Petra said in a very soft voice.

"Oh. Petra." Keira stopped and looked at her friend. She prayed to God to give her the right words to say. "It might not be that he is seeing someone else so much as..." Keira took deep breath. "You are his employer. He is acting professionally. Maybe, there is a certain line he doesn't want to cross. He knows this is the first year of the festival and is looking at the possibility of future DJ gigs. If he messes it up, the advertising, the fantastic venue, and possible contacts could go up in smoke." Keira wondered if she should say anything about meeting him on the dating website. She thought against it since she wasn't sure where the relationship was going. Why add salt to the wound so to speak?

"I wanted to have sex with him. I even shaved my legs. Thank God I didn't get a bikini wax that would have hurt like hell." Petra grinned.

"Hey, guys, can I walk with you?"

"Marla, how are you doing?"

"That was some fight last night. The out-of-towners got booked into jail. So, Keira, how is the dating website going? I have been dying to ask you, but there are always ears around." Marla questioned.

"There are a lot of scammers on there. It is horrible because they are so lovey and then hit you up for money. However, there are a couple of guys that really touch my heart. One is a sea captain for a cruise liner; another is a photojournalist..."

"You never told me you were doing the online dating thing," Petra complained.

"Oh, there is Micah. Come on, Keira, time for your meeting." Marla grabbed Keira's arm.

"Good Luck," Petra yelled.

Micah walked the entire perimeter of the marina. He inspected the asphalt, the palm trees, and the sturdiness of the engine picnic tables. Micah seemed to like the looks of the artificial grass, the indirect lighting, and the paver stone steps leading to the docks. As he continued to view his property, his features were hard to read. The marina had a professional building look in a beachy community atmosphere. Was he pleased, or did he hate the job Keira had completed with love and style?

He signed the papers, handed her the check for the asphalt company, and then sprinted to the office. That was it. Not, great job Keira. No, 'I love your work,' he just signed on the dotted line and left. Keira was completely dumbfounded and a bit hurt. It was hard to be totally professional and act like it didn't matter when she put her heart and soul into her designs.

When Keira took the copy of the contract into the office, Marla was red-faced and flustered like Keira had never seen before. What had happened in the hour since they had walked to the office?

"Micah seemed very preoccupied. Marla, are you ok?"

"Oh, an emergency came up in Sarasota. Micah is on a mad dash against time. I have to get this; the answering service is putting a call through. I will talk to you later, Keira. Yes, this is Marla. The engine number is…"

Keira got in her Jeep and drove back to the office. The next worksite to get underway was the St. Dominic Care Facility landscaping. Kraig was organized, ready to start the project on Tuesday after the Fourth of July holiday. All of the permits had been gotten and the electrical lines had been staked. Keira would orient Tina to the workings of the company. She was looking forward to not worrying about missed calls and scribbled appointments on napkins and blueprint paper anymore.

The furniture for the secretary's office had finally come in. Keira, at first, wanted her office to be the secretary's office. But she wasn't about to give up her small bathroom with the shower and the hidden Murphy bed wall unit along the outer wall of her office. In case of a hurricane, it was where she planned on staying when the island evacuated. No, the new secretary could be in the old storage room across the hall. Tina could still see the entrance when clients walked in. Keira was wiping down the new secretary's desk and straightening the computer when Kraig tapped his knuckles on the new office door.

"Why didn't you tell me; I could have moved all the office equipment for you? But I like that you are all sweaty; it's a good look on you." Kraig teased. He pulled her to him and nuzzled her neck. "Do you know how long I have wanted to ravage you when you are hot and bothered?"

"What about Tina? She has bigger boobs than me." Keira laughed and wiggled out of his grasp.

"Oh, burned in the prime of life." Kraig clutched his heart.

"You might have to clutch your 'something' else; I fear for it. Tina could whittle it down to a pencil." Keira laughed and dropped the pencil like dropping a mic, she had just picked up from her desk. Oh, she was on a roll, she thought. She knew she got him good. Keira one, Kraig zip, hehe.

The last words out of Keira's mouth before leaving the office were, I will have the coolers full of meat and all the trimmings at your house around two-thirty on Sunday afternoon. Do you need anything else for the party?

"Just you," once again, Kraig grabbed Keira around the waist and pulled her to him. He repeated how much he wanted her and kissed her lips. Only this time, he wasn't joking around.

Keira was tired of fighting off passes from Kraig. She kissed him back and ran her tongue across his teeth. Her arms skimmed down his back and rested on his backside. She slid her knee up the inner part of his leg and rested against his crotch. The surprise was quite evident with his intake of breath and then the wide-eyed look he gave her.

He leaned his head against the top of her head and whispered, "I want you, I want you so bad, but I want all of you." He kissed her again on her lips, turned, and walked out the door.

Keira cursed mercury in retro and slammed the office door shut. She wished Kraig would stop the nonsense. They had a great working relationship. He picked up the pieces of her, leftover from Peter's little tryst with a married woman. He knew she would never trust again, especially with someone who worked for her. She was frustrated once again. No, she couldn't skip out to a luxurious hotel suite every time she felt sorry for herself. But it was a good thought. A supreme pizza with extra cheese would help. That was a better thought. And then the perfect idea for a Friday night hit her, a big batch of popcorn and a night at the cinema. With a plan in place, she was on her way home.

Keira stopped at the stoplight in Cortez Village when she heard her phone's ping. Glancing at the text, thank goodness it wasn't from that creepy Scott guy.

"Would you like to go with me to listen to Kai's band, T De Novo? They are playing down at the Sarasota Yacht Club? We could pick you up at six-thirty. Lea Finn"

The Sarasota Yacht Club was hosting a gathering, recognizing all the sponsors, boat racers, and people who helped put on the festival each year. The Offshore Powerboat Grand Prix had started late in June and ran through the Fourth of July. So many people had worked hard on the jam-packed week-long festivities. Keira thought it was the best plan for a Friday night.

Finally getting onto the island with Friday afternoon traffic and zooming to the marina, she yelled hi to Jack and then rushed into her boat to shower and get dressed. What to wear? What to wear? It was the yacht club. She needed something sexy but classy. Finally, she slipped into one of the dresses she bought on her shopping spree a few weeks back. It was a dark blue glossy halter dress with layers of material and open slits up the sides of her legs. It was sexy but not slutty looking. She was just putting on a pair of silver sandals when she heard Lea and KC talking as they walked the steps down to the dock.

"Hey, you found me. Welcome." Keira said.

"Sorry, it was such short notice. I didn't want to stay home alone on a Friday night," Lea confessed.

"What a beautiful sailboat, Zac Karas would love to see your boat," KC said, with much awe in his voice.

"Thank you. I'm ready to go when you are."

The sun slowly set in the west, highlighting the beautiful sailing crafts in the harbor. With drinks in hand, many people milled around the banquet room overlooking the water. It was the cocktail hour; for the boat racers, boat owners, and sponsors to mingle. There were many people Keira knew from designing their mansions' landscape. She recognized some of the powerful money backers and charity heads. Lea Finn was well known and greeted as if she was royalty. Of course, she was one of the most beautiful women Keira knew; there wasn't a vain bone in her body. She was so refreshing to be around. KC Bradlow would stand out anywhere in a crowd. He was not only handsome; there was an air of sophistication surrounding him. He wasn't arrogant; he was debonair Keira thought, like a movie star in a top hat and tails.

Kristi Romanoff and Zac Karas showed up within fifteen minutes after them. Lea greeted her best friends and made sure Kristi remembered Keira. They had stopped at the buffet table and brought an array of beautifully decorated desserts for everyone to sample. When the host of the gala grabbed the microphone, a hush settled across the room. It was time for the recognition and congratulations for different sponsors and charity work to be honored. Luckily the speeches were brief. Then the band, T De Novo, began their first set. They were one of the best and sought- after local bands around. Their music was upbeat, with a few people stepping out to dance immediately. One of the band members named Jennifer sang. She had a sexy, sultry voice. KC not only played keyboard but also sang duets with Jennifer. His voice was clear and precise. The other band's members, Charles was on bass, and Joe played guitar like no other, were all well-known attorneys. Kenny, whom the band loved to tease, played drums. He had a law degree but also was a practicing physician.

Lea squeezed Keira's hand and whispered, "I know it sounds funny, but I find different ways of falling in love with Kai every day."

Keira smiled and knew that was exactly what she wanted. She dreamed of a lifetime of exploring love with someone. The conversation flowed easily between Zac, Kristi, and Lea. They explained funny things that had happened to them in the last couple of months so Keira wouldn't feel out of place. She was having fun watching people dance who really couldn't dance while sipping a glass of wine. Zac bowed dramatically and asked Kristi to take a whirl with him. Lea giggled at their craziness.

"They are such a striking couple. Kristi is so blonde in contrast to Zac's dark hair." Keira said to Lea.

"Yes, he may be of Greek heritage, but when he gets tired or is very nervous, he speaks French. "

"Why is that?" Keira asked.

"He spent many years in France, actually went to culinary school there, and didn't speak any English all those years," Lea explained.

Some lady walked up to Lea and asked if she would sign her copy of Lea's latest novel. During the signing, she confessed she saw Lea and walked back to her yacht and grabbed the book for Lea to sign. After the woman left, Lea turned to Keira and smiled as if she was embarrassed by the recognition.

"May I have this dance?"

Keira's mouth fell open as she looked into the beautiful gray-blue eyes of Micah Andreas. She slowly stood, turned to Lea, and excused herself. She saw the excited look in Lea's eyes. As she stepped into Micah's arms for the slow dance, she thought she had gone to heaven.

"You look beautiful tonight. Your dress reminds me of the midnight sky." Micah said as he looked into her eyes.

"Thank you. You cleaned up well yourself." Keira grinned. "For some reason, I didn't expect to see you here."

"I am a race boat owner and sponsor."

"The always drunk guys say, you are one of the best jet boat racers around." Keira smiled. She liked the feel of Micah's hand resting on her lower back. It sent tingles up and down her spine.

"The always drunk guys, at the dock space two piers down from you? Yes, I guess they are. That is funny you call them that, the always drunk guys." Micah laughed.

Keira had very seldom seen Micah laugh. With his black curly hair tied back at the base of his neck and those dark bluish-grey eyes, Keira thought he was beautiful. The color of his eyes was like looking across the horizon on a calm night at sea. She was amazed at how easy it was to dance with him. She didn't feel claustrophobic in his arms; she liked the way he held her. It was weird; why did many other guys' arms around her smother her and his didn't? When he raised her hand to his lips, she felt treasured, not ready to bolt from the room.

The song blended into another slow ballad. It was a seductive and alluring song only a female vocalist could sing well. Jennifer sang with passion and brought out the desired result of the song, which was pure lust. Her voice pushed the emotional lyrics of the song to the edge of yearning and craving. Keira closed her eyes, knowing the sweltering words and perfect background music was washing over Micah too. He showed no sign of wanting to end their moment together.

At the end of the set, Micah walked with Keira back to the table. Zac stood and greeted Micah like old friends. It was interesting. They seemed to know each other from long ago and chatted a moment before KC pulled an extra chair to the table for Micah to join them. The conversations flowed well.

"Ok, I have never seen Zac talk as much to anyone as he is right now," Kristi whispered to Keira.

"Kristi, you should have seen Keira's boat. Talk about a beautiful sailboat; she has it," KC said to his sister.

"One of her sails has a pirate with dreadlocks painted on it. The first time I saw it, she was pushing, what Keira, twenty-five knots?" Micah mentioned.

"I want to see that," Zac said with awe in his voice.

"Ahh, the sexy Mr. Andreas knows your boat. Delicious," Lea leaned over and whispered to Keira.

When KC's break was over, Keira watched him kiss Lea. And then the next set of songs started.

"Some of you may remember the last time I sang this next song. Lea, this song is for you, again." KC pointed to Lea and winked. "In Case You Didn't Know, by Brett Young."

Once again, KC's voice sang out clear and in perfect pitch. The flow of the lyrics was breathtaking. He may have been performing the song from of their play list but he seemed as if he was singing to each individual personally. The song ended with couples embracing and him smiling lovingly at Lea as he had once stated, 'the song was dedicated to the love of his life.'

Lea told Keira about KC singing the song to her right before

243

midnight on New Year's Eve. There was sadness in her eyes. Keira remembered reading the crash headlines online on New Year's Day, but the details of what truly happened were not known. Kristi explained the accident, which almost killed her brother and left Lea with temporary amnesia. They both had several broken bones. Keira felt sick to her stomach to think someone would purposely try to kill them. So much hate that person must have had in them. Micah put his hand over the top of Keira's hands, resting on her lap. She looked at him and smiled.

Zac and Micah discussed the merits of why some foods their grandmothers cooked; could never be replicated. Zac found it troubling that some secret recipes went to the grave with his Ya-Ya.

"I swear they were chemists. As easy as psarosoupa is to make, there is something she put in it, I will never figure out." Micah said in wonder.

"It has to be the Greek water. Just like loaves of bread made in different areas taste different. It is all due to the water used." Zac laughed.

Keira looked at Micah and had never envisioned him standing in the kitchen stirring a pot of fish stew on the stove. Racing his boat or helping a customer at the marina to get their engine She wondered if he ever spent time in the kitchen cooking with his wife.

"Keira, if Micah wants to leave and offers to drive you home, please feel free to go with him," Lea whispered.

"No way, that would be rude of me," Keira smiled.

"I can see the headlines now; romance writer impedes a potential romance, the story at eleven," Lea whispered, dramatizing her issue with her hands.

Keira burst out laughing but nodded her ok. She said, "I wouldn't want to hamper your book sales."

After the second set, Micah stood and thanked everyone for an enjoyable evening. He said he needed to check on his boats for the Boat Fun Run Race; in the morning.

"Keira, do you need a ride home, or did you drive here yourself?" Micah asked.

"Thanks, Micah, Keira came with us, but I am sure she doesn't want to stay until the end of the evening," Lea said with a smile to Micah and almost pushed Keira out of her chair.

"Thank you for inviting me. Let me know when you are sailing Zac, goodnight, everyone." Keira waved graciously. It was interesting how Micah seemed to take charge. He guided her through groups of people chatting to the right and others dancing to the left. She took one last look at the T De Novo band singing with the backdrop of floor-to-ceiling glass walls looking out over the marina behind them. Even the lounge across the entry hall had many people sitting at tables and standing at the bar. The sound of music and laughter slowly diminished.

As Micah and Keira walked out of the elevator of the yacht club to the parking area, Micah rested his hand on Keira's back. He had surprise-kissed her only moments before as the elevator had reached the ground level. Too bad the elevator hadn't gotten stuck between floors, Keira thought. She noticed the look of mischief in his eyes as they walked to his sports car.

"You dance extremely well for a tree hugger."

"I can sway like a palm tree in a hurricane!" Keira laughed as she sidestepped through the parking lot. The soft flow of the material of her dress whirled around her legs as she moved. Feeling sexy and alive, she wondered if Micah would get caught up in her playfulness. Instead of opening the passenger car door for her, he pulled her to him and kissed her again. So soft, so sensual, she loved the feel of his lips against hers.

On the ride back to the marina, Micah silently drove along the winding road of Longboat Key towards Anna Maria Island. Keira put her hand on Micah's leg and whispered, "The gulf is so beautiful tonight. I wish I was out there."

"It would be the perfect adventure to sail down to Naples. From there, plot a course across the gulf to Merida and my favorite port of Vera Cruz. You would enjoy exploring the old-world charm. Or not go to Vera Cruz; sail from Merida to Cozumel."

Keira was startled when Micah mentioned sailing to Merida and then onto Cozumel. She studied Micah's profile in the dark car. It was interesting; he talked of a yachting adventure across the gulf to Mexico. Three men, she felt special feelings for all had connections with the water. Theos was a sea captain, Micah was into offshore boat racing and owned a marina, and Michael was a photojournalist doing a surfing shoot in a few days. She was drawn to men of the sea. It was too soon to tell her true feelings for Storm, of course, his name alone resonated with water.

"You are very quiet tonight," Micah stated as he put his hand over hers.

"Just thinking of sailing with the moon reflecting across the water, it would be so beautiful. But you know I would have to find a hotel around one in the morning because I would nod off at the helm." Keira grinned and watched Micah once again laugh.

The drive along the beach was all too short. And when Micah parked his car on the freshly paved parking lot and opened her door for her, Keira slid her hands along his jaw and kissed him.

He wrapped his arms around her waist and pulled her to him. It felt good to be held by him. If only…

"Thank you for the ride home. Night, Micah."

Keira couldn't believe it was finally Saturday. The early morning sky was pink, and the boats in the marina gently rocked as the fishing trawlers passed on the way out to open water. She sipped a cup of tea since she was too lazy to walk to the convenience store for coffee. It had been late when Micah had dropped her at the marina. They had danced at the yacht club with the beautiful marina in the background. The drive home with the moon shining silvery on the gulf water was alluring as they talked of night sailing. He had held her hand as he drove. Yet, when he parked at the marina, he only hugged her and wished her a goodnight. He hadn't attempted to kiss her; she initiated the kiss in the parking lot. Nor did he walk her to her boat. She was puzzled and a bit hurt. She knew, in her mind, she needed to keep her relationship with him professional since he was her landlord. But in her heart, she had felt so sexy and beautiful at the yacht club, just a few minutes more of the illusion would have been fun.

Oh well, he had to get up early for the Fun Run boat race this morning. Speaking of this morning, she wondered if Petra had been able to get any sleep last night since today was the Wet T-Shirt Contest. The July fourth Coquina Beach festivities she had put together was all she had thought of for the past few months now.

Keira opened her laptop after getting a second cup of tea.

ExtremeLover – Michael

> *Dear Keira,*
> *I am sitting here in San Francisco waiting for the airline to call my flight. I am not sure how many times my mind has thought about all that needed to be taken care of and what I forgot to do. I am sure I have forgotten something in the mad rush to get it all done. Anyway, I called my mom to let her know I was waiting on the flight from San Fran to Australia. I needed to check to make sure she is comfortable and settled. She confessed she did not fall while I was out getting her pizza. She said she made the entire story up so that I would get on the plane. She laughed and said I was a loyal son, and she loved me for it, but I needed to fulfill my commitment to the company.*
> *So as I write to you, I keep shaking my head and laugh. My mother is one spunky woman. I hope when I get to be her age, I am as spry as she is. If I pull the same antics as she, will you still love me? I will email you after I get to the hotel. All my love,*
> *Michael*

Dear Michael,

I had to chuckle after reading your note. Your mother sounds like a very spirited person; but also very thoughtful. I am sure your sister is not going to be happy when she realizes the cleverness of your mother. Or maybe she already knew her spunkiness and stayed away so you could finally see and appreciate it (pulling your hair out in frustration at the same time!).

I hope you will be able to sleep on the flight from San Francisco to Sydney. Yes, email me after you have arrived and are settle.

Hugs to you, Keira

She watched as a fishing boat full of guys made its way towards the Gulf, for a day of fishing. She prayed Michael wasn't a scammer. It would break her heart if he, all of a sudden, dropped his 800 mm lens or had his camera stolen. Yes, it could happen. However, scammers always asked for money to replace their items. Never did they take responsibility for it on their own. The thought took her breath away. She had such loving feelings for Michael. She learned his love of extreme sports in effect, pushed her to appreciate her love of sailing all the more. Stepping out of the box and being brave and adventurous was a good thing.

"It's too early in the morning for such deep thoughts," Jack said as he walked out on his boat deck and stretched. "Is that coffee you are drinking?"

"Good morning. No, it's tea. I was too lazy to walk down the street for coffee."

"You looked really pretty yesterday evening when you left with your friends."

"Thank you."

Theseus – Theos

Dear Keira,

I wonder what you have planned for the Fourth of July holiday. Have you been watching the off- shore races? The other day one of the racers on my team blew the gaskets and damaged one of the engines. I scrambled to find a new engine and have it lifted into the boat. It was nerve-wracking trying to get it repaired in time to race.

Then this evening, I rushed back to Sarasota Yacht Club for the recognition gathering they have each year. I would have liked to have asked you to go with me to the reception. With the last-minute search for an engine, I lost track of time. All of a sudden, it was Thursday evening, and I figured you had made other plans for Friday evening. I am sorry for my lack organizational skills at the moment.

So, do you have family nearby; who will celebrate the holidays with you? It is interesting, in all the time I have talked with you, we have never discussed our immediate family or close friend. I wish you a safe and fun holiday celebration.

Love, Theos

Dear Theos,

Being around the marina when I was growing up, I remember hearing about owners of jet boats not breaking an engine in slowly and either throwing a rod or blowing gaskets. I found I loved the simplicity of sailing more; however, sails can be expensive. Nothing is worse than hitting a shallow area and snapping the keel or rudder. I guess, when you think of water sports or equipment, everything has a large price tag.

You were there, at the yacht club, for the recognition gala? I was there also. I came with some of my friends. It was an evening of champagne, fine wine, and fantastic music. I am sad that we crossed but didn't meet.

This weekend will be very busy. A friend of mine is hosting a weekend of festivities at Coquina Beach. She will have food trucks, a wet T-shirt contest, a DJ, and many other activities. Sunday, the fourth, there will be more activities. It will be a more family oriented theme with sandcastle building contest time for the children. The band T De Novo that played at the yacht club will be playing at the beach on Sunday afternoon. I have my company's Independence Day party to host. It will be at my business partner's home in Palmetto. I fear it will be a very long day, with fireworks both at the beach and at the green bridge on the Manatee River later in the evening. Thank goodness I gave all my employees the day off on Monday. I plan on doing absolutely nothing.

What will your plans be? I do wish we could get together, to know each other better. I have learned so much about you, but yet, so little.   Take care, love, Keira

Keira watched her brown tea water swirl around and around in her cup. Why couldn't Theos have called her, even at the last minute? She knew from his letters he was formal and seemed to follow certain decorum. What if she would have been dancing with Micah, and Theos walked into the room, and he made eye contact with her? Would she have made excuses to Micah and ran to Theos like in the movies? Micah hadn't asked her out on a so-called date. He asked her to dance. And Theos had never asked her for the evening out. Oh good grief, Keira thought with a laugh, such silly thinking. A month ago, there was no one in her life, and now, well, there was still no one beating down her door to see her. If one of them wanted her, they should step forward. And yet...no one had.

Peter Flynn's Friend - Basil

> *K Lee,*
> *I have to tell you about the most horrible thing that happened to me last night. I was out for dinner in town. On my way back to my apartment, I saw one of the workers walking along the road. I offered him a ride home; he gave me directions. It was on the more shady side of town. We laughed and joked as I drove. When we got to the house that he said was his, he took my wallet and laptop and ran off. I was going to run after him, but it was very dark and the wrong area of town to get out of your car. I drove to the nearest police station and registered my mugging and loss. They did not seem like they were very willing to help me. I don't know if it was*

because they thought I was a tourist or if this kind of behavior happens all the time. When I got back to my rental unit, I was in total shock from the entire experience.

This morning when I got to work, there wasn't any report yet from the police. Some of the workers, who know the guy who stole my credit card and laptop, said they had not seen him this morning. He has vanished.

While I was on the phone canceling my stolen credit cards, I was informed, an important piece of machinery has become disabled. When I searched online for the replacement part, the company will only take a credit card. I'm frustrated; my credit card will be replaced and sent to my home address. I need it here in Cape Town! I called my bank in Texas in need of emergency funds, but they will not send money without proper verification of who I am. My identification cards were in my wallet.

Please, will you help me? Will you drive to my friend's real estate agency in Brandon? He said he would loan me the money I need. He will give you a check. Please put it in your account. Meanwhile, I will send you the information to order the machinery part I need. If you will use your credit card and have it overnight express mailed to me here in South Africa, I would appreciate it. Also I will send you information on the type of laptop I need to have replaced. If you will, have that ordered; please have it overnight express mailed to me. I would so much appreciate it. I only ask this of you because I trust you with the check Peter will give you. Thank you, Basil

Well, there it was. Peter Flynn's friend Basil, if there was a basil, or a Peter Flynn, was initiating the scam.

Dear Basil,

I am sorry for the difficulties you have experienced in the last twenty-four hours. It must have been quite traumatic for you. I cannot imagine what I would do if I got mugged in a strange country. Did you have a contingency plan set up, so if anything goes wrong within the boundaries of your contract, you are covered? That is why, for any business, and especially those that work out of the country, American Express Business can help you. All you have to do is call their international office, and they can get a new credit card to you within twenty-four hours. Why don't you give them a call?

I don't feel comfortable receiving a check from your friend Peter. Why doesn't he overnight express mail it to you? There are several very reputable and international banks in your area: ABSA (with Chemical Bank), First National Bank, Nedbank (with Bankers Trust, Chase Manhattan, Chemical Bank, Citibank and Morgan Guarantee Trust), Bank of Taiwan Limited (South Africa), and ICICI Bank Limited. They are all American banks.

I hope this information will help you. K Lee

She was sure he, as a scammer, was not going to like her response to his plea for help. How did he know she wasn't going to take the check; that Peter Flynn was giving her and keep it? Then she realized, duh, the check draft was bogus. It would bounce, and she would have already used her credit card to buy the laptop and piece of machinery he needed. She would be out double. She would have to repay the bounced check plus bounce fees on her checking account plus the money she paid for the stuff he asked for. Once those items were shipped, there was no canceling that order. She couldn't call the fraud department on her credit card because she initiated the purchases herself.

Keira decided to send jimmy from JFlounderGig a note. She would let him know she caught another guy in a scam. It made her angry at how he did some smooth-talking and tried to play on her emotions. He told her how much he loved her and wanted to plan his future with her in a new home he supposedly just purchased in Brandon. That also was probably a lie. She explained how he left the country on a business contract to build a warehouse and office complex in South Africa. She told him about the pictures, well minus, the standing penis pictures. That was so embarrassing to even think about. Laughing while she was typing, she wondered who's penis that was.

"You are having too much fun over there on your laptop. Please don't tell me you are looking at porn or something like that." Jack joked.

"Nope, I don't do porn. Aren't those sights full of viruses and stuff like that?"

"Are you assuming I look at porn and know about that kind of stuff?" Jack asked.

Keira looked at Jack standing with his hands on his hips in an untied white terry robe and KISS ME stamped all across his boxer shorts. He was also wearing black socks and flip-flops. She didn't want to laugh; however, the evidence was in on the grounds for his divorce.

"Um, Jack, are you wearing 'kiss me' boxers to get the attention of the women who weekend on their cabin cruiser on pier 2?"

"Oh crap, sorry, Keira," Jack said and ran back down into his lower cabin.

At ten in the morning, dressed in her bathing suit with a T-shirt over the top advertising the Wet T-shirt Contest on the front and her landscape and lawn service on the back, Keira felt like a walking billboard. With her backpack and bottle of water, she hopped on the trolley that would take her to the festival at Coquina Beach. The cars were parked all along Gulf Drive and in the Coquina Parking lot. People were walking towards the beach area. Thank goodness it was a fantastic sunny day.

Petra, with her clipboard in hand, was talking to a couple the food truck vendors. She waved and trotted over to the market vendors. At this rate, Keira decided she would be exhausted by noon.

"Petra, what can I do to help you?"

"Hi Keira, nothing, I think I have it all under control. I am nervous about seeing Storm after I practically threw myself at him the other day. How stupid of me, you know?" Petra rattled off, not taking a breath.

"Petra, relax. You have worked everything down to the smallest of detail. You have this under control. Do you need a bottle of water?"

"No, then I will have to pee. Oh, here comes Storm. Storm, glad you are here. I would like you to meet my friend Keira. This is Storm, my DJ for the day." Petra rambled nervously.

"Hi, Storm." Keira smiled. "Petra, where are you having Storm set up?" She said, trying to focus on keeping her friend's stress level down and ignoring Storm.

"Storm, you will be at the same place as I showed you the other day. Are you ready to get started?"

"Yes, I just have to carry over my equipment, and then I can start on time. Keira, do you want to help me?" Storm asked.

Keira saw Petra deflating as Storm asked for her help.

"Actually, Petra had just asked me to check on the food vendors for her. Petra can help you while discussing any last minute ideas you may have."

Petra was eager to help Storm, and it gave Keira a chance to watch the interaction with her friend and Storm.

The Wet T-Shirt Contest got underway. Storm created loud and crazy fun music for the entertainment to help make the contest a success. Keira couldn't believe how many women participated in the contest, some for the fun of participating and some with the desperate need to win - anything. The local news team had it all on camera. The food vendors were super busy as the day and activities continued. Keira watched the squirt gun battles and kids dragging friends on beach blankets across a finish line to win colorful beach rafts and ice cream from one of the vendors. Susyn gave tarot card readings while Summer, from The Pet Shop, hosted a two-day pet adoption area under the shade of the pine trees.

Keira saw her employee who volunteered to work the festival passing out trinkets with her company logo plastered across each of them. It was a great marketing strategy to get her company name in people's homes. She had ordered a case of Wet T-Shirt contest t-shirts with The Landscape Architect and Lawn Care Service across the back. She planned to give them out at the party tomorrow to everyone.

"Chuck, thank you for working today, even though, it is on your day off. I hope two cases of key chains and sprinkle cans will be enough. Do you need a bottle of water?" Keira asked, looking at the cute keychain Chuck was holding.

"No, I'm ok. May I have a keychain for my wife and a sprinkle can for my daughter?" Chuck asked as he handed a couple, a key chain and a business pamphlet.

"Yes, of course. I will check on you later. And remember to have fun." Keira laughed.

"Si, I have already been asked if I was entering the contest." Chuck grinned, pointing down at his shirt.

Summer waved to Keira and encouraged her to buy a shaggy dog. Keira laughed and shook her head NO.

She sat down at Susyn's tarot card reading table under the protection of the pine trees dotted along the beach. It was nice to see her away from The Crystal Corner Gem Shop. During conversations at The Dive Bar, Keira had heard Susyn had helped a few people to understand and deal with out-of-control life situations. Many people from the island swore that Susyn gave the greatest tarot readings. One person raved about how beautifully decorated her after-hours tarot card reading room was. She knew some of the secretaries at KC Bradlow's law Firm read her daily horoscopes in the island newspaper and had natal chart readings.

As always, Susyn had a warm and inviting greeting for Keira. She asked Keira to choose one of the six different decks of tarot cards sitting on the carved oak table. Such a decision to make on a beautiful holiday! The black leather cards with a golden eye in the center could illustrate their all-knowing abilities, Keira wondered. One pack looked very medieval and old world. Another set proclaimed their celestial meanings were written in the heavens. Keira tried to ignore the woodland faerie deck even though its cover featured a beautifully grown tree with roots just as deep. The petite winged creature was cute sitting on one of the branches. She knew wood sprite folklore and didn't want to awaken any problems with her business. Instead, she picked the most exotic pack with vivid blues, golds, and reds across the front.

"Interestingly, you picked my voyager cards," Susyn said as she shuffled and placed five cards on the table. "It seems you; the high priestess is on a journey. A storm is brewing; it will feel like a major setback. Ah, but see, number 6 of the major arcana, the Gemini twin lovers, will protect you. And lastly, the Sun, of the major arcana shows me radiance, joy, and a spirit soul relationship."

"That was interesting," Keira said, although she was completely puzzled by what Susyn had said.

Susyn kept staring at the cards; she looked up and asked, "Haven't I mentioned the Gemini Twins to you before? The one who stayed in longer is more spirited with an older soul."

"Thank you, I think. How much do I owe you?"

"It's five dollars, but you don't owe me anything. You are one of my dearest friends. Do you have a booth; since I saw you are a sponsor?"

"Yes, one of our employees is handing out little shovel keychains, sprinkle cans, and pamphlets showing all the services we provide. I'm paying him time and a half, so he is very happy." Keira laughed. She set five dollars on the table and walked away with the promise to talk later.

Keira was sitting near one of the huge mounds of sand for the next day's sandcastle contest when Storm came and sat next to her. He let her know he was on a break and handed her a cone of Italian ice. They talked for a while. Keira sensed the awkwardness of their conversation. It wasn't like their dinner date at the Sea Hut, relaxed and casual chatting. She watched him watching Petra.

"You need to let her know she is special; you know that, right?"

"When you suggested she help me this morning, she was quiet and carried the equipment I handed to her." Storm stated.

"She felt like she made a mess of everything when she visited you at your studio. Why don't you ask her for dinner?" Keira suggested.

"Thanks, Keira," Storm studied her face. "I hope you find your special someone." He kissed her just as Keira saw Petra walking towards them. She almost cried when she saw the look on Petra's face.

"Petra, wait..." Storm hollered as he ran towards Petra, as she ran down the beach.

Keira took a dip in the warm gulf water. It wasn't refreshing at all as she swam almost out to the no-wake buoy. But she loved the feel of the salty water on her skin. The television news team had mentioned the gulf water was near ninety degrees, which was not cooling down the beach goers. Nevertheless, everyone seemed to be enjoying their day at the beach. Storm was back spinning songs and urging people to rock the music. Keira decided a beach-vendor ice cream wagon trolling along the shore would be perfect.

It was time to pack up her beach blanket. She was still hot after her swim in the water but was tired and ready to go home. Stopping at one of the food vendors, she picked up a couple of hot dogs. Hey, she decided it was the holiday; eating junk food was part of the celebration. And that was justification enough to buy the dogs. Keira spotted Petra standing looking at the puppies up for adoption.

"Petra, today was a great success. Congratulations." Keira smiled.

"Stay away from me. I hate you."

"Petra, it wasn't what you thought you saw." Keira pleaded.

"You lied to me. You knew Storm, and you let me ramble on and on and confess my love. I don't want your leftovers. Stay away from me." Petra spat at Keira before she turned and walked away.

Keira walked to the trolley pickup stop. She waited as others wearily found their seats; they too were near burnt and tired. The seats were even sweltering, but her wet bathing suit helped keep her skin cool. She found a dirty window seat and stared out across the water without seeing anything. The streetcar slowly lumbered towards the north end of the island. Keira couldn't wait to climb down the steps and walk towards the marina. She felt physically exhausted and mentally numb.

Rehashing the words over and over in her head that Petra had practically screamed at her, Keira walked past Marla without even seeing her leaving the marina office

"How was the festival?"

"What? Oh. Petra told me she hated me," Keira blurted out.

"What?"

"Petra is in love with Storm. I met Storm on the dating website a while back. We went to dinner one time. He just happens to be the DJ Petra hired. Well, I was watching some of the activities earlier this afternoon on the beach. He brought me an Italian Ice while he was on break. We talked, and both knew there weren't any strong feelings. Friends, yes, we could talk for hours, but a relationship wasn't in the making. I told him to go after Petra. He kissed me goodbye so he could find her. She saw him kiss me. A little later, I went to see if there was anything she needed and she told me she hated me. End of story." Keira confessed.

She couldn't believe she just told Marla of all people, everything. Keira was not one of those people who trash-talked anyone.

"Wow, what are you going to do?"

"What can I do? She has tomorrow to get through. I encouraged Storm to take Petra out to dinner. It all depends on if she accepts his date. But right now, her ability to listen to anything, especially logic, is gone. Oh well, thanks for letting me vent. I'm hot, salty, and tired, night." Keira wanted to kick herself for saying anything at all. She should have complained of being tired and left it at that.

Chapter 16
♥♥♥♥♥♥♥♥♥♥♥♥♥

Happy Fourth of July – America's Independence Day honoring the colonies of 1776 separation from Great Britain. People around the area had been setting off fireworks all weekend in celebration. With the constant booms during the late-night hours and all the drama from yesterday, Keira had slept poorly. She came out on deck before the sun came up and figured out how to hang a hammock between the two dock posts near her boat. It was then she finally slept well.

"Wow, look at you, hanging out as if you have not a care in the world," Jack said, no pun intended. He carried out a cup of coffee and sat down on one of his deck chairs.

"The day is young; things could change. What are your plans for the day?" Keira asked while she used her foot to rock the hammock. The waterway between the mainland and the island was already busy, with early morning boaters getting a head start cruising to the gulf.

"I am picking the kids up. We are going to watch the parade then go to the festival. The kids will eat until they are ready to vomit, swim, get sunburned, and roll in the sand, stuff like that. They are going to spend the night with me on the boat. So, if we are a bit loud, just let us know," Jack said with a shrug.

At ten in the morning, the city barricaded Gulf Drive off for the celebratory parade. The road along the beach was noisy, with the firetruck, the police cars, and parade cars honking and blowing their horns and sirens. A couple of Pirate floats, all decked out with patriotic flags, passed the people lined up on the sides of the road. Many children waited impatiently for the pirates to throw plastic beads at them. As soon as the procession passed, most of the bathing-suit-clad folks hiked back over the hot sand to the water's edge.

Keira took the trolley down to Coquina Beach to see if she could maybe help Petra. With luck, Storm persuaded Petra, they should get to know each other better. If not, Keira decided to search out KC Bradlow since his band T De Novo, was set to sing, starting at noon. Hopefully, Lea would be sunbathing on the beach and listening to KC's band's music.

The food vendors were ready for their hungry patrons to line up. She spotted some of T De Novo's band members setting up their sound system to a generator. Petra once again had her clipboard and was talking with KC.

"Oh, I hoped you would be here today." Lea wrapped her arm through Keira's arm, "I have the perfect spot over there under those pine trees."

"Cool, I will meet you there. I am going to walk over and say hi to Petra. I'll be back in a bit," Keira said as she handed her backpack to Lea.

Watching Petra talking to some of the festival newcomers, she seemed in a great mood, Keira decided. But that could be her professional business person facade.

"Petra, do you need me to help you with anything?"

"I think you have helped quite enough. Thank you very much." Petra glared at her for a few seconds. She flipped her hair over her shoulder and walked off.

So, she was still angry. Well, that was that, Keira thought and walked back to where Lea was sitting and sat down. The water was crystal blue as far as she could see. There was only a bit of white froth left from the boats as they passed by.

"Are you ok? You seem down."

"People were setting off fireworks all night. It was difficult to sleep." Keira pretended to complain. She didn't want to explain nor discuss the situation about Petra.

"Oh, I know. Kai bought me a little white Persian kitten for Christmas last year, and she slept almost glued to Kai's side all night long." Lea laughed.

"Aww, that's sweet; what is her name?"

"Holly. Hey, I have to tell you, you and Micah Andreas looked so good together on the dance floor Friday night. I hope you are serious about him because when he looked at you, the air practically sizzled." Lea grinned.

"Holly is a cute name for a Christmas kitty. As far as Micah Andreas, he is off-limits. He is my landlord, and I am not getting involved with him. If the relationship didn't work out, I would have to find a new place to live." Keira frowned as she saw a boat pulling children on a banana boat ride outside the no-wake buoys. It looked like fun. Wait that was Micah pulling them. Petra must have gotten him to donate his time.

"Well, you two looked fantastic together. And I have to say, you both sure blended in well with the four of us. Micah and Zac were like two little kids chatting. Kristi was amazed her man was talking so much."

Keira settled back on her blanket with her toes wiggling in the sand. She stared at the fluffy clouds slowly drifting by. "What a beautiful day," she whispered to no one in particular.

She worried about Petra. If she voiced her anger or whined to Storm, the relationship could backfire. After spending an evening with him at the Sea Hut, it was easy to tell he didn't have any patience for female drama.

Promptly at noon, the band, T De Novo welcomed everyone to the Fourth of July Celebration and started with a set of patriotic songs. Jennifer was handing out little flags and singing in her usual sexy voice. She could have gotten men to sign up for the military with her outfit and vocal cords! Or better yet, beach clean-up during red tide.

"You know Jennifer hated me when Kai and I started seeing each other," Lea mentioned.

She had her eyes set on the sexy KC Bradlow?" Keira teased.

"It was painful to watch her work through her feelings when Kai wasn't interested in a personal relationship with her."

"You know, he helped me through my divorce. After the initial shock of my ex sleeping with anything that moved, I got paranoid. I was afraid he was going to come after me. KC has a file on all the passwords, combinations of key locks of my business and boat. It was just in case something happened to me; I was that fearful for a while. It was more for my peace of mind to know I had a backup plan. I had to feel like I was doing something to protect myself. He has been a great attorney and friend to me." Keira said, looking directly at Lea.

"We talked on the way home the other night; he feels the same way about you. And I am excited to have you as a new friend." Lea smiled.

As much as Keira had enjoyed listening to KC's group sing and watching all the fun festivities, it was time to go. Lea understood when she explained her need to pick up all the meats and food for the company picnic at her business partner's home later in the day.

"Oh, I wish I could have helped you put your party together; we would have had fun."

"Thank you. We will have to figure out some excuse for a party soon. Have fun this afternoon. Bye." Keira said as she leaned down and hugged Lea.

The trolley was slow traveling north on Gulf Drive. People wanted to get on and off at different points along the way. But it was still faster than driving and looking for a parking spot or walking. Keira knew in her head what she wanted to wear and would have to rush to get changed. She wasn't sure how crowded the grocery store could be either, but she didn't have any place to store the food for the picnic if she would have picked it up yesterday.

There was a line of traffic trying to get on the island as she headed towards the mainland. She hoped she hadn't forgotten anything. Since the cars were bumper to bumper heading onto the island, there was no turning back. She had extra clothing in her backpack if she got thrown in the Manatee River, like last year.

At the store, she completely loaded the back of her car with all of the hot dogs, hamburgers, and sausages, plus the trimming for a huge feast. When she got to Kraig's house, a couple of guys were already there unloading tables and chairs.

"Jose, can you get the food out of Keira's Jeep and put the coolers by the grill? Maria is setting up the chairs around the backyard and pool. Baby, you got sunburned this weekend. It looks good on you. Where have you been?" Kraig asked.

"We were sponsors for the Wet T-Shirt contest yesterday. And today, I watched some of the festivities before driving over. It was a fun festival. My friend did well setting it up. I brought two cases of 'Wet T-Shirt Contest' t-shirts. I thought it would be funny to hand them out to everyone."

"Oh, the comments are going to be juicy. I forgot we advertised the company over the weekend there. How did Chuck handle handing out the shovel keychains and sprinkle cans?" Kraig asked, carrying the boxes of T-shirts to the dessert table. "So, did you win the Wet T-Shirt contest? Kraig grinned.

"Funny, very funny."

The afternoon started with Keira welcoming all her employees and their families to Kraig's backyard. Everyone brought their beverages of choice. Many workers brought cold beers and shoved them in the barrel of ice Kraig had set out. As the festivities got underway, Kraig lit the grills to get the meat searing.

Keira handed out the t-shirts. Thinking it was funny, some of the guys jumped in the pool with the t-shirts on. They paraded around the deck of the pool, attempting to walk sexy and flexing their muscles while others whistled. A couple of guys jokingly argued over who won the "wet t-shirt contest." It all ended good naturedly with them falling into the pool.

As soon as a batch of burgers and hot dogs were ready, Keira took the platter to the table. Keira was pleased with the amount of potato salad, macaroni salad, potato chips, baked beans, seven- layer salads, and all the other foods she had ordered for the day. She knew from seeing what the crew ate on any given day for lunch; how much food she would need for the party. Several kids grabbed hot dogs and ran to the dock to sit with their feet hanging in the river. She watched as her guests loaded their plates with hamburgers and beans. Some sat at the tables and some on blankets.

When Keira knew everyone had a plate of food, she sat down under one of the palm trees and ate a hamburger and a scoop of potato salad. Hot from grilling, Kraig sat down on the grass next to her. He took a swig from the beer he had grabbed from the barrel.

It was fun seeing all the workers with their families enjoying themselves. The children ran around the backyard and splashed in the pool. A couple of guys stood on the dock and cast their fishing lines into the river. Some of the younger men were getting a tag football game together. Kraig had hauled out corn-hole platforms earlier in the day. Two couples were laughing and pointing fingers at who cheated first. How do you cheat at corn hole, Keira wondered? Everyone seemed to be having a good time.

"I forgot to buy trash bags for the garbage," Keira mumbled

"Keira, I do own garbage cans and bags. You know you don't have to carry the weight of the world on your shoulders. Will you ever let me take care of you for a change?" Kraig asked.

"You have always been here for me. I rely on you all the time. You picked up the pieces of me when I couldn't." Keira said automatically. She watched several of the guys playing football in the grassy area on the other side of the pool.

"Speaking of pieces, who invited that piece of shit?" Kraig demanded as he stood and walked towards the table full of food.

"I see you are still trying to fuck my wife and on my birthday at that!" Peter slurred as he grabbed a beer out of the barrel of ice that everyone had contributed.

"You are not welcome here, nor were you invited. Leave before I call the police." Kraig growled as he took the beer out of Peter's hand.

"Miguel invited me, and I want my wife back, you fucktard." Peter yelled at Kraig as he tried to snatch the beer back.

Keira was furious. She walked over to Miguel. Keeping her voice low, she quietly said, "Take your friend and leave before I do something I will never regret. Trust me; you do not want to see my temper." She stared at him for a moment or two. She turned and slowly walked over to the side of the pool. One of the little kids was playing much too close to the edge for her liking.

"Honey, let's go play over by the tree with your dump truck. You can put sticks in the back of it, ok?" Keira said to the tot.

She kept an eye on Miguel as he walked towards Peter. But Peter was already out of control. It would be difficult for one guy to contain him and his vulgarity when he was drinking.

"Want my truck. Want my truck." The little one cried.

"OK, let me go get it, you stay here," Keira told the child before she walked back over to the pool edge to retrieve the toy dump truck. As she reached down, two of her crew playing football leaped for the ball and crashed into her. All three of them landed in the pool, with Keira at the bottom of the pile. Legs kicking to return to the surface and arms flailing, Keira seemed to receive the brunt of the thrashing around. When she finally reached the surface, she felt hands lift her out of the water. Two of the wives rushed to wrap her in towels.

"Keira, are you ok?" Peter said as he held onto her arms.

Kraig pulled Keira from Peter's grip and punched him in the nose. Keira trying to focus was still reeling from being hit in the face and head underwater. Peter, startled by the hit, let go of her, she lost her balance and fell backward into the pool. She fought to untangle her legs from the towels while several hands struggled to grab hold of her. She kicked her feet off the bottom and once again surfaced. It was Diego, who this time lifted her out of the water.

Keira walked dripping wet over to one of the chairs and sat down. She saw Kraig sprawled out on the grass and Peter cursing as Miguel led him around the garage and out of sight.

"Ay Dios! Lady boss esta sangrando! Kraig, come quick, date prisa!" Yelled one of the wives as she grabbed several red, white and blue festive napkins and shoved them against Keira's head.

"Ouch." Keira pulled away and then saw the blood on the paper napkin. She gingerly pressed a fresh couple of napkins against her temple.

Kraig pushed the others aside to get to Keira's side, "Let me see how bad that cut is." He pulled Keira's hand away from the side of her face and looked at the sliced skin as blood drizzled down her face. "Keira, it looks like you need to go to the emergency room to get a couple of stitches."

"No, I'm fine. I will just hold pressure for a little bit. It will stop. Can I search through your freezer for a bag of frozen peas? I got elbowed in the face." Keira mumbled as she slowly walked towards the house. Kraig hurried ahead of her through the back door. He rummaged through the sink cabinet of the small bathroom off the kitchen, pulling out gauze and bandages. "Do you want to lie down for a while or at least till the bleeding stops?"

"No, let me put some antibiotic ointment and a dressing over the cut, or do you have those bandage strips the hospital uses to hold suture lines together? Oh yes, cool, you have some." Keira said as she stood next to Kraig in the tiny bathroom. She let him slowly dress the wound and cover it with a small piece of gauze. He tried to place a larger gauze dressing over the side of her face.

"Geeze, Kraig, it is a cut, not a foot-long incisional line," Keira complained.

Once the dressing was on, they walked back outside, but not before Kraig hugged her to him. Keira thanked the women, who wrapped her in the beach towels. Looking around, she asked where the little one with the dump truck was? Abruptly, everyone stopped what they were doing and frantically scoured the property for the little boy named Mateo. They searched the pool, behind shrubs, bushes, and the entire backyard. A few of the men ran along the river, searching the edge of the water. Walking towards the water, Keira noticed the tether line from the pier to Kraig's fishing boat. The open bow boat was as far away from the dock as the rope would stretch. Keira reached down and tugged on the line. The little boat glided into the pier with a thump. There, curled up on a pile of life jackets, was Mateo sleeping with his thumb in his mouth. His chubby face was pink from the sun's exposure, and his little belly rose and fell with every breath he took. His mom, who had been sitting drinking under one of the umbrellas most of the afternoon, came running towards Keira. She was waving her arms and screaming.

Keira raised her finger to her lips, asking the lady to quiet down. There was no need to startle him; the toddler was resting comfortably. He had never been lost. The adults had selfishly disappeared from him in their want of an afternoon of fun.

Keira had cleaned the tables and removed the little dabs of food left in containers. She set out plastic-wrapped platters of cookies, donuts, and pastries all around the table. Some of the little kids were playing quietly in the shallow end of the pool. They hadn't seen Keira setting out the sugary treats yet. The adults started placing chairs closer to the river to watch the fireworks later in the evening. Kraig lit citronella candles so the area would be mosquito- free where they would be sitting watching the sky light up. Keira's face was throbbing in the heat of the late afternoon.

"Kraig, if you don't mind, I am going to head home. My face is hurting."

"No, please stay. Take a couple of aspirin for the pain. Watch the fireworks with me. Please." Kraig begged.

"I have already taken my quota of pain relievers. I don't want to take away from the celebratory fun of the light show. I need to keep ice on the side of my face. That is hard to do with the temperature outside in the nineties. Happy fourth, oh, I will be training Tina on Tuesday while you get the St Dominic project underway. Talk with you then," Keira said quietly.

After a long sigh, Kraig gave in, knowing there was no persuading Keira into staying. He hugged her and kissed her good evening. Judging by the whistles and hoots, the crew and their families approved of the kiss. Keira waved and retreated to her Jeep.

It wasn't even eight in the evening when Keira got back to the marina parking lot. The sun still had a bit of hang time in the sky before sinking below the horizon. It was too early to feel as tired as she did. It was one very emotional and physically draining day. The side of her face felt a little better since she had been in the air conditioning of her car. But it still was swollen and tender to the touch. Resting her head against the black leather padded steering wheel, she closed her eyes for a second.

"Keira, are you ok?" Micah asked as he yanked her door open.

"Yeah, I think I have a black eye. I am just going to rest here for a few minutes before I go to my boat."

Micah slid his arms under Keira's legs and behind her shoulders and carried her to his car. He gently set her on the passenger's seat. The soft leather seemed to hug her body like a protective cocoon while the air conditioner blasted cool air against her face. Laying her head against the headrest, she waited for the throbbing in her cheek to subside. It was annoying that her left eye kept tearing, but dabbing at the moisture dripping down her face hurt also.

Keira watched as Micah grabbed her backpack from her Jeep. He set it on the floor of his car and climbed in behind the wheel. Even watching him was exhausting for her; she just wanted to close her eyes and sleep a few minutes.

"Where are we going?" Keira mumbled "Where I can keep ice on your eye better."

Keira didn't know how long she had slept, but she woke as the sun started dipping into the gulf. The view was spectacular, with orange and red colors radiating across the water. There was a chill towel draped across the left side of her face and, what the heck? Her head was resting on a pillow across Micah's lap. She didn't want to move; nothing hurt at the moment. His feet were on an ottoman in front of her. She wasn't expecting to wake up to feet. But, she had to admit, they were even sexy-looking. She smiled at that thought.

"Are you going to tell me what happened?"

"We had the annual Fourth of July company picnic at Kraig's house. Some of the guys were playing football. As I was picking up a dump truck by the pool, someone caught a pass and crashed into me. We all fell into the deep end. Scrambling to get out, I got kicked in the head and side of the face a couple of times." Keira said once she had rolled onto her back. She looked at Micah as the last of the sun's rays were shining on his face. Lordy, he was beautiful to look at.

"How did you pick up a dump truck by the pool?"

Giggling and trying to sit up, Keira told him it was a toddler's toy dump truck.

"Hold on Wonder-Woman, you can sit or even stand at the railing to watch the fireworks, but for now, rest your eye. Your wound was starting to bleed again; I applied a new dressing to it."

"Thank you. I must have been sleeping soundly."

"You should have gotten a few stitches. It looks deep."

Promptly at nine-thirty, the fireworks show finally started lighting up the sky over the water. Keira sat with her feet on the ottoman and watched. Micah wrapped his arm around her shoulders and pulled her to rest against his chest. When some of the larger rockets exploded in the night sky, she oohed and aahed at the beautiful colors they displayed. They both laughed at the cheers she made because it was the expected response to a spectacular light show. The sound of crackles from the lesser fireworks could be heard, even on the upper level of Micah's home. Some of the booms rattled the glass hurricane candle holders on the coffee table. From Micah's balcony, she could see children running up and down the beach with extra-long sparklers.

Not wanting to sound ungrateful but curious, Keira asked, "Why did you bring me to your home?"

"Jack's three kids are spending the night on his boat. I saw you put your head on your steering wheel after you parked your jeep. I knew there was no way you were going to get any sleep tonight. When I opened your car door and saw your swollen eye, I brought you here." Micah quietly said as he stared across the gulf.

"Thank you."

Micah tilted her head up to his and kissed her. His kiss was slow and exploring as if he had not a care in the world. His tongue was silky smooth when he slid it along her upper lip. Fireworks continued to light up the night sky as he repositioned his lips against hers and deepened his kisses. Keira felt the caressing motion of his hands as he threaded his fingers through her hair. The massaging of the back of her head and neck was relaxing. If she had been a kitten, she would have purred. Unable to resist the urge, she ran the palm of her hand under his t-shirt along his rib cage. His skin was soft like buttercream leather but oh so firm. Her thumb skimmed in a circular motion around his nipple.

Once again, Micah gathered Keira in his arms and walked across the room to his bed.

"The fireworks?"

"Yeah, there are fireworks, alright," Micah said with a smile.

He pulled a pillow under Keira's head and stretched out on the bed beside her. She was thankful the only lights were from the light show outside the sliding glass doors. Her face still felt swollen. She knew it was probably an ugly purple by now.

"How was the Fun Run Race yesterday?" Keira asked. She rolled on her side and looked at Micah's silhouette against the illuminating backdrop of fireworks.

"I came in second. Some yahoo from Clearwater cut in front of me the last fifty feet of the race. I couldn't get around him." Micah pouted.

Keira laughed at Micah's competitiveness. "Then, the always drunk guys are correct; you are one of the best at jet boat racing," Keira said as she ran her foot up Micah's leg.

A large burst of fireworks flashed across the sky. Keira saw the sudden gleam in Micah's eyes as he pulled her to him. She loved the feel of his lips on her neck, her jaw, and finally coming to rest on her lips. His kisses were sinfully sensual. And then, Micah's hands began their travel from her waist to her bottom side. She could feel the heat from his palms through the material of her sundress. When she touched his leg with her foot, had that triggered his embrace? She didn't know, but the way he kissed her, took her breath away.

Keira rested her hand against the side of Micah's face and stared into his eyes. It was mind boggling to her how the slightest brush of his lips sent her heart racing. She wanted to caress his body, to feel his skin against her. The desire to touch him had been denied by her logic to keep him at arm's length for so long, she was almost afraid she was imagining this moment. Would she soon wake up and poof, she was watching the fireworks from her sailboat? The thought of Jack's kids bouncing around on his boat screaming, made her face hurt. Please, let this not be a dream. I want this piece of heaven, even if it is for a moment.

Tugging on Micah's shirt, she whispered, "I need your shirt off, I want to touch you here." She kissed the material covering his heart and watched as he pulled his T-shirt over his head. He dropped it on the floor next to the bed.

Some kids standing on the beach; lit off some loud fireworks as Micah's shirt hit the floor. Keira wanted to say something funny like what was in your shirt pocket to make that kind of explosion? But the temptation to run her tongue along his collarbone, then trailing it down to his breast, was too strong. She preferred teasing his sensitive skin and enjoyed hearing his very quiet moans.

Keira laughed when Micah slid his hands up her side, tickling her as he pulled her sundress over her head.

"It's good to know where you are ticklish for future times when the need for torture is required." Micah grinned.

Keira hoped he would forget how sensitive her sides were to the touch. Her focus was instead on unbuckling his jeans. She pushed them down his legs with her foot.

"Ok, that is the epitome of laziness. Just because you have a black eye doesn't mean you can't pull my pants off me." Micah laughed.

"Oh, so you are giving me permission to strip you of your clothing?" Keira questioned even though she knew it was a loaded question.

"Baby, you can rip my clothes off me any time you feel like it," Micah whispered as he pressed his mouth over her breast. He pulled her tiny wasp of lace underwear down her legs and dropped it on the floor. Trailing his hand back up the inside of her leg, very gently, he dipped his finger inside the warm moist area between her legs.

Was it the fireworks outside or the unbelievable feeling of Micah's fingers? When he touched her, her senses jammed, and her skin tingled. It was the same when he had kissed her the first time. Her body had felt energized when he had danced with her in Sarasota, at the yacht club. And, she felt nothing but pure excitement when he carried her to his bed. The magical sensations kept bombarding every part of her being.

She knew she was playing with fire. If she opened her heart

completely and Micah stomped on it, what would she do? Women drooled over him all the time; he could have any woman he wanted. Could she handle the consequences if and when he grew tired of her? She bit her lip, knowing she wanted to feel the same magic she had felt when he held her the other times. It had to be even more incredible if he made love to her.

Deep in her heart, she knew she wanted this moment with him. Micah groaned when Keira touched the tip of his shaft with her thumb and ran her fingers down its firmness. She liked knowing she was giving him pleasure. Rubbing her knee on his hip, she slowly slid her leg down his.

"Micah, I want you." Keira whispered as she looked into his eyes. And just as the finale of the Fourth of July fireworks exploded, one after another after another, Micah and Keira set off their own pyrotechnics.

It was a while before either of them spoke. "Keira" was all Micah could say in wonderment.

She was sure her body had exploded and showered back to earth as illuminating faerie dust. Never has she felt as alive as when Micah was making love to her. He was gentle, yet his body demanded and pushed her to heights she had never experienced before. She couldn't remember ever being so perfectly in tune with someone as she was with Micah. It was amazing. And, when he started to move off of her...

"No, stay, don't leave."

Micah rested his forehead against hers. Looking into her eyes, he said, "Babe, I'm too heavy for you."

Keira licked her lips. She was still breathless, "you feel good inside me."

"Some of your crew call you, let's see, um the Hermosa doncella de hielo." Micah smiled. He shifted off of her even though she tried to protest again. Bunching a few pillows under his neck and upper back, he pulled her to his chest.

"I don't understand what you are saying."

Laughing, Micah explained, "one evening after work, some of your crew stopped at The Dive Bar for a drink. One of them called you, 'the hermosa doncella de hielo', the beautiful ice maiden, and several of them agreed."

"What else did they say?"

"Peter was ah, excuse my language, fuckin ass, and Kraig is in love with you. Who is Peter?"

"My ex-husband."

"Care to explain?"

Where to start, Keira thought? Did she need to tell him anything, and should she? No, not really, she thought, but if she asked about his ex-wife, he wouldn't have to say anything either. "Have you ever heard of the Weinsworth mansion?"

"Oh yeah, that place is spectacular. The gardens and pools are out of this world; wait, you designed that landscape, didn't you?"

"I was finishing the last details before the final walk- through to sign off on the contract. My work on the landscape was going to be featured in a couple of design magazines. I was excited because my hard work would now bring me more clients, larger budgets, and greater flexibility in my designs. There was going to be a garden party and fundraiser for some senator running for re-election that weekend. Everything had to be perfect. The owner called me into his office and showed me a panoramic video of the work my crew and I had done on the estate grounds. On the screen, it was even more beautiful than I thought. But then, there on the white sofas between the fragrant flowers and the water cascading into one of the pools was my husband having sex with the owner's wife." Keira shook her head.

"I was the only one who didn't know," she whispered as if it was yesterday. She felt a wall of ice trying to encase her heart once again. Was it remembering Peter's betrayal or the ice stacking up that caused her pain at the moment? "The owner ripped up the payment check for all the hard work my crew and I had done. He suggested I protect myself by contacting my attorney immediately." Keira looked at Micah and realized, "I have guarded myself ever since, so maybe I am the ice maiden."

"My God, Keira, you are no way near an ice maiden. You have

more passion in you than anyone I have ever met." Micah said before his lips descended on Keira's with enough feeling to melt any ice that tried to freeze her heart yet again. He caressed first one of her breasts, then moved to tease the other with his tongue. Sliding his hand off her hip, Micah stroked her until she arched her back. When he felt her hand slowly glide over his already firm manhood, he knew she wanted him to make love to her, once more.

As he slid between her legs, Keira wrapped them around him and urged him deeper inside her. She pulled the band from his hair and watched as his dark locks tumbled around his shoulders. Slowly running her fingers through his long dark curls felt so erotic. She slid her fingernails up and down his back.

"I can't give you pleasure when your nails are driving me crazy," Micah whispered as he grabbed her hands and held them away from her body.

His rhythm was in sync with her as he increased his strokes. Keira felt exquisite. She moved her hips and changed positions with herself on top of him. There was much satisfaction for her to see the intensity on Micah's face when she slid down his shaft. She rose from him only to repeat her downward drive. Moving her pelvis against his, she watched as he took a deep breath. And then, he again repositioned himself over her and buried himself deep within her again and again. An electrical impulse shot through Keira's body.

"I'm sorry, I'm sorry, I've never screamed before." Keira tried to say as she gasped for air. She felt Micah slam inside her one last time before he dropped his head to her neck and intertwined his long fingers with hers.

"I," Micah said between deep breaths, "can confirm...there is no ice... in any of your veins."

Keira gave a small laugh as Micah rolled off her and laid on his back staring at the ceiling. It was late, and she felt hot and sweaty. Sliding out of Micah's bed, the marble tiles felt cold to the bottom of her feet. She slowly found her way to the bathroom and turned on the shower-head facet. Keira hadn't bothered with the light switch. There was just enough light coming in the window from the streetlamp across the street. She didn't want to see her bruised face.

Maybe she should have asked to take a shower, but what would she say? Hey, I feel grimy? About to step into the shower stall, a hand reached in and turned off the spray.

"You can take a shower any day of the week. Come take a bath with me." Micah said as he guided her to the tub that looked like the one in the hotel suite a few weeks ago. It was a deep stand- alone soaker tub. He held out his hand for her as she stepped over the edge and sat down. Expecting him to climb in with her, she watched as he kneeled at the side. Squirting some, what smelled like fresh pine and mountain water scented soap onto a sea sponge, not the fake ones she had seen in the stores, he started to lather soap across her breasts. The bubbles gathered across the water as he cleansed her body. Micah slowly kissed her and slid the soft sea wool down her abdomen and between her legs. No man had ever bathed her before. There was something so sensual about it.

Micah set the sponge in a bowl with other sponges and climbed in behind her, pulling her against his body. Although the water didn't splash over the sides, it did cover her breasts. Lying against him, she rested her head under his chin and closed her eyes. She would have never thought a tough guy like Micah Andreas could be so gentle. He gave soft kisses to her neck while the steamy mist rolled off the water. In the dim light from the window, she could see the silhouette of his hand as he fanned his fingers across her collarbone. Never had she anticipated his romantic nature to cause such excitement to parts of her body she thought were dead.

All too soon, the water began to cool. Micah placed his hands on her hips and pushed her into a standing position. He wrapped her in a bath sheet. It was thick and scented with the fragrance she associated with Micah. Again, he gathered her up in his arms and carried her to his bed.

"Micah, I should go home."

He laid down next to her and rubbed his finger across her lips. Gently he pushed her hair behind her ear and looked at the purple hue around her left eye. She wanted to turn her head, knowing it was swollen and ugly. Instead, he slowly kissed her lips.

"No. I want to hold you through the night and wake up next to you."

Keira stretched her legs alongside him and slid her arm across his chest. From the softness of the pillow, she watched him watching her. "The afternoon you towed the boat with no gas in the fuel tank, one of the drunken women said since you weren't married, she wanted you."

"They were all drunk."

"True." Keira yawned, "Was your wife beautiful?"

"Some say she was. Keira, stop thinking. Close your eyes and sleep." Micah whispered as he pulled the lightweight blanket over her shoulders and kissed her forehead. He watched her eyes slowly close.

Sometime in the middle of the night, Micah rolled onto his stomach, waking Keira up. She hadn't slept with anyone since Peter. And he, as usual, had fallen asleep on his back and snored. It had become so bad she had, on many occasions, taken a blanket and curled up on the sofa in the den. She studied Micah's relaxed features in the almost full moonlight. His thick dark eyelashes were what women tried so hard to acquire with gallons of black lacquer. His hair fanned out almost navy blue against the pale pillow covering. She usually didn't like long hair on guys; it reminded her of all the pony-tailed hippy-type guys in the keys. Their hair was dirty, greasy, and matted against their heads. Micah's hair was healthy-looking, clean, and had the kind of curls she wanted to run her fingers through. She eased out of his bed and walked out to the balcony overlooking the gulf. It was quiet, except for the occasional lapping of water against the sand.

"I dreamed we were diving for sponges. When I woke, you were gone," Micah said as he walked out and leaned against the rail. He looked out over the water.

"No, I'm here." She wanted to say and hopefully in his heart, but instead touched his jaw and kissed his lips. She remembered what Marla had told her about Nicola, his wife. She had demanded Micah give her everything she wanted and then walked out on him for someone else. Did he fear she too would walk away from him? "But it would be better if we were out there," Keira pointed across the gulf, "Sailing towards Mexico."

"You would like that?" Micah asked.

"We would probably talk nonstop and miss Mexico." Keira grinned.

With delight, Keira had noticed Micah had a new habit of picking her up in his arms. Only this time, when he picked her up, he sat down on the patio sofa and held her close. "Did I tell you? You look good in my t-shirt."

"And you look very good naked." Keira grinned.

Micah rested his head against the cushion and laughed. He lifted Keira and eased her down onto his firm shaft. Hearing her sudden intake of air, Micah stopped, "am I hurting you?"

"No"

They made love on Micah's balcony with the moon drifting across the western sky. This time when they headed back to bed, Micah rested his hand on her hip. Keira wondered if his hand placement was to reassure himself she was still there.

There would be no dreams the rest of the night. He would not lose her during his sleep.

It was after nine when Keira woke to Micah's stomach growling. She looked at his gray-blue eyes looking at her.

"I'm starving. Do you want to go to Hellas Restaurant? It is my favorite place to eat."

Keira wasn't familiar with the name of the restaurant. She, too, hadn't eaten since yesterday afternoon and was hungry. "I have never heard of the place. Where is it?"

"Not far up US 19."

Keira was amazed at how much energy Micah had with only a couple of hours of sleep.

"Come on. You told me you do not have to work today. I'm the boss too, so let's go. Micah said as he coaxed her from his bed.

They stopped for coffee and a donut on the way off of the island heading north. It was fun to watch Micah sip his hot coffee as he drove. The smallest of things she usually took for granted were giving her pleasure watching Micah do. Placing bits of the donut in his mouth was somewhat arousing. Interweaving their fingers or resting her hand on his thigh, Keira was starting to understand her parents' constant need to touch each other. Touching Micah gave her a sense of connection with him.

She thought the restaurant was a new establishment, maybe downtown Bradenton, but they continued heading north. Once on US 19, she watched to see if she could spot a billboard with Hellas name plastered across it. They passed the Sea Hut before the Skyway Bridge, so she decided it had to be in St. Pete.

As Micah drove north, she teased him about offering her a new toothbrush in every color this morning so she could brush her teeth before they left. He had explained with a shrug, his sister always forgot something when she came for a visit. It was usually her toothbrush. When Keira gave him a quizzical look, he reassured her no woman had ever slept in his bed at the beach house. He kissed her hand. Was that to shut her up, she wondered with a grin?

While they were at a stoplight in Pinellas Park, Micah answered his cell phone. She knew by his responses it was Marla with marina issues. Before he hung up, he asked if she wanted anything from Hellas. Keira giggled when she heard Marla scream across the car from Micah's cell. He told her he would not buy her one of everything and clicked the phone off. Keira continued to smile when he retorted, Marla loved Greek food.

"So where are we going, Tarpon Springs?" Keira joked.

"Yes, I was craving some good home-cooked Greek food."

As promised, they ate lunch at Hellas, which was a small feast. All the elders seemed to know Micah. They asked about Nina and Daria, Micah's sisters and how Markos was dealing with life. They pointed fingers at Keira, saying she needed to put some meat on Micah's bones. Only one inquired about Keira's black eye and bandage on the side of her face. Micah told the woman, a water accident caused the wound. The elder went into a rant about the harm caused by the sea. Keira wondered if the woman had lost her husband in some sort of boating accident in the ocean.

They spent the afternoon browsing the gift shops and the sponge factory. Micah took pictures of Keira looking at the different sponges and then purchased a few for her to take home. He photographed her eating a gooey dessert and laughing. She took a couple of photos of him talking with some of the sea captains on the dock and selecting a box of decadent pastries for Marla. The scent of the sugary and nutty cakes was heavenly. They couldn't resist taking an extra goodie box of Greek foods home. Micah said they both needed it for a late-night dinner.

The marina had closed for the evening, but the sun had not yet set when Micah parked on his newly paved parking lot. He kissed Keira in the car before she carried her gifts from Micah and the food he bought her for her 'late night dinner' back to her boat. She was relieved he didn't insist on walking with her to the dock. Exhaustion was setting in, and she hadn't wanted to stand around making small talk with Jack. Besides, life would have become unbearable if Micah would have walked her to her boat. The gossip on the docks would run rampant.

"Keira...we have a record to beat." Micah challenged before he laughed and drove away.

What did he mean? It took a minute before she realized what he had implied. She laughed as she walked down the steps. Still smiling, she was relieved as she walked the plank; Jack was not sitting on his boat. It wasn't that she didn't like him; she was beyond exhausted. Could it have been due to the three times Micah made fantastic, madly passionate, extremely magical, love to her? Or the fact, she had eaten enough Greek pastries to cause a carbo-crash into next week. By the time the decadent scented food was shoved in the refrigerator, Keira was past ready for her bunk. It wasn't Micah's extremely comfortable mattress, but she didn't care at this point. She stripped her clothes off and climbed beneath her soft sheets. No, the scent of Micah did not drift to her nose but she would dream of him instead. She planned on changing the dressing to the side of her face and brushing her teeth, but neither happened. By the time her face and brushing her teeth, but neither happened. By the time her head hit the pillow, she was asleep.

Chapter 17
♥♥♥♥♥♥♥♥♥♥♥♥♥

When a holiday landed on a Monday and Tuesday is the back-to-work day, it always seemed like double the work, trying to catch up. Kraig, with blueprints in hand, was starting the St Dominic Care Facility project. Keira was itching to be at the job site but needed to be at the office. It was orientation and training day for Tina, as the new secretary. Of course, if Tina worked out well, Keira would have more time to design landscapes and get her hands dirty at the work sites.

She had put antibiotic ointment on the gash next to her eye. Since it wasn't bleeding any longer, she didn't need the bulky thick pad of a dressing. This morning the bandage wouldn't stick because of the amount of oily antibiotic ointment on her skin. After wiping the greasiness from around the wound, the cut started bleeding again. By the time she got to work, she was frustrated beyond belief. She slapped a small bandage on, for like the umpteenth time in the private bathroom off her office.

Keira was happy when Tina promptly showed up at eight in the morning, ready for work. The problem was, she kept staring at Keira's eye. Orienting Tina was like talking to the wall. Why was her eye such a distraction? Walking into the small kitchenette, Keira started adding a filter and grounds to the pot to make coffee. When she turned around, blam she walked into Tina. Feeling frustrated, Keira finally explained how she got the cut and purple bruise. Finally, Tina settled down and focused. Keira showed her files on post clients, potential clients, and project schedules. Tina walked around the warehouse as Keira pointed out equipment and supplies. Keira explained, the crew order parts. By ten in the morning, Keira was talked out. She couldn't believe her jaws actually hurt. Thank heaven Kraig showed up at eleven.

"Hi Baby, oh man, your face is purple and yellow. I told you, you needed stitches." Kraig said as he hugged Keira.

"Um, Kraig, Tina is here, and I am giving her all the information she needs to know if we are out of the office on job sites," Keira said politely. What she wanted to say was, stop the huggy unprofessional shit in front of the new secretary. "Do you have any words of wisdom to offer?"

"Hi Tina, welcome aboard. But I have to tell you the other guy looks worse. Don't mess with Keira." He turned to Keira and said, "Do you have a copy of the St Dominic blueprint? I left mine at the site. I have some questions if we can make some changes."

Spreading out the design plan across the drafting table, Kraig pointed out changes he thought would work better. It was the makings of a headache by the time they had erased and re-plotted, erased again, and made more adjustments. Finally Kraig was satisfied with all the variations. The blueprint pretty much looked the same as when Keira first designed it. She didn't want to point it out, however; she had worked out all the kinks in the details after walking the potential job site two or three times. It was the last revisions before the presentation that made all the difference. Kraig would learn, not by her embarrassing him, but by seeing her vision. It didn't mean she was always right. There was, in any design, room for new ideas; she knew to keep an open mind when drawing a blueprint.

In the afternoon, Keira took Tina to the job site to see the work in progress. Tina met the crew. Then, it was onto the lawn service sites to view their side of the business. They returned to the office as the guys were returning the mini dozer. A couple of them teased her about her use of make-up. By the end of the day, her head was pounding, and she wanted to rip off the little dressing that tugged on her skin.

It was almost five when Keira got out of her Jeep and headed for her boat. She realized there had not been a moment during the day for her to think about Micah or their unexpected fantastic holiday evening. The marina was like a ghost town. There was no one around. But that was how it usually was after a long or celebratory weekend – dead. Grinning, she thought, gotta let the ole liver detox all the booze before starting all over again next weekend. She was sort of sad, though. It would have been nice to see Micah's car or at least wave to him. Stop, she thought, it would be painful to see him and not kiss him or feel his arms around her. Maybe he didn't want to see her. Stupid me, she thought. He had to stay away from her at the marina, her own rules, remember, idiot.

"Keira, Keira, wait."

Turning around after hearing her name called, she watched Marla walk swiftly across the parking lot.

"The mailman left this in your box. Oh, my, gosh, what happened to your eye?" Marla demanded.

"At my annual Fourth of July party, I got hit in the face in the pool."

"Gee, Petra sacrificed your longtime friendship over a guy. You get hurt at your party. The only one who had a great weekend was Micah."

"Oh, how so?" Keira tried to act casual.

"He may have had race boat problems last week, but someone saw him dancing Friday night at the yacht club, really close with some woman. You know, rich yacht owners have nothing better to do than gossip. He had the Fun Run Race on Saturday, which he loves to do. Sunday, he gave kids banana boat rides all day. Monday, he doesn't show up for work because he spent the day with a mystery woman. He even brought me pastries from my favorite restaurant this morning. He must have had some great sex because he was exceptionally happy today." Marla said as she recounted Micah's weekend on her fingers.

"Isn't he always happy?" Keira questioned. She hoped her face hadn't turned red.

"No, this was more of contentment, more relaxed, kinda happy."

"That is a good thing, and you got pastries, so it's a win-win all around. I will talk to you later," Keira said and walked towards her boat. She didn't want the conversation about Micah to continue. It would be too easy to slip up one word, and Marla would figure out she was with Micah yesterday.

When she opened the galley hatch door, she threw the mail on the chart table, took off her work boots, turned the air conditioner cooler, and flopped down on her bed. So Micah was content. If Marla only knew, making love with Micah was beyond contentment, it was magical. She sat up and remembered the food he bought her for her late-night dinner last night. So tired, she had fallen asleep and never thought about a midnight treat.

Eating every last bit of her Greek feast, she silently thanked Micah. The meal they had eaten on Monday was great. But, all the flavors had mingled after the dish had been reheated and were even better. Looking at the empty plate, she couldn't believe she had eaten all of it. She was pretty sure there were at least two meals she could have gotten out of the large portion sent home with her.

It was late in the evening when she decided to sit out on her deck and read her neglected over-the holiday emails. The sun had gone down and taken the unbearable heat with it.

"Hey Keira, did you have a good weekend?" Jack asked. He had walked out of his cabin and sat down on the stern cushion.

"It was good. How was your weekend with the kids?" Keira asked. She was so thankful it was dark; Jack couldn't see her black eye. If she had to explain the cause one more time, she was going to choke someone.

"I'm glad you went away. The kids were loud. They aren't used to voices traveling on the water."

"Hey, as long as they had fun."

SonicMusicMix – Storm

Keira,
I hope your holiday weekend ended on a better
note than when I last saw you. Petra was quite hurt
when she saw me kiss you. I am sure she blames you

for everything. I tried explaining. I am not sure if she listened to what I was saying. When she has time to cool down, she will realize you walked away from a relationship with me because she matters to you. I feel I damaged your friendship with Petra, and I am sorry for that. Storm

Petra's words, 'I hate you,' and then when she said, 'I don't want your leftovers', kept echoing in Keira's head. She knew Petra was angry and hurt at the same time. She must have felt justified in making those statements. However, her words could never be taken back. It was sad that Petra was willing to terminate their friendship. It especially hurt when they had discussed new relationships recently at the ice cream shop. She was worried about possibly hurting 'a friend' if a relationship would develop. Petra had reassured her if she found love with someone special, her friend would understand.

Keira wondered if she would have told Petra she knew Storm when Petra first told her about signing him on as DJ, would things have been different? Probably, but it wouldn't have been for the better. Petra would have ignored her immediate attraction to Storm or been frustrated for not meeting him first. Keira remembered Petra's instant excitement when she initially met Storm. None of that joy would have happened.

She knew she had done the right thing by keeping quiet. Storm was fun, charming, and witty. They enjoyed talking, but was there a long-term relationship between them? She honestly could say no. He was great, but could she see herself with him when she was eighty? There had been something missing; she didn't know what it was. She just knew she needed something more to hold her attention for the rest of her life. She understood that for sure now, and only hoped Petra's anger wouldn't push Storm away.

Dear Storm,

I wasn't going to email you back. I thought it would be better to let things settle. But then I thought, yes, Petra blames me. But don't don't give up on her. She is a very sweet, passionate, and loving person. She could bring you a lifetime of joy, I am sure. You owe it to yourself to have a bit of that kind of excitement. I wish you much happiness, hugs. Keira

Keira sat looking at her laptop and cried. Her heart ached for the friendship lost between Petra and herself. Together they had shared so many laughs. As for Petra and Storm, their relationship could be over before it started. Setting her computer down, she walked into the galley for a sheet of paper toweling. Why hadn't she bought a box of soft tissues when she was at the store?

PeterFlynn's Friend - Basil

> K lee,
>
> Why are you treating me as if I am a stupid fool? I don't have any accounts here in South Africa. I can't open an account here in Cape Town because my identification cards were stolen. So, that is why I asked you to help me. By depositing the check in your account, you would use my money to buy the things I need. How do I know you wouldn't take the cash Peter gives you and run with it? Because I trust you; I thought we promised to help each other, when in need. We discussed this; I thought I could rely on you. We have built a trusting relationship and love for each other. I can't believe you are giving me giving me a hard time.
>
> I have already made a lot of inquiries. Not one bank here will accept an out-of-country check. I am feeling so disappointed right now. I really can't deal with your negative behavior and the situation that has fallen on me.
>
> I wanted so much for us. While I try to get some sleep, I hope you will think about our relationship. Please, email me when you have come to your

senses and are willing to help the one who loves
and trusts you. Basil

Dear Basil,

I am not treating you like a stupid fool. I was merely trying to give you information on the banks in your area that catered to Americans. I was hoping to speed up the process of getting money so you can replace the broken equipment and your laptop. I am...

Keira decided to delete the note and let him stew a little bit longer. Being a scammer like he was, he had invested his time in her. All the time he spent copying and pasting those words about trust and love. Now, it was all about the money. Let him wait for her response.

JFlounderGig – Jimmy

Dear Keira,

I am sorry you have had to deal with a few of the many scammers out there. However, I am sure you have also met some genuine men looking for love just like you. I have to tell you; a woman contacted me. We talked; I was very leery of her. She wrote to me of all the places she would love to visit. Some of them were exotic. And others were camping in the middle of nowhere -extreme off the grid, shoot and hunt for your dinner kind of stuff. We burned up the nights texting and emailing back and forth. I kept waiting for her to ask for a plane ticket or money to finance these dreamscapes.

One night, she asked for my address. I was fearful she was going to come to Maine and steal everything I owned. She finally confessed, for my birthday she was sending me a plane ticket to visit her. I was shocked. I kept looking at the voucher and thought about it. Then, I feared while I was away, would someone torch my house to take my TV? You know like a setup. So, I hired a house sitter and went for a visit.

There was no scam. She was just looking for a friend. So, I am renting out my house in Maine for the summer. Carolina and I are traveling the country for the next two and a half months in her RV. She bought me a camera and a tablet, so we don't have to deal with paper maps.

Do you think one bottle of Viagra will be enough? Wink, wink. I will email you when I can. Best of luck with your men, Jimmy

Dear Jimmy,

What a fantastic story. I am so happy for you. Is her name actually Carolina? So, you tow adventure-seeking love birds are doing the RV thing for the summer. Well, maybe when the weather turns cool in Maine this fall, you and Carolina can do all the southern states. Although I am south enough to be considered the tropics, it is still FLORIDA. Come for a visit. You know there are drug stores across the country; I am sure, will carry the little blue pill. I am glad you will have the chance to put it to good use!!

I have met some very nice guys. Over the weekend, I realized, one guy will never be any more than a great friend. He is better suited for one of my best friends. She completely fell in love with him the day she met him. However, since I went out with him, she thinks I am a traitor to our friendship. What is sad is, it was a coincidence that we both met him around the same time. Hopefully things will work out.

I wish you all the best with your newfound relationship. Keep me posted. Keira

She sat back and looked up at the stars in the sky. Jimmy deserved a bit of heaven. She was glad for him.

ExtremeLover – Michael

Dear Keira,

I wanted to drop you a quick not. I arrived in Sydney and found my hotel without difficulty. I had meetings with my employer at noon. I was glad I was able to sleep on the plane. We are fourteen hours ahead of Florida. So I am sure you are out enjoying yourself on the perfect Friday night before the Fourth of July.

I have so much regret in my heart for not having the time to see you before I left. Things were so hectic. I hope you will forgive me. I will write when I know more about my surfing and photo sessions. I hope you enjoy the holiday weekend.

All my love, Michael

Dear Keira,

It is Monday. I am sorry I have not had the opportunity to write to you. I have been surfing non-stop, getting familiar with the surfboards I will be photographing. They are the next generation in extreme surfing (40-50 foot waves). The prototype board's speed is phenomenal. It has a super – smooth ride, but it is very temperamental. Maybe the board isn't as unpredictable, as much as I am learning to get used to the immediate response of the slightest shift of my body on the board. I am sure this is all confusing.

I will send pictures when I am not so amateurish looking.   *All my love, Michael*

Dear Michael,

Thank you for writing. I am sure you are exhausted and running on adrenaline. Thank you for trying to describe the surfboard you are testing. It makes me nervous. I know you need to pick up a lot of speed to get into the curl of the wave before it swallows you. I worry about you. However, I am sure you love every minute of it.

I had a great weekend, but you should see the side of my face. At my company's Fourth of July picnic, I was picking up a toy dump truck by the pool, when I got knocked in. Several other people fell in the water on top of me. I ended up getting kicked a couple of times in the head and face. I have a black eye as a result of it.

Because of all the activities over the extended weekend, I didn't see your emails until now. I can't believe you are fourteen hours ahead of me. So right now it is ten in the evening and noon for you. Amazing! Stay safe. I can't wait to see pictures of you surfing.

Love, Keira

Before she sent the email to Sydney, Australia, she looked at the words, love Keira. Love after the weekend had such different meanings. She questioned the love of her friendship with Petra. The love in her heart towards Micah was expanding. In terms of her relationships with Theos and Michael, she had yet to meet them. Did she have feelings for them? Oh, yes, very much, but it would be a test of time and or if they were scammers.

She was excited for Michael. He was back doing what he loved to do – extreme surfing. It was what he lived for, the rush he needed. Part of her didn't understand how someone could love living on the edge of an envelope without any safety net. Of Course, Summer, owner of The Pet Shop, panicked every time she knew Keira was lifting her sails in the wind. And although she never laughed at Summer's fear of sailing, she loved the thrill of it. So was she any different than Michael?

Theseus – Theos

Dear Keira,

It sounded like you had a fun holiday weekend planned. I spent Monday in the city, enjoying my day off. I ate at my favorite restaurant and talked with friends I hadn't seen in a while.

As much as I love my role as captain on the cruise ships, I have an offer to sail a private charter. I would not be quitting the cruise line, just not taking any assignments for a while. I cannot see myself passing up this opportunity.

I started looking at the details. I am working on plotting the course down the Gulf of Mexico and through the Caribbean Sea. How much food is necessary for the journey? When is the best time to go? Will the hurricane season be in full swing on my return journey?

Only you, with the love of the seas that courses through your veins, would understand the beauty of this journey. Tell me, would you take this leap of faith?   *My love, Theos*

Keira stared at the email Theos wrote to her. So, he was going to take on a private charter. Great, was Theos also a scammer? Was he going to get shipwrecked on some tiny atoll in the Caribbean Sea with only thirty minutes left on his phone? Would he ask her to send a ship or, better yet, buy him a helicopter? It was so bizarre; she couldn't rule out the possibility. She had lost all faith in these dating website guys. Of all people, she especially thought that Theos was a very genuine person. She wanted him to be her ship in the night, not to pass each other but to sail together.

Wednesday evening, she came home from work drained. Keira had gotten a request for a design for a new community development out east of Manatee County in Wauchula. Trying to focus when Tina kept asking questions and pointing to what she thought was a better design plan; was driving Keira crazy. Not to mention letting the phone ring and ring and ring until Keira answered it herself. Finally, Keira had taken her framed degrees off the wall and pointed to her name. She explained the client was paying for her signature designs, not Tina's. Kraig had walked in quietly and heard the conversation and did nothing. She was completely pissed off. Wasn't he supposed to back her up? Keira had locked her office door, which she had never done before, and walked, out of the office. It may have been a bit childish, or a lot, but she was the boss. Kraig didn't back her up and Tina didn't know her boundaries as, not only an employee, but a new one at that.

The only highlight of Wednesday was when she parked at the marina; she saw Micah working with his crew to remove a huge, at least fifty-foot yacht from a flatbed semi-truck. It was slow but fascinating to watch as they balanced the boat with the yacht crane and lowered it into the water. She wanted to cheer and hug him for his skills, but their relationship was a secret. No pom-poms, no cartwheels, and no public display of affection; he was focused and didn't know she was watching him, so it didn't matter.

As she walked to her boat, her cell phone rang. "Keira?"

"Is there a problem? Did someone get hurt at the job site?" Keira questioned Kraig. He never called her on her private cell; unless it was an emergency.

"I just wanted to let you know; I discussed with Tina the limits of her position. Until she has her degrees and certificates on the wall, her comments to you were inappropriate. Tina tried the 'I'm so sorry bit.' I let her know I was the wrong person to be apologizing to. I also told her next time I call, the phone better not ring six times and then go to the answering service." Kraig grumbled.

"Thank you. That has solved those problems. How is St Dominic coming along?" Keira asked as she unlocked her galley door.

"The astronomer?"

"No, you goofball, the job site?"

"Oh, I didn't know there could be so many roots in the ground. I actually feared if we pulled up too many, you could find us at the bottom of the aquifer. The mini dozer earned its keep today. I will see you tomorrow. And Keira..."

"I know. Thanks, Kraig. See you tomorrow." Keira smiled. At least some things were consistent.

Keira made a quick tossed salad and a pot of fettuccine Alfredo with shrimp. Carrying a tray out onto her deck, she enjoyed her evening meal watching the trawlers coming in with their hauls.

"Whatcha eating?" Jack asked as he walked the plank to his boat.

"Fettuccine Alfredo with Shrimp, you want some?"

"Oh please, that sounds good right now." Jack almost purred.

Keira went back to her galley and scooped out another bowl of pasta and shrimp. Thank goodness she made extra, she thought. When she brought it out, Micah was talking with Jack. "Micah, would you like a bowl of fettuccine also?" She asked as she handed Jack his steaming bowl.

"That smells so good. Do you have enough?"

As she scooped out yet another heaping bowl of pasta and shrimp, she smiled and thought, there won't be any leftovers tonight. She added extra Parmesan cheese and garlic butter. Walking back out on the deck, she noticed Jack had gotten Micah a beer. She watched him take a sample bite.

"This is to die for; where did you learn to cook like this?" Micah purred.

"My mama, and don't you forget it, capeesh?" Keira said in a very horrible Italian accent. And then she looked at the guys gobbling down her pasta. They were too busy enjoying their impromptu meal to comment on her mutilation of a beautiful language. What a group, a lonesome newly divorced guy, a Greek, eating Italian, and a palm tree hugger. If Brian came to eat, she could add a booze peddler.

When they finished, the guys sat and talked about the new boat in the water. She gathered the dirty bowls and bid them goodnight. While she washed the kettle, she thought about cooking with Micah and then dashed the thought away. Scolding herself for the happily-ever-after thoughts, she watched Micah walk towards the parking lot from her galley window.

Peter Flynn – Basil

> *K Lee,*
> *I can't believe I have not heard back from you. Peter has the check ready for you to pick up, but not one word. I was so in hopes you would realize how much I need you. My love for you is so strong, and it is breaking my heart that you will not help me in my time of need. If you were stranded*

anywhere and needed help, I would be there to help you immediately. Yet here I am, humbly begging for your help.

I figured out I had enough cash left in my rental unit the night of the thievery to sustain me for about a week. Then I don't know what I will do. I have no laptop. I can only use the computers at work. I have no extra funds, so I don't know where I will stay or how I will eat.

With the machinery down, the workers are not on the projected schedule at this point. So, I am in desperate need of the part, like yesterday. The monthly installment of the funding, set up by the Texas bank, will not be deposited into the account that we use to pay the bills until the fifteenth of the month. That is twenty four days from now. I am in a panic. Please, K Lee, help me.

Dear Basil,

I think you need to call your corporate attorney and have him verify who you are with one of the banks there in Cape Town. He can help you get a short-term corporate loan locally until your money comes through. Or he can pull strings and talk with your bank in Texas to advance you on your monthly installment of funds. That is why you have a corporate attorney. K Lee

That should shut him up for a while, she thought.

It was late in the evening. Keira had just climbed into bed when she heard her phone ping. No, she didn't want to extend the warranty on her Jeep. No, she didn't want to give money to some fake charity. She pulled the message up and was about to delete it when she read...

"Thank you for dinner. I miss holding you through the night."

Thursday, Tina had coffee brewing when Keira walked into the office. She tiptoed around Keira and answered the phone on the second ring every time. It rained most of the afternoon, so those who weren't cleaning the warehouse had gone home for the day. Keira handed Tina a stack of files. She asked her to call each of the clients. She explained it was to follow up or check on the quality of the plants and saplings. Kraig pulled up employee files and filtered through for candidates for the foreman position. Keira finished the design and set up a client meeting for the following week. She smiled and thought all they needed were sticks, marshmallows, and three-way harmony singing Kumbaya from her brownie/girl scout days.

After work, she picked up her laundry from George's Laundry Service; she bought groceries and stopped to get her Jeep's engine oil changed. It was almost dark when she got home. By the time she stored her groceries, ate a salad and grilled cheese sandwich, it was time to go to bed.

She once again heard a ping on her phone alerting her to a message coming in. She wondered what Micah would text her tonight...

Peter Flynn – Basil

> K Lee,
> If you don't want to drive up to Peter's office to pick up the check, can you float me a loan for about five thousand dollars? It will help so I can at least eat and continue to live in the rental unit. I am desperate. Please K Lee

Damn, she was so disappointed and irritated with that stupid scammer. She had heard on one of the radio programs that some eastern European men preyed on American women. They felt all Americans were wealthy, and that they were entitled to the money they scammed from women. She couldn't be sure, but it sounded like the radio program's person trying to drum up anger and a debate to boost ratings any way he could get it. She didn't know how he could have scientific proof all scammers were from eastern European countries or if some scammers worked as a group or individually. She had found the cut and paste paragraphs were sometimes identical on several guys' pages. And the sentence structure was not always the proper use of words. It was like some people in America do not understand British humor. Or, commonly used words of the English language in other countries are almost taboo in America.

Friday at work was mass chaos. The blueprint proposal Keira had drawn up earlier in the week, the customer called and needed to see them within the hour. She gave the drawings one last look before she rolled them up, put them in the carrying canister, and rushed out of the office.

"Keira, glad I caught you before you went into your proposal meeting." Kraig pretty much yelled into the phone.

"What's up?"

"You know those roots everywhere? Well, when we were cutting some of them, one lifted the water main fifty feet from where we were working. We had a geyser completely flood the back half acre. I called the county." Kraig explained.

"Wait a minute; they flagged all of the water lines."

"I pointed that out and threatened to call our attorney for damages to the facility grounds. So the county is scrambling to fix it. Hopefully, it will be dry by Monday. I sent the crew home earlier and told them to be prepared to work extra hours next week. They were happy. Oh, and the elders at the facility were cheering us on." Kraig finally said something which even he found funny.

By the time Keira got home, she was completely frustrated. The landscape proposal meeting had been a disaster. The client hadn't liked the layout of the trees. The placement of the shrubs felt awkward to him, and the pool was too "exotic." He did like the patio blocks, though. She crossed out a couple of the trees she had plotted to hide the neighbor's unsightly and trashy garage. Moving the shrubs, Keira erased and made changes to the blueprint. She asked if the owners wanted fast-growing privacy bushes able to block the view of the neighbor's property. Lastly, she sketched in a basic and very boring rectangular pool. It was the ugliest proposal she had ever drawn up, twice, but the client was happy. He eagerly signed the contract and demanded its start date by the end of July. Keira was worried; it would cut into the St Dominic projects' final days. Maybe she could hire some temporary guys to do the grunt work to get the new project started.

After a shower to wash away her irritated mood, Keira dressed in her favorite jean skirt and a gauzy shirt that hugged her chest. Did it make her boobs look bigger? Keira laughed and thought, only if she took a deep breath and pushed her chest out. Shaking her head, she walked over to The Dive Bar for a drink.

"Keira, what are you drinking, your usual?" Brian asked.

"Sure, make it a double." Keira laughed. She chose one of the empty tables and sat down.

Her favorite guitar player was just starting the first set of the night. His music was good and usually packed in a crowd on Friday nights. Tonight, there were not as many people around. Of course, some locals had taken the week after Independence Day, for vacations away from the heat. Brian set her rum runner on the table and sat down.

"So, how is my favorite Jeep driver?"

"Just because I just got the oil changed, don't get any ideas." Keira laughed.

"Hey, I saw your lawyer making a house call last Friday night." Brian grinned.

"And did you see the blonde he was with?" Keira asked, but when Brian looked puzzled, she explained, "KC lives with the famous romance author, Lea Finn. They picked me up to go to the yacht club in Sarasota. KC sings with the band T De Novo. They are good." Keira took a sip of her drink.

"I have heard that."

"Hey Brian, you have some thirsty customers," Marla yelled from the bar.

"Later beauty," Brian winked and walked back to the bar.

Keira closed her eyes and listened to the guitar music. Some of the songs were familiar from when she was growing up in the keys. Her mother had a few favorites that she played over and over on the cassette player. With the memories came a smile. She took another sip of her drink just as Micah extended his hand and asked her to dance...

She stepped into his arms as the guitar player began the first run of notes. The song told the story of a woman listening to a Spanish guitar player. The woman wished the guitar player would play her like his Spanish guitar. The lyrics were beautiful and mostly sang in Spanish. The flow of the words, along with the softness of the strumming, was very sensual.

Micah pulled her close and held her hand next to his heart. He rested his cheek on top of her head. They slowly moved around the dance floor, lost in their own world. Keira felt the electricity flowing from him through her body. His movements matched the rhythm of the song. The words spoken in Spanish reminded Keira of her youth, of listening to romantic Cuban tales on hot steamy nights. The arousing lyrics of the song floated in the air. The freshwater and pine scent Keira associated with Micah, wafted with the evening's humidity. Keira wanted Micah to make love to her as he had on the Fourth of July, fireworks and all.

"Wow," Brian said as he stopped mixing a drink and watched Micah and Keira dance.

"Micah has always been able to dance well," Markos said and turned back to the bar.

"He has made love to her," Marla stated quietly. Markos turned back around and looked at his brother.

"How do you know?" Brian asked.

"Look at how he is holding her. Their bodies are in perfect sync with the music and with each other." Marla smiled. "His body language never spoke to Nicola like that."

"I see the bitch has moved on." Petra spat out as she plopped down on one of the bar stools.

"Petra, we need to talk. Let's step outside." Marla said as she practically hauled Petra off the bar stool and marched towards the door.

"Ooo, Petra is getting schooled." Brian smiled.

"What did she do?" Markos asked, staring at the door.

"Not my story. I'm not talking. I'm the bartender. I listen to bleeding hearts; I'm not the local shrink." Brian laughed shakily, knowing Marla was giving Petra a piece of her mind.

The song blended into another slow and sensual ballad. More couples joined Micah and Keira on the small parquet dance space, dancing in the moonlight. The steamy night seemed to fit the mood of the music and those dancing.

Brian watched as Micah talked to Keira while they danced. He looked relaxed. In all of his nights behind the bar, Brian had seen Micah occasionally dance with other women. Over the last couple of years, he never held any of them like he was holding Keira. And thinking about it, this was the first time he saw Keira let anyone hold her close. He hated it when Marla was right.

"I'll have a vodka martini, please," Marla said as she sat back down on the bar stool in front of Brian.

"You know I will not let you drink a vodka martini."

"Why, not?" Marla asked with a look in her eyes like she could eat someone alive. She drummed her fingernails on the wood bar top.

"Because every time you drink vodka, you verbally abuse someone," Brian stated firmly. He set two beers and a shot of whiskey on a tray and handed it to his new server.

"I already did that a few minutes ago. Now give me the damn martini," Marla demanded.

"Where did Petra go?" Markos asked, looking around the pub.

"Hopefully home to write her apology. Shh, here comes Micah and Keira. Brian, come on, make me a vodka martini, please, just one." Marla pretended to beg.

"Night all," Keira said sadly. She dropped several dollar bills on the bar and walked out.

Once Keira had walked through the doors to the parking lot,

Marla slapped Micah on the arm and said, "So, what did you say to hurt Keira? She looked like she was going to cry."

"I don't know, have a good night? Or, maybe it was just, good night. I did thank her for the dance."

"Geeze, Micah," Marla said as she watched him drink the last of his, now, warm beer.

"Night, Marla," Micah said as he threw some money on the bar and walked out.

Keira grabbed her backpack and locked her cabin door. She walked along her dock to the main pier then turned left to quietly walk the slight incline to Micah's car sitting in the shadow of the boat shed. She watched Micah open the car door for her. He leaned in and kissed her before shutting the door.

"Your loyal friends think I hurt your feelings. Marla even slapped me, but I think she was drinking vodka again." Micah grinned as he drove along Gulf Drive.

Keira laced her fingers with Micah's in the darkened car. She could feel the electricity in the air. The energy she felt radiating through his hand was amazing. "I was so afraid of dancing with you, for fear Marla would catch on."

"I now understand why you don't want to talk with me at the marina."

Keira was confused. The last time Micah brought her to his home, he parked, and they took the elevator to his master bedroom and balcony looking out over the water. Parking his car tonight, he took her hand. They walked past the elevator door and through a side entry door. Keira caught her breath; the foyer was painted solely in white. Ironwork sconces and vivid artwork that looked like original oil paintings of Mediterranean Seascapes decorated the interior walls. If this was the side foyer, she wondered how the formal entrance looked. Micah led her up the stairs to the living area.

With a tap of his finger, lights lit up the kitchen to the right. Keira could see across the open kitchen, the dining room, and living room.

"Do you have someone living here?" Keira asked. She could hear what sounded like soft music playing somewhere.

"I forgot about the music. My niece was here visiting. She decided I needed more music in my life. She set up the sound system to start playing Greek love songs late in the evening. I am usually asleep by this time of the night and seldom hear it." Micah apologized as he walked to a panel to turn off the piped-in music.

"Don't turn it off. I like it, but tell me the words in English."

"This song is asking if the love is over before it ever started." Micah grinned.

As they walked through Micah's house, Keira was stunned by how beautiful it was. The artwork on the walls didn't look like prints. The grouping of sofas, she figured, was top of the line. They were designed for comfort and relaxing, not stuffy, hard to sit on, kind. The marble floors throughout the house were not ceramic. Micah hadn't spared any expense. He used a remote control to open the floor-to-ceiling drapes that had wrapped the living room in a cloud of white. Once the billowy material had recessed, the pool sparkled as indirect lighting bounced off the water.

"Would you like to take a walk on the beach or swim?"

"Oh, I would love to swim, but I didn't bring a bathing suit."

With the click of the remote, privacy drapes slid down the sidewalls of the pool cage. Micah clicked the lights off throughout the house and dimmed the pool lights. He looked at Keira and grinned, "Did I ever tell you I was the baby of the family?" He lifted Keira in his arms and threw her in the pool. Micah then leaped and curled into a cannonball position for a huge splash, next to her. They both surfaced sputtering and laughing. "I don't think my pool ever gets this much excitement."

"Oh, we will have to fix that." Keira pushed a wave of water towards Micah with her arm and then dove under when he tried to splash her. Although the water was warm, it was still refreshing. She grew up in Florida and understood, there is no such thing as cold water. They frolicked and swam the length of Mica's pool a couple of times. When she began to tire, she came up next to him; and slid her hands along his jaw. His lips were soft and so inviting. Was it too soon to rip his clothing from his incredible, muscled in all the right places, body? She unfortunately found out patience was not one of her virtues. It was very difficult to unbutton his shirt in the water. Yet she was able to release the buckle from his jeans; with ease. Go figure, she thought.

"Ha, you thought you could pull my pants down in the water with your toes. Not so easy, is it?" Micah said as he pulled Keira's gauze blouse over her head. Next came off were her bra, jean skirt, and tiny thong. The pile of soggy clothes grew on the pool deck, even though he still had on his jeans. Giving in, he helped Keira pull them down his legs and then off.

"I didn't think I would have to work so hard just to touch you," Keira whispered innocently and then slid her fingers around Micah's firm shaft. Her thumb caressed the sensitive tip. She got so much pleasure out of giving him pleasure. And by the look on Micah's face, he was enjoying her indulgence.

To Keira's surprise; Micah lifted her out of the water and set her on the tiled deck. Even though the pool water was warm and the night air was even, warmer; she felt exposed lying on the side of the pool. Micah's hands caressed her abdomen and breast while he trailed kisses up the inside of her leg. She arched her back when his tongue dipped inside her. Once again, she felt alive and wanted him to make love to her.

She smiled. In college, she remembered some women complained of men and their need for immediate gratification. Women wanted to be played with, long drawn out foreplay. Right now, she was impatient. Heck with the game playing, she wanted his body touching hers. Threading her fingers through his damp hair, she didn't want his neighbors to hear her scream. But what he was doing to her body was more than she could handle.

"Micah"

He lifted her off the pool deck and taking his time, slid her down his chest and abdomen. His skin was wet and silky smooth as he slowly eased inside her. The sensation was exquisite. With a sigh, Keira wrapped her legs around his back and settled her head on his shoulder. Kissing his neck, she wanted to hold him to her and enjoy the feeling.

Micah's hands leisurely lifted her and gently pulled her down on top of him, again and again. The intensity of his thrusts increased. He tilted his hips and ground deeper against her pelvis. Her hands were shaking as she pressed her fingers deep into the muscles of Micah's shoulders. With shallow breaths, Keira cried out. She climaxed with such force, the shock waves vibrated through her body. She squeezed her legs against his back as she felt him shudder. His breathing was erratic, and his heart was thumping almost out of his chest. His arms wrapped around her and held her close.

Micah whispered, "Just when I thought you had given me everything, you gave me more."

Keira loved how Micah held her loosely and walked around the shallow end of his pool. It was as if Micah was deliberately dancing her to the soft swishing music of the water. Was he aware he was creating a delicate symphony of sounds while he carried her; probably not. His intimate persona was far different than the characteristics of his personality he presented to others. Her heart did a flip flop knowing his soft side, others did not. Just holding her with the warm water caressing her exhausted body was relaxing. She rested her head on Micah's shoulder.

"It's late, my little dolphin; how about we put the clothes in the dryer. I want you to sleep in my arms." Micah whispered against Keira's ear, his hands stroking her back.

Sometime in the wee hours of the morning, the sun had yet to blush the sky, Keira woke. Micah slept on his side, his beautiful face relaxed. Deciding the rocking of her boat must lull and keep her asleep all during the night. A solid bed on terra firma took time to get used to.

Her body craved Micah's touch. She kissed his shoulder and nuzzled against him. The clean smell of chlorine and the scent of Micah relaxed her thoughts. She kissed his chest. It was then; he nudged her on her back and fulfilled her craving. There was no body slamming, orgasmic screams, just his mind-melting thrusts. She loved that he knew where to touch and trigger her kaleidoscope of feelings. Her last thoughts were of faerie dust drifting down over her in every color of the rainbow and Micah's whispers of love.

Keira woke to the smell of bacon and coffee. Micah was no longer asleep next to her. From his bed, she could see the vividly blue water of the gulf with small waves caressing the shoreline. A brown pelican was floating out near the no wake buoy, and seagulls cried in the distance. Oh, it would be fantastic to wake up every morning to Micah and this view. She hugged one of his pillows. And then she remembered her clothes were in the dryer. Looking around, she found a t-shirt of Micah's and slipped it over her head. The air conditioner kept the marble flooring cool, even a little bit cold beneath her feet. It took a minute to find her way down the stairs to the kitchen.

Her heart squeezed in her chest when she saw Micah standing at the stove cooking in a pair of sports shorts and nothing more. If her toes weren't so chilled, they would have curled.

"Ah, my sleeping beauty is finally awake. I thought you were going to sleep the day away." Micah said as he set the spatula down. He poured coffee in a mug and came to stand in front of her.

"Good morning," Keira said as she planted a kiss on his naked chest.

After eating an omelet of bacon and feta cheese, Micah apologized for not having cooked olives in it. He had eaten them for breakfast the day before.

"I was just happy you made a pot of coffee, thank you. I was not expecting a full meal. Zac Karas may want to hire you as his breakfast chef." Keira laughed.

"Keira, I took your clothes out of the dryer. Um, you know that top you wore here? Something happened to it." Micah tried to explain as he held her favorite, now shrunken, gauze blouse up.

"Oh my, gosh, I forgot when we threw all the clothes in last night; to keep the top out to drip dry. It is gauze. It shrinks to, well, let see, toddler size?" Keira tried to laugh even though she wanted to cry. It was her fault for not thinking, but she was preoccupied with Micah. Shrinkage of clothing had not been on her mind, body parts, maybe, clothing, nope. She walked over to where her backpack sat on the floor and rummaged through it. She found a t- shirt with her company logo across the back, but really didn't want to think about work this morning. At the bottom was a t-shirt with palm trees and a setting sun. That would be perfect for a Saturday morning.

As they drove back to the marina, Micah explained the new owner of the vessel they launched yesterday was picking up his yacht at noon. Remembering the urgency of Micah's crew to get the huge boat in the water two evenings before, she confessed she had watched the process. She asked him to drop her off at the corner; so their secret time together would remain private.

"Thank you for last night. All I wanted was a short walk on the beach in the moonlight with you. You gave me so much more." Keira smiled as she got out of Micah's car.

Walking along the street, she realized she enjoyed the secrecy they shared. There was something intriguing about their clandestine relationship. There was no speculation or gossip from the people around the pub and marina. She liked that.

Keira stood on the dock before climbing aboard her boat and talked with Jack. It was hot with the sun beating down on her head. She had dropped her backpack down onto the floor by the wheel. He was telling her about the woman he brought to his boat last night. She got seasick from the waves of one of the trawlers. Keira felt sort of bad for the unknown woman, but at the same time, it was funny in a sick sort of way. She remarked, Marla got seasick and wouldn't even walk on the docks. They were laughing at the irony of that when chaos broke out.

Jack whispered to Keira not to move. She looked up to see men scattered all around them in black uniforms and high-powered rifles aimed at her. Two armored swat vans were parked, by the steps.

"Keira St Cloud, stay where you are. Put your arms up. You, next to her, move away from her."

"Keira St Cloud, you are under arrest for trafficking illegal drugs into American waters." Another man shouted at her as he walked towards the docks.

"I am Nathan Jack, undercover narcotics division with the local police department. I have been keeping surveillance on this boat and have no evidence of trafficking or illegal drugs." Jack hollered, his arms still held up towards the sky.

Keira swung her head around and looked at Jack. Under-cover, she thought. He told her he was an administrator for one of the local hospitals. She thought she was going to cry. He lied to her. Why would he lie unless he was trying to catch her on her boat with drugs? Why? She had never done drugs. Her sailboat had been boarded and inspected time and time again. It was all so surreal. She saw Micah running across the parking lot. And Brian could be seen running towards the docks from the pub. People were starting to gather to see the commotion. She could feel sweat dripping down her back. Her mouth was dry. Don't panic, don't panic, she chanted in her head.

"I have cameras on each lamp post. There is no coverage of anything illegal on these docks. Everything is time and date-stamped." Micah yelled as he approached from the long dock. The crowd had parted to let him through.

"Micah Andreas, stay clear," yelled one of the swat team.

"You have no evidence. Keira's boat hasn't left its' berth in almost a month. I have proof." Micah yelled.

Yanking Keira from the dock, she almost cried out as one of the men in black jammed cuffs around her wrists. She felt someone from behind shove her head down as they placed her in the back of the black suburban with blacked-out windows. She yelled to Brian, "Call KC."

Chapter 18
♥♥♥♥♥♥♥♥♥♥♥♥♥

Keira was ushered into a holding cell. There wasn't much to see, just metal barred walls and a cold metal bench. Although she was alone, the place smelled of human waste and sweat. She sat down gingerly, not wanting to disturb the dirt mites, molds, and fungus. It sounded weird but this was one place she didn't want to leave a 'footprint'. She looked at her ink stained finger-tips.

Thinking about all that happened in the last several hours, she was having a difficult time comprehending it all. Why had Micah placed surveillance cameras on the light posts? The only obvious reason was to protect his business. He wanted to make sure if someone brought in drugs from out of the country, his business wouldn't be a part of it. And Jack, he had said he was an administrator of a hospital. Thinking back, he never said which hospital. She just assumed it was down the street in Bradenton. Smiling sadly, what happens when someone assumes anything? It makes an ass out of u and me, ass-u-me. Would she ever learn?

It was a big shock when Jack said he was Nathan Jack and part of the narcotics team. Did the Bradenton Beach Police Department put him on surveillance? Had they suspected she was hauling drugs? He had pointed to her mast. Had he illegally put an observation sensor up to view her boat for any activity such as bringing drugs on board? She hadn't had a clue. It hurt to know she was targeted, not only by the police but Micah and whatever his name was, Jack. All because her boat had at one time been a smuggling boat.

Staring at the wall, she wondered yet again. How could Micah make love to her, make breakfast for her and then believe she might have possibly been a drug smuggler? Did he develop a fake relationship with her to catch any possible information given to him as a lover? Her mind kept circling around and around as if trying to find some clue she might have missed. She couldn't think anymore. Her brains were scrambled.

A very large woman was brought in. She was loud and indignant. Her ranting made Keira's ears hurt. The lady, na, the large thing, she was no lady, paced back and forth. She screamed at the door. She cursed like a motha fucka, something a couple of the guys at work always said. It made Keira smile. She wore an exceptionally tight filthy gray skirt; it might have been white at one time, but not anymore. And a purple shirt that gapped at her breasts. Keira thought of her gauze top that Micah had shrunk in the dryer. She could have worn it four sizes too small, and maybe just maybe, her boobs would have looked gigantic in it. She almost laughed out loud at the thought. It was so sad she had to entertain herself that way. The woman's flip-flop-clad feet were almost dirtier than the holes they dug for Keira's beloved palm trees.

"What the fuck are ya'll lookin at?"

"The color purple looks nice on you."

"So, ya are the fuckin fashin poleleec?"

Keira decided; no more conversation. She didn't want to get beat up. She already had one black eye. And now that it was almost gone, she didn't need another.

"What the fuck were ya'll busted fur?"

Keira stared at the floor. What should she answer, DUI? No, there was no alcohol on her breath. She couldn't say prostitution; the thing would want to know who her pimp was or where her turf was. That wouldn't work. If she mentioned drugs, busty might badger her to learn her dealer's name, OR maybe she was an undercover cop planted in the cell to try and get a confession out of her. Oh lord; in the last couple of hours, she had become paranoid along with drug smuggler. Could she add that to her resume; paranoid, drug mule, tree hugger, and hole digger? Hmm, do jail chain-gangs dig holes for cemeteries like in the old days? Keira decided they had replaced them with backhoe equipment, dang no job security there. Wait, she owned a mini-dozer; would that work?

Still looking at the floor, Keira said, "I killed my husband and mother-in-law and was trying to slip out of the country with my three kids on a fishing trawler."

"I don't belief dat fo one fuckin minute."

Keira narrowed her eyes like in the movies, plastered a sardonic smile on her face, and slowly looked the women in the eyes and said, "Good."

That ended that conversation. The woman sat down as far away from Keira as humanly possible. It wasn't long after that the jail guard came and removed the purple shirt person. Keira wondered if her far-fetched idea was correct; the woman was taken out of the holding cell because she couldn't get a confession on drug smuggling from her. When the cell door clicked shut, she heard the woman telling the guard, 'dat skinny bitch murdered her husband. Thank you for gettin me outa dere.' Keira could hear the offensive chick all the way down the hall.

Once again, Keira was alone, and her thoughts were back in overdrive. It scared the heck out of her.She thought of Micah and what his hands were able to do to her body. Wait, he betrayed her. She had to stop thinking of him. His sole purpose was to protect his business. What if he was only close to her to find out if, in fact, she was a drug smuggler? The same with Jack whatever his name was. He might have been newly divorced, but he was on the job to see when the drugs came in. She never saw him during the day; he might have worked the night shift all along. And the boat was planted next to hers. She never saw him go to The Dive Bar because he was on duty. Yet, he and Micah drank beer on his boat. Maybe, his beer was water or a soda. Was the swat with the FBI, the DEA, ATF, or the local police? But they didn't seem aware of Jack when he identified himself. Of course, they may not have wanted to blow his cover with the gathering that had shown up on the docks. Her thoughts whirled around and around. She felt like she was being sucked down into an abyss of unanswered questions and despair.

A lock clicked. A guard's footsteps echoed as he walked down the hall.

"Keira St Cloud"

Keira stood as the guard slid the door open and escorted her out of the cell. He guided her down the hall and into another room on the other side of the locked door. For a few minutes, she stood looking at the grey walled room, with a table and two chairs in the middle. She felt like vomiting, but she hadn't eaten anything since Micah had made her breakfast, what seemed like a lifetime ago.

Finally, a side door opened, and KC Bradlow walked in.

"Keira, are you ok?" He asked as he sat down across from her.

All she could do was shake her head up and down.

"They are working on your paperwork right now. Once finished, we can leave." KC said as he searched her eyes.

"Did you bond me out?" Keira asked in a weak voice.

"No, the charges were dropped. They didn't have any evidence against you. I pulled a couple of strings, and the judge demanded the charges be removed immediately." KC grinned.

"May I ask what strings did you pull?" Keira inquired, looking at KC's button-down shirt that was open at his neck.

KC pursed his lips and exhaled, "Normally, with the charges connected to your name, you stay in jail until the judge sees you on Monday. If there are a bunch of arrests, it is when they get to your case. However, the judge owed me a favor and came in on her day off to review the charges. Since she could find nothing to hold you, the charges had to be dismissed. And of course, I reminded her, your lawn service maintains her beautifully landscaped yard. Incidentally, she ran a background check on you and your business before she ever signed a contract with your company." KC said as he sat back on the metal chair.

Once inside the butter-soft leather interior of KC's BMW, he asked if she wanted to go back to the marina.

"No, I think I will go to the office. I secretly installed a Murphy bed and bathroom in my office area for when there is a hurricane. Living on a boat, I would need somewhere off the island to evacuate to." Keira said, happy to be leaving the county jail and downtown Bradenton.

"No way am I taking you there. Lea would skin me alive if she knew you were sleeping on a Murphy bed when we have plenty of bedrooms for you to sleep in. You will stay with us until you decide what you are going to do. Oh, your backpack is in the back seat. I picked it up when I looked over the surveillance videos from the marina. I guess the swat guys didn't see it behind the seat." KC said as his car breezed down Manatee Avenue.

"Thank you. KC, I am not going to put you out, especially after all that you have done for me on your day off." Keira reached to grab her scruffy backpack from the back seat and burst out laughing.

"That is a backseat for tiny people. No person over four feet could fit back there."

"No doubt about that, but remember, before you look down your nose at my car, you haven't gotten my fees yet, have you?" KC grinned.

Keira was amazed at how beautifully Lea had decorated KC's house. The enclosed pool and patio were private but open. The bar and grilling area looked staged for a high-end photo shoot for Sarasota magazine. The kitchen granite countertop and cooking area was a chef's dream kitchen.

Lea talked excitedly with Keira as they cut lettuce, carrots, celery, and tomatoes for a tossed salad and set the dining room table for dinner. Lea had explained, Kristi and Zac had been invited previously and were on their way. She pushed for Keira to head upstairs to shower and change into one of the many outfits she left on the bed for Keira to wear.

When Keira walked back into the kitchen, KC had just set the swordfish and steaks on the hot grill. Kristi and Zac arrived shortly afterwards with Cuban rice and black beans, with sour cream and onions, and a dessert fit for the gods.

While they all dined on the feast in front of them, the talk with Keira was nonstop. Kristi was proud of KC for getting the charges dropped so quickly.

"They charged you, but I can't believe they didn't have any hard conclusive evidence against you," Kristi said before she continued with about a thousand more questions for Keira.

.   When Kristi took a bite of food, Zac started his round of questions about Keira's sailboat and hull identification numbers.

"I'm sorry, I'm sure you have rehashed this in your mind but, why didn't the DEA look back at their records? Your boat has been out of the business for a long time. The harbor patrol has searched your boat every chance they got." Zac ranted.

Lea finally asked the question Keira had most dreaded, 'why did Micah have surveillance cameras on the light posts?' All eyes turned to her.

"I don't know," Keira whispered.

It was KC who was noticeably quiet. He hadn't voiced his opinion, and no one seemed concerned. He poured wine, removed plates, and carried Holly, the Persian kitty, over to Keira to hold. But he never asked a question nor made his opinion heard.

After Zac and Kristi left for home, Lea handed Keira a glass of wine. "This will help you to sleep tonight when your mind refuses to shut down."

Keira looked through the two-story palladium windows towards the canal that ran beyond KC's yard. It was a beautiful setting with the evening's orange sky and the dark silhouette of the palm trees. Twinkle lights wrapped around each tree, creating an illusion of a magical forest. Keira smiled sadly at the beauty of KC and Lea's backyard.

Keira saw KC sit down at the piano. He ran his fingers up and down the ivory and ebony keys bringing the baby grand piano to life. The living room had the perfect amount of furniture and wall space for an ideal acoustic balance.

"I bet you never tire of KC's piano playing."

"Actually, at times, I can tell what mood he is in by the way he plays. His fingers have caressed the keys like new falling snow in winter. He has played blues and jazz as if it was a hot and steamy night in New Orleans. There is no doubt you feel you were sitting right there on Bourbon Street listening to him play. My sister and brother-in-law were visiting us from San Juan Island. I think she got pregnant that night after they listened to his music. Tonight he is upset and frustrated. His fingers are almost quarreling with the keys."

"I'm sorry. I should have encouraged KC to take me back to my boat. I am disrupting your life."

"No, Keira. He cares very much about you. Zac, Kristi, we all have come to love you."

Lea began to tell Keira the story of how Kia protected her when they first started dating. She laughed when she explained how he conned her into decorating his home. However, he left out one detail, why he wanted the house furnished. It was his turn to host his family of eighteen, Christmas Eve dinner. She was happy when Keira smiled. Lea finished her story by pointing out the nearly invisible scar that ran down the side of her face. The accident that caused that scar, her lost memory, and the possibility of never being able to give him children, through it all, he loved and stuck with her even in her lowest moments.

"Don't give up on Micah. Seeing him with you the other night, he loves you. Give him a chance to explain." Lea whispered.

With tears sliding down her face, Keira thanks Lea for telling her how she and KC started their relationship. "I think I will try and get some sleep. Thank you for dinner and for letting me wear your beautiful clothes. Good night." Keira whispered.

"Keira, I bought those clothes for you. You needed a little pick-me-up right about now. I want you to keep them." Lea said as she hugged Keira.

"Thank you," Keira whispered as she felt Lea's arms curl around her shoulders.

Keira chose the farthest bedroom in the house to sleep in. The soft coral color paint on the walls was so comforting, Keira thought as she walked around the room. There were touches of blue in the pillows on the bed and art on the walls. Lea's hand was in the color palette and décor of the room. Keira slowly closed the door. She was afraid they would hear her cry during the night. Puzzled, she wasn't sure what time it was but it had to be late. Hopefully the wine she drank earlier would help her sleep.

Later, wrapped up in a blanket and curled in a ball on the queen-size bed, Keira was so cold her fingers were pale blue. She wanted to sleep so badly, but her body was shaking. Not long after that, she threw back the comforter and ran to the bathroom, vomiting everything she ate for dinner. Hot tears burned her eyes. Fearful she would damage the lavish pillows on the bed with her tears, she draped a towel over them. The stars continued to move across the night sky; while she prayed for rest. Her body hiccupped and shuddered when her thought drifted to the molten current between herself and Micah every time they touched. She finally exhausted herself enough to sleep without dreams.

Sunday, KC and Lea had the boat ready when Keira finally woke up. With a cup of coffee shoved in her hand, they pulled her off their dock and onto KC's cabin cruiser. Thank goodness she had dressed in one of the cute bathing suits and beach cover-ups Lea had bought her. KC maneuvered his boat out of the canal bordering elegant homes and into the open water; he and Lea told Keira about John, their next-door neighbor.

"We didn't mean to be rude, but if John walked across the lawn for a chat, it would have been Wednesday before you could have gotten away from him. He is a very nice guy and would do anything for you, but he has the gift of gab." KC laughed.

"He won't stop talking. Nope, not even if you tell him you are late for an appointment. He will continue talking without taking a breath. I don't know how he does it." Lea said, shaking her head.

Keira laughed. KC pointed out where he almost drowned Lea, when they first met. In retaliation, Lea dropped ice cubes down KC's swim shorts. He jumped around the deck, water and ice dripping down his legs as Keira grabbed the wheel. It was one of those beautiful days to be out on the smooth-as-glass water. She loved driving KC's boat; it handled well as she cut across the bay towards the small island. She even laughed when she turned around to see KC and Lea sitting at the back of the boat, enjoying the view.

"By Jove, my dear Lovey, I think we found an excellent chauffeur." KC pointed out, in a horrible English accent. He and Lea tapped their red plastic cups together and kissed. They reminded Keira of Mr. and Mrs. Howell from the old reruns of Gilligan's Island.

When Keira neared Egmont Key, she turned the boat to head away from the beach. KC climbed to the front of the bow to throw off the front anchor. Once it was embedded in the sand, he threw a second anchor from the stern. The practice of throwing two anchors prevented his boat from drifting into other vessels if the wind picked up or currents shifted.

For a while, Lea and Keira floated on colorful rafts in the shallow water. KC scrubbed the water-line of the hull of debris and slime collected on the ride across the bay. Keira explained how she anchored offshore, downed in her scuba gear and scraped the barnacles off the bottom of her boat every couple of months.

"Do you realize you are murdering relatives of lobsters?" Lea informed Keira.

"And how does she know this?" Keira asked KC, in which he shrugged, and they laughed.

Lea almost fell off the raft while Keira told them about her cellmate in the jail. She didn't use the exact colorful language of the woman, but they got the hint. Keira put her hands on her hips and strutted through the shallow water like a boss, quoting what the f were ya'll busted fur? Explaining the dilemma of what to tell the other jailed woman became paramount. DUI was out of the question when there was no smell of booze. Being put in jail for prostitution couldn't be backed up. The busty chick bursting out at the seams probably knew all the pimps within a fifty-mile radius.

Keira asked KC if the DA or the police ever planted undercover cops in the cells to try and get a confession out of a person for drug dealing or trafficking. KC shrugged his shoulders and said he didn't know. Had she become suspicious, wondering if he really didn't know or wasn't telling?

To finish her story, and probably the best part was telling how she tried to convince the filthy feet person; she had murdered her husband, mother-in-law, and was fleeing the country on a fishing trawler with her three children. The woman didn't believe her. But, funny how she stayed far away from her until the jail guard removed her from the cell. Keira burst out laughing when she looked at Lea; her mouth was agape.

"I guess I don't have to worry about you in jail. Dang Keira, you are good." KC said before continuing with his scrubbing.

"Do you mind if I use that in a story line for my next book?" Lea grinned.

Sitting on the beach, Keira and Lea pushed sand with their feet into small mounds in front of them; just because they could. They chit chatted about insignificant stuff. KC brought two bottles of water for them after their pond digging expedition. He sat down between them.

"Keira, I need to tell you. I have talked to Micah a couple of times since your arrest. Wait, hear me out. He told me he placed the security cams because he wanted to protect you. He had heard during Memorial Day weekend that there was a possibility of smugglers bringing in drugs over the next couple of months, specifically to his area. He knew the DEA and the Bradenton Beach police kept an eye on your boat. He wanted to prove you were not a drug runner. Micah told me Nathan Jack is really on the undercover narcotics team. You see, he had gotten shot up pretty badly a while back. He was on limited duty, so Micah worked out a deal with Nathan's commander and paid him out of his own pocket. The deal was to protect you at night. He even hired a Mr. Benson on Sundays to keep a watch for anything suspicious.

"Micah pleaded with me to let him know if you were ok. Then, when your case was thrown out, he called me again, begging me to let him know where you were. Keira, he begged. Men like Micah don't beg. I let him know I couldn't give out that information without your consent. I know he has called Kraig. Kraig called me also. I told him you would be in touch. So, you will have to do some damage control there. I know you are hurt, and understandably so. But I also believe what Micah has told me to be true." KC explained, looking Keira in the eye.

She had spent so much time rehashing the sequence of events

from the day before. Sometime in the middle of the night, probably between her inability to get warm and vomiting, Keira realized it was over. All of it, she needed to restore her life to her carefree, enjoy life, hug a palm tree days. Her physical and mental health depended on it.

"Thank you, KC. I appreciate you telling me all of this. Answer one question for me, please. What does KC stand for?" Keira looked at KC and grinned.

"Wow, I wasn't expecting that question; after all I have just told you." KC shook his head. "Kai Christoffer. My mother's maiden name was Christoff. It was a mouthful to yell across the neighborhood, Kevin, Keith, Kai Christoffer, Kristianna Grace, come home, now. Our name-calling got shortened to Kevin, Keith, KC, and Kristi, get home. Zac then shortened Kristi to Kris, and Lea shortened my name to Kai. The family Thanksgiving Day dinner was unforgiving with the name shortening saga, but no one died, so all is well." KC laughed.

"Now that we have that solved. I have decided I am going to take a sailing vacation. I need some alone time to clear my head. I am going to sail to the keys to see my parents. It has been a while since my last visit, and it would be fun to surprise them. Yes, I will call Kraig and let him know I will pay the bills remotely since that was one thing that I held back on when I gave him the partnership. I need to step back a bit from Micah. Being around him is like a jolt of caffeine." She looked Lea in the eye when she mentioned the play on words describing Micah's presence around her. Lea would understand.

"Please, I don't want any of them to know where I am going. I don't want my parents bombarded with calls looking for me. I trust you both, and you know I have trust issues." Keira bit her lip. It was the first time in a while she felt like smiling.

"When are you planning on leaving?" Lea asked.

"I was thinking about tomorrow early before the tide goes out," Keira stated, feeling stronger by the minute.

"Then Kai, we should head home so Keira and I can go buy enough groceries to get her to Key West."

It was early Monday morning; the sky was beginning to turn pink when Keira, Lea, and KC carried her groceries and new clothes down the dock to her boat. Keira noticed immediately, Jack's boat was gone. She opened the cabin door, hoping to set the bags on the chart table and get underway before being seen on Micah's security cameras. But Lea wanted to see inside Keira's sailboat. She looked around the galley; peeked inside Keira's bow bunk at her bed, the bathroom, and even the storage room under the main deck.

"It is all done in whites and primary colors, very rich- looking. I love your sleeping quarters, so romantic; I would sleep there any day." Lea gushed. "Oh, I stepped on this envelope on the floor. I'm sorry." Lea said as she reached down to pick up the white piece of mail from the wood flooring.

"Lea, Keira is only going on vacation, not around the world. We will go sailing with her in a couple of weeks." KC said as he tugged on Lea's hand.

Keira hugged them both, "Thank you for everything you have done for me. I appreciate it and love you both. Yes, Lea, I will text you my locations along the way." Keira grinned.

As they stood on the pier, Keira untied the lines and pushed off from the dock. She maneuvered her boat out of its berth and into the waterway. The groceries could wait until she made it to the gulf waters and set sail. It was crucial to her to be as far as possible from the marina. She needed time to think, and the open water gave her the freedom and space to do just that. The winds were light, and the tide was going out. It was going to be a good day to sail.

She hoisted her sails, watching the top batten of the mainsail. The jib was taut; she then set her course on the wheel computer. It was time to put away her groceries and place in her wardrobe cabinet, her beautiful new clothing. Each item was chic and tasteful, like Lea. Keira decided she would be 'stylin' in the keys!

As she sat with a glass of white wine and orange juice at nine-thirty on a Monday morning, she laughed. Hey, she was on vacation for the first time in, like forever. It felt good.

She thought back to the conversation she had with Kraig the day before. It was intense. He was shocked when he learned from Micah she had been arrested and mad that she hadn't bothered to call him first. He accused her of being blinded by Micah, his money and looks, and not seeing his own love for her. He was concerned with the possibility of bad publicity for the company and questioned if they could handle the loss of clients? In all his fretting, not once did he ask if she was ok. It was assumed because she was strong mentally, she could handle anything. She let him know she was taking a mini-vacation and would be back in two weeks or so. It wasn't necessary to either discuss or debate any of the issues. He seemed to have more information on the subject than her.

Looking at the pirate with dreadlocks on her mainsail, she was glad she had chosen that design. It was most appropriate at the moment. Her sail would be a surprise to the marina in Key West from which her boat, Black Beauty, notoriously named after amphetamines, had berthed during its smuggling days.

She texted Brian: Jailbird freed. Skipped out on a vaca. I needed a privacy break, but you know where I'm headed. Margaritaville was calling my name. First stop: Pink shell – Ft Myers. Visitors not wanted right now. Xoxo K

By the time she cleated Beauty at her berth at the Pink Shell Marina, Keira was exhausted. The sun was setting, and the sea was calm. She grilled up some shrimp and ate a small salad. She realized she hadn't looked at her emails in a while. It wasn't that she had lost interest; her life had become complicated at the moment.

Peter Flynn – Basil

> K Lee,
> I ask one damn thing of you, and you can't do it for me. You think you have all the answers as if you were a business owner. You don't know squat about what is happening to me. You live in your sleepy little town planting petunias and geraniums

and think you know all the answers. I have a multi-
million dollar contract on the line, and you selfishly
will not drive up to Brandon to pick up a damn
check and help me. Or even float me a personal
loan, knowing I will be able to pay you back in a
month or so. I can't believe you won't help me. You
are a self-centered bitch.
I hope you rot where the sun doesn't shine.

Dear Basil,

I would like to inform you, I have been running surveillance on you and have your IP address. I have gathered detailed information on the scamming ring that you are a part of. Due to international money laundering and fraud, your little scamming gig is up. You will be receiving company at your front door within the hour. Oh, did I fail to mention... I work with the Federal Communications Commission? Sorry. Have a good life. Oh, by the way, my name is not K Lee, but you will know it soon.

Well, that felt good, Keira thought. She bet the minute Basil buddy read the email; he would be zooming to the pawnshop to unload his computer.

ExtremeLover – Michael

Dearest Keira,
I have enclosed some pictures of me surfing on
the new prototype surfboard. It is a light-weight
polymer surf-board. It has a coating underneath
with some sort of glossy resin for better speed in
the water. I tell you, it is wicked fast. The feel of the
board under my feet is different. Riding the curl of
the wave is like sliding down a wet piece of glass.
There is less resistance with this board. I am not
sure that makes sense to you. Let see, when you
walk on the fiberglass of your boat, your feet hug

the surface. When you wax the fiberglass, and it becomes wet, it is slicker. Even if you 'walk like a duck' and shift your weight even a little bit, the balance isn't there, and over you go.

I haven't done much more. I am on the beach or in the facility watching videos of stick people falling off the boards with various movements. The videos are so technical; they show what position on the board to stand at different angles in the wave. I feel like an amateur surfer.

My break time is over, time to hit the waves before sunset. Oh, yes, I have enclosed some pictures of the view from my hotel room. The food is great here. I can't wait to come home so I can see you.   Love, Michael

Dear Keira.

Enclosed is a picture of me. Yes, you guessed it; I am in the hospital. After I sent your letter the other day, I was scheduled to surf in a designated test range area. I had on my headgear, so I was able to talk with the shore crew, and they could see how the board was working the wave. Another surfer had drifted into the test range area. I wasn't expecting someone to be sitting waiting for a wave over the nest swell, and we collided.

I was told I was airlifted to a hospital. The doctors told me I have wounds to my chest, abdomen, and legs. I guess I have internal sutures and stapled together on the outside. One of the nurses used a mirror to show me the staples. I seriously look like Frankenstein in those old black and white movies.

I will write more soon. The nurse just came in with more antibiotics and painkillers. They make me sleepy. All my love, Michael

Keira looked across the quiet marina. The lamp posts lights had flickered on for the night. A couple was sitting on their cabin cruiser several slips down. She could hear them laughing over something funny that might have happened during the day. Over nine thousand miles away, Michael was lying in a hospital bed. She studied the pictures of him surfing, once again. He looked so vibrant, so happy. He was in his element, doing exactly what he loved to do. She was so happy for him. But then she saw the picture of him in the hospital. From the looks of his eyes, he seemed like he was in a lot of pain. His body, although he had a hospital gown on, looked swollen. Or maybe it was all the dressings to his abdomen. She prayed for his strength and asked that the Lord would heal him.

Dear Michael,

Thank you very much for the pictures. You explained the differences in the prototype surfboard versus a regular surfboard well. Even a novice like me could understand.

I have been sailing. I didn't receive your emails until this evening when I dropped the sails and berthed my boat at a marina for the night. I was in shock when you wrote that you collided with another surfer. My heart went out to you, and then when you posted a picture of you in the hospital, all I wanted to do was hug and hold you close.

You are still a beautiful person, even if it was obvious you were in extreme pain. I asked God for His healing power to make you better. I am sure your mother and sister are worried about you. I wish I could be there with you so you wouldn't be alone when you wake. Please stay strong, you can get through this.   Love, Keira

Brian from The Dive Bar

Dear Keira,

I came in early today to do inventory and reorder stock. I parked my dusty ole Jeep next to your sparkling clean Jeep. I saw Micah standing on the dock staring at your empty slip. One of his dock-

workers said he had never seen Micah so quiet in his entire life and couldn't figure out why. He said all the mechanics were walking around on eggshells expecting Micah to explode in a rant.

I know it will upset you since you like your privacy, but you have been the talk in the hood this evening. Petra came in after work, asking where you were. She demanded to know since she 'needed' to talk with you immediately. For the first time in a long time, Markos, who had wanted to take her out but never had the guts, told her not everything was about her and walked out.

Also, I have never seen Marla so quiet. I hope you are sitting down because I have to tell you, Marla was drinking ice tea, period. She even asked Micah again what he said to hurt you while you two were dancing the other night to make you disappear. For once, I wish she would have kept quiet. It crushed Micah. He walked out. Brian

Brian,

In my mind's eye, even from Ft Myers, I can see you standing behind the bar, quietly drying cocktail glasses. The rants of our friends and gossip of the uninformed probably are driving you to drink the tap water! DON'T DO IT BRIAN, don't drink the water. Oh, wait, even Sammy Hagar said you can eat the ice but don't drink the water. You're doomed.

I'm sad Petra has to eat a little, humble pie for a bit of time. And Markos, I too thought he had the hots for her for quite a while. He clammed up around her every time she walked within ten feet of him. However, I think he was never sure if she was authentic.

I am sure you have noticed I haven't said a word about Micah. I need your male logic and long-time, seen-it-all bartender's advice. So many mixed emotions, I don't know what to think: hence, my exile. Help me 'ole wise one. Keira

Although the latitude of Fort Myers Beach was ten degrees south of Bradenton Beach, the vastness and the beauty of the stars were the same. She reflected on the last time she had looked upon the heavens was at the railing of Micah's balcony. With regret, she remembered he had woken from a dream and told her she had disappeared. And then she did. She stood abruptly, almost spilling her glass of wine. Her heart felt like it was splintering into a million pieces; his fear had come true. Oh Lord, she thought, what had she done? She reassured him and then broke her word. Should she turn around and sail home or continue on her self-imposed exile, vacation?

Her boat deck was too small to pace. The walking back and forth thing in the alley had been done before, and it hadn't worked. She didn't want to sail during the night; it was too easy following the shoreline to hit a stray buoy, sandbar, or a drifting tree log. Opening the galley hatch, Keira felt the cool air. When indecisive, it was best to sleep on the problem and decide in the morning. That was if she could sleep. But before shutting down her boat for the evening, Keira washed and dried her wine glass and cleaned up the small kitchen area. Wiping down the refrigerator front, there sat the envelope Lea had picked up from the floor. Keira inspected the front cover, since she very rarely received any posts at the marina.

Ouch, Keira thought, as she slid her finger along the sealed flap of the mail Marla had brought her the other day. She hated paper cuts; they were worse than open heart surgery wounds, she was positive of it. When she pulled the white folded paper from its wrapper, a check fell to the floor. Bending to pick it up, Keira sat down on her cushioned storage seat against the wall. It was a check from the marina for thirty thousand dollars. She didn't understand... The paving company invoice had already been paid by the marina. Micah knew and understood she was covering the cost of the landscaping, not her company directly. In the memo was typed: landscaping property completed and the signature line was signed by Micah Theos Andreas. Keira dropped the check on the counter as if it burned her fingers. She felt like the bottom dropped out of her stomach. Micah was Theos, Theos was Micah; she closed her eyes.

Walking into the bathroom, Keira brushed her teeth with vigor like the dental hygienist had instructed. She stared at her reflection in the mirror, without blinking. Slipping her nightshirt over her head, she automatically set the security alarm and turned out the lights. Thank goodness she could do those tasks in her sleep because she couldn't think.

Keira curled in a ball with her pillows around her in her bunk and stared at the wall, Micah was Theos. She had poured her thoughts and dreams into the letters to Theos, and he was Micah all along. Why? How could he have done that to her? She slammed her fist against the mattress and sobbed until sleep took over.

Chapter 19
♥♥♥♥♥♥♥♥♥♥♥♥♥

Tuesday, Keira woke up not wanting to deal with Tina and her chatter all day. And then she remembered the nightmare she had been living through the last three days. How could she have forgotten? Still lying in her bed looking at the white beamed ceiling of her boat, she decided exile was a good word for her present state of being. She didn't have to get up. She didn't have to eat breakfast. She didn't have to do anything. That is what happens when someone is in exile; she was sure of it. Looking at the white walls, it was easy to think of nothing. Sitting up, she grinned, well that lasted a whole ten minutes.

Walking into the galley, she ignored the check staring at her from the counter. Coffee was out of the question; her stomach hurt. She grabbed the bottle of white wine and poured some into a red plastic cup. Shaking the plastic bottle of orange juice she pulled from the refrigerator, she added some to the red cup.

Looking at the check, she growled, "Don't judge me; I can buy alcohol in Florida after seven a.m., so that means I can drink it then, too."

Keira walked out on her deck and looked around. She had told the Pink Sell Marina she would be leaving in the morning. But it was still early. She opened her laptop to check the weather forecast for the day. A letter popped up.

ExtremeLover - Michael

> *Dear Keira,*
> *I wonder if you are heading off to bed. I wish you*
> *dreams of sleeping in my arms. But, I don't think*

that will ever be. I feel weaker today and see fear in the nurse's eyes when they change my dressings. I heard one of the doctors discuss with another, 'going septic'. I don't think I am responding to the antibiotics.

Keira took a drink of her wine and orange juice concoction. A feeling of dread came over her. No, Michael, come on, fight this. Please.

I wanted to take this one last assignment before I settled down with this woman I met on the dating website. She sparked my interest when she simply asked if my passion for extreme sports was participating in it or watching. She made me laugh. Little did she know that I had grown tired of the plastic Barbie-doll type women who hung out at ski resorts and beaches looking for a free-ride. I was also sick of the constant pushing of my body to find the rush from extreme surfing and Heli- skiing. However, over time as I opened emails from her, I felt the adrenaline rush I had been craving. Come to find out, she is a wind and sailing junkie.

Keira, you put the fear of God in me talking about the wind speed, the swinging of the boom, and the pitch of your boat. You have become the addiction I crave. But I had to fulfill this last contract.

A few minutes ago, I overheard the doctor discussing me with my best friend and agent. It was as I suspected, and that is why they had upped my antibiotics. They are now waiting to see if my immune system will kick in and fight the infection

The nurse just came in and drew blood from my arm again saying, they forgot a couple of blood test draws, the doctor ordered. But I know better, it is a

retest to see if my levels have changed. I haven't
lost my hearing, damn it, or my logic yet.

Don't morn for me Keira. I have lived my life as I
chose. My only regret is not meeting you in person.
I have come to love you and relied on the
inspiration you gave me each day. I know what I
am writing is causing you grief, and pain in your
heart right now. I am sorry I have caused it. I will
hold you close to my soul forever.

In your journey through life, look for the wind; I
will always be there for you. Live your life to the
fullest.

I will love you forever, Michael

Keira was in disbelief. No, Michael couldn't be dying; he had to get better. He wasn't that old. You die of sepsis when you are old, and your immune system doesn't work anymore. Not when he was young and just days ago so vibrant. She had pictures of him. She begged God to help him, she pleaded. But realizing it wasn't up to he looked at the time his email came through. The time difference between Florida and Sydney, Australia, fourteen hours, No, no, please, she thought.

She used her search engine on her laptop to look up one of the extreme sports magazine websites. And there it was.

Extreme Sports Enthusiast Michael Huntsmen Dead At 32.

The article was beautifully written, stating he had been testing a prototype surfboard that would revolutionize the surfing world when an accident involving another surfer occurred. He died of injuries sustained from the collision. There were pictures of him surfing extremely high waves and him holding trophies with beautiful women beside him. There were also pictures of him surfing extremely high waves and him holding trophies with beautiful women beside him. There were also pictures of him dropping from helicopters at the top of rugged-looking mountains with beautiful pristine snow-covered slopes. The photos of him kite surfing huge waves in Hawaii were amazing.

Another sports magazine only available at newsstands advertised a memorial issue featuring photos never seen before, taken by extreme sports photographer Michael Huntsmen. The sample photos were breathtaking shots of someone surfing inside the pipeline looking up, the dirt and grime of an undercarriage of a bike jumping over a ravine, with a full moon in the background, and other unusual snaps.

Keira cried for Michael. It hurt to realize there was a part of him, his personality she would never get a chance to get to know. She was gut-wrenching, deep down, agonizingly sad. She cried for what would never be.

"Miss, are you ok?" asked a man in bib overalls standing on the dock.

"I'm sorry, do I need to free up this slip?" Keira asked, recognizing the owner of the marina.

"No, I saw you crying and was afraid something might have happened."

"I just learned a friend, close to me, died."

"I'm sorry to hear that; take your time."

It was after ten in the morning when she finally removed her ropes from the cleats. With a heaviness remaining in her heart, she shoved her boat away from the dock. What looked like another beautiful day was oblivious to Keira. She headed south, needing the comfort only her parents and the lower keys could give her. She longed for her mother's over-cooked meatloaf and boxed mac and cheese.

By noon she was slowly passing Bonita Springs. There were such light winds it would be a week before she would be pulling into the Key West Marina. She was feeling dejected until a marine alert came across her phone. A small squall developed in the last few minutes over Naples; it was pushing inland. Keira hoped she could pull some of the breezes out of the outer bands. She watched the ripples in the water to show her any winds as the sky turned dark navy blue south of her plotted course. But instead of picking up speed from the squall winds, the air became dead calm. Quickly she used her search engine to find the nearest port. It was dangerous to be out on open water when lightning raced across the sky. She had heard stories of masts blown to bits and boats burning in storms. There was a deep enough safe harbor up the Cocohatchee River according to the map, she could take cover at. Keira just wanted to get off the gulf and past Wiggins Pass.

It was less than ten minutes after she cleated her boat and locked down her hatch, the rains came. She sat on her cushioned sofa and watched the storm move across the water on her navigational system screen. A ping echoed from her phone that she had a message. Turning on her laptop, she saw who sent it.

Theseus – Theos

> *Keira,*
>
> *Please come back to me; I never meant to hurt you. Although security cameras are always a good thing to have, my intentions were only to protect you. I am positive KC has mentioned it to you. My business was never under scrutiny by the DEA. And if it was, I am sure Marla would have eaten those who attempted to investigate.*
>
> *Rumored by the always drunk guys, you kept to yourself. You didn't socialize much at The Dive Bar, but those who knew you, loved you. I wanted to get to know you, but I had realized a while back I was jaded, damaged way past fixing. You see, my wife laughed at my integrity and ridiculed everything I worked for or gave her. Finally, after she thought she found someone better, I was released from my marriage vows. By that time, my love of life was beyond repair.*
>
> *One day you left a copy of your dating profile on the counter at the office. Creating a dating website*

account and profile, I could talk to you, get to know you and hope you would see me for who I really was.

I have to tell you when you congratulated Theseus as a Minotaur slayer and Greek hero, your humor surprised me. You made me laugh. I loved your description of sailing. They weren't just words scribbled in an email to impress someone. It could only come from one who truly loved sailing.

I grew up on an island in the Aegean Sea; saltwater is in my blood. I am a sea captain by heart and trade. I realized you were my kindred spirit. Your writing awakened and inspired me. You gave me hope. I wanted nothing more than to follow the light of the moon across the seas with you. You are everything I have ever wanted. You brought out the best in me.

Please come home, Micah

While she read Micah's letter, Keira giggled at the mentioning of Marla eating the DEA or anyone else threatening someone or something she loved. Marla was such a Pit Bull at times. And she laughed out loud when he talked of the always drunk guys. He remembered her name for them. As much as she wanted to be angry, she couldn't.

Posing as Theos, he had touched her heart. He was so romantic when he wandered through Cozumel, seeing the sights as she had described them. Who does that sort of thing? And when he flew to... WAIT, it was all there in his emails to her. When Theos said he was at sea or on board the ship, Micah disappeared for a few days from the marina. Marla had said he was in Miami looking at a boat. She was right. Micah was looking at the cruise ship and had probably sailed out of the Port of Miami.

Come to think of it, the day Micah signed off on the marina's landscaping, he left for Sarasota right afterward in a hurry. Marla had said he was stressed. Theos had mentioned in one of his last letters, one of his jet boats developed engine problems. Why hadn't she recognized the coincidences then? That was also why in the profile photo of Theos, she only got to see the back of his head; she would have known him to be Micah had she seen his face. Many of the guys on the dating site had long hair. Some had their hair tied back, but she could see their faces, but not Theos.

Micah had taken a gamble when he created his profile. Would she have ever taken the time to explore who he really was, otherwise? If she recalled correctly, she had told naked Len, well, before he was naked, that developing relationships took time. And, she wouldn't have followed her own advice on getting to know Micah over a glass of beer at the pub.

Watching the rain hitting the portal windows, it became clear. There were some topics when discussed, would have made her squirm. The innermost wishes of the heart are rarely, if ever, talked about in a bar full of loud and boisterous people. Someone's overzealous laughter would shatter the fragile journey of exploring her veiled dreams. Yet, when she typed late in the evening, she expressed thoughts and feelings from deep within her.

Would she have delved into a discussion of the romantic sights of Cozumel with Micah? No, the fear of being embarrassed or exposed or even laughed at was too great. But he, as Theos was able to put his spin on the exotic island tryst. He played along and fantasized about his thoughts and needs. She was sure he would never have done that in person. But under the guise of Theos, he could delete his profile if it was heading in an uncomfortable direction.

Outside, the storm had to be directly over the marina. The winds howled and shoved her boat against the dock. Thank goodness at the last moment before she locked down the hatch door, she had thrown out the bumpers. She didn't want her Black Beauty scarred and scratched by the wood planks of the dock. She could see lightning streaking across the sky and heard the snap hooks clanging against the mast. Stretching out on her bed, all she could do was wait out the bad weather.

Once the storm let up, Keira quickly maneuvered her boat out to the gulf. With full sails, she was able to pick up the last winds of the squall. Her new goal was to get past Everglade City by nightfall. Since she had slept, heading straight across the open water to Key West could be in the plan. But usually, the winds died down in the evenings.

For the first time in a while, she was looking forward to going home, to seeing her parents. She needed her old bedroom and the paintings of palm trees on the living room walls. Her mom had artfully hand-painted each of the beautiful palms to scale across the walls. And her dad, he had always been consistently and lovingly patient with the antics her mom pulled on any given day. She didn't know if her older brother and sister would be around. They had families of their own. She missed them and just wanted the familiarity of home.

Micah wasn't sure if Keira had received his email or if she would even read it or press delete without hesitation. It had been another day of wondering where she disappeared to. He had taken out his frustrations on one of his employees. All the guy did was drop a torque wrench in the bottom of the boat he was working on. There was no damage to the hull. Micah was plain and simply angry. He sat at the pub and stared at his empty beer bottle. Brian silently replaced it with an icy cold brew. Without moving a muscle, Micah watched as a drop of water trickled down the side of the substituted bottle. It pooled on the wood bar counter. Staring at the wet spot, he wondered how long it would take for the water to start lifting the varnished finish.

"You have to ask the right questions to get the answers you are looking for." Brian quietly suggested to Micah.

"You are right. Thanks, Brian." Micah said as he abruptly stood and threw some dollars on the bar. He knew Brian was loyal to Keira and would never tell him her whereabouts. He jumped in his car and drove towards Bradenton.

Just as Kraig was locking the warehouse doors of The Landscape Architect and Lawn Care service, Micah got out of his car. Micah saw him look over his shoulder and scowled. Well, that was not 'best practice' in business relations. Of course, the last couple of days, he hadn't been endearing to his clients either.

"How can I help you?" Kraig questioned. "Keira isn't here."

"Do you know what Keira's ex-husband's last name is? I think he has been trolling around the marina the last couple of days." Micah asked.

"Bastion, and if you 'talk' to him, give him a right hook for me." Kraig grinned.

"Will do."

As Micah drove out of the parking lot, at last, he had hope. Now, if he wasn't too late.

Keira sailed until she was exhausted and the winds had left the sails. She searched in the darkness for what she hoped was Pavilion Key. She would anchor on the south side. GPS promised the dark landmass to her left was the island she had decided would be safe for the night.

She heated a bowl of chicken and rice soup. As much as she wanted to stroll out on deck to eat, the mosquitoes were like vultures after the rain. She could hear them hitting against the porthole glass. She didn't feel like reading the paperback she found at the bottom of the storage chest. Her eyes were crossing from watching the radar on the weather screen. She hadn't seen a fishing trawler or the tri-hull catamaran boat that shuttled visitors between Key West and Fort Myers go by. Sometimes, if the weather conditions were poor, the trip between the two points was canceled. It even mentioned the weather condition cancellation policy on their brochure. So, she knew she was not anywhere near the shipping lanes or getting hit by another boat.

Micah's letter had been a surprise. Part of her still wanted to turn around and head for home. Yet, she needed this time to heal. It had been too long since her last visit with her parents, and she wanted some pampering that only Key West could give her.

She thought of Michael. The anguish of knowing his life had been on the verge of ending because of someone being in the wrong place at the wrong time must have been extremely distressing. He had died on the other side of the equator all alone. She would never get to know his zest for life. A tear slid from her eye before she silently sobbed in the darkness until exhaustion overtook her, and she slept.

Thank goodness she had thrown two anchors out in the night. The sky remained dark in the east with just a hint that morning was coming, but already the breeze was brisk. Seeing where she anchored for the night and where the mangroves were, she was glad she used her instinct. Her boat would have either had a cracked rudder or beached deep in the mangroves. Strategically pulling the stern anchor first, she was able to swing the hull away from the saltwater tree island. Lastly, she hauled in the bow anchor pulling her boat into deeper water before hoisting her sails. With aching arms from the early morning workout, she set her course for Key West.

It was after nine before she had the chance to grab a couple of hard-boiled eggs and a bottle of water. The wind was working her sails, and her average speed was about 20 knots. At this rate, she would be sailing into Key West in a couple of hours. Her excitement was building.

Keira got on her phone and requested a slip for her boat; she gave the length of her sailboat and the draft needed. After she gave the hull numbers, a voice from her past practically yelled in her ear.

"Keira, is that you? Welcome home. I can't wait to see you."

"George? Tell me I'm talking to my George."

"Yep, the one and only, see you in an hour or so."

If Keira could have stepped on the gas, she would have. She increased the space between the mainsail and foresail. Her foresail was tight. However, the closer she got to Key West, the winds changed direction. She watched her telltales and quickly changed the spacing on her sails, yet again. She was losing lift, so she had to make it up by increasing her sail area. She loved the challenges the winds were giving her. She felt alive. Maybe Michael was watching her sail. He said, look to the winds, and he would be with her. She smiled and thanked him.

George had kept a lookout for her also. When her cell rang, she heard a loud laugh from George.

"Only you would have a mainsail with a pirate wearing dreadlocks as big as you please across it," George yelled into the phone.

Keira dropped her sails as she headed into her port, funny how it was still 'her' port. George guided her to her slip. Once Keira's boat was cleated and her sheets were secured, she practically ran into George's arms. He had been in his thirties when she was young, learning how to sail. He had taught her so many tried and true tricks to sailing that the others refused to give out.

"I didn't think you could get more beautiful, but I was wrong. Look at you, Keira, gorgeous as ever." George gushed as he wrapped Keira in a bear hug.

"Yeah, and I was crushed when I was twelve, and you gave your virginity away to that blonde thing with big boobs." Keira laughed.

"I should have waited for you, she was a mistake. Now tell me, do your parents know you were coming?" George asked as he stood back from her with his hands on his hips.

"Nope, it's going to be a great surprise. Has anyone been asking about me?" Keira squinted before lowering her sunglasses over her eyes.

"Should there be?"

"Na, you know me, always one step in front of the law or however that saying goes." Keira laughed to hide her disappointment.

Keira grabbed her backpack that she had put a few of her new outfits from Lea in and walked the streets to her parents' house.

Nothing had changed, the place was as funky as ever, yet everything had changed. Some of the old haunts from when she was young were now restaurants and weird-looking, expensive artwork galleries.

When Keira rang the dolphin-shaped doorbell of her parent's pale yellow home, she could hear her mother's voice. She was complaining she would give anything not to drive Elsie Puchi over to the airport in the morning. And then she opened the door.

Keira had forgotten how strong her mother's lungs were. Her scream was ear piercing as she grabbed Keira and hung onto her as if her life depended on it.

"Hey, mom, I um can't breathe," Keira said as the door opened wide and her dad popped his face out the entrance. "Hi, Dad."

"Lizzie, Keira isn't going to float away." Keira's dad said as he tried to pry his wife's arms from Keira's neck.

"I am just so happy to see you, my beautiful daughter." Her mom said, leaning back to look at her and then hugged her again.

"Ease up, Mom. It's just Queera." Toby, her brother, said as he walked to the door eating a banana.

"Shut up, Tobyfrog." Keira sassed right back. She couldn't believe she had reverted to when she was ten and called her brother by his nickname. Geeze, was she in a time warp?

"Can we take this inside? I am about to grill hamburgers. Keira, have you eaten?" Keira's dad asked as he guided everyone into the foyer and shut the bold, in-your-face, royal blue door.

After eating burgers at the table by the pool, it was time to catch Keira up on all the happenings around town. Beth, Keira's older sister, started a new job as a manager at one of the fancy high-rise condominiums on the water across town. Toby had gotten a divorce a month ago. There didn't seem to be any remorse when he talked. Nor did Keira's mom or dad seem upset. Guess there was nothing to discuss on that subject. They asked several questions about her business. She told them how she made Kraig her business partner. She saw her father frown but quickly hid his feelings. Her mother asked Keira if it was alright to invite a few old friends over for drinks tomorrow evening to celebrate Keira being home. She was sure they would love to see her. What could she say? As night settled in, Keira realized how tired she was. And since her mother had converted her bedroom into a craft room, Keira grabbed her backpack and said she would sleep on her boat, not a problem.

"Come on. I'll walk you back to the marina. Is George still working there?" Toby asked.

Keira and Toby sat on her boat deck drinking wine. They talked late into the night, catching up on all the weird stuff going on in the hood and changes to the key.

"Say, does Mom still keep her stash of pot under the silk, potted plant in the living room?" Keira asked.

"Yep, same as Dad keeps his in the family bible next to his recliner." Toby laughed.

"Because no one ever touches the bible," they laughed in unison.

"How did we survive? They were stoned most of our childhood." Keira laughed, shaking her head.

"You lived through it by learning to sail and dive. And then, you sailed away. Beth worked and saved money to escape to the mainland for a while. Me? I didn't." Toby said as he polished off the rest of the wine. He searched the bottom of the bottle as if more wine would magically appear.

Keira stood and pulled Toby to his feet. She guided him down the steps into her boat. He plopped down onto the sofa while she opened another bottle of wine.

"What do you mean? You have one of the most lucrative construction companies in the keys."

"My ex owns half of it now, and I am sick of remodeling termite-infested shacks," Toby complained.

"Take some time off; get your head on straight."

They talked a little longer until Keira finally complained again that exhaustion was hitting her. She commanded Toby to stand, in which he stared at her like she was deranged. However he was soon amazed at how much room there was on the pull-out bed in the galley. She laughed when he immediately stretched out on the mattress before she had even gotten the boat alarm set. Climbing into her own bunk, Keira slid her feet against the side of the hull. She was afraid, with all that Toby and she had talked about, her mind wouldn't shut down. But within minutes, she was asleep.

Her dreams were of sailing. The winds off her star-board were reaching thirty knots. Michael was taking pictures of her boat heeling while Micah gave counter-balance. Michael clipped one of the sails to a bar, and kite surfed along the horizon as the sun set

She knew he was gone, never to return, when the sun dipped out of sight. She cried as Micah caressed her hair and spoke soothing words against her head.

Toby woke his sister early in the morning, asking for the alarm codes so he could get off the boat and go to work. Keira stared at him until she remembered he had spent the night. She yawned and walked back to their childhood home alongside him, complaining about getting up early on her vacation. But Keira was secretly looking forward to a shower. It would be nice not bumping into each of the walls as she washed her hair. She wondered if her mom still made pot pancakes like she used to.

It was the perfect day for walking along the streets, looking at all the changes. The chickens were still running free. Mallory Square was full of tourists, like always. She couldn't resist stopping at the shipwreck museum. When she was younger, it was her favorite place to go. She had spent hours looking at all the treasures salvaged off the bottom of the Straits of Florida after storms. She ate lunch at Hog's Breath Saloon and shopped at some of the boutiques. She bought a book on Ghosts of Key West for Marla. For Brian, she found a Whiskey barrel sign which she had personalized with 'The Dive Bar' written across the top. Rather than carry it, she had it mailed to his bar with a note that said, Thank you, love Keira. She bought a T- shirt for Kraig from the Hemingway Rum Company. She wandered into an antique shop. As she was browsing the numerous ancient and dusty items, she found an old nautical chart of the waters around Key West dated June 1889. The parchment paper was brittle but still in excellent condition. She had to have it. It was something she would love to give to Micah. If a relationship with him was not to be, she would cherish it herself because it was from home.

On the way back to her parent's home, she stopped and picked up two key lime pies from the pastry shop. At the fish market, she bought some special cuts her father would love. She thought she saw Micah walking down the street, but when the guy turned to cross to the other side, he had a full beard. Deflated, she walked up the sidewalk and rang the doorbell.

"Why are you ringing the doorbell? Come in, daughter of mine."

"Because Mother, I don't live here, and that would be rude. Besides, there were times when I walked in, you and Dad were having sex on the dining room table." Keira said as she handed her mom the key lime pies and fish packed on ice.

"Oh please, that was back then, now, we need the comforts of the sofa. Yum, key lime, how did you know I didn't make any pies for your party?" Keira's mom asked as she peeked inside the boxes.

"The last pie you ever made was the banana coconut pie, and dad tried to infuse marijuana into the pie crust. Remember, the Reverend from that church down the street came for Sunday lunch? I heard he never preached at the evening vespers service that night." Keira laughed.

"I forgot about that. You better go, get ready. CeCe and Dick will be here in a bit; you know they are always early to everything. Lord, they will be pounding on the pearly gates before God is even ready for them." Lizzie laughed as she wandered into the kitchen.

Keira took the stairs two at a time, up to her old bedroom, now craft room, to shower and change. She stripped off her sweaty clothes from shopping and hopped in the shower. Her parents hadn't changed a bit, still as crazy as ever. The soap Keira reached for was homemade, and when she washed her hair, the scent of exotic fruits and spices surrounded her. Slowly she toweled off while looking around the room. Her mother had created some very colorful and intricate stained glass window panels. They were beautiful. Her oil paintings were abstract by design, but Keira could see the features of the beach. It was as if she had painted a detailed scene and then lightly whitewashed over the top of it. Her mother, in all her flakiness, was surprisingly a fantastic artist. Hearing the doorbell ring, Keira rushed to dry her hair and select her outfit for the evening. The body-hugging sundress with splashes of purple, red, yellow, and pink flowers would look sexy but not over the top for visiting with a few friends and neighbors. She quickly pulled her hair up into a sloppy bun and zipped down the stairs just like when she was young and impatient to get anywhere.

Beth, Keira's sister greeted her at the base of the stairs. She had a puzzled look on her face. Was it because Beth remembered how she always repelled down the stairs? Or, maybe Beth's only memory of her was when she was scrawny and smelled of fish. After all, Keira was the runt of the family. It felt awkward for a moment. But as always, she smiled and hugged her sister.

"Surprise, I bet you didn't think I would be here. Mom said you were gorgeous, and you are." Beth complimented Keira while looking her up and down and then, hugging her again.

Keira could never remember bickering with Beth. Toby, well, he sometimes, ok, all of the time, without fail, teased her. But they always stuck together against the craziness of the times. Keira was the peacemaker whenever there was an issue between her brother, sister and parents, she recalled.

She and Beth talked for a minute or two before Beth pushed her into the living room to mingle with friends from her childhood.

The doorbell rang, and a couple with a bowl of potato salad walked in. Keira introduced herself. The husband quickly greeted her and walked off in search of booze. The woman said she was Margaret Williams, Keira's third-grade teacher. Keira covered her blunder with, 'I love how the tropics keep our skin so soft and smooth.' She reminded herself silently why plastic surgery was not always a good choice.

Keira hugged her way through the living room. A few friends usually meant four, maybe five coming for a visit. But she should have remembered, to her mother, a few friends turned out to be half of Key West. The doorbell rang yet again.

After a while of small talk with everyone her mother had invited, Keira set her now, warm bourbon and no longer ice, on the dining room table. She wandered out the patio doors. The small yard was completely surrounded with Areca, Pygmy Date, and Majesty palms. Keira smiled thinking they were all very healthy looking. Some friends were standing talking by the pool. She would have given anything for all of them to go away, so she could skinny dip in the pool like the old days. Keira realized it was bitter sweet to be home. The comforting feelings from her youth were soothing but she needed something left back at Bradenton Beach. As she stepped over to the table set up with hors d'oeuvres sitting in iced trays, the visitors, with help from her sister, seemed to part. Deck shoes, navy blue walking shorts, a Hawaiian shirt over broad shoulders, and hair hanging in a mass of black curls thanks to the high humidity, there stood Micah.

Keira's mouth fell open. Her heart seemed to flip flop in her chest. She blinked a couple times to make sure she wasn't dreaming. It was Micah; it really was Micah standing on her parents' patio. Her mind wasn't playing cruel tricks on her. She didn't know how he got to the keys or how long he was standing in her old back yard. She didn't even care if she didn't look graceful running toward him. She just knew she couldn't get to him fast enough.

"Micah, you're here."

So many questions flew through Keira's mind as she studied his face. "How did you find me, never mind? I love you." Keira cried before she wrapped her arms around his neck and kissed him.

She felt his hands press against her back. She wasn't dreaming; he was holding her for real.

"I was afraid I lost you," Micah whispered. "Thelo na me nioseis, please say that what we started isn't over."

"No, I don't want it to be over. I love you, Micah Theos Andreas." Keira said, as she ran her fingers through his hair and laughed.

"My Keira," Micah paused studying Keira's face, as if it had been years since he last saw her, "I love you."

So, then what happened?

Epilogue
♥♥♥♥♥♥♥♥♥♥♥♥♥♥

The party seemed to last forever. As much as Keira appreciated her parents hosting the get-together, she was dying to talk with Micah alone. Of course, everyone wanted to know all about her 'boyfriend'. To Keira, the word boyfriend sounded so high schoolish. Micah, however, was gracious and accommodating. He discussed the cost of construction projects and lumber with her father and brother. The neighbors insisted on filling him in on all the antics of Keira and her friends, when they were young.

After the party, Keira and Beth carried dirty plates and the leftover food to the kitchen after the last stragglers of the party left. Micah helped Toby tote the party's bags of garbage to the street for the next day's trash pickup. They lugged all the folding chairs back to the Harpers' home, next door.

"How many times have you slept with that hunk of a man?"

"Mom!" Keira whispered in shock

"Well, it's important that he is giving my daughter pleasure," Lizzie stated as she pointed the spatula at Keira. She pushed a few more prosciutto-wrapped scallops into a bowl.

"You did your disappearing act, didn't you? That is why he came looking for you, right?." Beth accused Keira while leaning against the kitchen counter.

"The DEA came after my boat thinking it was still a drug runner. I sat in jail an entire Saturday until my attorney got the charges dismissed. My 'ex' crashed the 4th of July party I was hosting. Kraig, my business partner, kept pushing me for a relationship, with him. A special someone I adored, died, doing what he loved doing the most and Micah completely overwhelmed me. I needed time to think." Keira said as she shoved containers of food into the already stuffed refrigerator.

"And just how did Micah overwhelm you? It sounds like you were running scared." Beth retorted, knowing her sister.

"Look at him, he's gorgeous, well off, and women drool over him. I rent my dock space for my boat at his marina. You know me about keeping my private life private. It is almost impossible on the docks to keep anything a secret. Well, every time he came near me, sparks were flying, I could feel it. I'm sure others could see bolts of lightning bouncing from him to me." Keira explained, trying to keep the s word out of the conversation.

"Just please promise me you won't burn dinner because you are having sex." Beth grinned at Keira.

"Who burned dinner because of sex?" Lizzie asked. "YOU DID!" Both daughters squealed at the same time.

The air was heavy; not even the slightest of breezes was stirring off the water, as Micah and Keira trekked to her boat for the night. So much had happened over the last week. Keira's head was swimming when she thought about it. She had found wisdom and appreciation in the slightest of things. The quirkiness of her childhood and zany parents made her smile. She loved them dearly. As sad as she was of the passing of Michael, she cherished what he had taught her about living life to the fullest. To honor his memory, Keira vowed to find adventures in everything she did. And Micah, it took guts to fly down to Key West, not knowing for sure if she was there or not. Maybe he had been trying to safeguard the marina from drugs, but he also had watched over her. He developed a dating profile to get to know her and for her to get to know him. She was still having difficulty, though, with Micah and Theos, as one person. Theos had deep feelings and an inner beauty she couldn't resist. He was a romantic sea captain who traipsed across Cozumel to visit the places she loved. She yearned for more of the amorous letters from his soul. Micah, on the other hand, had slipped into her heart. For a tough guy, he was amazingly gentle with her. He had caught her off guard with his cannonball splashes into the swimming pool one minute and carrying her to his bed the next. Making love with him was not just sex; it had been a magical exploration of love between them.

Did it take the devastating blow of Peter's infidelity for Keira to appreciate the beauty of Micah? Or, she may have never questioned or understood the depth of her own passion for life it hadn't been for the beautiful words of Theos' letters and Micah's romantic heart.

Susyn had predicted the Gemini twins would protect her. How was she able to connect Theos as a twin of Micah? Keira never mentioned Theos, from the dating website or the secret meetings with Micah to Susyn. She was amazed and baffled at the same time. The metaphysical realm of reality outside of the human sense of perception was staggering and far beyond her knowledge bank. But Susyn somehow knew.

Later that evening, Micah made love to Keira under the stars. He caressed and whispered his love for her in his native Greek, while she embraced and stroked his passion. Was their lovemaking, with the dark sky and twinkle of the stars above, more intensified because Micah had feared he lost her just days before? Or, had Keira finally admitted her love which freed her to share with him all that she was? Before the sun began its climb into the heavens, Lizzie's daughter had given Micah far more pleasure than he expected. Keira smiled, loving the feeling of the water caressing the sides of her boat while listening to the rhythmic beating of Micah's heart. There was one thing Keira knew for a fact; Micah didn't need Jimmy's little blue pills.

Keira spent the next day with Micah exploring Key West. She insisted they visit the shipwreck museum. Micah marveled at Keira's fascination with the sunken ships, littering the sea floor along the Straits of Florida. They toasted drinks to Brian in some of the pubs; Micah sent pictures to him as proof. They bought each other beach towels, books on Key West, and some colorful shirts. They took photos at the southernmost point marker on the Whitehead Street corner. She shook her head and told him only tourists took pictures at the Whitehead Street corner – how embarrassing for a local. Of course, she sent Lea a picture of her and Micah standing at the giant fishing buoy marker and texted, 'guess who showed up?"

That night Toby, coupled with his latest cute girlfriend, suggested they all take the ghost tour down the hidden alleys and back streets. He bragged of knowing scarier places than the tour guide could show them.

"Yeah sure, prove it, Toby!" Keira demanded.

Micah laughed at the brother and sister bantering, so like his own. However, when Toby took them to the Gato House on Virginia Street, his little blonde girlfriend swore she saw a man in a rocking chair on the balcony. But no one else saw him. Keira had always loved visiting the old cemetery full of people who died in shipwrecks. But on this night, she felt like someone walked beside her and Micah. And it wasn't Toby trying to scare her either. The brother and sister talked of the demon doll and the ghost of Geiger. Toby warned Micah his sister would be up all night with nightmares. He suggested hiding the dinner knives. Micah laughed, knowing their lack of sleep wouldn't be because of ghosts.

As much as Keira loved visiting her parents and especially having Micah with her, it was almost time to set sail for home. They were walking to meet her parents at Lizzie's favorite restaurant for breakfast. Keira stopped on the sidewalk and asked, "Do I look like we had wild sex last night?"

"Did we make love most of last night? Yes. Was it wild? I'm sure we rocked the boat. But I don't remember you swinging from the mast." Micah laughed and tugged on Keira's hand to keep walking.

Micah wasn't used to seeing chickens roaming the streets. A car actually stopped and waited while one rooster announced morning for the third time in about ten minutes. As Micah held the door open for Keira at the restaurant entrance, he wondered if the chickens would follow them in. He noticed Keira's parents were already seated at a table with a view of the street

"Good Morning. You look like you both slept well last night." Lizzie hugged first her daughter, then Micah.

"Mom!"

"We heard you had a wild night of ghost hunting." Keira's dad responded quickly.

During breakfast, they talked about places Keira had taken Micah the day before. Keira sent pictures of them at the southernmost point marker to her father's phone.

"Lizzie, look at the tourists!" They all laughed. Even the waitress, who had gone to high school with Keira, got a chuckle when Lizzie showed her the picture.

Keira's dad was concerned with the report of possible storms later in the day. He questioned where they would drop anchor in a squall? Not to be disrespectful, Keira shrugged and told him the nearest safe area along the coast. She didn't want to frighten her mother. She chose her words very carefully but told them of the storm she had to wait out in the mangroves in the everglades. Her mother didn't seem to notice the significance of getting off the gulf in a bad electrical storm. However, Micah gave her a hard-searching look.

"So Micah, when is your birthday?" Lizzie asked as she sipped on her mint tea.

Here it comes, Keira thought, the moment when her mother would declare Micah either the perfect lover for her or an astrological-incompatible loser. In which case, she would insist on Keira dumping him in the gulf for sharks to feed on.

"June third."

"Ahh, you're a twin." Keira's mom smiled.

"Wait, how did you know I was a twin?" Micah tilted his head and asked.

"Because your birthday is June third, you're a Gemini, the sign of the twins," Lizzie stated the fact as if everyone knew that.

Micah looked at Keira and said, "Markos is five minutes older than me. Most people don't know we are twins, only brothers. Did you?"

Keira was surprised by the revelation. "Actually… I thought you were related, like maybe brothers or yes cousins from listening to the stories Marla and you told at Brian's pub that one night," Keira said. As she stared at her plate, she couldn't believe the heavens were reminding her yet again of Susyn's predictions.

"So, is that a good thing or a bad thing?" Micah asked.

"Gemini and Leo are playful lovers. You don't like clingy women, so our independent Keira is perfect for you. The Gemini is creative and will bring out the best in August-born women. The Leo woman is full of grandeur and will shower you with love." Lizzie said with a faraway look in her eyes.

A ding sounded from Keira's phone. She wasn't going to answer it, fearing the text was from that crazy phone stalker, Scott. There would be fifty questions, plus a police report filed if her father or mother ever got wind of his shenanigans. No, no, it would be better if she just ignored it. However, it was Micah who questioned if she was going to check the text. Smiling, she was sure Micah was uncomfortable listening to her mother discuss the Gemini Leo astrological love connection.

Surprising everyone at the table, Keira nearly jumped out of her chair with joy after checking the text.

"Are you going to share? Don't keep us in suspense." Lizzie grinned.

"A while back, a homeless guy decided to steal one of our lawnmowers and took it on a joy ride. After a 'high-speed' chase driving maybe ten miles per hour, he rolled the mower down an embankment into a retention lake. The police caught him climbing out of the muck." Keira giggled. "Fearing he could file charges and sue my company if he was hurt, I filed immediately, claiming grand theft."

"When did this happen? Why didn't you ever say anything?"

Keira could see the concerned look on Micah's face. "I didn't want to jinx the charges. I was hoping it would stay out of the newspapers, since it would give others with nothing to do, something to try. Besides, you know how the gossip runs wild at The Dive Bar."

"Was the riding mower damaged?" Keira's dad naturally asked

"I'm not sure. The mower was impounded, as evidence. I filed a claim with my insurance, Dad. Anyway, the text was from my attorney. The guy pleaded guilty. So there will be no trial. He got five years jail time and all kinds of financial and court fees, which I will never recoup, my share. I am just glad he got incarcerated."

The look of sadness on Lizzie's face was apparent to Keira; she had said too much in front of her mother. "Mom, look at it this way, if he got away with a slap on the hand rather than jail time and fines, others would think it is ok to steal lawn service equipment when they got the whim. They could mow over a child playing on the sidewalk or kill someone fishing in the lakes or worse."

"I know, you are right, but I just wonder why the guy felt the need to steal your mower in the first place." Keira's mother pondered.

Micah stood and walked away from the table.

"Did I say something wrong?" Lizzie asked, looking from her husband to her daughter.

"No, Dear, they have to get sailing to stay north of the storm. Keira, what is your course?" Her dad asked.

"I think the storm will stay south of us. I wanted to island-hop, but the air is very calm right now." Keira shook her head.

"So we talked and will head out over the gulf to find the wind to get us home," Micah said as he returned to the table. "Keira, we have to get on the road so-to-speak. Sir, Ma'am, thank you for your hospitality."

"Let me get the bill; then we will walk you to the marina." Keira's dad looked around the diner for their server.

"I took care of it," Micah said as he reached for Keira's hand.

At the marina, Keira's mom wrapped her arms around Keira for several tearful hugs. Her dad smiled and gave her a tight squeeze with the promise of coming up north for a visit. George teased; he was going to block her boat from leaving port. But finally, after shoving off from the slip, Keira set sail with Micah at the helm. She could see her loved ones on the dock waving and laughing at her hoisted mainsail with the pirate with dreadlocks.

Their stay in Key West was over, for now. The journey north would be slow since the weather conditions in the gulf were unusually calm for late July. They would have time to laugh, make love and explore their feelings, ideas, and plans for the future.

Their biggest shock came when they were a few miles from their home port. As they approached the waters off Lido Key, Zac and Kristi, KC and Lea waved from Zac's sailboat. It was incredible to see them out sailing. Lea had texted Keira the day before, wanting to know when she was coming home. Never in a million years would Keira have guessed, Lea's request was so they could surprise and welcome her and Micah home.

Keira stood next to Micah at the helm. So much had happened since early June, but they had weathered the storm. The colorful sails from Zac's boat and her pirate sails were fun to see side by side. Keira loved watching Micah laugh and his enjoyment of the moment. He grabbed her around the waist and kissed her to the whistles and cheers of their friends.

Micah shouted to the heavens and anyone who could hear,
"I love you, Keira St Cloud!"

About the Author

♥♥♥♥♥♥♥♥♥♥♥♥♥♥♥♥♥♥♥♥♥♥♥♥♥♥

Scam alerts soundings on our phones, identity theft, and fraudulent online shopping hoaxes are on the increase. Even the desires of our hearts may be sabotaged by the trickery of others for self-gain. Scammers have learned how to seek out the weakest parts of someone. And instead of protecting that vulnerability, they have taken advantage of it. Thievery has become part of our lives. There are many such stories found in newspapers, magazines, and online pieces of text or videos. However, they gloss over the deep-seated trauma left in the wake of duplicity.

Tam Ahlborn has talked with a few women who lost their life savings to the convincing con games of deceitful individuals. Embarrassed, mortified, humiliated, crushed, and ashamed to admit they were swindled by smooth-talking people, are a few of the emotions some of the women felt. Anger and hostility were the latter feelings when realizing the authorities could do nothing to rectify the wrongs against them. The explanation given for their inability to help was the money was given freely and without a legally binding contract. Most scammers use false names or fictitious residencies, in which they will never be found. To bring awareness, is why Tam Ahlborn wrote **Lovers and Scammers**.

Made in the USA
Columbia, SC
19 February 2023

12355173R00212